W9-CDE-787

PARIS METRO

PARIS
METRO

A Novel

WENDELL
STEAVENSON

W. W. NORTON & COMPANY
Independent Publishers Since 1923
New York London

For information about permission to reproduce selections from this book, write to Permissions, W. W. Norton & Company, Inc., 500 Fifth Avenue, New York, NY 10110

For information about special discounts for bulk purchases, please contact W. W. Norton Special Sales at specialsales@wwnorton.com or 800-233-4830

Manufacturing by LSC Communications, Harrisonburg
Book design by Dana Sloan
Production manager: Beth Steidle

Library of Congress Cataloging-in-Publication Data

Names: Steavenson, Wendell, 1970– author.
Title: Paris metro : a novel / Wendell Steavenson.
Description: First edition. | New York : W. W. Norton & Company, [2018]
Identifiers: LCCN 2017052636 | ISBN 9780393609783 (hardcover)
Subjects: LCSH: Women journalists—Fiction. | Americans—France—
Fiction. | Mothers and sons—Fiction. | Terrorism—Psychological
aspects—Fiction. | Domestic fiction.
Classification: LCC PS3619.T43 P37 2018 | DDC 813/.6—dc23
LC record available at https://lccn.loc.gov/2017052636

W. W. Norton & Company, Inc., 500 Fifth Avenue, New York, N.Y. 10110
www.wwnorton.com

W. W. Norton & Company Ltd., 15 Carlisle Street, London W1D 3BS

1 2 3 4 5 6 7 8 9 0

For Three Linas. Lina Sinjab, Leena Saidi, and Lina Attalah. One Syrian, one Lebanese, one Egyptian; one Sunni, one Shia, one Christian. All journalists, all brave and strong and smart and indomitable. They sheltered me and fed me in Cairo and Beirut and Damascus, taught me, encouraged me, helped me in a hundred ways, and were my friends when I needed friendship. War and riots and arrests, boyfriends and broken hearts and road trips. If only the whole world was made up of Linas. What a brilliant party it would be.

CONTENTS

PARIS METRO

PROLOGUE

Zorro called at six in the morning.

"They're holed up in an apartment in Saint-Denis. The police have got them surrounded."

"Oh God, not again." I was tired red-rimmed sore angry asleep. I got out of bed and dressed automatically. Jeans and a sweater, windbreaker, sneakers, old habits, muscle memory; I pulled the laces tight and double-knotted in case I had to run.

Jean called, "I'm on my way now. Twitter says lots of gunfire. The address is 8 rue du Corbillon. C-O-R-B. Like *corbeau*, like a crow."

I went into Little Ahmed's room at the end of the narrow corridor. In the dark predawn, blue sailboats flew across the wall. I had painted them when we had first moved in. Blue is the color of sleep, his father once told me. Little Ahmed was lying on his back with his arms tight against his sides. His funny rigid sleeping position. I used to tease him he slept like a soldier. His black brown hair made paintbrush tips against the canvas of the pillow. His eyelashes—impossibly long, adorably, ridiculously long; we are going to have to mow them! Blink and you turn into a fly catcher!—made dark moons of his closed eyes. Dream boy. Thirteen years old, grown taller than me, his feet stuck out over the end of the bed, bear cub fur shadowed his forearms. Not a child anymore.

"Ahmed, wake up." I shook him gently. He made a trumpet snort but did not open his eyes. "I'm sorry. I'm sorry. I've got to go—" At this he opened his eyes, sleepy dust, and mad at me.

"Don't go again."

"You'll be OK. Breakfast, school. Call me when you wake up."

"You already woke me up." He propped himself up on one elbow. "Will you be OK?"

"No. I won't," he said, clear and accusatory. "I'll take all the emergency money hidden in your father's old copy of *Darkness at Noon* and burn the building down and run away and join my friends in Syria." I kissed him on his forehead and he wiped it off with the back of his hand.

"See you later," I said, and went out.

The streets were dark and empty. I looked for a taxi, but there were none. You can wait your whole life at a Paris taxi rank while taxis drive past, insouciant bastards.

There was a tent camp struck in the crescent park by the canal. A group of refugees—East African, high cheekbones, every face a sculpture—were drinking from cans of beer and throwing boules in the gravel courts under the streetlamp. The boules made dull steel thudding clicks against each other when they collided. The quayside cafés were closed, tables and chairs stacked inside or chained up for the night. Elegant stone swags above, below metal shop grilles covered with ripped posters and sprayed with #JESUIS, which I mistook, at first glance, for Jesus. The city was sleeping and not sleeping. Lying awake with one eye open pretending to be asleep. Breathing and holding its breath. On the wall I saw a stencil graffito of a gun with a croissant as a trigger firing plump little madeleines as bullets. A dog barked at another, smaller dog. Finally a taxi appeared.

Saint-Denis was only four miles away, but I had never been there. Maybe because it was so close. It would have been easy to go and therefore I didn't bother. I should have established a network of friendly imams and community organizers and deradicalization activists. I should have made Muslims and the *banlieues* my beat. But after all the years of living and reporting in the Middle East, I was fed up with the familiar. I kicked myself in the third conditional tense. Past; not done, can't be undone, is done. In any case, Paris was supposed to be a respite, *non*?

I had imagined the Saint-Denis of the Arabs-rioting-in-the-streets headlines would be a tower-block slum, but it turned out to be a pretty village consumed by the spread of the city. Cobblestones, tubs of geraniums, a *grand* Hôtel de Ville. In the gray haze of dawn, blue lights flashed and cast an eerie glow over the metal barricades and the white police vans. And over the police, hundreds of them: GIGN, CRS, RAID, which stood for Research, Assistance, Intervention, Deterrence—Zorro, our pricking conscience, chronicler of the surreal and absurd, pointed out it was a series of euphemisms that unwittingly made up an accurate acronym. Black-clad robocops, Kevlar helmets, shatterproof visors pulled down, neoprene gloves with jointed armor panels on the fingers, earpiece comms, Glock pistols drawn, fingers resting alert on the trigger guards. The gendarmes had covered up the identification numbers on their epaulettes with strips of black Velcro. I saw army too, balaclavas, camouflage combat fatigues, desert boots on city pavements.

The square was filled with the arms and armor of the French state. Behind the state, the press lined up in a row of satellite trucks, cables snaking underfoot, spotlights glaring at the clown faces of the stand-ups. Behind the press, the people. A milling, grumbly *banlieue* crowd, headscarves and beards, early-morning dog walkers, mothers holding the hands of their children very tightly.

I found Jean sitting on the steps of the cathedral where the French kings are buried. He was writing in his notebook with the steel ball-point pen that Margot had given him when they got married. He had never lost it; even when he left it behind, the pen mysteriously found its way back to him. A waiter would appear running in the street, panting, "Sir! you forgot your *stylo*," a taxi driver would leave it at the hotel desk. Its brushed matte finish was polished smooth in the places where his thumb and finger had rubbed against it, noting details of wars, for forty years.

"The gunfire stopped about fifteen minutes ago. There were two or three big explosions."

"Shit." I had missed it.

I always missed it. Zorro used to tease me about this in Baghdad. "Don't go out with Kitty," he would tell journalists who had recently arrived. "She has some kind of protective shield—nothing ever hits her."

"But I never see anything happen," I complained. (I complained!)

"Zorro went looking to find a way in. But it's a lockdown siege. They're saying that it's Abdelhamid Abaaoud. Zorro has nick-named him Baabaa Black Sheep." Jean's thin lips compressed into his habitual wry dry half-smile, *Oui c'est très drôle*, here we are again. A great and terrible violence has occurred. *Quelle surprise!* Clap your hands together; applause, thunder. Now the work begins! Ream-ing sentences into paragraphs of clichés and conventions. "It's a merry old go-round," Jean described it once, "like one of those tape machines we used to have, when you could watch history loop as you recorded it."

The local kids were already selling mobile phone footage. Three or four of them gathered around us. A girl with long black Kardashian hair, kohl oval eyes, diamonds in her sneakers, scrolled through her twitter feed. A guy in a Gucci baseball cap shuffled from one foot to another.

"Look at me! I look the same as him!" He showed me a screenshot of Abaaoud, smiling, thin moustache, guerrilla camouflage jacket, black ISIS flag behind him. They all laughed. I laughed too, because it was funny; he *did* look like him. Same long face, long nose, wet sand-colored skin. Not-Abaaoud cocked a thumb at the police line.

"I'm gonna turn myself in. Man, that would totally mess them up!" The kids were high and garrulous.

"My grandmother lives right opposite!" The girl tossed her long hair. She swiped the video on the phone; her multicolored fingernails clacked against the cracked glass. I bent to look closer, but I could only see a blank façade with two bullet holes star-bursted in the plaster. The girl gave me an earbud to listen. I heard gun shots, heavy caliber in clustered semiautomatic bursts, and an old woman's frightened, labored breathing. Then the video fell down to the street, where three policemen were roughly pulling and dragging a man. The man was bent over, his head was forced down, he was barefoot and naked from the waist.

"No wait here's a good one, my friend just posted it on Facebook." Another video of a blank wall. Through the earbuds I listened to a police voice shouting, urgent: "Where's your boyfriend?"

A woman's voice shouted back, angry, defiant: "He's not my boyfriend!"

"Where is he?"

"He's not my boyfriend!"

Gunfire sounded, flat percussive bangs, then drilling fusillades.

"I want five hundred," said the Kardashian girl, looking at me and tossing her head so that her hair swept up and fell back into a black crescent.

"We're just print," I told her. "Try the TV guys."

Jean was tapping on his phone. Long elegant fingers, a copper verdigris bracelet around his wrist, more white in his stubble than gray. He wore his experience of documenting man's-inhumanity-to-man as comfortably as an old pair of jeans. Dispassionate, long-lens perspective; he could get frustrated, but he was never bitter—he had no reason to be. He loved Margot, Margot loved him, his children had grown up kind and intelligent, he had a house with a sea view. No, he was never bitter; that was my trench, he chided. I followed his gaze as he looked up at a helicopter chopping the dawn overhead.

"It's like it's some kind of gratification for them," he said, pointing his steel pen at the Gucci cap guy and the kohl girls. "It's entertainment. Like it's cool to be in the center of the action."

"Of course it's cool. Why else would we have done it?"

Zorro appeared and sat on the step next to me. His blond dreadlocks were tied back with a pink sparkly elastic band. A Syrian girl had given it to him in Greece last summer. Zorro had been on the beach at dawn photographing the dinghies coming in. The girl had stood apart, shivering, he had wrapped his red and white keffiyeh around her, and in return she had given him her pink sparkly hair band.

"Bullshit. Police. Impossible to get anything except police. Oh, the police, there are hundreds; terrorists are more elusive."

I got up and wandered through the scene, notebook in hand. Hefty Maghrebi ladies, arms folded across their chests; old Berber men with gold teeth. Mothers worried that the schools were closed, what would they do with their kids? They had to go to work and the métro was not stopping at the station, and all of this—*this*. A woman with a flowered headscarf and gold dangling earrings swept her arm to encompass the invasion. A waiter was setting up tables on the terrace of the Café de Calife on the corner. Coffee would be good. A kid in a red leather jacket revved up on a *moto*, a group of police blocked his way, jabbing, pointing, ordering him back. He took off his helmet to remonstrate— Bambi eyes blinked, thick eyebrows, one razor-striped, and I thought for a second, It's Mohammed from the beach in Kos!

A crazy woman with curly hair pointed a claw hand at me.

"Whites! Look at them gathering like vultures. All of them! *Putains!* What are they doing here? Come to take pictures of us like we are animals in a zoo. This *quartier* is ours!" The guy on the *moto*, the groups of *flics*, everyone in the café and the kids hovering about the TV crews all turned to look at me as if I was the perpetrator.

When the Café de Calife opened, we set up our laptops on one of the outdoor tables. I had a habit of filing my stories under the names of Paris Métro stations, the better to confound hotel-room spies or officials at border crossings. The Paris Métro is full of destinations, forgotten heroes, old battlefields, and writers no one reads anymore. I kept a métro map tacked up on the wall above my desk, and it was fun to file things under apposites and to smile at correlations and ironies. *VOLTAIRE* for the Arab Spring, *BONNES NOUVELLES* for Gadaffi's undignified death, *PLACE DES FÊTES* for the Fall of Baghdad, *ÉCOLE MILITAIRE* for Afghanistan in the winter of 2001.

I opened a new file and began to type.

File: VOLONTAIRES
November 18, 2015

French police killed three suspected terrorists and arrested a further eight people in a raid on a house in the Saint-Denis suburb of Paris this morning. Among the dead was Abdelhamid Abaaoud, a 29-year-old Belgian national, who French authorities believe was the mastermind behind the attacks on Friday night in Paris, at the Bataclan theater and at several bars and restaurants, which killed 130 people.

"Another gangsta jihadi," I said to Jean as I typed, "radicalized in prison. Poor boy, he had to grow up as a second-generation immigrant in a suburb. Free education and health care and the protection of the rule of law. The miserable injustice of it! Having to endure the oppression of a democratic state! I am so fed up with this narrative—"

"Kit, stop ranting!" said Jean. "I'm too tired."

Zorro ordered another coffee, *un double*, fiddled with the catch on his pillbox and swallowed his morning dose of pharmaceutical heroin. His silver skull ring caught the first sun ray of the day.

"His girlfriend—she's the interesting one," Zorro said. "They are saying she's the one who blew herself up—"

"It's not confirmed," said Jean.

"There are pictures of her in a bikini all over the web. Beach-babe bikini. Her family said she only started wearing a headscarf six months ago."

Jean signaled to the waiter and said, "Bring me a brandy."

The waiter shook his head, *"Pas d'alcool, pas dans ce café non."*

"You see?" I said triumphantly. "The thin end of the wedge! Accommodate, accommodate. It's the opposite of assimilation. And now you can't have a drink when you want." Jean frowned. This was an argument we had been having for months.

Jean said he would have a coffee instead. The waiter made a curt smile. Jean looked at me over the top of his black framed glasses, but I kept talking.

"How many of these disaffected teenagers have to gun down innocent people before you stop saying it's just a few bad apples who have got the wrong end of the stick? What does 'radicalized' even mean? It's just one of those made-up media words that gets used to stand in for the bit you don't understand—"

"Shut up, Kit." This time it was Zorro who said it. Indignant, I went back to my story.

Abdelhamid Abaaoud was born in Belgium in 1987 and grew up in Molenbeek, an immigrant neighborhood of Brussels. His father emigrated from Morocco in 1975 and opened a shop in the area.

Abaaoud attended a prestigious Catholic school, but was expelled for reasons that are unclear. In 2010 he was arrested for attempting to break into a garage. Over the next three years he was known to the police for his connections with drug dealers in the neighborhood and was imprisoned three times for petty crimes.

By 2013, Abaaoud was in Syria fighting for ISIS. He appeared in an ISIS video, dragging corpses behind a pickup truck. Later that year, he recruited his thirteen-year-old brother, Younes, who traveled to Syria to fight with him. Sometime in 2014, Abaaoud returned to Europe (how is unknown) "in order to terrorize the crusaders waging war against the Muslims," according to an interview he gave to the ISIS magazine Dabiq.

French authorities now believe he was responsible for coordinating several previous failed attacks in France and Belgium over the past eighteen months. Intelligence sources have said that telephone records indicate he was in contact with Mehdi Nemmouche, who shot and killed four people at the Jewish Museum in Brussels in May 2014, and with Sid Ahmed Ghlam, who shot and killed Aurélie Châtelain in the Parisian suburb of Villejuif in April 2015 in the middle of a failed attempt to target a church in the area. He has also been linked to Ayoub El Khazzani, who tried to open fire with a Kalashnikov on the Thalys train traveling from Amsterdam to Paris in August 2015, an attack that was thwarted when passengers, including three American marines on holiday, wrestled the gunman to the ground.

After the attacks in Paris five days ago, Abaaoud's fingerprints were found on a Kalashnikov abandoned in a rented black Seat car that was identified as being the vehicle used by the group of gunmen who shot and killed people sitting outside bars and restaurants in the 11th arrondissement. At 10:14 pm on the night of the attacks, CCTV footage showed Abaaoud and a companion going through the turnstile at the Croix de Chavaux Métro station, in the suburb of Montreuil, in the west of Paris, 200 meters away from the street where the Seat was later found.

I looked up the footage from the métro on YouTube. Two figures moved in jerky slow-mo through the turnstiles. They were dressed in dark jackets and dark trousers and looked like anyone, *anonyme*. Except for Abaaoud's bright orange sneakers—

Paris Prosecutor François Molins has stated that Abaaoud took the No. 9 métro to the Place de la République station and that his mobile phone signal has been detected adjacent to the Bataclan concert hall, during the siege, from about 11:00 p.m. until 12:28 a.m.

In the early hours of this morning the French police received information that Abaaoud, and several others involved in the attacks, were staying at No. 8 rue du Corbillon in Saint-Denis. Hundreds of French police and army were deployed and cordoned the street. Witnesses say they were woken up by heavy gunfire at 4:30 a.m. A violent siege ensued. Between 4:30 a.m. and 7:20 a.m., when Abaaoud blew himself up with a suicide vest, the police poured five thousand rounds of ammunition into the house.

Along with Abaaoud, a woman named Hasna Aït Boulahcen—according to some reports, Abaaoud's cousin, according to others his girlfriend—and Chakib Akrouh, reportedly also a perpetrator of the Paris attacks, were killed. Five policemen were injured and a police dog called Diesel was killed. Eight people were arrested. One, Jawad Bendaoud, was the owner of the apartment in which the attackers were staying. As he was led away by police, he shouted to TV crews on the scene that he had lent the apartment to two Belgians as a favor to a friend.

"I said there was no mattress. They told me, 'It's not a problem.' They just wanted water and to pray."

I hit send. Oz was in New York, six hours behind; it was the middle of the night, but he never slept. Always hungry, always awake. Feed the beast, keep the news cycle turning, around and around like a hamster wheel.

"Kit, you done? Let's *yallah*." Zorro had finished uploading his pictures.

"Let's go," Jean concurred. "I'm going to go to the paper. Lunch later, Kit," he reminded me. "With Alexandre at Le Grand Véfour." My two godfathers had summoned me.

"Yes sorry. I forgot." I wanted to sleep. I wanted to forget everything.

Jean gave Zorro a lift; I said I wanted to walk for a bit. The Stade de France métro, half a kilometer away, was open. *One foot in front of another and maybe one day I'll get somewhere.* (Where did I pick up this endurance mantra? Tramping Moscow probably.) *Or maybe I won't because life is only a long walk to a dead end and the show will be over before I arrive.*

Here was Paris beyond the cordon of the Périphérique, low-rise bourgeois, plain, beige, walled. The idiom of the impenetrable French *non* was interrupted by a sudden cheery assertion.

"*Bonjour, Madame!*" said a woman walking her son to school; I had accidentally caught her eye. She was my age, thin, delicate crows-feet at the corners of cornflower eyes. She wore skinny jeans and a tailored yellow leather biker's jacket. *Tap-tap-tap* went the heels of her boots.

Her son raced ahead on his push scooter, like Little Ahmed used to do. It always terrified me. I would run after him gasping, and he would laugh with delight as if it was a great game of escape, oblivious to the cars and trucks and buses that could kill him in the split second of an accident.

The woman in the yellow jacket called out.

"Pay attention! Be careful! *Come back!*"

PART I
BAGHDAD

Ahmed refused to pay, there was an argument, and Ahmed slammed the door and got out of the taxi. He found himself on Haifa Street and decided to go to the Al-Rashid to call his mother, if the circuits were still working. And if he could get past the state security goons in the lobby.

"You cannot imagine, Kitty Cat," Ahmed recounted, some weeks later. "The place was absolutely deserted, it was like the hotel in *The Shining*. The storm was coming. I was excited. After all the years of hoping that this monster Saddam would die, that someone would assassinate him, that a SCUD missile would finally find him, I never imagined that the Americans would truly *invade*. It still seems fantastic to me that they are *here*, walking down our streets, going into all the ministries and throwing out the corrupt dinosaurs. The American invasion is the best thing that could ever have happened to the Iraqis! Most of them are just too stupid to understand. I am trying to get a conference of South Koreans and Japanese and Germans to come and tell them what a wonderful thing it is to be occupied by Americans!

"Jean says that he found me pouring myself a martini; but this is not true; it was brandy. And you don't put olives in brandy. I think he thought I was the bartender. He looked at the bottle and said, 'Ah, Napoleon. Very apposite for an invasion.' We began to talk and I explained that I was not the bartender. He said, 'You speak very good French and I need an interpreter, because my guy has vanished with all the others. So *Le Figaro* would like to hire you. How does a hundred dollars sound?' I was thrilled because I had been working for this air conditioner businessman who was paying me fifty dollars a month and five kilos of rice. I thought, That's double what I am getting! Then he shook my hand and said, 'A hundred dollars a day,' and I tried hard not to look completely amazed. And then I was really worried in case the Americans didn't bomb after all and Saddam somehow managed to wriggle out and survive as he had so many times in the past . . .'"

Typically, I missed the war. I was in Paris. My mother had died, and I was calling crematoria, furious with her timing, crying, confused, torn, watching the news and wanting to be in Baghdad, feeling guilty for feeling guilty.

We burnt my mother on a cold Tuesday afternoon. It was a desultory ceremony, not many people, and few that I knew. When the doors opened at the back of the windowless room for the attendant to push her coffin trolley through, I could hear the roar of the furnace. Margot squeezed my hand.

"*Courage, ma petite*. This is the first part, the trauma, shock." I shook my hand free; I didn't want to be consoled by her psychologist reasoning. Resentment was not one of the five stages of grief.

I took my mother's ashes to London on the Eurostar and scattered them in Hyde Park near the statue of Peter Pan, where we used to have rain picnics in the autumn. It was the day the Americans crossed into Iraq from Kuwait. I slept on the way back through the long tunnel under the Channel. In Paris there was a lot to do, and I was busy with the lawyers and the building residents committee. I packed her clothes in boxes for charity. I sent the curtains to the dry cleaners to get rid of the nicotine smell and threw away all her sheets. The British besieged Basra. I found the box of my possessions left over from Moscow that my mother had stored for me and I had never had time to open. The nostalgia was unbearable, as if episodes of my life had returned in a series of big heavy waves that swamped me. I found a packet of letters I had written to my father and never posted because there was never any address to send them to. I found the pink scarf I knitted for my mother when I was twelve and the mahogany tea caddy I had once hidden cigarettes in. I wrapped all her dusty trinkets from the Saigon years in newspaper and put them away in the *cave* in the building's basement.

In the evenings I drank her sweet Martini Rosso and watched the news. Tanks in the desert; ragged figures surrendering. I was missing everything! CNN was triumphant. Zorro was embedded with

the Marines and his pictures were all over the *New York Times*. Jean
sent emails:

> . . . I'm sorry for everything, your mother and the terrible timing.
> Margot says you were very dignified at the crematorium ceremony.
> I can't imagine how bleak you must feel, but you know you can call
> on her if you need anything. I'm holed up in the hotel because of
> the bombing. Comical Ali press conferences have become our only
> entertainment. Phone lines in Baghdad are mostly dead. All my old
> contacts/sources have disappeared. The Ministry of Information
> extortionists are trying to charge the TV crews $100,000 a week
> (Sebastian, BBC, told me) for their "visa extensions." They've arrested
> four foreign journalists from the Palestine hotel; a bunch of us went
> to try and find out where they had been taken, but the toads wouldn't
> say anything. Everyone is very worried about them. There is talk they
> will charge them for espionage . . .
>
> When are you coming? Come via Jordan, the border is com-
> pletely open now, Fitz came through yesterday and said there were
> no guards, a couple of American soldiers just waving everyone
> through(!) The road is pretty clear, a few bandits, everything cha-
> otic, but I'll send you a good driver. Can you bring me money? I've
> run out, everything is expensive, war prices. Suzanne at the paper
> will give you an envelope. You'll need a hundred a day for a trans-
> lator, more for a driver. I'm staying at the old Sheraton now, it's
> cheaper and they've got better internet than the Rashid, I'll get you
> a room. The food is bad, chicken and rice every night, but at least the
> room cleaners have come back now—they all disappeared during
> the bombing. Come quickly, before it's all over. You'll kick yourself
> if you miss this one . . .

When the Americans reached the banks of the Tigris, I left the
keys to the apartment with a rental agency and flew to Amman.

The driver Jean recommended met me at the airport and we drove through the night across the desert border.

Dawn drew a flat horizon. The road spooled a gray ribbon through a scratched-up landscape, dun and featureless. Nothing to see for miles, no other cars on the road. I was too scared to sleep, hundred-dollar bills stashed in my underpants. The driver was a big fat guy who chewed sunflower seeds to stay awake, splitting them methodically with his teeth and spitting the husks into a paper cup. When we got to the outskirts of Baghdad, we saw the first American tanks, great beasts sleeping in the shade under Saddam's triumphal arches. I held up my American passport and they waved us through. The driver dropped me at the Sheraton and there was Jean in the lobby with Zorro. Sitting next to them was Ahmed.

"You're late to the party," said Zorro. "You missed the fireworks."

"Thanks."

"You got across the desert alright?" Jean asked.

"No, I was kidnapped. I am in a basement in Fallujah right now."

"Not you, the money!"

"Yes, I brought the cash. And whiskey and an extra flak jacket and four new notebooks." Jean kissed me. "And two salami."

Jean and Zorro clapped.

"I am Ahmed Solemani," said Ahmed, standing up and extending his hand to introduce himself. He *was* golden, his skin shone, burnished. His eyelashes beat black angel wings. "Italian or French?"

I was confused, I thought he was trying to explain his background. "You are Italian and French?"

"Not me—the *saucisson!*"

———

Ahmed, my Aladdin. He smiled like a prince in a fairy tale, shining white teeth to the rescue. I think back to the beginning, to those early helter-skelter days when everything was new and exciting and the springtime sun was warm before the oven heat of summer, and I can hardly believe I was so naïve.

Ahmed was an educated, Westernized Iraqi. All the correspondents and diplomats were impressed by his erudition and his sophistication. He wore Diesel jeans and desert boots he said he bartered for a Saddam statue head with an American major. He was cool, he was fluent, he was one of us. He was an Iraqi anomaly. He could analyze Tony Blair's cabinet with a BBC producer, talk reconstruction with the neocons, roll his eyes with the French at the "coalition of the willing." They asked him where he'd learned such good English, such good French. Where had he read the novels of Romain Gary? How had he managed to watch *Sex in the City* under sanctions? Ahmed inveigled their condescension.

"Well," he would say, drawing his eager audience in, "if you must ask—"

Ahmed would explain that he was the only son of an Iraqi diplomat. He had learned his French and English from international schools in Paris and Caracas. In the early nineties his father was a senior political officer at the Iraqi Embassy in Washington and they lived in D.C. for six years. At the beginning of 1998 his father was recalled to Iraq. According to Ahmed, this meant he had to leave Georgetown when he was in his senior year, only a semester from graduation. Shortly after the family returned to Baghdad, his father was arrested. For several months they had no word of him. Ahmed called his father's friends in high places, but they all professed to know nothing and told him, insincerely, not to worry.

In the summer, at the beginning of Eid—Ahmed remembered because it was a holiday and everything was difficult to arrange—his mother received a telephone call telling her to collect her husband's body from the prison at Abu Ghraib. Ahmed went with her. The officials insulted them and made them pay for a coffin and would not help them carry it. Ahmed told me how he and his mother had wrestled with the dead weight of his executed father, levering, pushing, pulling the coffin onto the car roof while the guards watched and smoked and spat on the ground.

"At one point it fell and the lid came off and I had to go to a garage up the road and borrow a hammer to nail it back on. I understand why you don't want to look at death, Kit. His face was so familiar, and it was looking at me. They had not even closed his eyes. I wanted to close his eyes, but I couldn't bring myself to touch his body. Even now, I remember his face looking at me. I did not have the courage to close his eyes so that his soul could sleep."

He told me this sitting in a café on Mutanabbi Street. Dominoes clacked on the marble tables. There were many things he told me back then that turned out not to be true, but when he recounted collecting his father's body, he looked down, not to let me see his tears. This scene I believe.

A public funeral was not permitted. They took the coffin to the cemetery; they had to bribe the caretaker to say a prayer over his grave.

Afterwards came the sanctions years. As the son of a traitor, Ahmed was not allowed to apply for university, and government jobs were closed to him. His father's pension was stopped. They sold the family car, two gold-plated handguns Saddam had presented to his father, and the VHS player they had brought back from the States. His mother sold her jewelry until there was nothing left and she was reduced to begging from her sisters. After two years, a friend of the family helped Ahmed get a job with a businessman from Samarra who had some bogus concession that allowed him to sell Turkish air-conditioning units. They were difficult to come by under sanctions.

I long ago decided not to try to reconcile the misaligned details and ellipses in Ahmed's stories. But it was true that Ahmed's father was executed by Saddam for being a traitor. (There *was* an American-backed plot to oust Saddam in '98, cooked up by the CIA and Ahmed Chalabi; it was a complete disaster. But Ahmed always said he didn't believe his father was mixed up in it. "He was a patriot; he hated Saddam for what he did to our country, but he never would have joined a group of Baathie putschists.") But the part about Georgetown, for example, was not. After Ahmed and I finally split up, Alexandre made discreet enquires and told me that there was no record of Ahmed's matriculation.

The hard times, the misery years of sanctions? Yes, Ahmed was thin when I first met him (in Paris he would inflate to a satisfied tubby), and his mother's villa was large and empty of furniture. But the chronicles of Ahmed were inconsistent. Dates didn't add up, characters got swapped from one story to another. He had sold Turkish air conditioners, he had sold his father's books at the book market on Mutanabbi Street, he helped a cousin steal oil from a pipeline and sell it to a Kurdish middleman. He had tried to escape to Kurdistan, but the smugglers took his money and never showed up for the rendezvous. He was recruited into the Republican Guard, but when he reported for duty, the colonel realized he was the son of a traitor and sent him away. He lived for five years as a deserter (an offense that carried the penalty of having an ear cut off), he had three different fake ID cards, and once he was arrested for taking a picture of Saddam's son Uday's power boat moored on the Tigris.

He told these stories lightly, as comic illustrations of the mad Saddam years. Maybe there was some kernel of truth in them, but in his telling the episodes always had the quality of anecdote. From time to time in Baghdad we would run into someone he knew and he would be reticent to introduce me. I could not speak Arabic—at least not enough to understand low tones, dissembling, nuances. "Who was that?" I'd ask. "Oh, an old school friend," Ahmed would answer blithely.

One time, Ahmed and Jean and I had gone to Samarra—it must have been the end of that first summer—to investigate a report of two boys being pushed off a bridge by American soldiers; one had drowned. It was a long drive out of Baghdad—white skies strung with swags of telegraph wire. We interviewed the family of the drowned boy, and then Jean wanted to see the big Shia shrine in the middle of the Sunni town. I remember he was working on a long article about the Shia at the time. Ahmed didn't want to go to the shrine and was grumbling. He had wanted to go along the river to where he said there was the best kebab restaurant in the country.

"It's only because your father's family is from Samarra that you think that Samarra has the best kebab in Iraq. Every town thinks it has the best kebab in Iraq." Ahmed didn't smile at this; he didn't understand teasing yet.

A small crowd milled about the gate to the shrine, the popcorn seller, the beggar, a prostitute, an old man selling postcards. A man approached us under the colonnade. Brown trousers, white shirt, gold ring set with a turquoise stone on his pinkie. He was clean-shaven, angular, sharp face, knife blade nose. I saw Ahmed try to turn away, but the man reached out and held his wrist fast and I heard him say, in English, as if this was a language that would not be understood by passers-by, "Ah, I thought it was you. We haven't seen you for a long time, you have forgotten your cousins!" The man looked me up and down. I instinctively smoothed my hair under my headscarf, better to meet his approval. "You are friends with the Americans, I see. Yes, good. Very helpful."

Ahmed told me to go inside, and I did because I trusted he knew better. I asked him, "Who was that?" But he only said, "I'll tell you later," and then never did.

I fell in love with Ahmed that Baghdad scorching summer—throbbing temperatures, burning streets. I think he fell in love with me too. He said he did and I believed him.

"I am a monkey," Ahmed told me. "My father said I must be a monkey and a lion."

"You walk like a lion," I told him, stroking the underside of his chin. "Padding gracefully, prowling." Ahmed smiled at me and ran his hands through my hair.

"It's like gold," he said, drawing it softly through his soft fingertips. "Our children will be lion cubs with golden manes." I did not know yet that I was infertile. We drew the blinds against the beastly Baghdad sun and curled naked in each other's arms. A boom sounded, faintly.

"It's only the elevator," Ahmed reassured me. "When it hits the ground floor it makes a thud."

"Everything sounds like a bomb."

"Ah, my brave war reporter, frightened by the bombs."

"Aren't bombs supposed to be frightening? After all, they can kill you."

"No one is going to hurt you, my perfect American dream." He kissed the tip of my nose. "Let me count the spots."

"The *freckles!*"

"Freckles! One hundred, two hundred, a thousand freckles like gold dust. There are too many to count! I love you like the sky is infinite. I love you like waves in the sea. I love you from your ski jump nose to the bottom of your American ass."

"Half-American ass."

"American it must be, to be so big and generous."

"Are you saying that my bum is fat?"

"Soft and ripe like an apricot, Mish-mish."

He called me Mish-mish. Apricots and pomegranates and rosewater, the sweet scents of oriental courtship, pistachio baklava dripping in honeyed syrup from Abu Darwish's shop in Karrada. We made love one afternoon on a boat hidden in the reeds of the Tigris. A stork stood by and watched us with great fascination and Ahmed kissed my belly and said, "See, she has come to deliver a present to us." I felt the sun warm on my neck, heat pounding in my temples, pulsing hot blood, pumping lava through my veins, dizzy . . . heatstroke in May.

But how magical to fall in love, to carry a child, to feel love growing into physical form inside me. Ahmed was very handsome.

"But it's not that!" I later protested to Alexandre, sipping Campari in the embassy garden. "He is clever and speaks four languages and studied at Georgetown. He says I have been lonely all my life and I will never be lonely again. He understands me! I have fallen in love, Alexandre! Don't pout, be happy for me!"

"He is a very clever fellow, there is no doubt," said Alexandre, tinkling ice cubes into his highball glass. "But wartime romances are notoriously precarious."

"Like my mother and my father."

"Not a compatible couple," Alexandre affirmed. He looked at me intently, as if considering adding something—but he did not. Alexandre, who spoke in silver streaming paragraphs, stumbled. "They should not have—" he began and then corrected himself. "Well, it's an old story. There is no reason that history repeats itself—as I am always repeating myself! *Bien*. I am glad they did, *bien sûr*, because they made you."

———

Ahmed asked me to marry him, whirlwind. A sandstorm blew in from the desert. Wasn't love supposed to be like this? We posed for our engagement portrait in the garden of the French Embassy. Zorro fiddled with the light meter and said it would come out badly, visibility was too low. In the photograph I am looking up adoringly at Ahmed, smiling despite the grit in my teeth, and holding an apricot in my hand.

We came inside from the dust cloud and wind, Zorro polishing his lens with a chamois cloth, Jean pouring the champagne and laughing. He told Alexandre to stop being a naysaying old auntie, we were young and in love.

"I met Margot in Beirut. I asked her to marry me the day the

Israelis invaded. We got married in Cyprus and went on our honeymoon to the Turkish military zone because the beaches were empty. Kitty, don't mind the old bachelor."

"Humpf," replied Alexandre. Then he raised his glass and pointed a long elegant finger at Ahmed in warning. "You are welcome into the family. Such as we are—two godfathers and these two unruly adopted children." Zorro grinned and ran his hand through his long hair; his jangling copper bracelets tinkled like a wind chime. "You must know that we two old dinosaurs are *in loco parentis*. It is us you will have to answer to if you make her unhappy."

Ahmed only laughed.

TWO

Dad was my American half, Mum was my English. They met in the AP bureau in Saigon in 1974. He was a correspondent; she was a telex operator. I have a photograph of them taken just before the Fall of Saigon at the bureau Christmas party. My mother is wearing a Pucci minidress and a loop of tinsel around her neck; my father is wearing a wide-lapelled safari jacket. She is staring up at him adoringly and holding up (for some reason) a mango. Dad is wearing aviator sunglasses. I have only one photograph of him where I can see his eyes. It was taken in Tehran in 1979 during the American hostage crisis; it's black and white and it's hard to tell what color they are. My mother burnt all her photograph albums after her second breakdown.

They were happy together in foreign places. In Saigon, in Beirut—funny to think that they were happy there, where I was so unhappy thirty years later. Count back the months from my birth, I think I must have been conceived in Beirut because I was born in Boston in the summer of 1977. Dad had sent my mother to live with Granbet in the house in Good Harbor Bay when she was seven months pregnant. He stayed in Lebanon. "Abandoned me!" whined my mother through years of rambling complaint, mug of Martini Rosso on the coffee table next to an overflowing ashtray, TV on, droning melodrama. She loved *EastEnders* and wailed along with Angie because Den was a bastard rotter and he was going to run off and leave her. "Just like YOUR FATHER did!"

I don't know what happened between them. I know that he was not present for my birth. I know that my mother had postnatal depression. "They didn't call it that back then," Margot told me one Russian summer, pickling cucumbers at the dacha. Margot was a psychologist; her godmotherly sympathy carried the authority of professional reasoning. She gave me a way to see things from the other side: "repositioning perspective" was her clinical term for it.

"They just called it baby blues in those days. Doctors didn't do talking cures. I'm sure your poor mother was doped up with Valium."

I was born on July 2, 1977, forty-eight hours away from being independent—a metaphor I like to stretch to fit sometimes. When I was six months old, my mother left me in Good Harbor Bay with Granbet and went back to England. I think to a sanatorium there. Her mother would have still been alive then. After the sanatorium my mother must have moved in with her, because that's the house where I went when Granbet died. Granbet died the day after my eleventh birthday.

I lived in that narrow house in Paddington for seven years, in the guest room, my room, except my mother always called it the guest room. In bed, lights out, listening to the muttering television and my mother's snoring on the sofa, tiptoeing downstairs to make sure she had stubbed out all her cigarettes properly. I didn't like school, but I slunk out early every morning, better to have a few hours of lone freedom than suffer the grouchy breakfast routine. Zorro was my best friend because we were both bad at math and had the same blond bobbed haircut.

My godfathers, Alexandre and Jean, were my father's friends and not my mother's. I knew there was antipathy between them, but I did not know why. They sent me birthday cards and Christmas presents, and a couple of times Jean asked if my mother would let me spend some time with him and Margot at their house in Brittany, but there was always some logistical obstacle that my mother delayed into never happening.

When I turned eighteen, I finished school and the switch flipped to adulthood. I didn't have to anymore. I didn't want to go to university and sit in more classrooms and take more exams. My mother and I coexisted in the house by avoiding each other like repellent magnets. If she asked, I just said, "gap year."

"But where?" She became insistent. Eventually it erupted into a shouting match. I yelled back that I wanted to use my small inheritance from Granbet to buy a plane ticket to Thailand and go and find my father. Then the volcano really blew up, with all the rage and wrong and ingratitude and sacrifice and misery. Vitriol squeezed from her eyes and fizzed and turned to steam running over her red cheeks. In despair she called the godfathers, and Alexandre came over from Paris and took me to lunch at Le Gavroche to talk me out of it.

Alexandre and Jean had circled my universe as distant planets, as mysterious as my father's disappearance and somehow, gravitationally, connected to it. My mother always referred to them as "your godfathers" and in my childish imagination they appeared as a double act; in reality they were very different. Jean was practical and physical, vigorous—he surfed the Channel in the middle of the Brittany winter. Alexandre Delacroix was an effete diplomat.

At Le Gavroche, Alexandre kissed me affectionately hello on both cheeks and handed his thick navy blue overcoat and his homburg hat to the maître d'. His pale gray hair swept off his high forehead like a helmet of very fine cashmere. He wore a blue tweed jacket, an ivory shirt with silver dice cufflinks, and an apple green cravat. When we sat down, he ordered an aperitif of crème de menthe with champagne.

"And a Kir Royale for my dear companion."

Alexandre liked to say that he was a descendent of the artist Delacroix. When his audience smiled, he would continue, "And did you know that Delacroix was, in fact, the illegitimate son of Napoleon's chief diplomat, the great double-crossing Talleyrand?" (There was a certain plausibility to the rumors; Eugène Delacroix's father, Charles Delacroix, was minister of foreign affairs under the Directorate and had undergone testicular surgery in the year before his son's birth; Talleyrand was a close family friend.) Alexandre would clap his hands together with delight, a particular gesture of his, the looting joy of luxury that he did not have to pay for, he was a very model *roué* left over, like much of France, from La Belle Époque.

Alexandre was a perennial bachelor. Everyone *knew*, but he preferred to allude than to admit. Discretion, above all. I was never aware of any lover, although he must have had them. He had joined the French diplomatic corps in the days when homosexuals were not sent on foreign postings because they were vulnerable to blackmail. Outwardly he cultivated graciousness, politesse, but there was something of the costume in it, a professional garment. In the private residence of the French Embassy in Baghdad, his cadence was languid and indulgent, "but of course," "yes, I have often said so," "how marvelous!" If he wanted to chide, he would say, "come, come now" as if his interlocutor—whether belligerent Russian first secretary, ornery tribal sheikh, unblinking zealot—only needed a nudge to bring him round.

With eighteen-year-old me, that day at Le Gavroche, Alexandre was kind and concerned. He listened to my complaint attentively. He did not try to interrupt or intercede until we had finished our *vol-au-vent aux champignons* and the waiter had bought a bottle of Pommard.

"Explore, yes, this is your age and your nature; I wouldn't expect anything less of John's daughter. But don't go to look for your father. He has lost himself. He is lost to us." I felt my lower lip tremble. This was not how I had rehearsed Alexandre's part. He was connected to my father, he would help me find my father. Alexandre reached his hand across the damask, my hands remained frozen on my lap, and I regarded his five manicured fingernails and his gesture as if from a great height or from a great depth.

"It is very sad. We are all very sad, but the truth is your father doesn't exist anymore, not in any form that you can find him." The waiters put two plates in front of us and, with a nod, lifted the silver cloches at precisely the same moment to reveal a tiny nest of pigeon breast. My mouth tasted of zinc; I was biting the inside of my lip, trying not to move, trying not to cry. When I chewed the pigeon, it was as soft and dense as wadded tissue and tasted of betrayal.

"There, there," Alexandre said. "I've talked to your other godfather Jean. He is now bureau chief in Moscow. He says you can go and stay with him and Margot there—much more adventurous than Thailand, which is full of Eurotrash backpackers. Margot is a wonderful and wise soul, you can talk to her. You can learn Russian and how to drink vodka, take the train to St. Petersburg, white nights, Siberian tundra. You want to write?" I nodded, a single lead shot rolling under my tongue. "Very good. You will be in the land of writers and the new frontier of journalism. Stay for a few months and see how you feel. You can always go to university later."

————

"When did you first meet my father?" I asked Alexandre one evening in the dappled shade of the bougainvillea on his terrace in Baghdad.

"In Sinai," he said, but I could not see the expression in his eyes behind the emerald glass.

"Yom Kippur War?"

"Or the Ramadan War. Or the Six-Day War. Depending on which side you were on. That's where it all began," he said, and started to say something else—but gunfire sounded, *ratta-tatta*, quite close, and we went inside to be safe. The thread of his reminiscence was broken.

After dinner I asked Alexandre straight out why no one would tell me what had happened to my father. I had only a few photographs of him that had escaped my mother's wrath, and the thrilling memory of a rough pair of hands jerking me up on his shoulders.

Alexandre looked at me squarely and said he knew it was difficult to understand, but the truth was not being hidden from me. It was just that no one knew what it was.

"There are too many false leads down jungle trails. He got lost. There were drugs." He shook his head. "There were a lot of drugs." He sighed with the sadness of a great loss. "Your father was an extraordinary man. He was as sensitive as a grape skin, but he would carry a man across the desert under gunfire. Even a man he did not know. Jean. Did you know that? He found Jean in an Israeli trench in Sinai, after an Egyptian plane had just bombed. Jean's eardrums were blown and he was in shock. Your father carried him on his back out of the killing zone. He would save anyone except himself."

"That's how you all met."

"It's long ago, history doesn't care anymore. None of us were supposed to be there, I remember, that was the funny thing. I was working for French radio and managed to cross into the military zone with Israeli radio people as an extra sound engineer. Jean was a second lieutenant in the French Army, liaison to the Israelis, but officially unofficial. Your father, God rest his idiocy, was wandering about pretending to be a lost hippie. And then the Egyptians made their surprise attack. We were stuck in a medical base for three days under Egyptian bombardment until the Israelis scrambled a counterattack. We didn't think we were going to get out of it. Afterwards, we were friends, connected by horror and death, for life. War people understand these moments. We promised we would never tell what we had seen.

"Jean and I—we are not protecting your father, we are protecting you. It takes a few decades of experience—especially in this game, this hall of mirrors—and don't fall for Jean's sagacity, *Je suis le grand rapporteur!* In Sinai, I understood for the first time that we can *never* know, that there is no truth to be discovered by diligent investigation. It's why I changed sides, or rather I went from 'outside' to 'inside,' as Jean calls it. Just as he switched sides the other way. He thinks it is more honest to stand on the street with his nose pressed against the glass. But really it's only another perspective, a different angle, and one obscured by the reflections in the window."

THREE

Ahmed worked for Jean as a fixer in the early months of the occupation. At the end of 2003, he secured a job in the Green Zone, as a translator for the Development Fund for Iraq. His mother was against it; she worried about his safety.

"People are spitting on those who work for the Americans," she told him, "soon they will start killing them." She was right. But Ahmed, annoyed, told her to stop fussing as if he were a child.

"Your father would not like you working for the Americans," she said, falling back on good old emotional blackmail.

"If my father had worked for the Americans instead of being loyal, he'd probably still be alive," Ahmed replied glibly.

I liked Um Ahmed, but she was skeptical of me. Ahmed told me she was conservative and would disapprove if I was his girlfriend, so it was better that I was presented as just a friend, a colleague, one of the journalists he had met through Jean. I don't think she was fooled, but she kept up her end of the pretense, a convenient complicity.

Um Ahmed had lived in Caracas and Washington as a diplomat's wife, but she never lost the tenets of propriety and obedience that the second daughter of a sheikh of Samarra was brought up to observe. Ahmed told me she would sit at dinner tables and make conversation when her husband commanded her to, but she never accompanied him to cocktail parties. She would not drink alcohol nor take off her headscarf in mixed company. She made friends with wives from Muslim countries, but she was always suspicious of the loose ways of the European women who drank and flirted. She prayed at home and would not have thought of going by herself to a mosque. But after Saddam fell and it was possible for Iraqis to travel again, she applied for the haj lottery and was accepted with a group of other widows. When she came back, she said that it had been very fulfilling, but that the crowds had been overwhelming and uncomfortable.

"There were too many Arabs" was how she put it. Which I thought was hilarious.

I knew that Ahmed had been married before. Early on, when we were still discovering each other, I had gone to use his mother's bathroom, and caught sight of a photograph of Ahmed, younger, with a moustache and a formal black suit and a carnation in his buttonhole, standing awkwardly next to a bride. His mother was in the kitchen preparing lunch and I asked him straight out, hands-on-hips, what's going on here? He had hung his head and sighed. They had married in 1998, he said, when his father was missing. He told me she was a nice girl from a good family, a suitable match arranged before his father's arrest. The wedding was very small because of the cloud hanging over his father's fate. A few months later, he said, she had an ectopic pregnancy and died in the hospital because a surgeon could not be found to operate on the relative of a traitor.

I asked him, "Did you love her? Are you still sad?" I reached for his hand and he let me hold it for a moment before withdrawing. He spoke between rhythmic drags on a cigarette. Inhale, pause, smoke, puff. He kept looking towards the door to the kitchen. His mother was slicing onions and we could hear her, exclaiming, "Ow-weesh," sting-ing eyes and weeping. Chop, chop, "ow-weesh." He lowered his voice.

"She was only the second daughter, not the pretty one." I had the sense that he had been pushed into the union against his wishes. I asked him what her name was, but he wouldn't tell me. He said that he felt guilty and he closed his eyes, as if retreating into some private interior torment. I thought that he felt guilty because she had died and he had not loved her. I told him that guilt was of no use to anyone—that her death was not his fault, that he must not allow the past to poison our future. That he must live his life and be happy and that was all anyone could do. I gathered my love into a force that would wipe away his pain and would lead us, together, towards a new and better future. I moved to put my arms around him, but he was stiff, stuck, somewhere else, and would not look at me. I knelt at his feet and rested my head on his knee. He started to say I'm sorry, but he said it in Arabic, "*Ana asif*." I heard it in English, "as if."

"As if what? Ahmed, don't worry. Everything is possible," I told him, my American dreaming half who believed, back then, in love and happy endings.

———

Ahmed was very gratified with his new job. The Development Fund for Iraq for was responsible for dispersing monies and contracts for civil projects. This was rebuilding, he thought, a Marshall Plan for the Middle East. His boss was a Vietnam vet Arabist on the State Department's Iraq desk. Colonel Don was in his sixties with plenty of salt in his wisdom, a Vermonter, a fisherman; he had optimistically packed his rods. "One of these days I'm going to get upriver, out of the Baghdad sewage stream, and haul in one of those mythical Tigris salmon." He treated Ahmed like a sidekick son-in-law. They barreled around the country in a white SUV convoy meeting tribal elders and dispensing wads of cash.

At the beginning it was a grand adventure. Sheikhs came out into the yards of their compounds and lined up their sons to greet the new rulers. A wary deference, bowing, welcoming, *Yes, yes, it is very bad in our town, Saddam punished us too much.* Coffee was poured into small thimble cups and the foreign entourage was ushered into the formal reception room.

Sometimes Colonel Don let me tag along. We'd take off our shoes and sit cross-legged, careful not to display the soles of our feet. A succession of coffee, tea, coffee, tea. Low concrete houses, chickens scratching in the yard. Small children throwing stones at crows and shooting each other with plastic Kalashnikovs. Inside, endless talking as a fan swirled the flies about. Hours of this. Interminable lunches, whole lambs slaughtered in our honor on giant mounds of almond raisin rice. The old men wore their tribal robes and sat beneath portraits of their fathers and grandfathers. *You can see we have no electricity, the bridge is in need of repair, the road was washed away in the floods last year. We are humble men who want to serve our people with your freshly printed bundles of green dollars that arrive shrink-wrapped in million-dollar blocks on cargo planes twice a week.* Colonel Don shrugged and nodded at their demands; this was the policy.

Ahmed was contemptuous of them. Backward, greedy village idiots, everything according to *inshallah.* Classrooms were repainted, but the school walls fell down; incubators were ordered, but there were no generators to power them. All those billions and good intentions ran into the sand and seeded IEDs. Like some strange greenhouse effect, as the weather got hotter the violence grew. Ahmed rolled his eyes that the first thing a sheikh would ask for was an air conditioner before any work could be done.

———

In the winter the car bombs began, slowly at first—perhaps one a month—but then more frequently. One day Zorro turned a corner and the street blew up bright orange! His photograph made the front page of the *New York Times*. Zorro became obsessed with finding the Baghdad golden hour, when the sky would be blue and the shadows could cast faces into bronze. He never did. The sky was white and it leached all the colors away so that only shades of ochre and yellow, beige and sand remained. Dust, dust, fucking dust.

Helicopters veering overhead all the time, ping-pong gunfire, constant, nothing to turn your head about. Pink globs of flesh wobbling like jelly on the tarmac after a bomb. Women wailing, flapping their black nylon wings, too heavy to fly away. But mostly when I think back, I recall that time in Baghdad as halcyon. I was in love, the story was the center of the world. Oh, happy days.

To think that we used to laugh at Zorro's luck, to always be next door to the explosion! He would tease me about my "bad" luck. "She goes up to Sadr City in the morning and buys tomatoes and chats to the neighborhood militia Moqtadr men and sits in a café and has a glass of tea with the mullah. I go up two hours later and the whole place is exploding and there's a Humvee burning." Zorro had all the luck. Until he got caught in crossfire under an overpass. And even then we continued the myth of Zorro's luck, because the bullet hit only his left arm and he got second prize in the World Press Photo Spot News category.

I was never struck by the violence in Baghdad. I lived there for two years after the American invasion and I never saw a dead body. Partly this was my bad luck, partly it was deliberate. I didn't go to count corpses in the morgue. I didn't want to look closer when they pulled up the sheet covering the dead fighter so that we could see how his face had been blown off by a mortar. I didn't want to have PTSD like all the old guard. I didn't want those war porn images in my dreams. I never watched the beheading videos, even when it was all the rage.

I was the girl who stood by the side of the road and wrote down what I saw in my notebook. Observe. That's what Jean had taught me in Moscow when I was new and green. He would take me along on reporting trips, Ingush orphanages, oil cities in Siberia, political campaigning in the Urals.

"Just write what you see and what you hear. Think about the word *reporter*. That's what you should be, the person who reports, tells what they have seen. Just that. Leave all the editorial guff— *What does this mean for XY and the future of U.S. foreign policy? et cetera, et cetera.* Don't worry about context, trying to compress history into subclauses—the editors will cut and paste their boilerplates. Editors—god rid the world of editors, I would say they are a necessary evil except I cannot see the necessity—an editor must edit, otherwise he has no job, so he edits, which means he fusses about all these irrelevancies and others—like what the foreign minister said this morning. Another thing to avoid is press conferences. Press conferences are the way of the politicians to put journalists into a zoo. The most important thing is to keep your eyes and your ears open. You must *notice*."

Soot-blackened chassis. Another car-bomb crater. Tiny silver triangles of jets overhead. Puffs of thunderhead smoke rising between tower blocks. Trails of red tracer in the night dark. Wailing black abaya triangles. I ran out of synonyms for rubble. I sat in cafés by the side of blasted roads and listened to people tell me what had happened to them. My pencil tip looped across the page, pages and pages of gunfire and wounded brothers hiding, arrested, tortured, fighting. I wrote down their terror and outrage and pain and noted the details: *three tribal tattoo dots on the bridge of her nose . . . fingernails missing from his right hand . . . Osama Bin Laden screen saver on his mobile phone . . .* I took their stories and sold them.

I was, Ahmed once told me, unkindly, the mistress of aftermath.

On panel discussions in the safe parallel world of New York or London, I was asked why I went to war zones. I answered that I felt a duty to understand and explain the Other to readers at home. This is not "an Iraqi," this is a person, even if he is called Ahmed, I would say to the interlocutor on the panel. Let me add something more to his identifying subclause beyond his age and occupation: *38, taxi driver.* For example, there is an Ahmed I know who is funny and wry and does a very good impression of George W. Bush, *Mission Accomplished! Let's go back to playing golf with the heads of Iraqi babies!* This Ahmed is hospitable and always invites me for tea and his wife bakes pistachio cookies that are delicious. You cannot imagine how friendly they are! This is a real Ahmed, with a life and family and a sense of humor. He has copper hair, and he laughs that they used to tease him in the army about being the descendant of a lost crusader tribe or those mythical long-lasting batteries that you could never get under sanctions. Yes, that Ahmed! His son has bright copper hair too and his wife calls him "my little orange." Ahmed, you know, the one who worked as a driver on the road to Amman and was hired by Reuters. Yes! Him! Funny lovely guy. Shot on the road to Fallujah last week. Another dead Ahmed.

I once said to Oz: "I want to give Iraqis a real, three-dimensional life. Not to lump them into a group of villains or victims and label it *them.*"

"Yes, characters. We need good characters," Oz replied. The satellite phone connection cracked. The exigencies of the newspaper's style manual impinged on the clean blank page of Jean's idealism. "Find me a donkey," said Oz. A donkey was a character whose own narrative carried the bigger issues of the story on his back through a feature story.

I reported, I wrote. It is true that the stories were all unhappy—war, injury, pain, loss—each an episode that peeled back another onion layer to reveal a previous misery. Iraqis were scabs over wounds that had never healed. I listened and diligently wrote down ruined lives in my notebook. When people cried, I found tears in my eyes too. I would hold their cracked and callused hands in mine and tell them it was all going to be better now. There would be reconstruction, renewal, redress. I was a fool.

———

Fire ringed a black hole crater. Everything was covered in a thin film of gray dust except for bright red pools of blood. The foreground was jumbled and full of lies. The women scratched their faces and ululated grief for the foreign cameras. The men stood beside the blasted scrim, smoking. When I asked them what happened, they pointed to the sky and said, "American helicopter!" Despite the irrefutable evidence of the burnt-out carcass of a car bomb.

The ambulance men picked up a severed leg and wrapped it in a sheet. The white bloomed red. A boy, perhaps eight years old, watched with the dispassionate fascination of little boys with war. I asked him what he had seen. He looked me up and down and asked for ten dollars, and when I rolled my eyes and walked away, he yelled after me, in English, "We will kill all you foreigners!"

I walked back and stood in front of him.

"OK," I said, pulling the scarf off my head. "Kill me then."

The kid laughed and said, "I will spare you if you give me a cigarette." I made a show of pulling a cigarette up from my pack and offering it to him, as politely adult as if we were at a cocktail party. He took it, made a small ironic bow, produced a lighter from his pocket and lit my cigarette before lighting his own. We got talking. He was adamant that the Americans were responsible for the bomb that had killed two of his neighbors and supported every attack on the occupying imperialists.

"You just blame everything on the Americans," I remonstrated. "It was a car bomb! Iraqis did this!" But the boy shook his head as if my version was as absurd as his. Truth has two points of view. Jean had told me to look through the looking glass.

"It's as if all Iraqi emotion is expressed by gunfire," I complained to Ahmed. "Angry at the occupation? Shoot at the Americans. Frustrated, stuck in a traffic jam? Fire off a couple of rounds in the air just to let off steam. You've had a son? Spray the air with celebratory bullets." When the Iraqi football team won an international match, there was so much gunfire all over the city the Americans thought the insurgents were staging an offensive.

"And another thing. What about all the looting, armed break-ins, carjackings, routine banditry on the roads." Ahmed reasoned that it was the breakdown of law and order.

"And the kidnapping?" Thousands of children were being ransomed by gangs of extortionists. "I mean, stealing I can understand. But taking a four-year-old boy and locking him in a garage until his father sells his house to pay? Making a business out of threatening to rape a teenage girl? This is not just opportunism, it's something much nastier."

I decided to focus more on the backstory and delve into recent history. What had happened to Iraqis in the terror time of Saddam? How had violence become so inculcated?

"I'll introduce you to an old friend of my father's," Ahmed offered. "He grew up with my father in Samarra, they were the bright young generation sent abroad to be educated while the oil money still flowed. This man became an army doctor, very senior. He is a slippery kind of chameleon, he has a different face for every occasion. He refused to answer my mother's calls when my father was arrested. I saw him the other day, by chance, at the Haifa Street checkpoint next to the Green Zone. They wouldn't let him in, and he was stranded there with the flares of his ridiculous three-piece suit left over from 1976 flapping and snagging on the barbed wire. Our roles were reversed. It was his turn to ask for help, and my turn to say I couldn't. But I took him for coffee at that place around the corner you like to go and find sob stories, the one Jean calls the Salon des Refusés. He saw my lanyard and that I was working for the Americans, so he became full of apologies and crocodile smiles. 'I swear on my eyes, there was nothing I could do.' They all say that. 'On my eyes, you are like a son to me!' He has three sons, all officers in the Republic Guard! I decided to play along, so I said, 'But I am not as brave as your sons, the lions of our country! May Allah have delivered them safely from the defense of our nation!' Ha-ha! Of course they were all burying the gold and hiding in some relative's compound in the countryside when the Americans invaded. Naturally this loyal man now wants a job with the Americans. I said I would see what I could do. I can try and talk to Colonel Don about him. You should not trust him—he is full of slander, he will pry any crack to his advantage. But if you want to talk to someone who was on the inside, he might be interesting. His name is Muntazzer."

———

I first met General Muntazzer at his house, a well-appointed concrete villa in one of Baghdad's middle-class suburbs of walled houses. An old man was washing a Mercedes in the forecourt. I buzzed but there was no electricity, so the old man helpfully honked the horn and Muntazzer came to the door. Stiff bearing, thick black moustache. He wore a tan suit with crisp pleats in his trousers, a burgundy shirt and a matching burgundy tie secured with a tie pin. On his wrist he wore a chunky brushed-steel watch ringed with pavé diamonds. A typical Baathie military type.

He showed me into the public reception room of his house. There did not seem to be any wife at home to bring us coffee. Instead he had set out two glasses and a bottle of Johnnie Walker Black Label, ice cold from the fridge. It was the middle of the afternoon. The room was decorated in Louis Farouk luxury: satin sofa covers, tasseled cushions, gilded claw-foot coffee tables laid with gold plastic doilies. Two photographs hung on the wall. In one Saddam was pinning a medal to Muntazzer's chest, in the other Muntazzer stood at the end of a line of eight generals. The second picture seemed to have been taken hurriedly. It was badly composed, the generals were too small for the landscape, and the camera had been held at an odd angle so that the line of commanders tilted as if they were about to fall over. Underneath was handwritten "1991." It must have been taken during one of two ignominious episodes, Kuwait or the uprising afterwards. Muntazzer proudly pointed out that he was wearing a red, black, and white sash, which had been awarded for his participation in the "Mother of All Battles."

He smiled easily and appeared friendly, but his eyes were still and his lids flickered. I could not tell if this was because he was blinking slowly or fast. From time to time his tongue licked at the side of his bottom lip.

Pleasantries: had I found the right crossroads easily? Most taxi drivers knew the blue minaret, but the Americans had closed the access road to the highway, so now you had to take a big loop around.

"I am very happy to help any friend of Ahmed. He is like a son to me. How did you meet?" His eyes narrowed. I demurred. Ahmed had warned that Muntazzer would probe, but I shouldn't let on that we were engaged, because he would gossip and Ahmed's mother still didn't know.

(I went along with these games. I loved Ahmed, I trusted him, I knew Iraqi society was complex and honor-bound. I swallowed his plausible explanations and did not add them up into any accountancy. Ahmed divided his life into compartments, but I did not know that. The idea that I was kept in a separate folder, cross-referenced with other personnel files only occasionally and with caution, was impossible to imagine. To this day I don't know why he risked introducing me to Muntazzer. Perhaps because by connecting him to Colonel Don he had indirectly connected him to me anyway.)

I sipped my cold Johnnie Walker and asked Muntazzer jokingly where Saddam was hiding. He repeated the more colorful rumors. House arrest guest of the Turks, eating caviar in Riyadh. I asked him directly about the big Baathies like Izzat al-Douri, the King of Clubs. Muntazzer spread his hands wide and empty and told me he was out of the inner circle these days.

"I am living very quietly in my house," he said. I asked him about his sons, but he only said, vaguely, "They are out of Baghdad."

Muntazzer's medical specialty was psychiatry. This was unusual in Iraq because mental illness was taboo and very few admitted themselves or their relatives for treatment. As the senior psychiatrist in the Iraqi Army during the Iran-Iraq War in the eighties, Muntazzer told me he had been responsible for evaluating officers as mentally fit for the front line. Despite the stigma, it was a common ruse to try to get a "mentally unfit to serve" certificate to avoid deployment. He said he had helped many of his friends' sons in this way.

I found I oddly liked Muntazzer. He was shallow and callous but every so often a flush of resignation, regret—even something that might approximate compassion—would wash over his face. He said he appreciated that I wanted to tell the stories of real Iraqis; so many journalists (he flattered me) were only interested in the Americans. I told him that I would very much like to talk to some of his patients. Muntazzer told me, indeed, he had many patients with different kinds of mental disorders. He had, that very morning, visited a woman in her thirties whose hair had turned white overnight and her body had gone rigid as a board. Her husband said it happened when bandits broke into their house and tied up their children and threatened to cut their necks.

"I diagnosed psychosomatic paralysis." Muntazzer made a compressed smile, pleased by his own professionalism. "Yes-yes, these things are quite common. Once I saw an executioner who had turned blind for no medical reason."

"And you must have treated many victims of torture," I said, my turn to probe.

Muntazzer was in the process of pouring more whiskey into his glass, the amber flow halted for a moment.

"Yes, all of us have suffered." I thought I saw a tremor in his cheek muscle.

We talked about my theory that Iraqis were suffering an epidemic of trauma. He nodded gravely. Yes, this was evident, but nothing could be done.

"There are only a handful of psychiatrists in the country. I am only one man, I cannot treat a million people. And now there are drugs coming in through all the open borders, people are buying Valium, diazepam, lithium, ketamine, even antipsychotics in unlabeled packs from street vendors. People eat them as if they are sweets."

The plight of the people, yes, yes, it was all very sad—but he seemed to accept it as axiomatic. It is what it is. About his own fate, he was more alarmed.

He told me that in the past two months he had survived two assassination attempts. He had sent his unmarried daughters and his wife to live in Amman. He railed against the Americans and the lawlessness that accompanied their occupation. A gang had stolen his other Mercedes ("a gift from Saddam!") and when he went to the police station to report it stolen, they had just shrugged and turned him away.

"These thieves are all Kuwaitis!" he declared, almost spitting on his own carpet. "They have come on the coattails of the Americans. They pretend to be from Basra, but it is obvious when you talk to them, from their accent and their noses, that they are only Kuwaitis who have been waiting for their revenge."

He began to rant about the state of the country. "Nothing is working! Imagine it. You have a driver who takes your children to school, your wife to shopping, everything the state provides for you so that you can concentrate on your position—and this is all gone and suddenly there is nothing—and in addition to nothing, worse than nothing, there is the collapse of everything. No petrol, no water, no telephone, no electricity, no leader."

He told me, with some indignation, that he had to sell his wife's gold jewelry to pay for the small apartment in Amman. "Two rooms with windows facing a wall!"

He had been reduced to driving his remaining Mercedes as a taxi. "Should I wait for hours just to fill my taxi with petrol? When Iraq is full of oil? This is our shame! Should I wait for hours in the street queuing for my army pension? Who can endure this? I am not a proud man! I try to work!" He lit another cigarette and pulled a lungful of smoke to calm his indignation. I sat back and let him recover his emollient smile.

"I must find work," Muntazzer continued, quieter, supplicant. "I hope that my good friend and yours,"—again he watched me carefully to see if I would give anything away—"Ahmed, will help me in this endeavor. My knowledge and my experience, I feel confident, could be of great help to the Americans. They are making many mistakes, they are trusting the wrong people and employing the thieves."

———

Muntazzer did not introduce me to any of his patients, but he did set up a meeting for me with the head of the Saddam Psychiatric Hospital.

It was a place of cinder block and iron bars full of raving figures, squatting, walking in circles, hollow cheeks and half-moon brands on their temples from electroshock therapy.

"Oh yes, it can be very effective," the director, Dr. Farhid, told me cheerfully. "One of my patients, his name is Ahmed Merry. He is our most interesting case. He was arrested for throwing paint on a picture of Saddam. In prison he was tortured. To protest he continually banged his head against the wall—hard enough to bring blood—and after several weeks of this behavior they sent him to us. He told us he hurt himself just to get out of that place. We said, we are sorry, but if you are not really mad we have to send you back. He said, OK, I really *am* mad, and he made all the actions of a madman. He went naked, he scratched himself.

He *went* mad. We administered electroshock therapy and immediately he became better. We said now you are recovered you must go back to prison. So he went mad again. After many years of playing mad I think he really did go mad. But I think he must have been mad all the time, because it is a madness, no? To throw paint on a picture of Saddam—"

I retold this story to Ahmed later as I cooked him lamb chops. He had pretty much moved into my minisuite at the Hamra Hotel. Beige curtains, beige carpet; in the winter the bathwater was tepid, in the summer the air-conditioning was feeble, but it was our first home-place together. We tacked up maps and sepia prints of Ottoman-era Baghdad on the walls. Ahmed made me take down my portrait of Gertrude Bell—British imperialism he could not forgive. Of French imperialism he was more indulgent (I don't know why); American imperialism, I teased him, was his worldwide dream. Ahmed laughed at my account of the mental hospital, trying to follow the circle of mad-pretending-to-be-mad and came up behind me and put his arms around my waist.

"It's something very disturbing," I said, "it's a mirror game; but it's not funny not to be able to know sane from insane, real from not real. It's like Muntazzer, a psychiatrist who is on Prozac," I said. "I saw the pills in his bathroom."

"Did you?" Ahmed took his hands away from my waist, went to the minifridge and took out a bottle of arak. He cracked ice cubes out of the ice tray and poured two glasses, clear turned to cloudy. "Interesting. But I'm not surprised he needs medication to maintain some kind of equilibrium, to keep the mask on. I've been trying to persuade Colonel Don that we should start to bring Muntazzer and some of the other Baathie dragons into the fold, put them on the consultancy payroll, keep them close. We will need them to counter the Shia. The Shia think it's their show now because democracy means the majority rules and they are the majority."

"What does Colonel Don say?"

"He thinks it's a good idea, he understands the danger of alienating the old state apparatus—such as it was, it held some kind of government together—trying to reconstruct without scaffolding is just foolhardy. But he says the de-Baathification program is the official policy. We can't be seen to be supporting Saddam's henchmen."

"So they will just let the Shia take over?"

"They can't." Ahmed drained his arak and poured another. "It will be civil war."

"Don't be melodramatic." Ahmed on the subject of the Shia was intractable; he sighed and went back to talking about Muntazzer.

"He is like mercury, he will find any slot to slip into. Did you know he was arrested? In the eighties, during the Iran-Iraq War. The matter of a prescription for amphetamines for a general. The general was arrested for retreating and then implicated him under interrogation. My father spoke up on his behalf, despite the risk. Did he tell you this? No, of course not! He is still clinging to his friendship with Saddam, as if it was a badge of honor instead of shame—worse, he is trying to sell it as if it had any value!"

"Muntazzer didn't tell me he was arrested," I said. "But it makes sense in a screwed-up way. The rope that twists to make a loop; the psychiatrist who has treated so many victims of trauma—he is his own doctor and his own patient."

"Prison No. 1, the cushy prison—Muntazzer was only locked up for three months, the kind of arrest they used to call 'a holiday.' After he came out, do you know what he did? He was taken straight to the palace and he fell on his knees in front of Saddam and kissed his ring."

———

Sometime around Christmas, Muntazzer and I met again at the Hunting Club, once the preserve of the elite, now down-at-the-heel. The swimming pool was cracked and drained; the patio was covered with moldy plastic-grass carpet. There was a metal articulated Christmas tree in a corner of the dining room, dragged out of storage, a leftover from a bygone secular era. The crabby bent waiter took an age to bring us two beers. Muntazzer's shirt was frayed at the collar, but he would not allow me to pay. *Iraq is my country, I am inviting you.*

He sat back in a scuffed leatherette armchair.

"How is your wife?" I asked him. "How are your daughters?"

"Al hamdillullah. They are safe in Amman." His voice was more relaxed than before, he drew his vowels out; sanguine—or perhaps resigned. There were pouches under his eyes. I saw that his belly strained against his belt, he had let go of his upright military formality and crossed one leg over the other.

He told me his wife had been diagnosed with bowel cancer and needed radiation treatment. He complained that it was very expensive. He'd gone to Amman to take the money from the sale of some land because he did not trust anyone else to carry that much cash through the desert road. There were bandit attacks around Ramadi and Fallujah all the time.

"How are your sons?"

The club library (there were no books) was almost empty, but he looked behind himself to a corner where a woman with a bright headscarf was sitting with a small child, feeding it Pringles one at a time, which the child ground into dust with little fists.

"They have chosen a difficult path," he said. He looked directly at me as if he was going to tell me something, but then he seemed to decide not to. He called the waiter to bring an ashtray and began to talk about Saddam's capture the previous week. Muntazzer was upset at Saddam's humiliation.

"To show our president being dragged out of a hole in the ground by common soldiers is a national shame." He shook his head sadly, angry. "This is not right, this is not respect for a head of state. When a general surrenders, he must be given all dignity, it is against even the Geneva Conventions to make him look like an ordinary criminal. And the Shia went out onto the streets and celebrated! I do not know where the honorable Iraqis have gone." I commiserated. Then the conversation devolved, inevitably, to what was universally referred to as *the situation*. Muntazzer railed against the ascent of SCIRI, the Supreme Council for the Islamic Revolution in Iraq, an Iranian-sponsored Shia political party, which had set up an office in Karrada, black flags flying on the roof and guarded by men with black balaclavas. He was indignant that Americans had blocked off Abu Nawas and the traffic jams were worse than ever. A bomb hidden in a horse cart had gone off next to the Palestine Hotel. The Armenian supermarket had stopped selling alcohol under pressure from some Imam. Ambushes on the Qanat road, gunfire in Saidiya, a friend of his had survived another assassination attempt. But! Muntazzer grinned heartily. There was now a mobile phone network up and running! He showed me his new Nokia and gave me his new business card: *Muntazzer al Samarrai, Medical Professional, Consultant at Large,* in smudged serifs. The phone number underneath had a blue biro slash through the 8.

"The printers made a mistake," said Muntazzer, "it should be a 3." He had gone through the whole stack and amended each one by hand. But nevertheless he was cheered by the black and white evidence of his self-styled title. "We are finally joining the twenty-first century. My daughter has email now in the apartment in Amman!"

A certain veneer of forced jollity, urbanity, pretense. Muntazzer was bluff and calculating. But perhaps because he was so obviously so, I didn't mind. It was like a pantomime act; every so often he would offer an aside, a confidence, a morsel of sincerity, as if to acknowledge, wink-wink, the ruse and, in doing so, plead indulgence for the pride of an old washed-up man. He played his part, victim of history, wise elder, and I mine, his deferential audience.

Friendly, but only as much, I suspected, as I was useful, as a connection to Ahmed, who was a connection to the Americans. In the meantime Muntazzer was happy to stretch his nostalgia and tell me stories about Ahmed's father when they were at university together, both middle-class boys from Samarra. About the nightclubs and pool parties from before the wars, the time no one could remember anymore, when an Iraqi dinar bought three dollars, and the young women wore skirts and blouses in the streets and there was a discotheque at the Hunting Club every Saturday night.

"When I was training I lived in Vienna for six months in 1979 and this was the most beautiful time in my life." Muntazzer took off his gold-rimmed aviator sunglasses and wiped a wistful tear from the corner of his eye. "I fell in love with a woman even though she was Jewish. I had to go back to Baghdad because my father died and I promised to take her to Paris when I returned. But when I was home, the war against Iran arrived suddenly and everyone had to put on the uniform and *khalas*"—he made the gesture of finish, wiping one palm over the other. "Now maybe, I can dream of Paris again." He smiled. He looked at me. "Ahmed tells me you are a good friend with the French ambassador?" (Ahmed told me afterwards that he had not told him this. But, thinking back, how else would Muntazzer have known about my connection to Alexandre?) He leaned forward to pour a little more whiskey in my glass. I did not answer directly, but I made an assenting sort of smile. I wasn't going to lie, but I didn't want to encourage a quid pro quo. That was Ahmed's domain, he understood the form; when we were haggling in an antique shop, he always took over the negotiation.

"It's the different mentality," Ahmed had explained. "In Europe you go to a shop and the price is displayed and everyone pays the same. This is democracy. An Arab shopkeeper would never stoop to make his price public. He will make up a different price for each customer. Every transaction is a negotiation, not about a sum of money, but to determine the relative status of buyer and seller, who is more powerful, who is wealthier, who is the dominant one. Don't ever think that you are just buying a kilo of lamb or that the butcher is happy to see you as a valued customer. You think that you are patronizing him because you have money, but he is overcharging you and boasting to all his shopkeeper friends that he has put one over on the foreigner."

I did not understand the rules; Muntazzer was forced to show me a glimpse of his hand to encourage me to play along. He said, "Perhaps my son can be persuaded to talk to you."

"What can he tell me?"

"He will tell you himself."

"Is he—*involved*?" I asked, couching my words carefully. Muntazzer raised his finger to his lip, circumspect.

"At least tell me his name."

"Oberon." said Muntazzer. "I have three sons, Oberon, Othello, and the youngest one, my favorite, is Caesar."

"Seriously?"

"I love very much Shakespeare," Muntazzer admitted. "I called my first daughter Regan, she was born in 1984, we were still friends with America. But after the Gulf War we had to change her name to Raghad."

FOUR

When the Hamra Hotel was bombed, Alexandre bent all the rules of protocol and persuaded me to move into the French Embassy. Inside those well-guarded blast walls the talk was high-handed. Oil executives and Kurdish PR operatives, visiting senators, American technicals from the Green Zone—the man responsible for health care in Iraq, the man responsible for electricity in Iraq, the man responsible for education in Iraq. "The earnest evangelicals," Ahmed nicknamed his colleagues, "they are just like the Iranians: very polite, they sit forward on the edge of the sofa and refuse to drink alcohol."

Alexandre was a gracious and accommodating host, variously cynical, synthetically corrupt, or sympathetic, as required. The French had abstained from the invasion and were now able to spread their hands wide, I-told-you-so, the-world-is-never-as-we-would-wish, *quel dommage*. Alexandre sat on his mezzanine, above the fray, courted by all sides as a go-between. No one ever refused an invitation to the French Embassy. The chef had oysters flown in once a week; his specialty was quail stuffed with fois gras. The Russians clapped with delight at his Stroganoff Rossini.

After dinner we would gather in the Sykes-Picot salon. It was decorated with a hand-painted orientalist wallpaper landscape of palm trees, elephants, and pagodas.

"Saddam was a great leader," Alexandre said to the Russian ambassador there one night. He raised his brandy balloon in ironic salute. "Who else can control these unruly Iraqis? The Americans have made a grave mistake. One day, mark my words, one day we will all wish Saddam back. After all, who doesn't now lament the demise of the Soviet Union, even with all its imperfections? Who can say all those little countries have brought better prosperity and security to their people?"

Under strict pain of excommunication, I was not allowed to report on anything I heard inside the embassy walls. This frustrated Oz, but as I always reminded him, the stories were only as true as their sources believed them to be, and therefore entirely unconfirmable. When the guests had gone, sealed into armored SUVs with tinted black windows and driven back to air-conditioned compounds, Alexandre would sit on the terrace, swirl his glowing cigar coal against the mosquitoes, and rue that there were more conspiracy theories inside the diplomatic corps than on the streets.

Ahmed often stayed overnight because it was dangerous to drive back to his mother's house late at night. Baghdad in the dark had become a lottery of carjack, car bomb, random bullets. His mother lived in Mansour, and the route home took him through the SCIRI checkpoints in Karrada. "Scary-SCIRI-we-are-so-silly," I used to singsong mock the Supreme Council for Islamic Revolution in Iraq. "Shia who want their revenge on us," said Ahmed. He had started to keep his father's old pistol in the glove compartment.

Alexandre liked to discuss *the situation* with Ahmed. He found he was a useful analyst of the political culture and mood inside the Green Zone, that strange UFO bubble dome constructed out of razor wire wrapped around portacabins held together with duct tape. Ahmed said it was like *Star Wars* being shot with extras from *The Hobbit*. All the same he was grateful for his daily Starbucks latte and sometimes he would bring me back a congealed Bacon Double Cheeseburger from the Burger King as a special treat. Ahmed did not have the right pass to access the PX store, but Colonel Don would take an order for Oscar Mayer hotdogs and bacon and I would implore the French chef to cook them up for us, which he did with an expression of indulgent contempt for *"cette choucroute nue."*

Ahmed and I had a long-running joke that we should write a series for HBO called *The Diplomat*, which would fictionalize all the comic ridiculousnesses that the title character, an erudite ambassador from an unnamed European country, had to navigate in occupied Baghdad. Alexandre pretended to be aghast when we made up storylines at the dinner table: The Wahhabi gardener and the Argentinian ambassador's wife who wore a yellow polka-dot bikini to swim in the embassy pool. The donkey cart bomb outside the North Korean Embassy; working title, "Donkey Kong." The sheikh who refused to check his gun at the door and ate his dinner with the pistol next to his plate. The American hard-knock raid on the Hashemite pretender to the throne who lived next door. The strange nighttime comings and goings into a First Gulf War bomb shelter on the other side of the street, which turned out to be a Blackwater interrogation site. The one about the invitation to invite Moqtadr Sadr to a dinner party in honor of Jacques Tati.

Alexandre said that no one would believe such plotlines. "The trouble with fiction is that you cannot make it as absurd as real life. Reality is not credible, it is incredible!"

———

In late spring, after a hot Eid weekend, slaughtered lambs in the streets, insurgent attacks on the airport road, black helicopters hovering, flies over carrion, Muntazzer called.

"My son Oberon is ready to meet you. I will pick you up from outside the Embassy in one hour."

The traffic was terrible, clogged in an inching, honking mass; a lake of sewage had flooded Karrada, no traffic lights, because the electricity was off. The thick hot air smeared my skin; I stared out of the grimy car window I dared not wind down in case anyone saw strands of foreigner blond hair escaping from my hijab. A man was selling gasping carp from a wooden handcart, a beggar with one arm waved his stump at the cars, an explosion boomed somewhere, a jet whined far above; there was a line of twenty-five cars at the 14 July Bridge checkpoint into the Green Zone.

It took us an hour and a half to get to the sprawling car market on the highway. The King of the Faeries was sitting in a plastic chair outside a prefab sales cabin. The rows of secondhand cars radiated heat. Oberon was tall, with hooded eyes like his father, stubble, swarthy. He wore jeans and a T-shirt and black sneakers. Leaning against the portacabin was a Kalashnikov. He shook my hand. Polite, serious. (Sexy.) He asked if I wanted tea, I nodded, and he clicked his fingers for the boy to fetch it.

He told me he had come from Samarra that morning and they were very well organized there. He wanted me to understand this. They were not kids, they were not terrorists. He told me they were attacking the American FOB, the forward operating base set up in the old Baath Party administration building, with mortars every night. He said that the Americans were too frightened to leave their fort even to patrol the streets. Once a week they resupplied their garrison with an armored convoy from the battalion at Camp Beast outside the city, but they could only do so with the cover of Apache helicopters.

"We now control Samarra," Oberon told me. "The Americans cannot go out in their Humvees without being hit. They used to drive their tanks down the main street. Now they don't dare. Their tanks sit on the edge of the town and drive a little way in and destroy houses because they cannot do anything else. At night they arrest people in their homes, they arrest anyone their informers tell them to. They are looking for us but they cannot find us."

There had been very little news from Samarra for three or four months. The roads north had become too dangerous for Westerners to drive. I asked him if he could verify any of what he said. He brought out a white envelope containing photographs. Several were nighttime shots, streaks of red and white tracer against black sky—unidentifiable. Several were of a burnt-out Humvee, but this was not exceptional and could have been anywhere. The last few pictures were of an Apache helicopter, crashed on its side in a winter wheat field, crumpled like cardboard. One was a close up of the stenciled registration number on the tail. There was also a shot of the rotor blades sheared off, and lying, like a decapitated ceiling fan, on the nearby riverbank.

"You must tell the Americans who read your newspaper that we are in control of Samarra and we are fighting the Americans, that we are defeating them and that we are not terrorists."

I nodded.

"This is important and interesting, but I need to see this for myself." Oberon smiled. His father, I noticed, did not.

"We will arrange it."

The traffic on the way back was even more interminable. I sat in the passenger seat of Muntazzer's white Mercedes with my forehead resting against the scorching glass of the car window, listening to the shushing whirr of the AC fighting the heat. The car crawled and stopped. The endless street moved past slowly like a trundling stage set, grime and dirt, misshapen structures. A series of garages set up in shipping containers made a row of rotting teeth. Among these ruins, men in rags beat panels into rough satellite dishes, black horned toes hooked over the edge of sandals, black lines etched on foreheads, a small boy balanced a tea tray on his shorn and scarred head. Men sat on warped plastic chairs smoking cigarette after cigarette. Paper and leaf to ash, each cigarette butt trod into the dust.

All this misery went past, and I congratulated myself that I was in the right place to bear witness to it. I felt a burp of excitement nestling in my sternum. My own personal insurgent! All the people I could see out of the window were fucked, but I was buzzing. The stupid thing is that I don't remember being frightened.

———

I sent my Oberon file to Oz. He was skeptical. He asked me to confirm the downing of the American helicopter. I had copied down the registration number of the Apache in the photograph, but the American military spokesman would not even verify that this helicopter was in Iraq.

"I have to go to Samarra," I told Alexandre. "It's a proper scoopy-scoop." Alexandre pressed his lips together, pulled on a fleshy earlobe. In his breakfast kimono, he looked like my worried aunt.

"Zorro and Jean are coming next week."

"Oh are they?"

"Wait until they come. I don't want you going up there alone."

———

All the time, time-lapse chrysanthemum spreading its petals into full-blown flower, the violence blossomed. And with it came its corollary, spiritual attrition. The quotidian horror ground us down into contempt, black humor, cynicism. I did not notice at first that my periods had stopped. At first I was elated, but the French Embassy doctor confirmed that I was not pregnant. He told me that my blood test indicated idiopathic perimenopause. When I asked him what this meant, he said it was not clear, perhaps the hormone imbalance was due to stress, I should wait six months and see if I my period returned.

Ahmed began to deride the Americans almost as much as he

derided the stupid Iraqis and their mendacious sheikhs. His callow Green Zone colleagues, ciphers in blue button-down shirts and chinos, revolved on six-month secondments to the Development Fund for Iraq, as if a posting to Iraq was like a semester abroad, he complained, CV filler for young Washington insider wannabes. They were only in the office long enough to pick up the mannerisms of occupation, never long enough to actually do anything. They tossed around in-country slang, "towelheads" and "bedsheets." Ahmed told me, incredulous, that one of them, a real asshole named Brogan, used to carry a bottle of antibacterial gel to wash his hands after shaking hands with an Iraqi. I met Brogan at one of the Sunday barbecues by the pool in Saddam's old palace. He took off his T-shirt to swim, and I saw he had a Marines tattoo, a giant eagle with semper fideles across his back, even though he had never enlisted.

"You're our terp's fiancée. Cool. Yeah, he's one of the good-uns," he said to me, cuffing Ahmed on the shoulder. "Shit, man!" He twirled a pair of tongs in an accidentally aggressive loop. I took a step back. "We got like all sausage and ribs, like all pork. I forgot."

"It's no problem," said Ahmed, "I eat pork."

"Like I said, he's one of the good-uns!"

Embrace the suck.

Then Ahmed found out that the Americans were being paid ten times more than him and this really stung. He confronted Colonel Don, but Colonel Don only shrugged and nodded in his equitable way. He said he would do what he could, which turned out to be nothing.

Ahmed redacted these slights when he gossiped about Green Zone shenanigans with Alexandre in the embassy. Was it water-off-a-duck's-back or denial? At the time I didn't think Ahmed took them personally, but maybe these barbs stuck more than I guessed.

It took me a long time to see that Ahmed's Achilles heel was his pride. He was, after all, an Iraqi, an Arab. But I never thought of him this way, partly because he was accentless and Westernized,

FIVE

Muntazzer had given me a story. Now it was my turn to reciprocate the back scratch. At the same time Ahmed wanted to find some way to introduce Muntazzer to Colonel Don, to stop him calling him every two days to ask when his invitation to the Green Zone would be ready. Colonel Don had said no, there was no point, discretionary funds for "sources" had been stopped. Confluence of interests, I persuaded Alexandre to invite Muntazzer for dinner at the embassy. Ahmed oiled the wheels by telling Alexandre that Muntazzer "knew people" and then, when he had reluctantly agreed, suggesting that he ask Colonel Don to come too.

Muntazzer arrived first bearing a large box of chocolates and a bouquet of carnations. He wore a brown suit with a brown shirt and a brown tie secured with his gold tie pin. He had been to the barber; his moustache was neatly trimmed and he had dyed his salt and pepper hair black.

"You look very natty," I said.

"What is *natty?*"

Alexandre poured him a Johnnie Walker with ice. Muntazzer smiled like an iguana in a sun spot, gold incisor gleaming.

"Monsieur Ambassador, it is very kind of you."

"Please call me Alexandre. I hear you are a psychiatrist?"

"It is not an easy specialty in my country," Muntazzer sighed, lapsing into his professional lament. "Most Iraqis have sustained some kind of psychological trauma. It comes from different origins and triggers, at the base there is a generalized national psychosis. What I call *Saddam paranoia*."

Ahmed arrived with Colonel Don and one of the ciphers. Josh had blond hair parted on the side. Introductions were made. Wine was poured. Josh asked for juice. We went out onto the terrace. The gendarmes patrolled the roof and their shadows made gargoyle silhouettes on the lawn.

"We were discussing Saddam paranoia," explained Alexandre.

"Some people were socially withdrawn, they were afraid to go to work," continued Muntazzer.

"No one talked to anyone," agreed Ahmed, looking directly at Muntazzer. "When my father was arrested, all our friends ignored us."

"It was between social phobia and agoraphobia," Muntazzer continued. "You would see normal people displaying signs of paranoia, not wanting to talk on the telephone, afraid of the doorbell. You never mentioned Saddam's name. Especially in front of your children."

Ahmed added, "Every conversation was a half conversation or an avoidance."

"Yes," said Muntazzer, as if they were in agreement. "For a long time we had to lie in every situation. For example you would never tell your father that you smoked cigarettes or drank whiskey with your friends. You lied to your boss because he was under obligation to write an official report about you every six months. You must never admit to going to a mosque, because this was officially frowned upon. Within your own family it was dangerous to say what you really thought about anything, especially about the regime, the system, the ruler. Especially in front of your children who could repeat something to a teacher and you would be investigated. As a result Iraqis became expert liars. Yesterday I was questioned at a checkpoint by an American soldier and I was afraid to give him my ID card because I am a former Baath Party member and now they are arresting people like me. It feels as if we have just swapped one kind of fear for another."

"That is very interesting," said Josh, blinking behind his Harry Potter glasses.

"Do you think this kind of national fear accounts for the resurgence in religiosity?" asked Colonel Don.

"Iraqis have been turning to Islam for several years now," replied Muntazzer, gratified to find his opinion solicited. "It is partly a defense mechanism," he explained. "The stress of the situation draws us back to religion. It is also a surrender to divine responsibility. Islam is not like Christianity; we believe what happens is written on your forehead; fated. This occupation is a catastrophe." I saw Josh wince at the word "occupation." Colonel Don only nodded. "But somehow we blame ourselves as if Allah is punishing us. It is a manifestation of insecurity. This chronic frustration will lead to aggression. I don't know if the Americans understand the Iraqi mentality."

"Well, it's a difficult learning curve for a lot of people," said Colonel Don. Josh stood by, junior, listening. "We old-timers in the State Department don't have much sway with the hotbloods in the DoD."

Colonel Don was an Arabist, one of the old Middle East hands, scholarly, intelligent, well informed. I had heard him chafe at the Defense Department before.

"We have our hotbloods too," said Muntazzer. He put on his wise, grandfatherly voice: let me tell you, you naïve new arrivals, twisting your ankles in our potholes, stumbling into our sinkholes. "There are no maps of Iraq; did you know that? Saddam would not allow them, in case of spies and foreign invasions. Saddam drained the marshes, but don't imagine there are not still swamps and quicksands that can swallow whole armies."

Muntazzer puffed out his chest and pressed his advantage.

"The young Iraqis see their country humiliated. We cannot stand by and be patient. Don, my friend," Muntazzer held Colonel Don's gaze as he spoke, "in Samarra—" Some kind of warning glance passed between Ahmed and Muntazzer. I felt a queasy tremor. A delicate cat's cradle of acquaintance was looped around the fingers of the assembled. Which string was Ahmed tightening, which was he playing out?

Ahmed interrupted. "The insurgents claim they are fighting the great enemy America, but they are killing more Iraqis than Americans."

"They are resisting," said Alexandre, nodding at Muntazzer with an expression that wore kid gloves. Alexandre was ever the grand master diplomat. It occurred to me—fleetingly—that he and Ahmed might have rehearsed this scene, so that Alexandre could appear to come to Muntazzer's defense and draw him into his confidence. "Resistance is never pretty," said Alexandre, full of sympathy, *tristesse*, and wisdom, "it is only glorious afterwards, when you have won. Resistance is fought in your home, and therefore the bleeding is internal."

The majordomo announced dinner. We sat in the dining room with the shades drawn against the evening's slanting sun. At each place was a small menu card, handwritten in ink. The chef had made a gazpacho. Muntazzer asked me why the soup was cold. The conversation turned to the problem of the Shia. Josh, looking around to see which spoon to use, said he thought it was a natural part of a readjustment to democracy. The Sunni would have to get used to the idea of being a minority.

"We cannot," said Ahmed. "It is one thing to be a minority in a democracy, but Iraq has never had democracy. Iraqis have no idea what it means to agree to disagree! The Shia will turn this country into a Persian colony."

"But Shia and Sunni are intermarried in Iraq, even some tribes are mixed," said Josh.

"Everyone always lives perfectly happily together before a civil war," observed Alexandre.

The butler served filet mignon with ratatouille. Muntazzer pushed his pink meat uneasily around the plate. He did not drink the wine and instead asked for another Johnnie Walker. The conversation continued: Shia, Sunni, bombs, insurgents, hard-knock raids, the Abu Ghraib scandal, de-Baathification, Paul Bremer III, Bush the Younger, Ayatollah Sistani, Moqtada Sadr, the Iranians, the Kurds, the British in Basra. Push and pull, a good discussion. Dessert was lemon sorbet with fresh fruit. After dinner we moved into the library and the discussion broke up into pairs. Muntazzer, who had not spoken much since the beginning of the meal, now turned to Colonel Don again.

"I want to help my American friends," he said. A black eyebrow raised in a scimitar arch; powdery clumps of beige makeup were caught in the bristly hairs at the bridge of his nose. "I have information about the situation. Your colleagues in the 2nd Armored Division are having difficulties in Samarra. I am originally from Samarra, I have many relatives there. Perhaps I could visit you at your office, I am sure you will find what I have to say very interesting."

"Samarra is out of my area, but why don't you give me an idea of what you know." Colonel Don kept his face very straight. Noncommittal, direct. Blond hair razored close at the back of his neck, graying at his temples, frank wide-open blue eyes, square jaw. He stood, arms folded, opposite Muntazzer's coiffed and lacquered beehive. The crusader and the orientalist cartoon. A perfect racist portrait in black and white. One supplicant, groveling, inveigling, the other standing, legs akimbo, half-listening, indifferent. I looked over to the corner where

Ahmed was talking to Alexandre and saw the reverse negative of this vignette. Ahmed was leaning against the mantelpiece with the languid elegance of confidence. Against the backlight of the sunset, his profile was cast as a silhouette, a handsome marble bust. Alexandre, by contrast, was pale pompadour, lace handkerchief in his top pocket, vestige of an ancient regime.

Each of us wanted something in return. Ahmed wanted Alexandre to write him a recommendation for a position at the U.N. Muntazzer was desperate for money and medical treatment for his wife. Alexandre needed leverage with the Americans. Colonel Don was gathering information for his final report, due before his retirement in a few weeks, that would indict the ideological zealotry of the Defense Department's Iraq policy. (Not that it would do any good, he had confided to Ahmed, but at least for the record.) Dinner discussion dispensed with, now we came together to horse-trade in euphemisms. I was stuck with Josh earnestly describing an imaginary hospital renovation program. Over his shoulder I could see Alexandre nod and smile; a written recommendation for Ahmed's U.N. application was in his easy gift, I knew. Then they began to talk about Muntazzer; both looked over towards him.

Muntazzer's hands were pressed together in a gesticulation of obsequiousness and prayer. The glints of gold in Ahmed's eyes caught the lowering rays of the sun and flashed. There was something unfathomable about the way he looked at Muntazzer and Don and then back to Alexandre. Did he feel caught between two sides, fearful of betraying one to the other? Probably this was my own sensitivity that I superimposed on Ahmed. Ahmed was playing to his own rules, as he always did, making them up as he went along, expedient, opportunistic.

I am sure Colonel Don understood what was being offered, but he seemed reluctant to take Muntazzer's heavy swinging bait. His expression was neutral, but his hand kept going up to pull on his earlobe, a poker signal or for keep-awake sake.

"Even in families," Muntazzer continued, leaning forward on the edge of the silk sofa, "things are breaking down. Sons do not obey their fathers."

"Do you have sons?" Colonel Don asked pleasantly, as if making a small-talk enquiry. Perhaps Ahmed had told him about Oberon after all.

"Yes. They are my pride and also my painfulness," said Muntazzer. "They are the hotbloods, they are the future of Iraq, and I fear for them as I fear for my country. This younger generation wants revenge and they will destroy everything in their thirst for it!" Muntazzer made a sweeping movement with his arm and slapped his palm against his forehead in a theatrical display of despair. "They do not like to listen to their fathers anymore! We are just the stupid old men who led them into this disaster. They think only of avenging our mistakes. They think they are all Salah ad-Din! They grew up in Saddam's classroom and they think war is glorious, because we, we who saw it and fought it and suffered when our friends and families were killed, did not tell them how it was, because we could not, we did not dare. And now when I tell them no good will come, they say we are cowards and do not listen to us. What can we do? We did not teach them to trust us because we lied to them and now they despise us. For family and nation, when old traditions of honor and respect are broken, is the destruction of family and nation, everything is torn down—how do you say it—the material, the cloth?"

"The fabric of society," supplied Colonel Don. Muntazzer wiped the tears from his eyes. He had poured out a great torrent of anguish and now threw himself at the feet of Colonel Don's mercy.

"Yes, exactly. You understand! I am, like many of us—the old men, the failed generation, we must find a way to protect our sons and serve our country, even as our sons ignore us and our country burns with their fire!"

Muntazzer's performance and the tragedy he described were worthy of the Bard. But he overplayed it. Colonel Don was going home soon. To Vermont, where the air was clean and cold and the apples grew crisp and plentiful on the trees. He did not want to be drawn into an emotional stew of conflicted and conflicting filials. ("He has seen this before, after all," Ahmed told me later. "At the beginning he thought reconstructing Iraq would be an expiation of the sin of Vietnam. He was enthusiastic, he wanted to help. Then he was angry when he saw how the idiots at the Defense Department were screwing everything up. After the fuck-up in Najaf he became resigned, and then he actually resigned. Now he just wants out. He goes through the motions at the office, compiles his 'list of stupidities,' as he calls it, counts the days.")

Colonel Don, a good man, faced with his own inutility, gave Muntazzer a shoulder squeeze. "I am hearing the same thing from a lot of people." Muntazzer sat with his palms upturned on his lap, waiting for something to fall into his hands. But Colonel Don stood up and said he was sorry, it was time to go, curfew and all. Josh shook my hand, dry and formal. Colonel Don thanked Alexandre for such fine French hospitality and told Ahmed he would see him tomorrow, bright and early worm. Muntazzer did not get up because he was scowling into his whiskey.

When the door closed behind them, Alexandre and I went into the garden. Jasmine flowed into the cooling purple dusk, the sparrows in the jacaranda squawked nighty-night. Muntazzer took Ahmed aside and they walked along the lavender hedge.

"Muntazzer is asking Ahmed for something," I said to Alexandre.

"Hmmm," said Alexandre, lighting a cigarillo.

They walked, talking, to the far end of the garden, to the swimming pool. I saw Muntazzer make a chopping gesture with two hands. Ahmed put both his hands out in front of his chest as if to protect himself. Threat, remonstration, appeal? Ahmed's legs made ambulatory triangles against the blue glow of the water. I wondered for a moment if Muntazzer would push him in. But by the time they returned and sat beside us on the terrace, it was all smiles and congeniality. Alexandre poured balloons of brandy.

"Ah," he said, settling into his seat and turning to Muntazzer. "My dear general. Now do please, I pray, if you think I can be of some assistance, tell me what my American friend didn't want to hear."

"It is a delicate position," said Muntazzer. "How to explain?"

"You are worried about your family."

"Yes. I am worried about my family. I have three sons." He paused. Alexandre did not prompt him.

"Beware of Iraqis asking favors," said Ahmed. He was either trying to make a joke or inserting himself into the conversation; there was something bitter in his tone.

"Ahmed." Alexandre was irritated, the rhythm had faltered. "Dr. Muntazzer, please continue."

"My wife is very ill and the doctors say she needs radiation treatment. It is very expensive."

Alexandre nodded. "Of course."

"I am driving my car as a taxi. I am not proud. In every life, sometimes fortune smiles, sometimes she is angry with us. I can bear this for myself, but for my family—"

Muntazzer did not say that his sons were fighting the Americans in Samarra; Alexandre did not say that he knew this already.

"We, in France, have some latitude to provide medical visas," offered Alexandre.

"I would be very grateful, my friend. On my eyes," said Muntazzer using the strongest Iraqi expression of sincerity he could muster, "you can see the difficulty of this situation. A husband must protect his wife. A father must protect his family."

SIX

I went to Samarra to meet Oberon at the end of September. Jean didn't come after all—he was in and out of Iraq; I think he had gone back to France for a while. Zorro drove me in an orange-and-white-quartered taxi we hired. He took off all his jewelry, dyed his beard dark brown, tied up his dreadlocks in a keffiyeh and wore a checked shirt and a tired pair of suit trousers, Iraqi mufti. I wore a black enveloping abaya and sat in the backseat. We had IDs from Alexandre that said we were Moroccan nationals working for the French Embassy to get us through the checkpoints. No guns. A satellite phone in the glove box, a hundred dollars in small notes in our pockets, enough for a robber to take, be satisfied with, and go away. Zorro kept two hands locked on the steering wheel all the way out of Baghdad, until I told him it looked too rigid and suspicious and so he let one arm dangle over the gearshift. Between us and them, only the frame of a metal chassis, inside outside, safe to not-safe, was only half a misunderstood exchange, a pothole, an overheated engine, a minor accident, anything. I repeated to myself:

as long as we are in the car together, as long as the car is moving forward . . . but the car kept stopping in the jams and security funnels. We got stuck behind an American convoy with signs that read: KEEP BACK 100 FEET OR YOU WILL BE SHOT. We lugged a heavy silence for twenty kilometers before the convoy turned off to Balad. Further north, the road became emptier and emptier, the occasional pickup, a boy behind the reins of a horse cart mounted on truck tires.

Samarra was quiet. It was high noon, no shadows, shops shuttered against the midday heat. Groups of gunmen sat in cars at crossroads, engines idling; sentinels sat on broken chairs on corners and watched who went past. They knew we were coming. Two foreigners asking for Abu Omar, Oberon's nom de guerre. Frown, nod, rifle barrel, surly wave-through. At the third checkpoint we were told to leave our car, we would be taken the rest of the way.

Zorro and I sat in the back of a dust-bucket black sedan, no windows or license plates. The driver was a jolly fellow and gave us the grand tour.

"Here is the house Americans raided two days ago, they took away the father and the elder son." Smashed windows, orange glow sticks littering the garden. "No one knows why they leave these orange things, for marking or signal, or maybe to make intimidation." We drove past the house where Jean and I had interviewed the family of the boy who had been thrown off the bridge and drowned. When I asked about them, the driver shrugged and said they had gone to relatives in Mosul. "Many people leaving." A row of run-down shops, an old man selling tomatoes from a tarpaulin spread on the ground. The market was closed, he said, because the Americans wouldn't let the farmers come in with their vegetables. I asked him if they were under siege. The driver only grinned and pointed straight ahead to a modern cracked concrete building. "Here is the hospital, the Americans paid a thief to rebuild it and he took the money and nothing happened, not even a single brick. The head doctor has gone."

"What do you do with your wounded?"

"We have our people."

The houses became more spaced out, compound walls turned into rough fences, wooden posts patched with corrugated iron. A mother duck led her ducklings along the ditch; the driver kindly swerved to give them room. The river, fringed with tasseled bulrushes, came into view.

"Our mighty and great Tigris!" announced the driver. "Our mother and our life."

"These days full of corpses," Zorro said to me in an undertone.

"Look, the bird!" said the driver, stopping the car so we could see. A large and beautiful heron stood on one leg on the piling stump of an old abandoned jetty. It was pure white, a zeppelin ballerina, pointing its yellow beak like a spire into the azure sky. It gulped and a fish bulge traveled down its long sinuous throat.

"When I was a boy, we caught fish here by the basketful. We call them sun trout. Samarra is the most beautiful country in the world, we have water, oil, and fertile land. It is a paradise!"

Here was the mythical land between two rivers, the origin of writing, city, bread, and law. Of civilization. The river flowed by, seemingly eternal, constant, and impartial. But not. Dammed, tricked into irrigation channels, diverted into pipes. Subject to man's ambition and its own vagaries, looping detours, dead-end oxbow lakes, rushing headlong over eroding cliffs. One of the Green Zone technicals, the man responsible for water in Iraq, had told us, one evening at the embassy, about the Mosul Dam. "It's held together with duct tape. The original design was totally flawed, its foundation is made out of soluble gypsum. And if it goes—whoosh, eleven trillion cubic meters of water will flood Iraq in a giant tidal wave and wash a million people away. Like God flushing the whole country down the toilet."

But for now it was bucolic: blue water flashed with rippling crescents of gold sun. The heron spread its great wings and ascended, pure and fluid, into the fathomless blue sky. Jean liked to say that war was a conservational preservative—killing, migration, abandoned houses, no tourists; fewer people to disturb the herons, nature left alone to grow over the ruins.

The driver turned off the rutted track onto a paved road. We looped back towards the town. Green river verdancy gave way to the always encroaching desert. The land was dun and camel-humped, scarred with tracks and random, abandoned excavations. The famous spiral minaret came into view.

"Wow!" said Zorro.

"It is our best feature!" said the driver, grinning at the climax of our tour.

"It looks like an upside-down ice-cream cone," said Zorro. The driver stopped the car beside it.

"We get out now."

I looked up in awe. A thousand years old—conquerors, empires, vainglory, history. Let it stand, extant! The driver ushered us forward. We walked up, winding around the cone of gently ascending curves. A warm breeze billowed my abaya behind me. Above, a hawk wheeled in the clear sky, feather trousers luffing in the wind, Iraq left behind on the ground. My boots made prints in the fine layer of sand dust and the wind blew them away. We climbed slowly, in reverent silence.

We arrived at the summit, a small crenelated circle. There, alone, dressed in black combat trousers and a black T-shirt, black bandana tied around his forehead and a new big black pirate beard, was Oberon. Glock pistol on his hip, Kalashnikov rested against the low wall.

"Welcome." He opened his arms wide, to embrace us and the view, master of all he surveyed. "This is my favorite place in the world!" he said. "Do you like it?"

He stood on the rampart and pointed out landmarks among the grid of streets spread before us. The Shia shrine, the market, the former Baath Party Headquarters which the Americans held as their forward operating base.

"There, further, where the river bends, do you see?" I followed his index finger to the outer edge of the buildings. "That is the main bridge into the town. The Americans have a checkpoint there, but we attacked it last night again. They sent two tanks against us—there, can you see? Where they blew up that building, it is still burning." A faint haze of smoke hung in the air below his fingertip. "But we were expecting this and attacked the tanks from the roofs behind—the old bus station—and they retreated."

"What did you attack them with?" I asked. Oberon wagged his finger, mock admonishing me.

"Aha, you want to know our weapons and capabilities! So you can take this information back to Colonel Donald Goodman in Baghdad."

"You have been talking to your father."

Oberon smiled but did not reply.

"He's not a colonel," I said. "He used to be, but he's a civilian now. He's an infrastructure officer. He's on the construction side, not the destruction side."

"For us there is no difference. The Americans will be defeated, as all invaders in our country will be defeated." He said this without any particular animosity. "I have sworn to free Iraq from the occupiers. This is what I want you to write in your article. The American people think we are the supporters of Saddam and we will crawl into our holes and hide—like that coward!—that our fighting is only—what do they call it?—teething troubles! Are we babies? Are we learning to walk? It is better the American people understand who we are so that they can tell their politicians so that they can tell the army to leave. This is the way democracy works, am I correct?" He smiled again, even white teeth. Lion stalking a hippo. There was a merriness in his eyes, an intelligent twinkle, he was teasing me and teasing me out.

"What's the point in attacking Americans, blowing up a helicopter, killing a few soldiers? You are only provoking, creating more violence."

The back of his hand wiped his smile into a sneer.

"You have been listening too much to what that Americano—Ahmed—says." He saw my expression, discomfited; the character in my story had crossed the line into real life. It had not occurred to me that Oberon knew Ahmed. "We are relatives, from the same tribe. He did not tell you? Ahmed was the foreign boy who visited one summer with his father. He had a big bag of Lego, and my brothers and I told him we should roll dice to see who can play with it. We were three and he was one and he could not beat all of us. That is the law of probability. When he lost, he cried that it was unfair. His father was furious and slapped his face. Ahmed was so surprised he stopped crying. My father pretended he was angry with us, but after they left he laughed and told us we were his lion cubs. Ahmed's father was from Samarra, he understood that his son had shamed him, but his son learned at the school of Americans and has no shame." Oberon picked up the Kalashnikov and propped it against the parapet, idly sighting a distant, putative target.

"Shame and honor, these are the central pillars of Iraqi society that the Americans will never understand," I said.

"Because they do not have these values. Their minds are shallow, their souls are hypocrites. Ahmed—and he is not the only one—has been seduced by American toys. What is this game called democracy?" The rifle stock had a Bush 2000 campaign sticker on it. Oberon saw me looking at it. "Did you vote for him?" I said I was British, I couldn't vote. "I thought you were more intelligent, Catherine Kittredge. The half-American, half-British woman who has come alone into the territory of the terrorists should not tell lies."

Zorro had been taking pictures, but now he took a step forward.

"She is not alone."

"I'm only trying to understand," I said. "That's how journalism works. I ask questions to understand."

"Perhaps. Or perhaps you are a spy."

"We are in Samarra at your invitation," I said, invoking the sanctity of Arab hospitality. "As your guest."

This Oberon conceded. He clapped his hands together and shouldered the Kalashnikov, "Yes. Come! It is time to eat!"

———

We ate in the garden of a house nearby. Fig trees heavy with red rotting fruit; wasps buzzed over the table in droves. Oberon relaxed and played the diligent host, insisting Zorro have the fattest chicken leg, spooning more rice onto my plate, clicking his fingers for one of the men to bring dates and yogurt. Zorro was allowed to take pictures as long as there were no faces in them. One of the fighters was assigned to watch him, and once or twice, when he caught an edge of smile or a thick eyebrow, made him delete the image from the flashcard. We continued our discussion of the Arabs and the West and our misconceptions of each other. We talked about media and conspiracy theories, about public debate and demonstrations and freedom. Oberon said he had never been out of Iraq except once, recently, to Amman.

"It was very modern, very clean, but their rice is not tasty like our Anbar rice and the Jordanian Mukhabarat are all CIA." He did not have memories, like his father did, of the old days, of wealth and prosperity and European capitals. He had no experience of the good life to lament or miss or wish for. He had grown up in the hard-bitten sanctions years, in an atmosphere of humiliation and betrayal, schooled in violence and suspicion. He was sure of himself in his little fiefdom of Samarra, but of the wider world, of its possibilities and complexities and profusion, he was ignorant. For him it was a blank territory beyond the borders of his imagination. At the same time, he knew there was much he did not know and I think, in part, he wanted to talk to us to find out more. At the same time, he insisted he had read many books about the West and knew a great deal, but when I asked him which books, he waved away my question.

"Many, too many!" He was alternately sun and thunder, courteous and aggressive, curious and defensive.

"I consider myself a democratic leader," he announced when the other men had gone into the house and left the three of us alone in the garden. Zorro looked sideways, his cigarette hung from his bottom lip. "I would like a glass of cold beer, but my men disapprove of alcohol and so I do not drink for their sakes and to provide the good example that they want to look up to. I tell my men we must learn from the Americans. *Know your enemy!* But they say this is heresy, we must resist Western culture and anything that is not the true path of the Koran." Oberon lit a cigarette as if to waft away these didactics with its smoke, and leaned forward.

"This is what you must understand. Spy or journalist, it is the same to me! Tell the Americans this: For me the fight is for my country, for Iraq. But for many of my men the fight is against the Western infidel. They say kill them in their homeland as they kill us in our homes. For them every kaffir is an enemy, for them every Shia is a kaffir. They watch the foreign imams on the internet. They are inspired by Al-Qaeda. They think Osama is their prophet. I tell them Mohammed was a warrior. He knew there was a time to pray and a time to fight and a time to plant fields and raise a family. But for them it is a jihad and their eyes burn with their desire for martyrdom—"

The driver returned and Oberon stopped talking. He looked at his watch and nodded.

"Excuse me," he said, sighing, a little reluctant. "I must pray now."

————

"He is charismatic," I said to Zorro when we were left alone. "See how his men are around him? Disciplined, deferential. Soldiers, not terrorists."

"Terrorist, freedom fighter; same diff," said Zorro. "He wants you to make a distinction, but there isn't one. He will fight using whatever means he can. If he thinks he can get money for us, he will kidnap us."

"He hasn't kidnapped us."

"Yet."

"Why would he bother to persuade us then? To talk to us?"

"You are telling him more than he is telling you."

"What am I telling him?"

———

When Oberon returned from his prayers, he apologized. He had wanted to take us to see the helicopter wreckage on the other side of the river, but the Americans were patrolling in that area and it was not possible. More tea was brought. We waited for an escort back to our car. Only ten more minutes, we were promised several times, half an hour, soon.

Oberon went in and out of the house issuing orders, listening to a crackling walkie-talkie, making calls on his cellphone. In between he sat with us and chatted. He asked Zorro about his dreadlocks but shook his head, perplexed: reggae? dope smoking? hippy? I asked Oberon about his childhood, but he only said, "My father is the old man, he has time for old stories." I tried to ask him again about the number of men under his command, weaponry, tactics, supplies, coordination with other groups. He smiled disingenuously or frowned or put his hands out to stop my spy questions and repeated his main point. "We are soldiers, not terrorists."

A teenage boy, a lookout, incipient moustache shadow, came running into the garden, panting, pointing. "Amrikan Amrikan," he said, and delivered a rush of urgent Arabic. Oberon barked at us, "Stay here." The men all came out of the house with their guns, ready. Oberon shouted orders into the hissing walkie-talkie, dispatched his men in ones and twos. The metal gate banged. I saw Zorro use their distraction to angle a few discreet table shots. I kicked him; nervous-nelly me, left over from school; I never liked to break rules. He kicked me back. *Look.* Oberon signaled to the driver and pointed at us. The driver nodded, all politenesses gone, pulled me up by my armpit, jabbed at Zorro who was pretending to put his camera away while taking out his flashcard and hiding it in his boot. Pushed me into the house, into a corner. Pushed me hard. We heard the door lock. We sat there, not talking, hugging our knees to our chests to make shields of our own selves. I felt the residual imprint of the driver's thumbs in my shoulder socket. It had finally touched me, physically. Torn through the cobweb of my own invincibility, my penciled sentences and earnest observations. It was nothing, not even a bruise, but it was shocking to me because I was the unlucky girl and immune. And suddenly not. I leaned against the gray plaster wall, leaned against Zorro, warm, next to me.

"It's alright, I think, it's alright," he said, taking my hand in his. "Something happened and they got spooked, that's all. It's alright."

"How do you know?"

"They've put us in a room with a window."

We sat there for two very long hours. The sky darkened into a somber sienna twilight. But Zorro was right. Eventually the lock turned and the driver reappeared and took us back to our car. We asked him what had happened, but he said only, "Amrikans. You go now." We drove back to Baghdad in the dark, in silence. There were no cars on the road.

———

Later, as a wedding present Zorro gave me one of the prints from the series he'd taken. It was of Oberon's broad back, leaning forward to hand a piece of bread to the black abaya (me) sitting next to him.

I wrote the article about our trip without mentioning being locked in a room for two hours. Journalist sin of omission; my own denial.

The sensation of the driver's thumbs in my flesh faded. The flash fear of the locking door was replaced by the relief of our safe arrival (several cognacs and a played-down description of events for Alexandre) and the get of a good story.

Oz ran it under the headline, "Lunch with the Enemy." We had a huge fight about it. I remember screaming at him down the phone: "They are not my enemy!"

Oz shouted back at me. "Well, just whose side are you on, Kittredge?"

SEVEN

In October 2004, Thomas Sligo, a stringer for the *Washington Post*, was kidnapped from his hotel room in Basra. He managed to escape after three days. I didn't know him; Basra was in the Shia south, under the British, a different kind of demographic and risk. Then Marla was killed by a car bomb two weeks later and that was awful because she was my friend; in the early days we used to swim laps together in the Hamra pool. In November, Celestine Cornudet was kidnapped—I had only met her a couple of times, but Zorro and I had been in the same area in Sadr City only the day before. It took Alexandre two weeks of nail-biting negotiations via the Iranians to get her back. The French government paid three million euros. Alexandre told me never to print this. The president himself had directly intervened; the Quai d'Orsay was in uproar about it.

It became very dangerous to go out. Most of Baghdad was no-go, either seriously Sunni or Shia militia in balaclavas. After my Samarra insurgent story, I tried to work on something about orphan street urchins. Ahmed rolled his eyes derisively and called it my "shoeshine boys" story. He thought it was sentimentalist nonsense when the real story was the mysterious Ayatollah Sistani and Moqtadr; the Shia and the Iranians and the upcoming elections.

I had not left Iraq for twenty months. Ahmed was waiting to hear about a U.N. position in Beirut he had applied for and in the meantime had only a Coalition Provisional Authority document, a stamped, misspelled piece of paper with his headshot stapled to one corner, and no passport because there was no Iraqi government to issue one. Alexandre kept telling me to take a holiday, to go to stay with Margot in Brittany, rest, recuperate, but the outside world was far away—the other side of a long desert road cut with bandits and insurgents or a dog-legged plane ride, spiral ascent from Baghdad airport to avoid missiles, via Erbil or Amman. Like Oberon, I could no longer imagine that somewhere else existed. I had a spot of blood in my underpants one day and I thought my periods had returned so I didn't go back to the doctor and forgot about it. I lived in a brocade-lined bunker well stocked with black humor and green chartreuse. Sometimes Alexandre and I would sit up together watching CNN and laugh at their reports on subjects like "Cats on Prozac" or "Sugar: A Deadly Killer?" I went to bed drunk on brandy because I could no longer concentrate long enough to read a single sentence of a book.

Nonessential staff were evacuated from the embassy. The gendarmes were replaced by French Special Forces who imposed new security protocols. Alexandre gave lunch parties because no one wanted to be on the streets after dark. I spent days sitting in the residence, eating cheese sandwiches, getting up the courage to go out to report. When I went out, I used one of the embassy drivers and never stayed anywhere longer than an hour.

———

One afternoon, close to my second Baghdad Christmas, I went to the SCIRI headquarters to find out about the candidates on their party list for the election in January. Ahmed had been offered a position as a protocol officer for the U.N. in Beirut. A pale blue U.N. passport was in the works. We were going to stay for the elections—Iraq's first free and fair!—and then go.

It was raining. The Tigris was swollen and turbid, the streets were flooded, mud slopped against the concrete block chicanes at the checkpoints. Khalid the driver was irritable, he hadn't wanted to go out. Someone had posted a threatening note on his door because he was working for foreigners. At SCIRI headquarters we met a barrier of young men with trim beards and clean white shirts and no ties. They were southern Shia grown up in exile in Iran. They were not friendly. They told me to wait and didn't offer any refreshments. Khalid the driver did not want to wait, he kept saying: "We go now? We go? Not good people." He was jumping up and down, very antsy, and I realized he was Sunni and suddenly this whole expedition didn't seem like such a good idea. Jean always said: Pay attention to your driver's mood, they always have better exit instincts than you do. So I conceded to the nugatory, threw up my hands, OK, OK! and we left. I was angry with the unnice SCIRI boys, the hoppity driver, the rain. A wasted, pointless afternoon. It took us two hours to get back through the checkpoints and the traffic. A bomb boomed somewhere and all I could think was: For fuck's sake.

When I got back to the embassy, I found Alexandre with Ahmed and Muntazzer sitting in the Sykes-Picot salon having coffee. They were in the middle of a discussion, but when I came in they stopped talking. I had a sense of negotiation and complicity; my arrival was an interruption. I sat down, but Alexandre said, in his sharp pince-nez voice, "Kittredge, would you mind waiting for us in the residency?" I looked at Ahmed, but his expression only confirmed my exclusion. I stomped out.

Ahmed stayed for dinner. Alexandre kept the conversation going with tales of Beirut in wartime and the legendary Johnny's Bar.

Ahmed asked him questions about the different factions; I was too tired to follow the intricacies of Lebanese politics. Alexandre and Ahmed kept up a jolly talking show. I kept quiet; shadow premonition. It was cold and I cupped two hands around my soup bowl. The coldest I have ever been was Baghdad that winter. The embassy had no heating system and the floors were tiled to keep cool in the summer. The generator was needed to power the communications systems and there wasn't enough capacity for electric radiators. I went up to bed before coffee.

An hour later, Ahmed came up. I was hunkered under the covers wearing a thick sweater, socks, and a ski hat. Ahmed got into bed and put his arms around me to quell my shivering. I was not in the mood to be mollified.

"What was that all about?"

"Nothing."

"It wasn't nothing. You were all sitting there conspiring."

"Muntazzer was upset, that's all."

"Why? What was he doing here?"

"It's a security clearance thing. It's better you don't know. Alexandre wants to keep proper protocol." Ahmed put his finger to his lips, hush-hush. I sat up straight, resistant, suddenly furious. He looked surprised.

"What's wrong?"

"Muntazzer is doing a deal," I said. "That's what's happening, isn't it. He tells Alexandre the identity of insurgents in Samarra, Alexandre takes the information to the Americans, you are the bridge. It works out very nicely for everyone. Muntazzer and his wife get a humanitarian medical visa to France." Ahmed got up from the bed. He did not answer, but he did not deny my guess either. His face was turned away from me. "I'm right, aren't I? Muntazzer has sold his son."

"And you bought him." I had not heard this tone from him before; sharp, cornered.

"What do you mean?"

"The brave resistance fighter," he mocked. "He is taking money from the Iranians, did you know that? You think you know this country, Kit, because you are fucking an Iraqi—" I was startled, it was the first time Ahmed was mean to me. I tensed. "You think people are the same everywhere. You believe in your universal humanity—but humanity is a luxury, you need prosperity to have humanity. It's about money. The doctor wants to take Muntazzer's money to operate on his wife. The insurgents need money for rockets, they don't care whose money. They will take it from Saudi, American, Israeli agents, they will take it from the Pasdaran who want them to fight the Barzani Kurds who are being sponsored by a different Iranian intelligence cabal. Oberon and his group are too stupid to see that it is a Shia trap. War is only money. Today the insurgents are full of pride and boast they are killing Americans! But if the Americans pay them, the same people will find other infidels to fight. They will happily sell their own brothers to the Americans for the right price, for bounties and visas and green cards. They want to kill Americans on one day and the next day they want to move to America. It is the dream of every Iraqi to kill an American and to be American."

I cowered. I could not make sense of what he was saying, and as I tried to untangle the knots of his screed and understand his hostility—against the Shia or against the insurgents, against me?—I forgot about Muntazzer and the invidious triangular arrangement I had witnessed in the Sykes-Picot salon.

"Beware of unintended consequences," I remember Alexandre telling Josh the Earnest Evangelical during dinner.

"But the consequences of doing nothing are worse," Josh had said.

"Seldom," Alexandre had replied.

———

I did not see Muntazzer again. Once or twice over the following years, I asked Alexandre what happened to him. He offered only a broad sketch: Muntazzer had indeed moved to Marseilles, but his wife had eventually died. And Oberon? Lost in the maw. Almost certainly dead or detained. The Oberons and his Shakespearean brothers-in-arms fought, refought, changed sides, realigned with or against the Americans, the Shia government in Baghdad, Al-Qaeda. Shuffling loyalty jihad God and country; half of them ended up commanders in ISIS.

In January, Iraqis voted and dipped their forefingers in indigo ink and held them up for the cameras. Democracy for a day. The Shia won, of course. The following week Ahmed and I left for Beirut.

PART II

BEIRUT

ONE

Ahmed and I got married a month after we moved to Beirut. February 13, 2005. When I try and remember if I was happy on my wedding day, I am not sure. Perhaps already the niggles of unanswered lacunae had begun to undermine my in-love certainty, perhaps I distracted myself with bridal details of dress and guests and cake.

Alexandre came from Baghdad. Zorro came from London, Jean and Margot from Paris. Ahmed told me his mother had given us her blessing but that she was suffering with bronchitis and couldn't travel. He said he had finally told her about our engagement just before we left Baghdad, but between all the election hoopla and organizing a leaving-Baghdad party and the logistics of arranging an armed escort to drive to the district where she lived, my hope to visit her had somehow been thwarted.

We found a liberal imam who agreed to convert me and marry me on the same day. (A matter of legal expediency; interconfessional marriages were not recognized in certain Arab states.) The imam was also a dentist and we signed the contract in his surgery. *Qabul, qabul, qabul,* I said three times—I accept, I accept, I accept. Alexandre and Jean signed as witnesses. The dentist-imam gave us each a date to eat and wished us well and excused himself because he had a patient waiting for a root canal. We went out on the street to get a taxi. I had bought a floor-length ivory slub silk evening dress in Aïshti, the fancy department store in Downtown, and I wore new white sneakers I glued all over with pavée diamante. It had rained overnight and the streets were muddy, so Jean and Ahmed lifted me up and carried me to the car so I wouldn't get them dirty in the gutter.

We had rented the private room at the restaurant Casablanca overlooking the sea, and Alexandre made sure there was plenty of champagne. Zorro took the pictures. They are put away now, in an album in a box file in the closet at the back of the laundry room. Am I smiling in them? Was Ahmed smiling? Fizzed up, drunk on bubbles, in the swirl and center of attention, congratulated. I think I thought that everything would be alright, whatever stresses of organization, whatever nerves of commitment, the blowups over the previous fortnight—these were done, it had been settled, we were married, happily ever after.

One moment, though, comes back: Zorro staggering against the wall of the spiral staircase down to the bathroom in the basement. He was doing a lot of white at that time, cocaine and alcohol, up and down.

"Are you OK?"

He looked through me with crystallized eyeballs and said, "Are you?"

The next day a giant car bomb blew up Prime Minister Hariri's motorcade, killing him and several others. Zorro, typically, was walking past. I, typically, missed it because Ahmed and I had left early to drive to Syria for our honeymoon.

———

We found an apartment on the second floor of an old Levantine mansion abutting the rock cliff next to the Gemmayze steps. It was elegant and neglected, its high ceilings were marbled with water stains because rain leaked into the porous stone. The green-and-blue-tiled floors were patched with concrete; triple arched windows let in the winter drafts. It was light and bright and big and cold and dusty. Ahmed had rented it unfurnished—"It's an orientalist dream, you're going to love it!"—and we looked in the secondhand shops along the bullet-pocked old Green Line for tables and chairs and a sofa. I liked the idea of flea-market chic; Ahmed said the stuff was junk and the shopkeepers wanted too much money for it. He sulked until I agreed with him and we ended up at the ABC shopping center buying modern pine and cream chenille. I tried to tease Ahmed that his taste was nouveau riche footballer.

"What about rush mats?" He thought I was mocking him.

"Are we living on a riverbank? I didn't leave Iraq so that I could end up living like my grandfather in the village."

The apartment was jerry-rigged with faulty wiring. The washing machine gave me a shock when I put my hands inside the drum. There were not enough electrical sockets, and we made a giant web of extension cords plugged into extension cords to get a router set up in the second bedroom that I used as a study. There was a third, smaller bedroom, and I found an old claw-foot tub in a builders yard and paid a plumber to connect it through the wall to the kitchen pipes.

"Cat needs to be clean," I'd said.

"Yes, but cats don't usually like water," Ahmed had reminded me.

"I need a bath. I can't read in the shower. I can't think in a shower."

There were a few months of pretend marital bliss. I was pretending, I don't know what Ahmed was doing. I learned how to make kibbeh and outlined a novel. Ahmed went to work and came home late.

The level of tension rose, drip-fed. Ahmed began to travel, at first just to Damascus, spending a night or two, then further, back to Baghdad, to Ankara, to Abu Dhabi, Bahrain, and longer gone. He said it was U.N. business, but his absences were often unexplained.

"Where are you?"

"I'm with a cousin in the north."

Which cousin? Which north? The phone line cracked and my heart cracked. Sometimes I could hear gunfire in the background as the winter rain seeped through the roof and spread clouds of green-black-edged mold across the ceilings like thunderheads.

I didn't have many friends in Beirut, I was lonely. After Hariri was killed, the streets were full of protests, but I walked through the forests of cedar tree flags and could not engage. I wrote daily pieces for the website, counterposing vox pops, but every time I tried to expand the roiling Lebanese politics into a feature, I got tangled in subclauses of shifting alliances. Oz asked, "OK, so who should we be focusing on? The March 8 alliance or the March 14 alliance?" And I would just say, "I don't know." It didn't feel like my story.

When Ahmed came back from a trip, I scratched at him with whittled splinter resentments. I nagged. I wanted the version of Ahmed I loved in my imagination, my golden dream boy, warm and burnished and caressing me. But he was distant, distracted, and when I polished up my mood into happy wife and made plans, all I got was, "I can't. I've got an early flight tomorrow."

I tried to construct a different narrative in the unreal conditional tense. On weekends, we would walk along the Corniche to Rawda and have lunch, eat grilled sardines and French fries with garlic labneh, and drink beer. Ahmed would make me laugh with absurd U.N. acronyms and stories of diplo-gaffes. We would talk and walk through the city, postprandial peregrinations through someone else's half-forgotten war. We would mend our two halves. We would make a bridge between East and West as we walked from West to East through the half-rebuilt downtown, dodging cars crossing highway lanes, tramping acres of parking lots asphalted over bulldozed bomb sites. We would make clever political commentary out of the lack of pedestrian crossings.

I put on this hope like a veil each morning. I did not realize that I had made love into a kind of costume. For a long time I blamed my self-deceiving artifice for provoking Ahmed's diffidence and recalcitrance. But it was not my fault that I didn't know what he hid from me. He had put on his own disguise and it was stretched taut and wearing thin.

———

One Saturday morning I woke up late. The sky was so impossibly high and blue and perfectly clear that I almost expected something terrible to happen. I think I actually said to Ahmed, leaning over him in bed to kiss his earlobe, "It is a beautiful day. Nothing could possibly go wrong."

I sounded lighthearted, but it was an effort. I thought by being so I could make us so. Love is delusion. God, how long it takes, how painful to let go of it.

Ahmed was still asleep. I wrapped myself in a warm robe and felt the February chill of the tiled floors against the soles of my feet. I went into the kitchen and turned on the kettle. When it boiled, I steeped dried hibiscus flowers in the teapot and tried to read a book about the civil war, each complicated chapter dissolving as soon as I had completed it. I thought: When Ahmed wakes up, I will make him an omelet and he will smile at me. We will not fight. We will go and have coffee and then we will walk along the sea and it will be sunny and he will kiss me.

"It's a beautiful day," I said, leaning over, kissing him in my realizing fantasy, awake, hello there, I am here and I love you, love me back please, like you used to. Ahmed turned away from me, sleepily, heavily, grumpily. I touched the back of his neck—

He turned around sharply.

"Kit—"

"What?" I sat up like a good Kitty Cat, waiting to be fed. He swung his legs over the side of the bed and got up. He seemed to have gone from sleepiness to wide awake at sixty miles an hour, as if my kiss had been a bucket of cold water. I followed him meekly through the living room into the kitchen. He kept his back to me. He stood in front of the refrigerator as if deciding what he wanted.

"Do you want an omelet?"

"No."

"I can go and get us coffee."

"No."

I struggled for words. "You can't just, you should be more . . . You should . . ."

Ahmed turned around and I saw that he was angry. I was confused, his anger was out of nowhere, out of a nightmare he hadn't shaken off on waking. He took a step towards me and for a moment I thought he was going to hit me. Instead he picked up a jar of pickles on the counter, swung his arm up and smashed it against the tiled floor. The noise startled him away from fury. He looked down at the mess he had made, sharp glass shards, green cucumbers splayed out like limbs. There was a crack in the terracotta tile.

He did not look up at me, but he said in a resigned, honest, small, tired voice: "It's not true that my wife died. But now she is dead. She was killed yesterday morning and I have to go back to Baghdad to collect my son."

Stone cat, very cold. Carved out of marble. Ahmed walked out of the room. I heard him turn on the taps in the bathroom and begin to brush his teeth. I had no blood or thought in me at all, so it seemed very odd that my ears were singing.

I went into my bathroom, ran the bath and undressed. I was cool, lightheaded. I imagined a faint, faked nonchalance even as my denial crumbled like a sand castle. I lowered myself into the aquatint water and watched my body disassociate from its surroundings, pale, submerged. I didn't need to talk to him, I didn't need clarification. He had only said what I had known, but had refused to know, had lied to myself as much as he lied to me.

His wife was not dead not dead not dead.

The cast-iron bath drew the heat out of the water, so I had to sit up and turn on the hot tap to recharge the temperature. My brain remained icy. I lay flat against the floor of the tub, legs hooked over the tap end. I shimmied down into the pale blue, water swallowed me without a ripple, so that I was drowned and blind, save for the island tip of my nose.

Ahmed must have finished brushing his teeth because I could hear him on the other side of the wall. The shared pipes banged and I heard a metallic echo in the carcass of the old tub as he turned off the tap. I heard him lean against the metal sink and clink his wedding ring—my wedding ring—against the rim.

I continued to listen carefully in my peculiar position of underwater snorkel spy. *Beep-beep-beep.* Ahmed tapping numbers on his phone. I heard him talking in Arabic and I instinctively put my head out of the water to hear better. But in the clear still air—steam coming off the surface of the water like a lake in a frozen dawn—I couldn't hear anything. So I went under again and heard him talking, now in English, in a tone of familiar intimacy.

"I told her, she knows. Wait for me at the café, I'm coming now . . ."

I held my breath. I could not imagine what aural trick of plumbing and wall cavity had produced this strange eavesdrop phenomenon. How did sound travel? Could it bounce like shock waves? Like when a bomb hit and a house three streets away would have all its windows smashed because the blast had bounced in a tangential coincidence of angles.

". . . no, he's with her relatives. I don't know . . . He is very young. He won't remember."

The talking stopped. I heard him pull on his boots, scraping them against the floor, and bang his heels into them with his habitual double tap. I heard the door open and his footfalls going down the stone steps.

I stayed very still. Bloodless, sterile. The bathwater provided an amniotic suspension. I could not think or I did not dare to. For some moments everything was quiet and blank. Then I began to recall his individual words. They fell like the cuts of a chisel against my nerveless statue self. *"It's not true that my wife died. But now she is dead. Killed."* I tried to unravel the sequence. At first her death appeared to be more terrifying than if she were alive. But then, at the same time as the obvious and astounding deception presented itself, its own solution appeared in the mirror, almost as if I had wished it. The wave of dread knowledge washed into relief, even gratitude, that his wife was dead. Then the relief cooled. His words continued to chip at me. I knew, I knew, I knew. Wife not dead, now dead, and the woman—for it must have been a woman, a lover, on the other end of the phone—a second jagged betrayal. Chip chip chip. To draw, in slow comprehension, finally, the full shape of Ahmed's revelation. Not just a wife. A son. A son! Not mine, but had fallen to me, Icarus spark, phoenix egg.

I opened my eyes and they filled with water, the washed watercolor blue of a New England dawn from my childhood. From underneath, the surface of the bathwater reflected a memory of a silver sky. Northern limpid light. I recalled the weathered gray clapboard of Granbet's house, sea foam between my toes, stealing lobsters from the fisherman's pots for supper. Lost world, a world where I could come in from the cold. The sea was freezing, even in the sunshine of a sparkling July day, and Granbet would hold my hand so that I couldn't chicken out and we would run into the sea together.

"The shock is the best part," said Granbet. "If you can make friends with the shock of it, we will be swimming buddies." I wanted to be her swimming buddy, so I held my breath not to scream or yelp or give way to any kind of childish reaction. "Jump in. Never hesitate.

You can talk yourself out of something you want to do a hundred times in the guise of anticipating doing it. You might as well do it. There's very little efficacy, I have found, in waiting. There is even less in worrying."

The curious thing was that after the first moments of needling, freezing shock the water felt delicious, like an ice cube was licking you. The best bit was when you got out and your whole body felt on fire. A miracle that turned cold to hot.

Come in from the cold, from the sea, from the snow, come into the kitchen and sit by the fire and drink hot milk, rugs underfoot, layers of ancient fleece blankets to snuggle into. This was the assumption of my childhood; cold was not to be feared because Granbet would make me warm again. This was the color I was always trying to get back to, the transparence of an Atlantic wave. Fluid, fleeting, I would catch it in the tint of bottle glass, in a window shadow, reflected in a spring rain puddle, but I could never find it in paint or Pantone; it was unprintable.

The color of Ahmed was the color of Iraq, yellow. My opposite. Take all the reserve and spite of my childhood, take all of the longing, the gaps and silences and unsaid things that a child cannot yet even articulate as missing. Take all of that and imagine how much I loved Ahmed at the beginning when the summer burnt yellow and it seemed as if I could never be cold again.

Ahmed was the sun. A son!

I don't know how long I lay in the bath. The water cooled, but I did not notice. I lay there, incubating, inert and still, careful not to move, not to make any splash that might ripple against the warmth of the rising—

The door hinge squeaked.

This was strange. Ahmed had gone—

In the instant the man walked into my bathroom I realized I had not heard Ahmed lock the door behind him on his way out.

I got out of the bath very fast and dragged a towel around my wet naked body. The man was wearing a leather jacket, a wool ski hat and he had a bushy reddish beard. He saw me, hopped. Stopped.

"Who are you?" Crystalline adrenaline poured through me. I shouted again, "Who are you?" I thought Ahmed might hear and come and rescue me. But Ahmed had gone. The man seemed to be startled; his hands juggled a nervous panic and he quickly removed himself to the other side of the door, saying, "I am sorry, very sorry, sorry."

I pulled on my jeans and a sweater and wrapped the towel around my wet hair. I looked at the screen of my phone. There was a text message from Ahmed: *don't go out stay at home, lock the door.* I put the phone in my pocket. I thought about putting on my shoes so that I could escape but they weren't in the bathroom. I could try to get out of the window and run in bare feet. But the window was two stories above the alley. All of this I thought through very fast. Possible, not possible; fight or flight?

The intruder stood on the other side of the door repeating, politely, in accented English, "Sorry, sorry." For the moment he did not seem threatening. I went out into the living room.

"Who are you?" I looked around for a weapon. There was nothing, of course, but books.

"My name is Ahmed," the man said. I almost laughed. He looked embarrassed. My phone vibrated again: *riot going on. Gunfire.* I had been going to run out of the door onto the street, but now I hesitated.

"Are you Denmarkan?" asked the man.

I said no, I was not Danish. I was English. (Which was better than being American; an identity I had learned to disown in the Middle East). I told him I was married to an Iraqi. Everyone, after all, was afraid of Iraqis. I held up my platinum wedding ring. He took it for silver, the choice of a modest believer.

"You are a Muslim?" he asked tentatively.

"I am," I answered tentatively. I was. Technically. "But my husband has not taught me very much."

The intruder Ahmed apologized for stumbling into my house, he said he had run away from the tear gas and found my alley by accident, climbed the steps to avoid the police who were looking for people to hit with their sticks, and noticed the door was open. His eyes were red and streaming. He rubbed them with his fists.

"No, don't do that." I reached out and touched his hand. He complied, crying, childlike. "It will only make it worse," I explained. "Come, I've got some Coca-Cola, that works the best." He followed me into the kitchen, blinking meekly, and let me hold up a cloth to catch the drips while he flushed the bubbly black Coke over his eyes. When he was finished, he tipped his head forward and blinked.

"Thank you. It is better. Coca-Cola!"

"I don't know why it works," I said, laughing. "It rots your teeth."

"It was American gas so maybe it needs American medicine."

"Create a problem and sell them the solution!"

We grinned at each other. My eye caught the raw crack in the floor tile, the pool of vinegar, shards of glass and pickles. I took a dish cloth and bent down and cleaned it up. He watched me awkwardly.

We could hear the helicopters vrooming overhead and the distant roaring of the crowd. Ahmed the intruder tried to call his brother-in-law, who he had lost in the melee, but the network was jammed. I said he should stay for a bit to catch his breath.

"Are you hungry?" I asked this other Ahmed. He nodded. So I made him an omelet. He ate it sitting at the kitchen table.

He was a big man and I remained wary, even as we became accustomed to each other. He politely asked me where he could wash his hands to pray and in which direction was Mecca. (I made an educated guess somewhere south and pointed towards the airport.) His movements were slow and deliberate, but he carried a grace that was expressed in long elegant fingers and a habit of pressing them together to make a steeple. He spoke English haltingly. He told me he lived up the coast in Tripoli, where he had a mobile phone shop; he had learned English to navigate the handset settings. His wife, he said proudly, was educated and spoke much better English than he; in fact she had taught him. He had two children, a boy and a girl.

"Do you have children?" he asked me.

"No."

"It is a shame. How old are you?"

"I am twenty-eight." Ahmed the intruder frowned. For some reason I told him the truth I had not yet told myself, let alone confessed to Ahmed. "I cannot have them."

"Ah," he said, looking sad for me, fingering his teacup.

"It is God's will," I said, playing my part.

He looked discomfited by this.

"I do not have children but my husband has a son by his first wife, who died."

How easily I repeated this lie! Then I realized that it was—strangely, wonderfully true.

———

I turned the television on to watch the riot we could see from the balcony. The footage showed an angry melee, fists in the air, clots of protestors breaking into a run, lines of Lebanese riot police advancing. Black flags and green Saudi flags and burning red and white Danish flags. Ahmed the intruder asked if I had a charger that would fit his Nokia because his battery was low. I found one and he plugged it in and began to text, to his wife to tell him he was OK, to his brother-in-law to try and find him. I made another pot of tea and sat with my laptop on my knees, Googling news reports so I could file something quickly for Oz.

File: SAINT-PLACIDE
February 5, 2006

A demonstration held in Beirut today to protest the publication of political cartoons depicting the Prophet Mohammed in the Danish newspaper Jyllands-Posten, turned ugly. Several thousand protestors, Sunnis, many bused in from other towns, gathered in the center of the city. Towards the end of the morning, when a group began to march towards the Danish Embassy in the upscale Christian district of Ashrafiyeh, clashes occurred with Lebanese police.

Tear gas was used and protestors say they were fired on with rubber bullets. A small section of the protestors, some armed with Molotov cocktails, some carrying sticks, managed to push through police lines and begin to break into the office block that houses the Danish Embassy on the sixth floor. Windows appeared to have been smashed, but the main door remains locked and protestors have not managed to get into the building. After a similar crowd burnt the Danish Embassy in Damascus yesterday, the diplomatic staff had been evacuated, and as it is a weekend, very few of the other offices were occupied. Frustrated, the protestors set fire to cars and attacked a Maronite church next door. Gunshots were heard as protestors ran through residential streets to avoid police. The mostly wealthy Christian residents of Ashrafiyeh were terrified to see Al-Qaeda flags and a religious mob in their neighborhood. Many of the protestors have expressed dismay at the violence.

"We came to demonstrate our rights, and to ask for the respect to our Prophet. We did not mean to do any harm," said Ahmed Khalil, 32 years old, a mobile phone shop owner from Tripoli. "Those who made violence are the police. Most people in the crowd were just trying to defend themselves."

Ahmed Khalil, Ahmed-the-Intruder was, like all of us, an apologist for his own. His awkwardness at finding himself alone, unchaperoned, with a woman, a foreign blond woman without a headscarf, put him in the pigeonhole I used to label "Seriously Sunni." His moustache was carefully shorn above his top lip, while his beard was left luxuriant below. His trousers were three-quarter length and showed a good three inches of white athletic sock before his Nike sneakers. When I got to know him a little better, I amended his moniker from Ahmed-the-Intruder to Ahmed-the-Wahhabi. He was very polite; he was very certain of his religious tenet.

We talked a lot of Us and Them that afternoon, watching the riot in stereo, on TV and from the balcony. Islam and justice; might and right and human rights. For Ahmed-the-Wahhabi, Islam was a universal law so obvious and extant, God's word enshrined in the Koran, that he simply could not understand that there was any other point of view or another way of looking at things.

"We can agree to disagree," I said. But he shook his head at this kind of compromise.

"No, no, there is no disagreement between right and wrong." Publishing an image of the Prophet Mohammed, Peace Be Upon Him, was *haram*. Mocking the Prophet Mohammed, Peace Be Upon Him, was blasphemy. Blasphemy was a crime. He was not insulted by the cartoons because he had not seen them. He was simply outraged—but more than that, incredulous, hurt, genuinely pained—by the idea that Danish people would deliberately blaspheme and that their politicians would support such a heinous atrocity. He understood rights as respect and this was the opposite. One group of people, he argued, should not trample on the rights of another group of people and call it their right. I tried to explain it in a different way, in the way I knew, had been taught, inculcated.

"I have the freedom of speech to say what I like, and you have the right to be upset and complain about it." Ahmed-the-Wahhabi shook his head, sadly, disappointed.

"I don't understand your freedoms," he told me quietly.

Despite our inability to make each other understand, or perhaps because we were both earnestly trying to understand, we found a kind of friendship. We saw in each other someone to answer our questions about each other. It was the continuation of the conversations I had begun with Muntazzer and Oberon, but in Ahmed-the-Wahhabi I thought I had found a purer subject because the Americans hadn't invaded his land and he was not reacting to geopolitics and sectarian muddles.

I was oversimplifying. I was in Lebanon, for god's sake, the greatest practitioner of geopolitics and sectarian muddles. Religion is always politics, sectarianism, nationalism, bollocks; jumble up the semiotics, same diff, as Zorro would say. But still, we had made a little island in the middle of the storm. He had needed sanctuary and I had given it to him. I was pleased because I had been rewarded for my liberal values and he was grateful with a sweetness that was humble and endearing.

———

By the end of the afternoon, when the riot had burnt itself out and he had managed to contact his brother-in-law, we had agreed to meet again, to discuss these great matters further.

I went out a few minutes after he left and walked up the hill to Ashrafiyeh to survey the damage. An elderly lady with a chic blond coiffure and a Chanel jacket with a mink collar was walking a small dog around a smoking overturned car. She looked not in the slightest deterred or dismayed as she carefully picked her elegant Ferragamo feet through the rubble. Picture-perfect Beirut ridiculousness.

TWO

That evening, I found Johnny, sitting in the corner of the bar in his habitual pose of patron. He had a telephone and a cup of coffee in front of him, a stack of old copies of *Time* magazine at his elbow. "The news never changes," he liked to say. One of his favorite party games was to open one of the magazines at random, read out a headline and make people try and guess which war it was. He poured himself another glass of wine and cursed the Wahhabi marauders stirred up by idiot imams.

"Sons of Mohammed's dogs!" Johnny said. "Jesus H and his apostles, Kittredge, if they come into our side of the city again, I swear I will shoot these bastards myself."

I sat at the bar, typing my notes into my laptop. He had decided he would open the restaurant after all, because his chef had come in to work, diligently on time as always, despite the sirens and the mayhem.

"Hussein is a Shia from the South. Ask him what he thinks about these turbans and beards. They want to dress like it's the seventh century and brush their teeth with sticks because that's what Mohammed did. But of course they watch television and drive cars and they all have mobile telephones and are very happy to get their hands on a Kalashnikov. Did Mohammed use these things too?"

I folded myself into the concentrated effort of organizing facts into sentences. The waiter brought me a Negroni without my asking and I drank it.

When I looked up, I saw a few journalists I knew coming in.

Johnny opened his arms wide. "Ah yes, welcome, welcome to the thirsty vultures!"

The Beiruti hack pack: Jeroen, Emilie, and Imma. A Dutchman, a Frenchwoman, and an Italian walk into a bar—Jeroen ran his hand over his shorn head. He had a cut over one eye, a yellow bruise along his brow.

"Oh dear," I said. "What happened to you?"

"Hit on the head by a pirate with gold teeth and a scimitar in one hand," he said equanimously. He showed us pictures on his camera. "I didn't realize I was sheltering in the doorway of the building where the Danish Embassy is. There is only a tiny plaque next to the main door, no flag or anything." I wrote the details of Jeroen's observations into the story and hit send.

Johnny held up a bottle of wine and the newcomers collected their glasses underneath it.

"Saudi money. Saudi religion!" Johnny poured forth freely. "They are sending all their imams to tell our Sunnis that the rest of us are all heretical apostates! They broke the cross off the shrine next to the Armenian church, did you see it? They are fanaticals. God deliver us from the fanaticals! We must defend against them! If they come here again, I will fight them."

"Very good idea," I said to Johnny, "look how well that worked last time." I tossed the civil war back at him as if I knew what I was talking about. Johnny was sixty years old, he had brilliantined hair and he was having an affair with the new waitress. I took his reaction to be the hollow words of defiant machismo.

"Ha!" said Johnny. "Look around. This is the last place in the Middle East where there are still Christians. If the Christians don't fight, they will die. So I will fight."

"It's always a minority of nutty," I said, reasoned by an afternoon of Ahmed-the-Wahhabi's sincerity. "They have the right to protest if they don't like something."

Ping. Oz emailed me back: *Thanks for this. We'll run it on the website now.*

"Is this protesting?" Johnny pointed up at the TV on a bracket above the bar. The news footage was a repeating loop of police clashing with the menacing mob. A woman in a black abaya was screaming into the camera, her face frenzied and contorted. "They are crazy! Bulls in this china shop Lebanon!"

Ahmed appeared. Jolt.

"Are you listening to this old Phalangist?" He walked over to kiss me hello, I ducked his embrace. He was clean and shaved and smelled of a scent—honeysuckle treacle; something sickly sweet—I did not recognize.

The revelations of the morning had been superseded by the events of the day. I had been too preoccupied to think about Ahmed, his wife and son and lover.

"Where have you been?" I asked him.

"At the U.N. Mission," he said, addressing everyone. He began to retell gossip from the antechambers to power. His favorite kind of conversation, the kind in which he held court. (Ahmed was always at the center of his own stories; Alexandre once used the word *diva*.) I watched the semicircle of faces nod and drink it all in.

Apparently the Lebanese prime minister had spent most of the morning reassuring the U.N. ambassador that everything was under control. Until Ahmed told his ambassador that he had just come through Ashrafiyeh and the demonstration was out of control and there was black smoke coming from the Danish Embassy building. His ambassador relayed this to the prime minister, who muttered, "The bastard Syrians," and hung up and did not call back. Now they were saying that the interior minister was going to resign in the morning.

"It's your crazy coreligionists!" Johnny said to Ahmed. Ahmed spread his hands in a gesture of mock surrender.

"Don't blame me, I'm an atheist," he said, laughing, deflecting. "It's obviously a Zionist plot."

"Syrians," added Johnny. "The prime minister is right. We are always at the mercy of our neighbors."

"Everyone is always trying to get their hands on little Lebanon because it has the most interesting parties." Ahmed grinned at his own pun and poured himself a glass of wine. Charming, charming, charming; that was the word everyone used. Except Zorro, who had remained uncharmed, even the first time they met. "Photographers are hard to fool," he said. "We listen with our eyes. Charming? Nah." His word, dredged up from our London childhood, was "smarmy."

Ahmed put his arm around me. Warm palm snug in the empty small of my back. "How was your day, Mish-mish?" My face tucked into the familiar contour of his neck, underneath the syrup I could smell his smell, frankincense embers and leather. I knew I would forgive him. Not for the lie, which was unforgivable, but for his son.

"People are being manipulated," said Ahmed. He had put on his serious diplo-expert face, ready to analyze events.

"People are upset," I said. Ahmed-the-Wahhabi had been very upset. He had wept over the Danish insults to the Prophet.

"They are upset because someone tells them they are upset."

"But all over the world—Pakistan, Indonesia, London—everywhere."

"Don't be fooled by crowds. Crowds are easy to buy," said Ahmed, the son of the Baathie traitor.

"Don't underestimate people, popular sentiment."

"So do you agree with them?" Ahmed turned to me. We were back in our marital to-and-fro, discussing. The world to rights again.

"I have sympathy for their outrage," I said, measuring my thoughts. "Just because we don't think it's insulting doesn't mean it isn't insulting. They are clearly insulted. But on the other hand, insulting someone shouldn't be a crime. But it is something we try and avoid doing."

"The trouble is," said Ahmed, "insult is in the eye of the insulted."

"But we all have our red lines. Like France and Germany, where Holocaust denial is illegal."

"Free speech is an absolute," said Ahmed. "On this point I am a fundamentalist!"

"Maybe that's OK in theory," Jeroen came over, shaking his bloodied head. "But in practice these things have consequences."

"If you give them an inch, is the beginning of the problem," said Johnny. A crescent of light shone across his shiny hair. "You say, OK we agree not to be offensive, and then they decide that everything is offensive so that by the end you are not even allowed to eat salami."

"It's important to think with your stomach," mocked Ahmed.

"Yes it is," replied Johnny, who ignored the reproach. "If everyone's stomach is happy, then many other problems would be less well fed."

"Yes!" said Ahmed, agreeing with Johnny. "I always say it's the economy, stupid. Free markets and good financial infrastructure. This is the answer to the Middle East."

"Yeah, yeah," I said. "A chicken in every pot, a refrigerator in every kitchen. But they have plasma TVs in Saudi Arabia, and all they watch on them are religious shows."

"It is deeper than the superficials of white goods," said Ahmed. "It is the difference of mentality. It is the divide between Islam and the West." Then I regretted challenging him because now he went into full pontification mode. He was wearing a blue button-down shirt, khaki trousers, and suede loafers. He looked almost presidential, and then I remembered his talent for dissimulation and thought, maybe not quite presidential; Ahmed was more praetorian aide.

"If not these cartoons, then it would be something else," he continued. "They will find any issue to wave about like a flag. A headscarf is a flag. A flag is just a banner with a stick. Why are we Arabs poor and oppressed? We Arabs, who once ruled as far as Andalusia and invented arithmetic! What happened to *our* empire? They say we are brought low because we are not godly enough. If we return to the piety of the good old days, we will be delivered from these humiliations. But they never question the source of our poverty and our rotten societies. It does not occur to them that religion is the problem. Submission, obedience. No, no! You cannot question the Koran!"

I had often heard Ahmed rail against the shibboleths and superstitions of Islam. For Ahmed, the West was successful because it had done away with religion as a political authority. The American Constitution separated church and state, Henry VIII had divorced England from Rome, the French Revolution had destroyed the power of the bishops and established *laïcité* as a fundamental principle of the Republic. I used to argue back that by opposing all Islam, he was only playing into the hands of the Islamists who said that the West wanted to destroy it. Jihad needed an enemy in order to exist; why give them what they wanted?

I felt the red wine curdling in my stomach. Ahmed continued his stump speech.

"Arabs will beg and lie to get a visa to live in the West. But when they get there, they want to live according to the same values of the society that they left. Where women are less than men and everyone has to suffer all the tropes of family and honor and obedience because they are written in this surah or that hadith. The Koran is the word of God. So they are stuck in a tautology, don't you see? They are stuck because they won't allow their belief to be questioned even as they demand that their beliefs be respected. But how can you respect something that can't be questioned? They complain that their rights are not respected; but they're in Denmark! Try and have your rights respected in Damascus!"

Jeroen and Emilie and Imma stood listening intently. Ahmed was very convincing. I had seen the same expressions on the faces of bespectacled Western government officials in conference rooms in Baghdad and London and Washington. Ahmed was the perfect Arab because he confirmed the opinions they were leery of voicing themselves. There is nothing more compelling than an argument you already agree with.

"None of which means we should not uphold our values of accommodation," I said. "It's freedom *of* religion, not freedom *from* religion. It's not right that the French don't let women wear the burqa, it's not right that the Swiss have banned minarets. Of course Muslims feel discriminated against."

"Do you feel discriminated against as a Muslim?" Ahmed teased me.

"Only because I am married to an apostate atheist!"

"Are we still married?" he whispered, turning me away from the group for a moment, husband to wife. He took my face in his hands so that the tip of his nose touched mine. I looked into his eyes wanting to be comforted by their caramel softness, but they looked back at me clouded and turbid as a Martian magnetic storm. I took his troubled look for concern about me, about us. All I wanted to do was reassure him.

"I have a ring on my finger," I replied.

"I will explain everything," he said very softly, kissing my forehead. "And if you are the woman I love, you will forgive me."

"Take me home. I'm sleepy," I said. But he didn't want to leave yet.

"Go home, I'll come later."

That night I wept tears that spread mascara blooms on my pillow and I waited but Ahmed did not come.

THREE

The weekend after the riots, Jean came to Beirut to report on the cartoon crisis. He took me to Johnny's. "When Terry was released, this is where we all celebrated," Jean said. "It was open every day. If the shelling was bad, he turned the music up. If there were Israelis around, he would lock the doors and there would be a special knock that would open sesame it." Johnny beamed at Jean from behind the bar. The good old days.

We sat in one of the corner booths, and Jean laughed that nothing had changed, not even the red velvet curtains that made the place look like a brothel. "I think it *was* a brothel during the war—Johnny's brother used to run a backroom 'poker game' during the afternoon bombing hours." He called over, "Whatever happened to Basil, Johnny?"

"Went to Melbourne like the rest of them," replied Johnny with a shrug.

"We would come here and drink Negronis."

"My father too?"

"Yes, sometimes." Jean looked into his glass. "Johnny could get Campari even at the height of the blockade." Johnny came over and put his hand on Jean's shoulder and winked at me.

"Did you know my father?" I asked Johnny.

"Old war stories!" he said. "All bullshit! That Campari was only wine and cherry juice."

"Ah, the rose-tinted glamour of wartime when the war is over," said Jean. "Kit, don't be beguiled by the 'I-was-here-and-the-tank-was-there' war reporter stories. I know wartime is a crazy kind of happiness, but it's also a sickness. You think you are at the center of the world when you are covering a big story. You are seduced by the excitement. You are standing right next to death and you are alive; it tingles. People say they get addicted to it. People get addicted to drugs—*ouf*—Zorro. I know, I know. How is Zorro? Where is Zorro? I saw his pictures from Somalia—The drugs take away the pain of life because life is shit and you know this and it is agony to live with this knowledge. And when you know you are an addict, you are ashamed and so you take more drugs. War is an avoidance too—I am sure, for Zorro it is like this. Because everything in a war zone seems more important than real life. When you are in the field, you have no responsibilities, no routine, there is only running and getting the story. You don't have to go to dinner with your in-laws and take the kids to school and spend your Sunday afternoon working out your taxes. You are excused all of this. It is a kind of holiday. So when you go back, it all seems unbearably mundane and pointless and you want to leave again. So you leave again."

"Like my father."

"But eventually you are not happy because you realize that all of these everyday family things are actually more important than dead strangers. Some idiot with a gun is just another fighter and there are always thousands of these idiots and they are nothing special. But now you are stuck because this is what you do."

The distraction of violence. Jean was right, Jean was always right.

He had seen it all before in another revolution, a previous war. But then again, Alexandre always said it was wrong to think that history repeated itself. History didn't know what it was doing, any more than its protagonists who made it up as they went along.

Jean tipped the rest of his wine down his throat.

"How is Ahmed?" he asked kindly, a little worried. "The first year of marriage can be difficult."

"Ahmed is traveling a lot," I said, noncommittal. "The ambassador sends him on trips and he can't discuss them."

We ate the infamous boeuf bourguignon and ordered baba au rhum. Johnny put a bottle of Captain Morgan on the table and we kept pouring. We talked Shia and Sunni and civil war and Iranians and Alexandre taking up the ambassadorship in his beloved Damascus. I avoided talking about Ahmed because I didn't know what was happening. He had gone to Baghdad and had not called. I suspended myself in limbo, waiting, wishful thinking in the future perfect. "Things to figure out," as he had said when he left, would be figured out. I didn't want to admit to his lie, I had absorbed it as my own secret too. Jean did not probe.

Perhaps it was the rum, perhaps the comfort of old haunts and old friends who haunted them. Lulled, Jean became mellow and reflective. He smiled as he told me his regrets. He said he had made peace with them.

"Or perhaps it is Margot that made peace with them," I said. He nodded, acknowledging his debt to his wife's forbearance.

"Maybe it's just time that sands down all the rough corners and resentments," he replied. His children were grown now and at university. There was the house in Brittany, where the waves made navy blue taffeta ruffles in the winter. Pewter tones, duller grayer skies than Granbet's Good Harbor Bay, but on a fine day, blue, good strong northern blue. Margot pottering in the garden; planting, pruning, composting, whispering to her dahlias, nourishing her plants as she nourished me with her gentle advice. Maybe I could grow straight and true too. I loved their house in Locquirec, vicarious home. All my father's books were in the bookcase there.

"What are you working on, Kitty?"

"I don't know. I was working on something about the reconstruction of downtown. How the hole in the middle of the city is being filled up by ersatz façades and luxury fashion brands. It's a metaphor for the whole Lebanese post-civil-war denial and amnesia. But I met an interesting guy, an ordinary everyday Wahhabi. He took shelter in my apartment during the riot. I thought he might make an interesting profile, a case study—"

Jean nodded encouragingly.

"This is what we do," I said to Jean. "We are reporters. A fine thing to be, no?"

"Well," he replied. "It is either this or the dark side. Become an editor."

———

I rang Ahmed-the-Wahhabi in Tripoli the next day, by chance, he was coming to Beirut soon to buy circuit boards and suggested we meet for coffee.

A week later we sat in a café near the American University during the quiet midmorning, and he told me his life and times. As an experiment, I tried to write the story from his point of view, not inside his head, but in the third person. "To understand the other, walk in their shoes, stretch my mind to see the world from different perspectives," as I wrote to Oz when I sent it to him.

File: CONCORDE
March 2006

Ahmed Khalil was born in the city of Hama in Syria in 1977. His mother was his father's second wife and much younger than him.

His father's first wife had died and left him a son, Ahmed's brother Mohammed, who was twenty years older. When Ahmed was five, the Muslim Brotherhood rose up against President Hafez al-Assad and was brutally put down. His father and two of his uncles were killed in the massacre. His older brother Mohammed was in his last year of his studies in hydro engineering at the University of Damascus, and when he graduated he returned to Hama, took a junior position in the irrigation department, and supported his father's second wife and son.

Ahmed grew up believing his brother was his father because his mother and his brother were the same age and they shared a bed. After the uprising, Hama was a silent, cowed city, there were tens of thousands of missing fathers and brothers. Nothing was said because no one could speak. Rage was stifled, grief had been bulldozed into mass graves and paved with asphalt. Cry at night when no one can hear and do not forget, never forget. For several years, on the anniversary of the crackdown Ahmed's mother left a white carnation at the edge of one of the empty parking lots. She was not the only widow who did this. One year a wreath was laid, and after this transgression soldiers were posted so that no one could leave flowers anymore.

Ahmed did not know any of this until he was eighteen and went to the municipality to register for his adult ID card. The official behind the desk told him to come back next week. The next week he told him to come back the next week, and the next, the week after. Ahmed had the sense that something was not quite right by the way the official continued to stamp, stamp, indigo stamp, moving forms from one pile to another, without meeting his eye. On the fourth week, the man referred him to a colonel in the Amn Security office in another part of the building, and with a fearful heart Ahmed found the right corridor and door number 43. The secretary told him to sit and wait and he sat there and waited for four hours without daring to go to the bathroom, without even asking for a drink of water. Finally the Amn Colonel handed him his blue laminated ID card with a line of XXXXX crossing out his father's name, Mohammed, the same name as his brother's name. When he asked why, the colonel said, "Your father was executed as a traitor."

Ahmed suffered the turmoil of deception, betrayal, anger, and youth. He vowed to himself that he would never serve his national obligation to the army that had killed his father. He refused to speak to his mother or his usurper brother or to live under the same roof. As a way out of the family crisis, one of his widowed aunts arranged for him to marry a cousin in Tripoli. And so he left Syria and went to live in Lebanon.

His fiancée was called Fatima and was the same age. When he met her among her family, he was happy and relieved. She was plump and pretty and she smiled a little mischievously while trying not to look up at him. Her brother owned an electronics shop in Tripoli and Ahmed went to work for him. Another cousin rented them a small apartment with a catty-cornered view of the sea. Ahmed had never seen the sea before and he marveled at the bigness and blueness of it.

When he came to live in Tripoli, it was only a few years after the end of the Lebanese civil war. The city was scarred by the fighting, but he could see signs of new building that gave him a sense of fresh beginning and optimism. Radios and TVs and personal stereos were very popular, he learned fast, and his brother-in-law was a good man. Soon Fatima was pregnant.

When they married, Ahmed had agreed that Fatima could continue her studies to become a pharmacist. She was more modern than the girls he knew in Hama; she wore jeans and liked flowery silk blouses. When she became pregnant, she said she would continue working in a tone of voice that did not seem to invite any argument. But as she grew bigger, she stopped wearing trousers and began to wear a long gown for comfort. After Mohammed was born, she adopted it as her everyday dress. She had always worn a headscarf, but now she was very careful to make sure that not a single hair was showing and secured her scarf with pins. Ahmed was pleased at her modesty. It was better for his wife to be modest, closer to God, closer to the right way. He was a Muslim, this was his identity, but he did not consider himself especially pious.

When Al-Qaeda flew airplanes into the World Trade Center on 11 September 2001, Ahmed felt bad for the Americans who were killed. There was a Palestinian refugee camp in Tripoli and Ahmed heard that some of the Palestinians had rushed into the street victoriously waving Palestinian flags as if they had won a football match, but he did not like this reaction. People dying was not a cause for celebration. His brother-in-law did not believe that it was Arabs who had done this because the buildings had fallen down too neatly and too perfectly. His brother-in-law said he was sure that it was IsraelAmrika because everyone knew that they had told all the Jews in the building not to go to work that day. Ahmed did not agree, but did not like to contradict him in front of customers.

He did not pay much attention to the war in Afghanistan; it was far away. But when the Americans threatened to invade Iraq, he began to feel a sense of grievance. Iraq was a sovereign Arab country. Iraq had nothing to do with September 11, and in any case what were weapons of mass destruction? Didn't Israel have weapons of mass destruction that the Americans had given them? Some of his friends in the café said it was their duty to fight the American infidel and defend Iraq. Ahmed thought this was a stupid idea. They would not be able to do much against American smart bombs, and he couldn't see that there was any reason to get yourself killed to defend a Baathie idiot like Saddam Hussein—even if he claimed to be the defender of all Arabs (they all said that anyway)—who was just the same kind of Baathie idiot as Hafez al-Assad, who had killed his father.

But when he watched the bright explosions light up the Baghdad night and saw American tanks driving over cars and laughing, when he saw the frightened faces of the children watching firefights from doorways and their tiny limbs torn and bloodied, when he held his sleeping son or carried his baby daughter in his arms, when he saw the pictures of Iraqi men blindfolded, naked, humiliated, he began to feel differently. The anger he had buried in the bosom of his family began to resurface.

It was about this time that his mother wrote a letter to him asking that he bring his family to visit in Syria. Hafez al-Assad had died, his son Bashar was president now, and the Amn Security were no longer questioning or detaining Syrians with Lebanese residency permits.

Fatima convinced him they should go to Hama for a visit. Even, she reasoned, if only out of curiosity. It had been several years now, it was time for forgiveness. So he bought bus tickets and a baby sling for traveling and a new suitcase with wheels and they made the journey back to the home that he had once vowed he would never set eyes on again.

His mother and his brother received Ahmed as a prodigal son. The women of his family gathered and cooked all the dishes he loved from his childhood, the quince kibbeh and makkdous and mohammara with Aleppo pepper. And the lamb! He had forgotten the taste of the fat-tailed lamb! Layered with yogurt and pinenuts and raisins, there was nothing to compare with the fat of the lamb from the land of Hama.

His brother had married his mother and they had a daughter who was the same age as little Mohammed. His brother was more confident and more friendly than Ahmed remembered him. The city seemed to have changed in this way too. His brother was now a manager in the Department of Irrigation, but at home he changed into a dishdasha and wore a white prayer cap. He had become an unofficial imam, preaching in the apartment of a neighbor, because he did not want to be registered with the Ministry of Religious Affairs and affiliated with a mosque. "All the imams are only mouthpieces for the government," he said.

His brother's new piety had conferred on him a certain authority. His brother explained to Ahmed that everything that had happened was according to God's plan and said it had been necessary to protect him from the truth in the years when the agents of the government were watching the families of the slain Brotherhood. He talked a lot about politics, and he spoke with a fervor and outrage that was new to Ahmed, who was used to the mild dronings of the imams in the mosque which he attended in Tripoli.

At that time there were many Iraqi refugees coming over the border into Syria. The men brought their families to safety and then went back to Iraq to fight the Americans. It was their duty, his brother said, to help them as the Ummah should, and listening to him, Ahmed felt proud that there were Syrians who would sacrifice themselves to defend their Arab brothers.

After he returned to Tripoli, Ahmed began to attend a new mosque where a young Saudi imam preached. This imam was a friend of his brother's and his message was the same. He spoke of a battle between infidel and believers, between the godly and the apostate, between the Crusaders and the righteous. The cartoons in Denmark were only the latest insult. Should we stand by as our Prophet, Peace Be Upon Him, was insulted?

In Beirut, I concluded my story about Ahmed-the-Wahhabi with a description of the cartoon riots, from his point of view, how he had been blinded by tear gas and lost his brother-in-law in the stampede and stumbled into an apartment for safety. I left out the incident in my bathroom and folded our debate about Islam into the narrative. I sent it to Oz.

He did not run it.

———

Ahmed was away in Baghdad for two weeks. He was never good at answering his cellphone and the reception at his mother's house was conveniently patchy. In his emails he wrote that he loved me. He wrote that he had been separated from his wife when we had met. He had wanted to get a divorce, but his wife's family refused so he had paid an imam to pronounce the divorce. His wife's family had not accepted this as legal. At this time the baby, Little Ahmed, was only a year old. According to Iraqi family law, based on Sharia, a father was granted custody of a son at the age of two (girls stayed with their mothers until the age of seven). His wife's family wanted to keep the child beyond that age and they refused to let Ahmed see him.

In his emails Ahmed painted a portrait of an avaricious family who had kept him away from his son and prevented him from talking to his ex-wife without their supervision. The word "bigamy" did not enter my head. I waited for Ahmed to return. I dared not ask if he would bring his son.

The day after he came back, we drove up the coast to Tripoli. Ahmed-the-Wahhabi had invited us to lunch with his family at their home. He said that Fatima wanted to meet me.

Beirut fell down the mountain into the blue sea. The Christian suburbs scrolled past, a cubist jumble of dense apartment blocks.

"What is the Lebanese obsession with concrete?" I wondered aloud as Ahmed drove. "It's as if they have poured a tub of cement over the most beautiful place in the world."

"Development," said Ahmed. "Do you know that property prices have never gone down in Beirut. Not even during the civil war?"

Ahmed told me news from Iraq. Things were very bad in Baghdad, it was now a Shia-Sunni civil war mixed up with an insurgency and spiked with Al-Qaeda spectaculars. The Americans had begun to realize that they couldn't fight everyone, and almost as if they had taken Ahmed's advice ("War is only money—it's what I have been saying all along!"), they began a policy of paying Sunni tribes to fight Al-Qaeda.

"They are calling it The Awakening," Ahmed told me, laughing. "Which sounds like it's going to gross a million on its opening weekend."

"What else is going on?"

Ahmed grinned, turned down the volume (he had put in one of his old tapes of N.W.A., left-over teenage rebellion from his Georgetown high school days) and entertained me with hair-raising stories of the airport road. The Americans had decapitated all the palm trees to widen their fields of fire. There was the wreckage of burnt-out Humvees all the way along one stretch. The mercenaries liked to hang out of their bubble helicopters like Magnum, P.I. Checkpoints every ten meters and they had only one question: Are you Sunni or Shia? Ahmed told me that he would answer that he was a Christian because he was clean-shaven and looked the part. All the journalists were still in the Hamra Hotel, but it had been hit again and now the swimming pool was full of rubble.

"How is your mother?

"She is fine. She still refuses to leave. She barely goes out. She has the generator, and old Nawal's husband brings her gasoline for it so she can watch TV all day long. She told me that they kidnapped the boy next door and his mother went mad because the father refused to pay the ransom so they killed him."

I did not ask him about his wife. I did not ask him about his son. It was sunny. He kissed me.

"I tell my mother every week to leave, that it is too dangerous. She agrees, but she says: it is my country." Ahmed shook his head.

"She will never leave," I said. "She has her sisters."

"The three witches."

"She has her home."

"But there is no one else left. Everyone has gone—to Amman, to Dubai, to Beirut."

"People have been leaving Iraq since 1958."

"My father should have left." This was an old refrain. His father should have defected to Jordan or made some excuse and stayed in America when he was recalled to Baghdad. He should never have trusted Saddam. He should have, should have. When he could have, he wouldn't, and then it was too late.

"Soon," said Ahmed, turning up the volume again, "there will be no one left but angry boys with guns."

I took Ahmed's pessimism for indulgence, for Iraqi fatalism. I didn't know how bad it would get, because back then it already seemed worse than anyone had imagined it could be.

"Lebanon is not far enough," said Ahmed after a while. He had been thinking, I could see. His future was now untangled from his past. "I want to get out of Arabland, I want to get away from all these seething idiots. My father told me once: 'I did all this so that you could live in the West.' He didn't want me to come back to Iraq. He wanted me to stay in America and go to university there. Maybe he knew what was coming—"

"We could go to Paris," I said. "There is my mother's apartment. It's small, but I can give the tenants notice."

FOUR

Ahmed-the-Wahhabi lived in an ordinary block behind the fish market in Tripoli. We walked up the raw cement stairs and rang the bell. It made an electronic chime. When the door opened, Ahmed made his lopsided smile that said, I am a humble man to be so honored as a guest in your home.

Ahmed-the-Wahhabi introduced us to his wife Fatima, and I gave her the chocolates we had brought and went with her to help prepare lunch in the kitchen. Ahmed and Ahmed-the-Wahhabi sat in the living room and Fatima brought them tea and then after a little while, coffee, and then after another interval, two glasses of sugary orange juice.

Curiously enough, the two Ahmeds got on like a house on fire. They found common currency in their executed fathers. Good men whom they revered and loved and could not live up to. They both, I think, strived for an approval that could never be affirmed. This was their original trauma, the scars that warped their souls and changed them. Ahmed's father had always told him that to get on in the West he would have to be twice as good as they were. This was the ambition that goaded him. Ahmed-the-Wahhabi had grown up with a lie that could never be expunged and a great and buried guilt; he could not remember his father's face.

Ahmed and Ahmed talked in Arabic together, and in the kitchen Fatima and I talked in English. Fatima was an intelligent woman. She still worked part-time as a pharmacist. She was proud that she had a husband like Ahmed who allowed her to work outside the home. She felt that this was progressive; her brother, she admitted to me, would not let his wife out of the house, even to visit the mosque. Her two children, Mohammed and Zeinab, ran in and out, between the kitchen and their bedroom. Mohammed had the same slanted eyes of his mother that flashed from side to side and saw everything: his little sister hiding behind the door, an abandoned cookie on the counter. Fatima sternly chased them out of the kitchen, settled them in their room in front of a Disney cartoon, and returned with a wry smile. Kindly, she did not ask why I did not have children or make the usual mock apology about childish interruptions. Instead she seemed to have another agenda.

"You became a Muslim for your husband?" she asked me. Head cocked to one side, fingers moving neatly, precisely slicing onions.

"Yes."

"But Islam is not in your heart?"

"I respect the ideas of justice," I said. "I respect the pillars of faith, of charity, of prayer and fasting." I sat down in one of the kitchen chairs and pulled my hair into a ponytail because I felt a certain opprobrium, as if I should have covered my hair in front of her husband. Fatima waited for me to continue. "I appreciate the wisdom of Mohammed."

"The wisdom of Mohammed is not something to be appreciated. It is not a flower in a garden that you can pick it up or leave it be. He is the example for us all."

I tried to redirect the conversation. "Ahmed and I—my Ahmed—often discuss this: is it culture or religion? Because the Koran is one thing, it is the word of God, but the Hadith is the sayings and deeds of Mohammed—"

"Peace Be Upon Him," Fatima reminded.

"Peace Be Upon Him," I added mechanically, "—are an interpretation, are a way of doing things, not the fundamental principles of the religion. They are more cultural."

"There is no difference," said Fatima authoritatively. "The way of Mohammed is the example for us all. It is difficult for you to understand because you did not grow up with this idea. For guidance you must ask your husband's imam."

I had a rule in the Middle East: however tempting it was to dissemble, I tried not to misrepresent myself.

"To be honest," I said, perhaps with an edge of provocation in my voice, "my husband is not very religious. I am not either."

"You were a Christian?"

"I was, but I did not go to church. I always found it hard to believe that Jesus was the son of God." Fatima said she thought it was a shame that I did not know my own religion. For Muslims, Jesus was a prophet, not a deity. She would have preferred it, I think, if I had been more respectful of him, instead of agnostic. Christians were people of the book, after all, but ambivalence was apostate.

"I am worried for you." She looked genuinely sad for a moment, but then her bright smile reappeared, "Ah, but that is why it was easy for you to give your Christianity up. You were convinced by the Koran and its message!"

"The Koran—"

I had tried to read parts of it once, in Tora Bora by the torchlight. "It's a good read, actually," Zorro had said, tossing his copy to me as the fabric of our tent trembled with the explosions in the caves. "Lots of battles. God and War. More relevant than you would think. It's all quite progressive and reasonable and wise enough. For the seventh century."

Fatima looked up from the pot of fatteh she was stirring on the stove. I said, carefully: "I was always impressed with how fair the Koran is. That everyone must be taken care of, daughters as well as sons must have their inheritance, widows and orphans must be provided for. Everything is laid out clearly, how to wage war, how to solve disputes, how to make sure the poor are fed." Fatima nodded encouragingly. "But there are parts that are difficult for me," I said. "Because women are counted for less than men." Fatima nodded again, this was self-evident; she did not hear the "but."

"Yes, everything is written," she said, pleased.

"But what do you do when you disagree with something?"

"Ah," said Fatima, very happy to be able to explain to me. "If you disagree, it is because you have not understood the reason; God is wise and we must respect this."

"But what about your rights?" I said. "As a woman. You have Ahmed, who is a good and kind husband, but if you were not so lucky—" She turned around with a small paring knife in her hand. I was going to say: because we both know plenty of women who are stuck in terrible situations, whose lives are made miserable, who will lose their children if they try to leave, women whose fathers refuse to support them when they are divorced, whose brothers beat them in the name of honor, women who have to navigate school, university, work, marriage, street, careful to make sure that every strand of hair hidden, under the constant threat and judgment of a society—of a society that is policed, inevitably, by women.

I was going to say something like that, but not in that tone. But then I saw the knife and in the same instant Fatima saw my confusion and rushed to apologize she had not meant—

She had only been slicing tomatoes for the salad. Red pulp stained the chopping board.

"Can I help?" I asked.

A wave of laughter came from the living room. Ahmed and Ahmed had each bent to light the other's cigarette and discovered that they had the same lighter. A brushed chrome Zippo.

"An American classic," said my Ahmed.

"My brother told me it saved the life of one of his friends who was shot in Iraq. It stopped an American bullet!" said Ahmed-the-Wahhabi.

The Ahmeds looked up at us, the women, coming into the room bearing plates of food.

"We are reorganizing the world," said my Ahmed. "My friend here is a political pragmatist. He is willing to give Israel to Israel and move the Palestinians to—to where?"

"To Sinai," said Ahmed-the-Wahhabi in all seriousness. "It is very unpopulated."

"The same could be said of Montana." Ahmed winked at me and whispered, "It's a very Zionist solution—find another homeland! Genius." He put his arm around his new friend's shoulders as they rose from the sofas to come and sit at the table. "What else, what else. You have lots of good ideas!"

"Iraq and Syria must unite," said Ahmed-the-Wahhabi. "We are one people, one history, divided only by the lines drawn by Europeans."

"And Ottomans," reminded Ahmed.

"The capital of the Caliphate should not be in Istanbul," agreed Ahmed-the-Wahhabi. "It should return to—"

"To Baghdad!"

"To Damascus!"

"You see there is already disagreement between the allies," said Fatima. "Come, eat. It will be cold."

"Ah, Um Mohammed, look at this feast!" Ahmed began to spoon it all onto his plate. He was happier and more relaxed than I had seen him for a long time.

We ate and talked about the weather and the fish market and the crusader castle on the hill and the clock tower next to the harbor that had been recently restored.

Fatima, I saw, held back during lunch. Her thinly plucked eyebrows pinched the bridge of her nose.

"You have lived in America," she said, finally, to Ahmed. "And you are English and have lived in France," she said, turning towards me. This was not quite true; my mother had lived in France, I hadn't, but I didn't correct her. "Can you tell me please why the Denmark government allows to publish those drawings?"

Ahmed took a deep breath and explained the principles of freedom of religion, freedom of speech, and the independence of the press. The newspaper had printed the drawings; the government had no right to stop it doing so.

"I don't understand your freedom," repeated Ahmed-the-Wahhabi, sadly. "They want us to accept blasphemy as a right and this is what they call integration. There is always this word, *integration*."

I had the impression that, for Ahmed Mohammed and Fatima, the episode of the Danish cartoons had only reinforced the idea of a Europe that wanted to force Muslims to drink, take drugs, and allow their daughters to sleep with men, using the word "integration" as euphemism for subjugation. I tried to redress the balance. I spoke about the good parts of a multicultural society: intermarriage, social diversity, individualism, people being able to choose for themselves. I don't think either of them bought what I was saying—I realized as soon as I had said it that intermarriage was like a red flag to them— but they seemed to acknowledge my right as a Westerner to defend my own culture.

"And how is it for Muslim people in France?" Fatima asked. "They make the women take off their hijab." Ahmed replied that it was not a general ban, it was just that girls were not allowed to wear a headscarf at school because it was a religious symbol and all religious symbols were banned in state institutions, crosses and stars of David as well. But Fatima did not understand this logic. "Christians and the Jews are also people of the book," she said. "There is no problem in Lebanon for a Christian to wear a cross and for a Muslim to wear a headscarf." I did not like to point out that there were no Jews in Lebanon anymore and that Muslims and Christians lived in separate neighborhoods in a country still divided by the mistrust of a civil war.

"The idea is that the state should be a place where no religion can interfere," continued Ahmed. "The Republic is above religion." But *laïcité* only sounded like lassitude or licentiousness to our hosts.

"Nothing is above God," said Ahmed-the-Wahhabi severely.

I did not say anything. It could have been an awkward moment, but actually at the time, in Lebanon, in Damascus, in Aleppo, it was a conversation that Ahmed and I were used to having, with each other, with our friends, with journalists and Arabs, with Seriously Sunni imams, with ordinary people when I did vox pops on the street, interviewing politicians or Hezbollah commanders—it was as if we were all trying to figure it out: what are we and who are you and why do you think that? Our debate around the table that day was in this spirit of inquiry; there was no acrimony to it. Fatima wanted to try to understand a society that seemed to make a virtue out of mocking that which she held precious and reverent. I wanted to understand: why do they mind so much?

Just then little Mohammed came barreling into the room followed by his little sister. He was waving a toy gun around and Zeinab was crying, "Give it back, let me have it, give it back!" He held it high above his head, taunting her, "Girls can't play with guns anyway!"

Ahmed-the-Wahhabi picked his son up by the scruff of his neck and shook him like a bear cub. "What's all this noisy jihad!" he said, tickling him. "It's time for you to play jihad of the quiet obedient boy!" Mohammed yelped. Zeinab jumped up onto her mother's lap.

"It's time for ice cream!" said Fatima.

———

When the time came for us to leave, we all said goodbye very warmly and agreed we must meet again in the summer for a picnic at the seaside.

Ahmed gunned the car down the highway. Jay-Z turned up loud. *99 Problems*. Everything would be alright now. *But a bitch ain't one.* When the song finished, he turned the volume down and said: "My son is with his mother's family now. They want to bring him up, but I have petitioned the courts for custody. I don't see how the rights of a father can be refused. So," he said, looking over at me, "I will bring him to live with us." He waited for my reaction. In his own way, by not asking, he was asking for my permission.

I leaned over and kissed his cheek and affirmed. "So we will be a family."

FIVE

Ahmed brought Little Ahmed out of Baghdad on July 4, 2006. (My favorite date, my password to everything.) He was four years old. I went to pick them up at the airport in Beirut and saw him come through the electric gates in the arrivals hall. His father held him by the wrist. He was very small and solemn. When I crouched down to say hello, he put out his hand to shake mine and said, in carefully practiced English, "Yellow my name Ahmed." Yellow-hello.

"*Ahlan wah sahlan*," I replied. Welcome.

Apart from yellow and no, Little Ahmed said nothing for the first week. He watched us silently. He nodded for yes and said "no!"— loudly, clearly, definitely—for no. He was not rude; he was not biddable. His father and I were strangers to him, but he seemed to accept his new surroundings without much complaint. Such was his world apparently different today. He ate, he slept, he watched Teletubbies DVDs, he went round and round on the merry-go-round so fast it made my heart stop. Twice he woke up in the middle of the night crying in his sleep, but he did not remember his dreams. I put food in front of him and he nodded or said "no." I dressed him to go outside and he nodded or said "no." I tried to teach him English by repeating words, singsong voice, "You-r name is Ah-med. My-y name is Kit." He watched me curiously and did not reply. When his father tried to play with him, he made his arms stiff next to his sides and assumed an expression of sufferance. He did not like to be touched. I told Ahmed I thought he had the demeanor of a political prisoner. He was testing us.

After a week we went to the shopping mall to buy him a bed. Little Ahmed was suspicious of this trip, which required a car, and refused to have the seat belt fastened. He squirmed.

His father threw his hands in the air and said, "OK, tough boy refusnik. Sit in the back with no safety belt, and when we crash you will fly through the windshield and break your neck." Little Ahmed glared at him. Ahmed put the car into drive with a long-suffering sigh that belied his single week of parenting.

"Don't yell at him," I said.

"You don't need to teach him English, Kit. He perfectly understands."

We chose a wooden bed with a headboard painted with two sailboats.

"It's a sailing boat," Ahmed said, pointing.

"I no," said Little Ahmed. His father misunderstood. He thought he was still refusing.

"It is the most beautiful bed in the store," he said, throwing up his arms at his son's ingratitude.

"I know," repeated Little Ahmed.

We took the bed home and Ahmed spent all afternoon assembling it. I made spaghetti for dinner, and Little Ahmed ate it with his fingers even though his father tried to insist that he use a fork and twirl it in the correct Italian manner. Little Ahmed tucked the snaky strands into his mouth messily slurping. Globs of tomato sauce spattered over the table.

I laughed; eventually Ahmed laughed. Little Ahmed didn't like being laughed at and threw the bowl on the floor in defiance. As I sponged it up, I saw that the tangled spaghetti had landed on the pickle jar crack.

I hosed him down with the shower head in my bath. Taut little limbs, bowed back, funny pot-belly tummy. He smelled like chamomile. He would not let me hug him as I toweled him dry. I put him into his pajamas, tucked him into his new blue bed. He arranged himself carefully under the sheets and I sat respectfully on the edge of the mattress. I read him *Where the Wild Things Are*. By and by he fell asleep, eyelashes quivering, dreaming. We were his prison-guard parents now, the Wild Things were banished to the land of memory dreams.

Ahmed said he thought it was a stupid book to read a four-year-old, it would only give him nightmares. He opened a bottle of wine and turned on the news. Hezbollah had kidnapped two Israeli soldiers on the border.

"He already knows that bad things happen," I said. "He's an Iraqi."

"I don't want him to be an Iraqi. I don't want him to assume every fatalistic horror that country will impose on its people."

"He can be whatever he wants to be."

"Can he?" Ahmed looked at me, candidly, concerned and tender father, worried for the future. "Can any of us?"

"You are," I pointed out. Ahmed snorted, refilled his glass of wine. He fell silent for a moment.

"Are you going to tell me how she died?" I asked.

"I don't know if Little Ahmed should know. I don't know what to tell him. His grandmother told him that his mother went to paradise and it is a beautiful place. Now he thinks she is going to stay there forever because she loves paradise more than him. What can I tell him? That paradise doesn't exist? I don't want to tell him what death is. That his mother is buried in the earth and being eaten up by microorganisms."

"How did she die?"

"You know he hasn't cried once! Oh, he is a brave little Bedu!"

"Did the Americans kill her, did my people kill her?"

"No one knows," said Ahmed shaking his head. His eyes clouded khaki. "Crossfire gun fight on the Qanat Road. No one knows if it was your people's bullet that killed her or mine."

———

That night the booms woke us up at three in the morning. Little Ahmed came into the room and stood beside our bed and announced, matter-of-factly, in Arabic, "Bombs, Aba. We must go to the basement."

"You see?" Ahmed said to me, almost laughing at it, nothing to be done but open your arms wide to embrace your own complicity in the absurd; stop trying to run because you were only running in circles chasing round and round like the rainbow wheel on the desktop. "From one war zone to another. You can take the Iraqi out of Iraq . . ." Another shuddery, thundery window rattle. "The Israelis are bombing the Shia suburbs," said Ahmed, as matter-of-fact as his son. "We'll be alright here. Come in, little man," he held up the corner of the duvet. "Crawl in and come in beside us."

We could not sleep, and so we went out onto the balcony and looked for the planes that we couldn't see because it was nighttime. I watched Little Ahmed's fragile silhouette, tender stem, little rib cage puffing in and out counting the seconds between detonations.

"That was a big one!"

"No, Aba, it wasn't as big as the one before!"

I had missed Little Ahmed's very beginning. But we had our own story, didn't we? Once upon a time there was a boy without a mother and a woman who could not have children of her own. The light from the streetlamp turned the edges of his ears translucent pink, and I knew that I would do anything to take Little Ahmed away from war.

PART III

PARIS

ONE

I grew up half-and-half, the American kid in the English school. Until I settled in Paris, I had copied my peripatetic father. Hopscotch: three years in Moscow interrupted by a year in New York; then I followed the War on Terror bandwagon from Afghanistan to Baghdad, lived in Beirut, detours to Syria, reporting trips to Cairo, Gaza, Dubai. Most of my friends were also journalists and similarly displaced. We seemed to form a new itinerant tribe: half Iranian, half German, Egyptian-American, born in Afghanistan and grew up in San Francisco, Congolese-Belgian but went to university in Edinburgh. Our lovers were Dutch or Russian or Lebanese; our children were trilingual.

When Ahmed and I fell in love, we thought of ourselves in this way, blissfully removed from nationality and borders. When we moved to Paris after the July war between Hezbollah and Israel, it did not seem odd to us that neither of us was French. Ahmed spoke French fluently because his father had been stationed in the embassy in Paris when he was small. I spoke French pretty well from school. I had a British passport and therefore EU rights. Because we were married, Ahmed had French residency, and when I legally adopted Little Ahmed, he got a British passport. I had an American passport too, because I was born in Boston. But we both decided that there was nothing to be gained by applying for Little Ahmed to have American citizenship except a tax liability.

Such were our identities; forms and applications, photocopied documents of attestation, notarized signatures. Little Ahmed spoke French at school, Arabic with his father, English with me. He had the brown hair and green eyes and amber skin of his father. He didn't look different or out of place; Paris was a cosmopolitan city, and his classmates were all sorts of colors. France was a secular republic. No one was legally allowed to ask us what our religion was. Until his mother's family insisted he take Koran lessons, I did not have to explain to Little Ahmed that we were, that he was, a Muslim. Certainly his father, who loved pretending he was Italian at hotel check-ins—spelling out his surname with an exaggerated accent. "S-o-l-e-m-a-n-i! Yes, almost a salami"—never bothered to mention it. We had come to Paris so that Little Ahmed could live in a society where no one would take any particular notice of his hybridness.

I wanted him to grow up unbounded, a citizen of the world. Ahmed was keen to give him an upbringing that would be far from the tenets of obedience and honor that would have enmeshed him in Baghdad or in exile with his mother's family in Amman.

I don't know if we were naïve or if the world just changed around us.

"What am I?" Little Ahmed asked us, aged six, when we picked him up from his first day of Big Boy school. "Am I French? The teacher asked me where I was from."

———

My mother's apartment, now ours, was on the fifth floor of a grand Haussmann block on the Quai de Jemmapes on the edge of the 10th arrondissement. It had a narrow slice of balcony that looked out over the Canal Saint-Martin. When we moved in, I painted clean white walls over all her wallpaper and installed a double-sized water heater so that I could always have hot water for my bath. It was a funny kind of neighborhood, on a transitional line between the commercial offices around République and shabbier streets on our side of the canal where rabbit-warren apartment houses were inhabited by Algerians, Vietnamese, and young *Bobos*, Bohemian bourgeois. When we first arrived, it was still a working-class *quartier populaire*, with old-time bars like Le Carillon, scuffed and easygoing, where Coco, the white-haired patriarch of the Algerian family that had run the place for forty years, set out plates of peanuts every evening at six o'clock to signal *l'heure de l'apéro*. Within a couple of years the hipsters opened up wine bars, and in the summer droves of pretty young things sat along the canal with bottles of rosé and baguette picnics. I liked our netherworld mix, but Ahmed complained the area was run-down and there was no supermarket nearby; he would have preferred the more haute international climes of the *sixième*.

I wrote expat stories for Oz about the Paris that Americans wanted to visit on their vacations. I found the city was largely unchanged since Hemingway had shot himself. It was easy enough to paint a glaze of faded glamour nostalgia over the city's deliquescent slide, because the Parisians did. It all looked the same as it did when the Lost Generation had camped there, but now the bistros were staffed by Sudanese reheating magret de canard and poulet chasseur in the microwave, and the accordion players were Romanian beggars. Aspic, petrified, stuck. Nevermind said Oz, Paris is the eternal city of rose-tinted foreign spectacles; send me Audrey Hepburn, Edith Piaf, and lilac blooms. Paris was almost a parody of itself: chocolatiers and bonbon vitrines, wrought-iron café tables under the horse chestnut trees, red-and-white-checked tablecloths and a carafe of rotgut Brouilly. All the young people had given up

and moved to London. I derided my version of "twee Paree" to Jean
one postprandial afternoon.

"Ah yes, the popular Anglo-Saxon pastime of French bashing.
Have another Café-Calva, my dear, and then I'll take you to the
Rodin Museum."

Ahmed worked for the U.N. Political Mission. He was away a lot.
For Little Ahmed, his father's returns were great occasions. He would
paint big WELCOME HOME ABA! banners and I'd help him pin them up
in the hall. He would hug his father and hang on to his legs and help
him unpack by carefully folding up his socks and arranging them, in
rainbow color coordination, in the sock drawer. His father was like
the moon to him, a bright being that waxed and waned, full spotlight
attention or diminishing slivers of phone calls. Of me, the everyday
sun that rose in the morning to wake him up and fell into a glass of
wine at dusk, he was less enamored. I watched him follow his father
from room to room, not to spill a moment of precious Aba-at-home
time, careful to be quiet if Ahmed was working, to be still if he was
watching TV, and to remember to ask politely if he could sit on his lap.

At first I tried to persuade Ahmed to apply for a post that would
keep him in Paris. I said we were a family, Little Ahmed needed his
father. Ahmed came up with various obstacles, U.N. internal politics,
the contractual complexities of local hires over international staff. But
something about Paris never quite knit into home for him. Because
of his traveling, he remained a visitor always caught out by the city's
particular rhythms: shops that were closed on Mondays or Tuesdays
or alternate Thursdays, restaurants that didn't open on weekends.
He would come home in the evening irritated, irritable, thwarted. A
shuttered shop, a rude waiter, an abrasive encounter with an official,
a shove on the métro, muttered tutting in undertones.

"We should have gone to America," he said. But he didn't apply
for a post in New York either.

"Why did you call your son Ahmed?" I asked him during one of our difficult conversations. His packed rolling suitcase waited like a tombstone in the front hall. Ahmed had his coat on and was rifling through the pockets for his ticket. "Didn't you call him after yourself because you are his father? Don't you want to *be* his father? Where are you? Here, there, nowhere."

"I am late," Ahmed replied and left again.

His absence became normal and I devolved into indifference. We did not grow apart, we simply *were* apart. I stopped asking him about particulars; there was always some glib excuse. He wasn't in Istanbul that weekend when he said he was going to be because of a last-minute change of ambassadors, the conference had been delayed, the flights to Erbil had all been grounded because of fog, the hotel switchboard got the wrong Solemani in another room and the woman who answered his phone was just a secretary with the Geneva mission.

I let go nagging, reminding, justifying, self-recriminating. I got used to being alone, took solace in my own routines and small discoveries, my friends, in Little Ahmed's little hand in mine. I took him to McDonald's on Friday afternoons as a treat, and he liked to make an artist's palette out of blobs of ketchup and mustard and mayonnaise and then swoosh his fries through them to mix them into a happy mess. His father always said that when McDonald's opened in Baghdad, it would mean the wars were really over.

"See Kit-ma, the mustard is English and the ketchup is American and the mayonnaise is French."

"All we need is some labneh and you would be the perfect poster child for multiculturalism."

Every Christmas, I marked Little Ahmed's height on the back of the bathroom door. I took him to school in the mornings and picked him up at three-thirty in the afternoon. He hated football and loved drawing and demanded great quantities of paper. Always, the cry went up, "More paper! Another pencil! Not that kind, I want a red one!" He was implacable, he would not bend for my convenience, yelling and begging and bribing made no difference. He could be convinced only by the logic of his own benefit.

"If you eat all your green beans now, you won't have to eat them cold again tomorrow." Silence as he considered this before he began to eat them, one by one, glaring at me.

How they grow so fast! And other banalities of motherhood. Washing machine, dishwasher, make the beds, pick up, tidy up. I did not mind. I learned to nod in acquiescence at the school gates with *les autres mamans*. Except I was not Little Ahmed's real mother, as Little Ahmed reminded me when we argued.

"You're not my mother!"

"I know. I'm sorry. I'm trying."

"I want my father!"

"He's away."

———

Rousse was my first Paris friend. Jean introduced us. Margot said she thought we wouldn't get on because we were too alike, but for once she was wrong—well perhaps not completely wrong, because there was always an element of competition between us, or at least that I felt when I scratched my ego against Rousse's success. I don't know what similarities Margot discerned—maybe of ambition, of trying to stretch reportage into something more artistic. But Rousse *was* an artist, this was never in doubt. I was just a journalist and whenever I tried to color outside the lines Oz sent it back for a rewrite.

Rousse had grown up in Strasbourg. Her father was *pied noir*, her mother was an Algerian Jew who went to church at Christmas, so she was a mongrel like me. We both felt as if we didn't fit somehow. Like Little Ahmed, I always hated it when someone asked me, "Where are you from?" and so did Rousse. "It's not important where you are from, it only matters where you are *going*!" she declared one day. (Little Ahmed had nodded at her and then asked, "Yes, but where are we going? If we go to the zoo, does it mean I can be a tiger?") But while I secretly wanted to belong—but belong where? to whom?—Rousse reveled in her unbelonging.

"I never want to *join*," she declared. "We must remain independent!"

Once, feeling lonely because Ahmed was away again, I said, "Independent together!" Rousse physically pushed me away to make her point.

"*Non!* You are independent and I am independent. Separately. It's what I said to Charb. He said, 'Ah, but you cannot make love separately.' But of course you can, it's what telephones are for."

"How is Charb?"

"I don't know. I have refused to answer his calls for a week."

Rousse was an eclectic eccentric, drama and ice, the moth and the flame. She was always late, always dashing, alternately a stray cat hanging around my kitchen mewling she was hungry ("where is the pasta? can I open this bottle?") and aloof, working for weeks alone in her studio without calling.

Rousse had gone to art college in Strasbourg. Her graduation show had been a series of paintings of famous reportage photographs. When she graduated, she was twenty-two, she didn't know what she was interested in, but she wanted to paint real stuff, not conceptual stuff. She was mesmerized by the violence of Old Master paintings—rapes of the Sabine, massacres of the innocents—and she was frustrated by the banality of the photojournalism of the day, the repetition of Kalashnikovs as props in every shot of fighters no matter if they were Taliban or Congo rebels. She told Zorro once that she had really wanted to be a famous war photographer like Lee Miller but that she knew she wasn't brave enough, so she hid behind paint. When Zorro repeated this conversation to me, he added, "You see, Rousse wants to be you and you want to be Rousse."

"But Rousse *is* brave! And anyway she is a better painter than she is a photographer."

"Actually," said Zorro, "although it gives me great pain to admit it, she isn't."

Rousse met Jean the very first day she moved to Paris to become an artist. She arrived at the Gare de l'Est with her six-foot portfolio under one arm and manhandled it all the way to the École des Beaux Arts, where she had a place for a masters in plastic arts. Her drawing professor in Strasbourg had told her to go to the 61 bar because it was the sort of place where war correspondents and photographers hung out, so she went to see what it was all about. It was early evening, and by chance Jean was having a drink with Charb. Charb noticed her immediately and invited her to join them. Rousse was a little shy. She said, "No thanks, I'm waiting for someone."

"No you're not," said Charb. "Come over and tell us your life story. What's the worst that can happen? Do you think I am going to seduce you?"

"Are you Emmeline?" Jean asked, standing up and offering his hand. "Yes, you must be! Your professor told me to look out for you. Come and have a glass with us. Don't worry, I'll protect you from this rogue!"

And so it happened like this, happenstance, that Rousse sat down and changed the course of her life. Jean introduced Charb, the hot new cartoonist making his mark. Rousse, of course, knew his work. A shy smile drew across her rosy lips.

"You should come to the magazine and meet Charlie!" Charb said, warmly encouraged by her freckles and the generous amplitude of her breasts. "Come by on Wednesday, after we have our editorial meeting, and you can see what's going on. We need young talent!" He had not seen any of her work at that point. "I am practically the youngest person in the place, all those old '68-ers huffing about!"

Rousse had a knack for the simple single line, and her style was so elegant and cool and sharp that Charb did not have much trouble convincing Vals, Charlie's editor at that time, to use her when an illustration was needed for a story. Rousse had come to the capital with the ambition to mix media, to blur the line between paint and photo, art and reportage, to do no less than reinvent the image of the world and how it saw itself. Cartoons were her apprenticeship, a way to learn to draw fast and narratively and make crazy ideas into funny shapes that refracted the news and all its absurdity. She fell right in with Charlie's crew and became a regular.

It was Charb who gave Rousse her moniker. He came up with it the first time they went to bed together. Tousling her copper hair, intimate afterglow, they were having a conversation about progressive tax. Charb was a Marxist, for whom all property was theft; Rousse had no politics because she hated politicians, but she did have a house in Strasbourg she had inherited from her grandmother and was paying tax on every year. "Rousse," said Charb, kissing her deeply. Rousse for red and to echo Rousseau and his old-fashioned *égalité*. Charb always said that Rousse was too moderate.

——

"Who is Charlie?" I asked Rousse once when we were early friends. Summertime, picnic at the Buttes Chaumont, perched on the steep slope overlooking gothic follies. Little Ahmed had wandered off to make friends with a spaniel.

"Who is Charlie?" Rousse repeated, considering the question. When she had talked about Charlie, she used personal pronouns as if he were a person, so I assumed he was. She smiled at my mistake, wriggled her toes in the grass, and continued the ruse. "Charlie, let me think how to describe *him*. Charlie is a naughty schoolboy, a subversive radical, a wheezing old lefty. A Gavroche of the '68 barricades, a Peter Pan who never grew up. Charlie is the one who says Fuck the President and Fuck the Pope and Fuck Mohammed and Fuck All

Authority. We are going to laugh at everything! At everything, do you hear! Even if it's not funny!"

"A satirist."

"More than that. He's the mutt who steals the sausages and pees on the mayor's ankle. He likes to giggle at his own jokes. He is like a ridiculous, offensive, tittering, prurient adolescent, tit-obsessed and scatological. The pope takes it up the arse!"

"Is he funny or not funny?"

"I don't know. But it's somehow important to be irreverent—not just irreverent, but tasteless too, to not have any limits."

"Do you like him?" I asked.

Rousse threw up her hands at me. "It's not a *him*! Oh, I can't tease you anymore." She poured more rosé into our paper cups. "It's a magazine."

"Oh." I felt foolish and also disappointed.

"But you're right in a way. It's a personification, a state of mind, a rebellion. So yes, you can think of it as a person. We gather together and draw Charlie's world."

"So how did it start?"

"Charlie was always a mutt, really. Like Snoopy."

"Snoopy was the wise one." I reminded her. "It was Charlie Brown who was the underdog."

"Exactly, which is how Charlie got his name. So the story goes: In 1970, de Gaulle died in his home town of Colombey. The headline in the magazine was *"Bal tragique à Colombey, 1 mort"*—Tragedy at ball in Colombey, 1 dead. The week before, two hundred people had died in a fire in a nightclub. So that's why it was funny. But the interior minister was not amused. He banned the magazine and so they just changed the name to Charlie and kept publishing. Same stuff. Still obsessed with tits and arse. They cut up a photograph of Brigitte Bardot and dressed her like a Christmas turkey. The authorities covered up her naughty bits with black censor bars. *Bête et méchant*, said the naysayers. Oh yes, I am very *bête* and very *méchant,* said Charlie. I think they were pleased to have caused such offense.

"Charlie was popular in the 1970s, but then the radical generation who had been its readers all got jobs and Charlie closed down in the eighties. Came back in the nineties. After all, the world was still being run by a bunch of ridiculous dinosaurs. Mitterrand got it in the neck a lot. A scrawny neck, pulled up out of the collar of his shirt like a chicken head. The right-wing Le Pen was also a favorite. There were also plenty of nuns and cocks and bishop's miters shoved into obscene places. I hate the porno stuff, it's too easy. Charlie is still such a boy's club. They are deliberately silly. Throwing ink around their playground. Cheshire cat grin, the complacent and the obese; the sanctimonious and the successful. Mockery, smash all the crockery. *Wallop!*"

"Did you get into trouble with the Danish cartoons?" I told Rousse about the riot in Beirut, about being in the bath when Ahmed-the-Wahhabi came in.

"Charlie was never particularly interested in Muslims, any more than he is interested in any group of people who cling to their own dogmatics. But, of course, sanctimony begs to be ridiculed."

Sometimes when I picked Rousse up at Charlie's offices, she would give me old copies of the magazine that were lying around. For the first time I found myself looking properly at the infamous Danish cartoons. There was a picture of Mohammed with a bomb for a turban, Mohammed in a white robe holding a curved knife with a black censor bar blocking out his eyes, Mohammed with a yellow crescent behind his head that poked up like a pair of devil horns.

In fact the cartoons were not supposed to be funny. The Danish newspaper had asked several different cartoonists if they would submit a drawing of Mohammed for an editorial that would discuss whether mocking Islam had become a red line taboo in a free society like Denmark. One drawing showed an artist holding up a stick-figure drawing of Mohammed while wearing a turban with the label "PR Stunt" tucked into its folds.

Charlie had shrugged at the finer points of the debate (to be fair, everyone did) and gleefully reprinted them, saying, "It's the first time the Danes have been funny!"

The Grand Mosque of Paris and the Muslim World League and the Union of French Islamic Organizations were not amused and they sued Charlie. Charlie's response was to put Mohammed on the cover weeping and saying, "It's hard to be loved by jerks!"

There was an excellent hoopla around the trial. Rousse was especially gratified that many of the people the magazine had loved best to lampoon, the vulgar pols like Sarko and Hollande, supported their right to lampoon. Charlie won the case. Sales shot up.

Ah, red rags to bulls, who can resist? When France debated the law banning Muslim women from wearing the full face veil in public, Charlie published a cartoon of a naked woman cavorting with a slip of fabric dangling from her ass. *Yes to the Burqa! On the inside!* Charlie dedicated a whole issue of the magazine to Islam and invited Mohammed to guest edit it. It was called *Charia Hebdo*. "A hundred lashes if you don't die laughing!"

Then someone firebombed Charlie. Rousse was away when it happened. She called me, shocked and confused, she couldn't get through to Charb. I reassured her: it was OK, it had happened at night when the office was closed, no one was hurt. "Jesus, Kit, we've had threats, but we never imagined—not in France!"

Their offices were trashed, and for a while Charlie had to squat in the *Libération* building until they could find a new space. Charb, now editor, was assigned a police bodyguard for protection and Rousse tried to hide her concern by being irritated by him. She knew that Charb would not be cowed and she didn't want him to see her worry. The cover of the issue published after the attack was Charlie wearing round John Lennon glasses, holding a pencil and sloppily kissing a Muslim in a prayer cap. *Love Is Stronger Than Hate* ran the caption.

Everyone loved it. The issue sold out.

"Laughter," Charb liked to say, "is a human right."

Rousse had a regular feature for Charlie called "picture of the week." She took reportage photographs and copied the well-worn news images of bomb blasts, gun-toting insurgents, stone-throwing teenagers on the West Bank, and put them into a London street with black cabs and double-decker buses going past, or next to a Parisian café full of tourists or against the backdrop of the Colosseum in Rome. She redrew Zorro's famous picture of the detained Iraqi, hooded and on his knees in front of an American sergeant, at the foot of the Lincoln Memorial.

———

On the first Sunday of every month, entrance to the Louvre was free, and Rousse and I began a tradition of taking Little Ahmed along to introduce him to the art. We would let Little Ahmed choose in which direction we would get lost. "Let's go here! Up this staircase! Kit, why does that Roman woman have a pee-pee? Was this statue a good emperor or a tyrant like Saddam? Who cut her arms off? What's a Pharaoh?" We had only two rules: we avoided the *Mona Lisa* and we always stopped in front of Géricault's *Raft of the Medusa* on the way out. Rousse was obsessed with *The Raft of the Medusa*. For her it was the hinge between fact and representation, between the depiction of horror and the squeamishness of the news magazines.

There are a million million stories in the Louvre, there is a story in every brush stroke, every chip and carve of marble lip and lintel, stone and stellae, pottery shard, porcelain plate, silver ring, and golden crown. The museum contains the flotsam sum of all civilizations, of all the world. One day we found the Cy Twombly ceiling above the ancient Greek bronzes and we stood amazed at his eternal cerulean blue circles. Then we went into the next room and looked up and there were Braque birds flying above us! Another time we couldn't find a way out of rooms and rooms and rooms of Poussin. "So repetetive!" Rousse said, "these monumental classical allegories, pompous *pompier* pictures." Little Ahmed discovered the gallery for the blind, where you could touch the sculptures. We counted the large number of severed heads of Saint Denis in the medieval French painting wing. "Was my grandfather tortured?" Little Ahmed asked, looking sideways at a multipunctured Saint Sebastian.

One day we realized that what we had thought was a mossy tarpaulin in an abandoned courtyard was in fact the undulating verdigris roof of the new Islamic wing. This prompted a long conversation about cultural appropriation represented by the Baptismal Bowl of Saint Louis that was formerly a Mamluk banqueting piece. We showed Little Ahmed the proud lions of Babylon and told him all about the laws of Hammurabi.

Another Sunday, when Little Ahmed was about seven, we found ourselves standing in front of a monolithic Easter Island head. Rousse took his hand and gently explained the concept of abstraction. Little Ahmed listened in his carefully attentive way, head cocked, twirling a dark brown curl with his forefinger. A woman pushing a stroller came in. The toddler in the stroller was squirming and yelling, and his mother bent down and unbuckled him to let him go free. He stopped crying and pushed past us, marching towards the huge face. He stood there with his arms folded across his chest, looking at it intently. The eyeless face stared back. The toddler reached out and pointed and then touched his nose. He seemed to instinctively recognize himself in it. Rousse bent down and whispered in Little Ahmed's ear, "You see, that is art. Who we are and what we see and how we understand. He sees himself, do you see?" Ahmed nodded up and down several times emphatically; he saw it too.

"Yes," I heard him reply, "he thinks it looks like him but it doesn't. But in a way it does."

———

Despite all my efforts, probably because of them, Little Ahmed looked up to his father as the ultimate authority in the whole wide world. Ahmed had designed the architecture of this relationship: he never talked down to his son but only up, of grand ideas.

"You see, *habibe*, when the Arabs can believe in themselves instead of an old book, they will be great again. Do you believe in yourself, *habibe*?"

"I believe . . ." Little Ahmed sucked his bottom lip, searching for something to believe in. "I believe I am not good at divisioning," he said. (This was true, Little Ahmed was not a natural mathematician; when he was doing his homework, he drew faces in the circles of all the 8s.)

"Don't worry, it is better to be good at adding," said his father, who retained a supreme and absolute belief in the academic brilliance of his progeny. (How could it be otherwise?) "You are an only child, you don't need to divide things up!"

"I believe I am good at drawing animals, though. Rousse says I have an eye."

"You have two eyes."

"Yes, two. But also *the* eye, which is not a real eye but what happens inside your head which makes you see, because you need two eyes to look but a brain to see."

"What is this nonsense?"

"It's my imagination."

"Ah yes. Imagination!" Ahmed drew a circle in the air with his fingertip like a mime drawing a balloon. "Let's imagine, *habibe*, the perfect world and you can draw me a picture of it."

This was one of Ahmed's favorite games to play with his son. In their own way, both dreamers. Ahmed had no patience for Monopoly, he didn't like going to the playground, he had not grown up with computer games so Minecraft completely defeated him. "But you can build your own houses and cities and civilizations," Little Ahmed had explained one rainy afternoon, pulling on his sleeve, trying to show him his world.

"OK, how do I build a house?" Block, block, block. "No, not there! I don't want to put a wall there." Block, block, block. "How do I delete? Where are the instructions?" Ahmed was irritated because he could not do something that was intuitive for his son. His son had not been irritated back. In this friable heartbreak moment, Little Ahmed was only disappointed. His bottom lip trembled imperceptibly.

"It doesn't have instructions because you are supposed to figure it out for yourself," he explained to his father.

This was such a perfect mirror of Ahmed's own philosophy of autodidacticism and self-discipline that he got really angry then. "It's a stupid game if it doesn't tell you how to play it!"

"So imagine, *habibe*, the perfect picture. Can you draw it, you clever boy?" Elder head bent over the younger, parallel, two heart-shaped hairlines, bronze where the sun touched their temples. Little Ahmed drew a tree and a house and a blond woman and a red-haired woman with a boy standing between them. He colored his hair with his favorite royal blue Crayola crayon.

"Why is your hair blue?"

"Because I am a punk! Rousse has red hair and Kit has white hair and Rousse says if I dye my hair blue and we stand together we can make the tricolor!

"And where am I?"

Little Ahmed considered this. I could see he felt bad that he had left his father out of the picture, so he improvised and drew him sitting in a tree cross-legged like a swami.

"What am I doing up there?" asked his father.

"You are looking down on everyone and telling them what they are doing wrong," said his son, as accurate and uncompromising an observer as Rousse.

I framed the picture and hung it on the wall above my desk. It made me smile to think that as much as Little Ahmed looked up to his father, his father would never be able to fool him as he had me. Little Ahmed had X-ray vision for bullshit.

TWO

In the spring that Little Ahmed turned eight, Ahmed finally moved out, into a U.N. apartment near the Eiffel Tower in the bland, grand 7th arrondissement. Little Ahmed went back and forth between us. He didn't like the new arrangement. He couldn't quite grasp the idea of two homes, he kept forgetting his colored pencils "in the wrong house"; two or three times he wet his bed and we all worried how he would adjust. At the end of each week he grew anxious and concerned. "Is Aba coming for me tomorrow? Is Aba coming tomorrow or tomorrow tomorrow?" Ahmed kept changing the schedule, and since I was the one who had to tell him and let him down, I was the bad guy. Aba he wanted to please, but could never manage to please enough to make him stay. I was his constant nag: bathtime, bedtime, brush your teeth, say thank you.

Rousse was the fairy godmother. She took him on special just-you-and-me outings to art supply stores when Ahmed canceled, and explained pastels and chalks and oils and watercolor, the ancient mysteries of lapis blue and the modern technology of zinc white. She brought him two boxes of fifty-six different colored pencils so that he could have them in both his homes. She took him to cafés and let him order Coca-Cola and drew cartoon outlines on paper napkins for him to color in. She told him, "You are helping me with my preliminary sketches." Little Ahmed would nod earnestly, her devoted apprentice.

One Saturday she arrived to pick him up and walked into the middle of a giant fight between us. I had told Little Ahmed that he could not watch *Revenge of the Sith* because it was time for lunch, and he became completely enraged and screamed at me. I lost my temper—at Little Ahmed's intractable fury, at his father who had dumped him with me, at my own lonely impotence, a single parent faced with a tantrum. I smacked him on his bottom. Not hard, but hard enough to sting his baby Arab pride. Red-faced, he drew himself upright and hurled his favorite nuclear weapon at me.

"You're not my real mother. I don't have to do what you say!"

"You deal with this!" I said to Rousse, and slammed my bedroom door behind me.

"Kit is your other-mother," I heard Rousse try to explain to him. I was curled up on my bed, hugging a pillow, listening to them in the living room. "Can't you think before you speak?" Rousse asked him gently. No reply. I could imagine his screwed-up stubborn face through the closed door. Pomegranate-mottled cheeks, tears caught like dew drops in his long glossy eyelashes. I listened to Rousse's patient remonstrations; I heard Little Ahmed pause and imagined his quizzical blank expression when he could not grasp something.

"What do you mean, think before you speak?"

"I mean you don't say words without considering the effect they will have."

"But she isn't my mother."

"She is your other-mother," Rousse repeated.

"She's not my real mother." Painful, adamantine truth.

"She is real, just as much as the woman who gave birth to you and loved you when you were little is real. She is real because she really loves you."

"Do you love me, Rousse?"

"Of course, my Medio."

"Call me Frank."

"Frank whatever your name is this week."

"Then why can't you be my mother instead of her?"

I put the pillow over my head.

Later, after we dropped Little Ahmed off at the pottery studio around the corner, I talked it through with Rousse. We sat in Le Carillon with a plate of charcuterie between us and two glasses of beer. I said, in despair, "Why does this hurt more than anything else in the world? More than Ahmed's betrayals and his Swiss cheesy blonde, more than my mother dying. More than leaving Granbet and Good Harbor Bay. It hurts in a terrifying way. It scares me."

Rousse only smiled, as if she was pleased with me.

"Don't you get it?" she said in her charcoal gravel and coffee dregs voice.

"He is always going to hate me."

"It doesn't matter if he hates you," said Rousse. (In my dreams I can hear her saying, "Forgive, forgive," and I wake up feeling guilty. Or angry. I can't separate the two.) "It only matters that you love him. And you love him. That's the only thing that you can do."

————

One Sunday, Alexandre was in town and I invited him to come with us to the Louvre. He and Rousse, as I was sure they would—both aesthetes—hit it off like a house on fire. Alexandre told her his story of being the descendant of Delacroix and Talleyrand.

"You see, I have blood of a great statesman and a great artist in my veins."

"And a great homosexual." Rousse, *provocatrice*, liked to throw darts to see if their points would stick. ("Alexandre of-the-Cross," she would tease him when they had become friends. "Alexandre Cross is very *cross* with me!)

"Eugène Delacroix, my dear," Alexandre insisted, "was *not* gay."

We wandered through Napoleon III's apartments and Alexandre looked so at home among the crimson velvet and chandeliers and gilt stucco that Rousse begged him to sit on one of the plush chairs for a portrait. Even though there was no *gardien* in view, Alexandre refused with a puckish smile. "Transgressions are more properly practiced in private."

On our way out, as always, we went to see *The Raft of the Medusa*. The gallery was tall and painted dark maroon, the crowd was thin, and standing there in the somber winter light was like being cocooned in a dim vaulted womb. We peered at the shiny swirling oils. I was trying to hold Ahmed's hand, because he was going through a phase when he thought it was a great lark to run off.

"Let go!"

"No."

Rousse was drawn to *The Raft of the Medusa* because, as she explained to Alexandre, it was the first piece of visual reportage, the first example of photojournalism before the camera was invented. In 1816 the *Medusa* had run aground off the coast of Mauritius. There were not enough lifeboats, so the captain had ordered a raft built from its timbers for the remaining 150 passengers and crew. The raft was cast adrift and floated, partially submerged, for almost two weeks. A barrel of ship's biscuits were eaten on the first day; the remaining supplies were a single barrel of water and six casks of wine. People drank themselves drunk, fought, became delirious, were thrown overboard; there were reports of cannibalism and murder. When the raft was rescued, only fifteen people were still alive. When reports of the tragedy, with all the lurid details of saturnine barbarism, reached France, it became a tabloid sensation.

In preparation for his epic painting, Géricault interviewed survivors, built a partial replica of the raft, and plundered the morgue for body parts to understand the pallor and rigor of corpses. He changed his mind several times about which episode of the drama to depict. The survivors wave towards a ship on the far horizon. It looks like they are about to be rescued, but in fact the ship is too far away to see them. It looks like it is a picture of hope, of deliverance, but it is a false dawn, the moment before the reality of disappointment and despair.

Rousse was transfixed by the story of the shipwreck and by the story of the painting and how people had paid and queued to see it when it was first exhibited in London. And by the work itself—the petrol blue color, the triangle composition, the bitumen paint that was spreading a black void at its center.

"The restorers don't know what to do about it. It is eating the picture. It is a metaphor, *non*?" She pointed out the Christ agony of the splayed corpse in the foreground, caught awkwardly in the timbers of the raft.

"Look at the angle of his bent leg. Unnatural and *horrible*."

Rousse moved along the gallery to the right of the *Medusa*, where a much smaller shipwreck hangs, sea-swamped and indistinct, painted by Delacroix.

"It is a pathetic attempt to be Géricault! But he cannot match such majesty!" She looked at Alexandre, an amused smile playing at the corners of her mouth. Alexandre raised an eyebrow, as if to say, Bravo, but I'm not taking the bait. Rousse continued to the next painting.

"And now look!" Little Ahmed let go of my hand and ran over to catch hers. They stood together in front of the huge canvas of Delacroix's *Liberty Leading the People*, her breasts bared, tricolor aloft, striding over the barricade of corpses.

"Do you see?" Rousse nudged me. But I didn't. Little Ahmed tugged at her hand.

"It's the same dead man!" he announced. He was perfectly right. Delacroix had copied—almost exactly—Géricault's bent dead leg.

On the opposite wall is Delacroix's extraordinary masterpiece *The Death of Sardanapalus*. Alexandre turned to look at it and we all followed him.

"Just look at the whirl—it's more of an orgy than a massacre, the great fat arse of the king, the giant bed—"

"Emmeline, my dear, your salacious mind! Tut-tut." Alexandre pulled up the white mink collar on his winter coat, exaggeratedly, as if the very thought of sex made him shudder.

Little Ahmed wandered off towards the steps at the far end of the gallery. I went after him and held him by the wrist. He scratched at my knuckles to release him.

"Let me go!" he said, whining.

"I've got to take him home," I said. I could tell Little Ahmed was hungry.

"Take the monkey away!" encouraged Alexandre.

"I am not a monkey," said Little Ahmed, hands on hips.

"But monkeys are clever and they climb high," protested Alexandre, pretending to look affronted. "Your father asked me for a job once and he said, 'I can do anything. I am a good monkey, I learn fast.'"

"That's true," I said.

Little Ahmed regarded the ripe and terrible scene of Sardanapalus's deathbed. "There's a monkey there," he pointed.

"Don't stick your arm over the red rope, they will think you are trying to steal it."

"It's too big for me to carry," said Little Ahmed reasonably. "There in the corner behind the big divan is a monkey trying to get out of the picture frame. He's trying to escape . . . look!"

We three stared hard and could not see what the child saw.

"It's a man with long arms," said Alexandre.

"No, they are his big long monkey arms pulling him up, do you see?"

"So monkeys are clever to try and escape," said Alexandre, giving in to his opponent's logic to get him to concede his original point, an old diplomatic trick.

"OK, so it turns out that you are right this time," said Little Ahmed. "My father is right. Monkeys are clever. It is better to try and escape than to beg the king for your life, especially if the king has already decided to die and kill everyone else as well. Aba said my grandfather would not beg and that's why Saddam killed him. It would have been better if he had escaped."

THREE

I missed the Arab Spring in Egypt, Tahrir Square and the toppling of Mubarak. Rousse and Jean came back from Cairo with shining amazed faces, full of revolutionary zeal.

"Kit, you should have seen it!" Rousse swirled her finger in the foam of her beer. I scrolled through the pictures on her iPad. They were crammed with faces, so many faces in every frame.

"Everyone together, young and old, Copt and Muslim, the fancy Zamalek girls with Fendi sunglasses and the poor from the slums. Everyone shared food, fought together. The atmosphere—oh, Kit, I cannot describe it."

When the protests began in Syria a few months later, I convinced Oz to send me. Ahmed was in Damascus on a short-term contract, ostensibly advising the U.N. on the protocols for a conference between the government and opposition parties. I took Little Ahmed out of school for a fortnight. Zorro and Jean were there reporting for *Le Figaro*. Rousse came too. The whole family gathered. It was the last time we were all together.

Alexandre was ambassador. I had expected to find him optimistic. First Tunisia, then Egypt, now the West were backing the rebels in Libya and thousands were massing and marching against the old dictators in Bahrain, in Yemen—even in Baghdad! But he seemed only more cynical.

"The Arab street, *pah!*" Alexandre said as we sat on the balcony overlooking the garden of the Iranian Embassy. "The streets are mosques. Listen, listen to what people are actually saying. *Down With!* Oh, they are all very excited. But they are not talking about parliaments; they are not asking us how to write a constitution, like the Eastern Europeans did when the Wall came down. They are circling the empty thrones like packs of hungry younger brothers in the Ottoman Sultan's palace." He fingered his cigar. Gray smoke serried against the blue sky. "I miss Nasser," said Alexandre, as if he was recalling an old flame. "I even miss Arafat." A different generation of chess players. He lamented the passing of the great characters of that era; things were so much simpler when you could pay off the Saudis and outmaneuver Khomeini and play the Americans against the Russians. When terrorists took over passenger jets back then, you could *negotiate* with them. "Negotiate! Imagine, this word is almost entirely forgotten now."

"What will Assad do?" I asked.

"He will do what his father did." Alexandre looked out over the rooftops. Puffs of black smoke rose over the riots in the suburbs. An Iranian on the opposite balcony watched through a pair of binoculars. "He will kill them," he said with despair. "My old friend Father Angelo agrees and I always considered him an optimistic man."

I had heard Alexandre telling stories of Father Angelo and his monastery at Deir Mar Mikhael, in the Syrian desert, for years. Alexandre had first visited when he was economic secretary at the embassy in Damascus in the early nineties and found respite from the geopolitical game in the wide spaces of the desert. Father Angelo was the restoration of simple piety in a world frenzied with blood and banners. Even after he had left Syria to take up posts in Africa and then Washington and then Baghdad, Alexandre returned almost every year to Deir Mar Mikhael. When Zorro overdosed in Kabul and his father wanted to put him in a mental hospital, Alexandre arranged for him to convalesce at the monastery and Zorro had also come to love the place. Peace after war, sanctuary.

Alexandre said we should go up to the monastery for a few days.

"I think it might be the last time it will be possible for a long time," Alexandre said. "And there are things I need to talk to Father Angelo about."

Ahmed was in Hama, talking to dissidents; he said he would meet us at the monastery.

———

We took the highway from Damascus, driving out of the brown pollution haze, over a smudged horizon. We passed a convoy of eight tanks being transported on lorries and turned right at a bronze statue of Assad the father; his arm outstretched, pointing to the future. We drove through a town of straggling concrete houses that ended in a landfill gorge full of garbage and across an area of cracked dry earth littered with black plastic bags caught on thorns and scrub.

We left the embassy SUVs when the road ran out, and began to climb. The path was rocky and the sun was high. My hat trapped the heat and my face puffed as puce as the purple thistles that grew among the stones. Little Ahmed kept asking, "Where is this place anyway? Is it *all* uphill?"

"Stop whining."

"I'm not whining."

"If you want to go back, go back," said Alexandre equitably, and Little Ahmed fell quiet after that.

Zorro carried a bag of tangerines as a present for the monks. After a couple of hours' slog, we stopped for a break and he broke one open and shared out the segments among us.

"Can I have another one?" asked Little Ahmed.

"No."

"But it's the best tangerine I have ever tasted."

"It tastes so good because you are hungry. If you have another one, it won't taste as sweet."

"It will!" Rousse relented and gave him one of hers.

The climb became easier. The air thinned and cooled and the breeze swept our hair into salt strands. Little Ahmed tied his keffiyeh around his head in the fashion of a Bedouin road worker toiling in the noonday sun.

"Where did you learn how to do that?" I asked him. *Shrug.*

At the top of the path were a hundred steps carved into the living rock, worn smooth by centuries of pilgrim footfalls. We picked our tired feet carefully upwards and mounted the final step, crossed the thick stone lintel and ducked through the low arched doorway. We came out onto a wide-span terrace and there was the world laid before us, woven in ancient striations of gold and rose. An infinity of sky fell away from the edge of the parapet. Beneath us an eagle glided along thermals.

Father Angelo came towards us in greeting.

"He looks like he is about to fight Conan the Barbarian in a movie," Little Ahmed whispered in awe. Father Angelo was six feet four, heavy-boned, with a square jaw and steel gray hair cropped close to his scalp. He bear-hugged Zorro, shook Jean's hand heartily, kissed Rousse on both cheeks, bowed solicitously to Alexandre, and held out both his hands to take mine in his. Then he knelt down and motioned Little Ahmed to sit before him and take off his sneakers. A young monk brought a copper basin of water and a towel, and Father Angelo began to wash Little Ahmed's feet. This was his ritual welcome to newcomers. Little Ahmed watched Father Angelo very carefully with a quizzical look on his face. When he was finished, Little Ahmed ran over to the balustrade and terrified me by walking along the stone lip that overlooked the steep chasm below, leaving a trail of little wet footprints.

Father Angelo sat with us and poured us tea. He wanted to know the news from Damascus and shook his head gravely when Alexandre told him about the arrests and underground prisons.

"They have circled Deraa with tanks, no one in or out," reported Jean. "There are Alawite gangs of thugs in the squares in Damascus—kids pretending to sell cigarettes, lookouts. It's almost impossible for people to protest. Not in the capital."

"In the capital, no—and the capital has always supported the regime," said Alexandre. "Assad was careful to make alliances with the urban Sunnis." Father Angelo stroked his thick gray beard, listening. "And the Christians—the Orthodox bishops will support him until the end," Alexandre added.

"The danger for Assad is going to come from the old Muslim Brotherhood strongholds," said Jean. He looked at me, "Isn't that why Ahmed has gone to Hama? To talk them into talking instead of fighting?"

"Who knows what Ahmed thinks he's doing," I said.

Zorro leaned back against the wood frame of the vine canopy. He held his Leica in his lap and lazily pointed the lens at Little Ahmed, who was sitting on the wall and tossing stones into the ravine.

Rousse whispered to me, "Isn't this the most beautiful place in the world? Doesn't it fill your soul with an extraordinary floating happiness?"

I leaned into her warmth and felt her joy, stilled by the wonder and magnificence of the view and the limitless horizon. Little Ahmed jumped down from the wall, tired of stone throwing. He ran to me and for no reason at all threw himself into my lap and hugged my neck. There was a bowl of hazelnuts and Zorro showed him his trick of crushing them between his palms.

The bell rang for vespers. Father Angelo clapped his big hands together.

"*Andiamo! Yallah!*" He stood up to his mighty height.

"You boy!" Little Ahmed looked up, startled. "Stop eating all the nuttiness or we will feed you to the squirrels!" Father Angelo had lived in Syria for more than thirty years. He spoke in a fluid mixture of his native Italian mixed up with English-Arabic-French-Italian and interspersed with Latin, Greek, and Koranic surahs. This would have been comic, but his charisma, combined with an imposing stature, invested him with the authority of a regimental sergeant major. No one would have dared to laugh at him, even though he often laughed at himself. Father Angelo was stentorian and wry; he bellowed his kindnesses. Zorro (whom Father Angelo mysteriously loved in the tradition of saints always loving the greatest sinners) could not stop photographing him. Father Angelo was different in every portrait: glaze-eyed mystic, muscled rock-splitter building the new guest dormitory, bon vivant with a jug of wine in his hand, martyr reflecting the agony of a woman with bowel cancer whose sons had carried her all the way up to the monastery on a stretcher. The lines on his face were as deep as the runnels that sudden rainstorms carved in the desert parch, and as myriad.

"Are we going into the church, too?" Little Ahmed asked.

"Yes. Follow Zorro."

"But we're Muslims. We can't go into a church."

"You'll see."

The floor of the chapel was overlaid with carpets and strewn with cushions. There were no pews or wooden furniture. The altar was an ancient stone slab. Orthodox saints lined up in ranks along the wall clothed in vermillion and ochre against a lapis sky, each surrounded with a golden halo.

"Is this going to be boring?" Little Ahmed asked.

"Probably, a bit."

"Zorro, can I borrow your camera?"

"No."

We found a niche in the wall and Little Ahmed nestled himself between me and Rousse. I took a Bible and opened it and Little Ahmed did the same. Zorro squatted to the side, his camera raised in expectation. The roof was full of holes and let in shafts of sunlight filled with dancing dust motes.

Father Angelo began to sing a psalm.

"Oh Lord I have cried."

Alexandre stood straight as a sentinel, clean-shaven, white wings in his hair. Jean stood with his hands clasped in front of him. Zorro shifted his weight from one leg to the other, and the key chain that looped over his trouser pocket tinkled. Little Ahmed stuck his forefinger in his ear, a habitual gesture which I nagged him about and which he claimed helped him hear better. Father Angelo's handful of disciples, a dozen monks, made a semicircle of swishing gray cassocks.

I opened the Bible at random and read:

They shall hold the bow and the lance: they are cruel, and will not shew mercy: their voice shall roar like the sea, and they shall ride upon horses, every one put in array, like a man to the battle, against thee, O daughter of Babylon.

Father Angelo called us to prayer, intoning the solemn rise and fall of liturgical cadences . . .

Then the Angel of the Lord went forth and smote in the camp of the Assyrians a hundred and fourscore and five thousand: and when they arose early in the morning behold, they were all dead corpses.

Brother Thomas held a morsel of bread and dipped it in oil and offered it first to Father Angelo, before repeating the sacrament along the line of monks. Jean stood back. Alexandre went forward and bowed his head and received the blessing. Zorro followed and Little Ahmed got up and asked him, can I go too? Zorro nodded and they went forward together. I watched my son bend his graceful neck to receive a piece of bread. When he turned to come back, I saw that his eyes were shining. The smoke from the incense unfurled dragons in the sunbeams. The monks softly sang a tuneless song of ancient origin. I opened the Bible again at random and I read:

Then three thousand men of Judah went to the top of the rock Etam, and said to Samson, Knowest thou not that the Philistines are rulers over us? What is this that thou hast done unto us? And he said unto them, As they did unto me, so have I done unto them.

I opened the Bible two or three more times but could find no consoling verses in between the battles between the Babylonians and the Israelites and the Assyrians and the Philistines and Hittites that historied an endless bloodletting as if nothing would ever change amen.

———

Zorro was entranced by the high desert light. He said it had a special clarity, especially at dawn. We woke for Matins at 5 a.m., tumbled from our narrow pilgrim beds in the cold dark dormitory, and stumbled down a stone spiral staircase. The bell rang out, cassock figures crossed the courtyard, gliding quietly on sandaled feet. Zorro lay in wait, facing east, to catch the first prick of daylight. Father Angelo shook his head at this ambition, but with an indulgent smile. He said that trying to capture the first sun ray was a vainglorious folly. An endeavor, like landing on the moon, that served only to exercise man's own belief in his ability to master the universe. "But by all means," he said to Zorro, "you must try. Otherwise how can you learn to respect the impossible and the miraculous?"

Rousse was fascinated by the ruined frescoes in the chapel and spent hours tracing the outlines of angels and saints. She sketched the orthodox oval shapes of their chipped faces and complained she could not capture the fragility of their beatific smiles because she could not render the effect of time on stone and tinted plaster. Alexandre perused the library where the monastery had amassed a collection of texts in many languages on interfaith dialogue. "We, here," Father Angelo had told me, "are not the first to try to preach a larger ecumenicalism—to embrace all faiths."

Little Ahmed had the run of the place and, as the only child, everyone's adoring attention. He ran off in all directions exploring and the monks indulged his curiosity. Brother Thomas showed him the beehives.

"You have to move your hands very slowly," said Brother Thomas, holding his hand out level and still to illustrate. Little Ahmed watched him carefully as he moved his hand towards the wooden box beehive. "Because if you move fast, then they attack. They are suspicious. You must move as if you are a butterfly, not like a bear!" Brother Thomas made a violent swiping motion with his hairy forearm to demonstrate. Little Ahmed laughed. "Now you try." Little Ahmed held his hand out. His thin fingers trembled delicately. "They must trust you, do you see?" Little Ahmed advanced his hand slowly towards the metal catch that secured the front panel of the beehive. A few plump and furry black-and-yellow bees hovered near the hinge. He inched his hand a little closer—

"YOW!" Little Ahmed withdrew his hand sharply. Brother Thomas smiled.

"I was stung many times when I was first gathering honey. But now I know how to move slowly, so the bees accept me. Now I am never stung."

We watched as Brother Thomas carefully drew out a wooden frame of honeycomb swarming with bees. They clung to their hexagon cells for a moment and then, finding themselves in the bright sunlight and open air, flew away.

"I do not know if they are free or if they are bereft," said Brother Thomas. "I worry about this: am I the thief or the caretaker?" He cast his eyes over his several hives. "I give them a home and then I take it away from them." He made a small laugh. "In this I am like a dictator. I am Bashar of the bees!"

We walked back along the stony track to the monastery. The siege of Deraa, the gunfire cracking in the Damascus suburbs, the terrible stories of arrest and torture that filled my notebooks, seemed another world away. And yet, part of the same world, a world of natural robbery and savage retribution, the order of things, that we were all part of. We and the bees and the ants and the scorpions and the desert rabbits that the monks gleefully trapped too.

All around us was mayhem and violence. The monastery was a strange ethereal interlude. Silence. A bright red lonely poppy growing between two stones, the translucent iridescence of butterfly wings, the cool replenishment of a sip of water. I pricked my fingers on the thorns of a terebinth tree. A zephyr gently blew away my thoughts. I emptied and the air filled my lungs.

I watched Little Ahmed feeding a tortoise with a lettuce leaf. He had grown into a lean and wiry nine-year-old. He had his father's eyes; they bowed towards the bridge of his nose like gently tipping rowboats, dark green, evergreen, flecked with gold tinsel. They were so dazzling that I would stare into them until he caught me looking and scowled at the intrusion. What is contemplation? Redux, my beautiful boy, only love.

In the desert I listened. We all came together and listened.

"Everyone without exception is loved by God," said Father Angelo. The terrace shimmered gold in the afternoon sun. "This is universal salvation. You can explain the concept from a theological point of view. But there is also a purely logical route to arrive at this conclusion which does not rely on God or faith. That is: If you search for truth, you must accept that there are different truths—that there is not one truth. This is self-evident. This is obvious to everyone who has ever had an argument with anyone else. Having an argument with a fellow human being is a universal experience. And arguments teach us that there is not conformity, that there is not consensus. If we are free, we argue. The only way people do not argue is if they are physically threatened. This is the nature of dictatorship."

Alexandre bowed his head to acknowledge the wisdom in his friend's words. But he was looking for examples of practical application among the grander ideas.

"And now what can we do? How can an *idea* stop the conflict that is coming?"

"But the conflict is between two *ideas*," declared Father Angelo. "Fear of the other, the creation of an enemy, is only a mental construction. The only way to defeat this way of thinking is with another idea! The 'idea,' he smiled, exultant, answering everything, and echoing my heart, "of love!"

Little Ahmed stood on the stone parapet and pointed to a figure toiling up the steps.

"It's Aba! He's walking up the path! He said he would come!"

Soon Ahmed appeared on the terrace, out of breath. He was swinging an enormous bag of tangerines. "Here!" he announced triumphantly, red cheeks puffed out. "Zorro said the thing to bring was tangerines. I have carried up five kilos of tangerines!"

Little Ahmed dashed over and pulled on his father's hand and brought him over to us. Alexandre stood to greet him, courtly as ever. Zorro gave him a mock salute.

I said, "Hi, Ahmed." Rousse squeezed my hand. Little Ahmed eagerly introduced the others to him. "This is Brother Thomas who makes honey and this is Father Angelo who gave me bread in the church."

Father Angelo came forward in greeting, "You are welcome, come, sit," and rolled up the sleeves of his robe.

"He's going to wash your feet, Aba. It's for humility." I think Little Ahmed had confused humility and hospitality. Or maybe not. Father Angelo smiled.

"Would you like to help, my boy?" he asked. Little Ahmed nodded enthusiastically. Suds and splashing ensued. The hems of Ahmed's chinos got soaked.

"It tickles!" Ahmed laughed and looked over at Rousse and me, watching him. "Is this what it's like getting a pedicure, girls?" Rousse frowned. This was old grist between them. Ahmed would play the Arab male stereotype to prick Rousse's feminism. She knew very well it was an act; it still drove her bananas.

Little Ahmed ran to the edge of the terrace.

"There are more people coming!" he yelled. Two men had reached the final flight of steps and we peered over the stone lip of the terrace to see their progress. They were bulky and huffing. One had a pistol tucked into his waistband.

"Friends of yours?" Alexandre asked Ahmed. "Did they follow you from Hama?"

"I parked at the cistern near the bottom," said Ahmed. "I didn't see anyone else."

"Mukhabarat or thugs?" asked Jean.

"Same diff," said Zorro.

We all peered over the wall. The monastery had always had a strained relationship with the government authorities. It was a barely tolerated outpost, anomalous. Father Angelo told everyone to sit down and gestured for the samovar to be brought out. He went through the low stone doorway to greet the two men. They had reached the top of the steps on the other side of the gateway where we could not see them. We stood uncertainly, waiting. I held Little Ahmed tightly by the hand and for once he did not squirm.

After several long minutes, Father Angelo emerged, the two men following as meekly as lambs. The one with the gun had put it away. The one with the stick held it deferentially behind his back. Father Angelo called for a basin of water to be brought. He knelt before them and washed their feet. We stood, watching, wary. No one spoke.

Father Angelo had a big head and bright blue eyes as if he had stared at the sky for too long. His size alone was enough to fill your vision. His stillness and those eyes, blue like the planet earth seen from space, were mesmeric. When he looked at me, I felt myself subject to an all-seeing laser. Instinctively, I wanted to please him. His trick of replacing your own desire for supplication with his own humility—his ritual feet washing—was deliberate and disarming.

When he had finished washing their feet, the big square man sat down on the low stool and pulled his socks and shoes back on. I could see the gun bulge under his leather jacket. At first he kept his hand on it, proprietary, but slowly he relaxed and his hands came together in his lap, like a patient boy listening to his catechism.

I marveled to see the threat overcome by sheer charisma. I have never seen it since. I have seen violence back down, threatened with other violence; I have seen violence break its stride, dissimilate, bide its time for another day. But I have never seen it *persuaded* like it was that day on the terrace high in the Syrian desert.

At first the two men would not say who they were and none of us asked.

"You are welcome, my friends," said Father Angelo, opening his arms to them. "Please honor us with your company."

We each introduced ourselves, as formally as a diplomatic reception. Alexandre assumed the role of majordomo. We were all foreigners and that seemed to satisfy them in some way.

Little Ahmed whispered in my ear, "These are not the droids you are looking for."

Ahmed put out his hand and said his name.

"You are Arab," the large square one said. He had a bristle beard, a thick gold chain around his neck, a black bomber jacket made of expensive supple leather. When he took it off, I saw it had a Dolce & Gabbana label.

"Yes," admitted Ahmed, with a sigh, as if he wished he were not.

"Iraqi," judged the square man.

"Yes."

"You live in Syria?"

"I work for the U.N."

"With the ambassador?" said the square man jerking his head in Alexandre's direction.

Ahmed said, "No, but we are old friends."

"No pictures!" growled his sidekick at Zorro, who had tentatively raised his Leica in their direction.

Zorro spread his hands innocently: "I'm only cleaning it."

"And the boy?" The big square man pointed a stubby finger.

Little Ahmed looked up, alarmed.

Ahmed and I answered, at the same time: "He's my son."

The gong boomed for supper. An hour earlier than usual. Ahmed and I stood up, each taking one of Little Ahmed's hands as he walked between us, Rousse behind, Zorro in front, Jean and Alexandre flanking.

We sat on benches around the low wooden table which the two Assyrian sisters had set with small wooden plates of olives, goat's curd, bread, and a few precious tomatoes. Our two guests sat either side of Father Angelo. He bowed his heavy head, pressed his hands together, and said a prayer in Arabic.

Brother Thomas passed a bowl of honey to the square man, smiling and recounting the histories of his hives and describing the bees and the flowers of the desert plateau. Father Angelo poured wine from an earthenware jug. He raised his glass and spoke a homily to friendship among all men. The smaller man with fleshy earlobes and a low hairline pulled down to his eyebrows like the brim of a hat, loosened his suspicion and made a small salute and drank.

The larger one hesitated before he raised his glass, in countertoast—almost, it seemed, to challenge Father Angelo's dominion.

"To our country! To Syria!" he pronounced. He looked around the table expectantly. We complied and raised our glasses with him. "To the president, who protects us from our enemies."

"To peace," said Father Angelo, amending, parrying.

"To freedom," added Ahmed. As usual, he couldn't help himself.

"Freedom is a Western conceit," replied the square man. "An Iraqi should know this. How are you enjoying the freedoms that America has brought you?" He made a piggy snort.

"Democracy," Ahmed conceded, "cannot be built in a day. The most stable democracies have evolved over many decades." The big man laughed heartily.

"God keep us from your democracy! I have studied political theory! Freedom and democracy are only words on paper. The Americans want to use them against us, but what does a good Syrian, taken care of, kept safe and secure by his government, need with these words? They are shouting them on the streets because they read them on foreign websites. But they don't know what they mean. I'll tell you what freedom means. It means the destruction of safety and security. Ask the Egyptians and the Libyans how much their freedom costs and what is its reward."

"Where did you study political theory?" asked Ahmed, mock polite, making conversation.

The square man said he was a professor, but he didn't teach anymore. He said he had written many books, but when Jean asked him about them, he said their titles were not important. He said he had lived abroad, in Europe, in America, in Arab countries and other places. He gestured in a large circular wave of his hairy hand.

"I am known as the most generous man in my village. Everyone loves me there. When I return, they come out of their houses and slaughter their sheep. My hospitality is known in the whole district. If you were guests in my home, I would make a feast that would cover three tables and last for days . . ." He opened his mouth wide as if to gulp the meager monastery fare in one swallow, and I saw that his molars were rotten black.

Alexandre contributed platitudes, Jean inserted questions (and indicated to me, in an aside, that he was recording everything on his iPhone). Zorro played stick-your-tongue-out with Little Ahmed. (A game of facial contortions they had devised together one lunchtime in a smart bistro when I was trying to instill some table manners into Little Ahmed; a game with rules so impenetrable and complex that they constituted a whole private language.)

Father Angelo fetched more wine. The two intruding rectangles softened around their edges. The large one put his elbows on the table, comfortably expanding his territory. He seemed to have decided to enter into a wry duel with Ahmed. Syrian to Iraqi, brother-cousins; an internecine relativity.

"Don't make the mistake," Ahmed said to him, "of underestimating religion."

The square man touched his breast and looked up into the night sky, reflexively, only half joking.

Brother Thomas whispered to me, "He's an Alawite. Only God knows who their God is."

"It is the most powerful force in our region. But now we need another ideology," Ahmed continued, warming to one of his favorite think-tank conference themes. "We need a vision that can supersede the superstition of religion—"

Father Angelo frowned. "Man's violence to his fellow man is not the responsibility of his religion."

"I don't think you can ignore God," Ahmed said.

"I never think that I can ignore God," Father Angelo replied drily.

"Religion. God. It does not matter," said the Alawite. "Communism. Democracy. It does not matter—"

"After all," said Alexandre, who had also understood quickly (as I had not) the political proclivities of our two intruders, and was now able to inveigle accordingly. "Al-Assad—the father—a great man, whom I had the great honor to meet," he added with impressive emphasis, "on several occasions—was able to lead his country through all of these temptations." The Alawite smiled, but saw through the emollience and continued to focus his gaze on Ahmed.

"We need something that can supersede the politics of democracy or dictatorship or East versus West. Even to supersede the imams and the clerics." Ahmed paused for effect; his small audience waited for his utopia. "More important than all of these is the universal unifying medium of—money."

I had heard this all before. Alexandre had too. He raised his usual objection.

"We have tried this, but you cannot have free markets without free and fair institutions to regulate them—"

"Money," Ahmed winked at the Alawite bomber jacket, "will co-opt even the most fervent ideologues, even the pious ones. Especially the pious ones! Not because money is corruption, but because they need it to achieve their goals. Give them money."

"Which is the same thing as giving them guns," Alexandre warned. What did Alexandre know of Ahmed's dealings in Hama?

"He is right!" said the Alawite, laughing. "You must give them money and guns, because otherwise someone else will give them money and guns." Ahmed grinned, an alliance had formed. "And then you can direct them—"

Ahmed stood up. He held the world in the palm of his imagination (in the palm of his nonsense). This was a perfect audience: a Western diplomat to navigate the geopolitics, a journalist to disseminate, a photographer to record, local partners to provide logistics. Only the monks had no purpose—except someone would have to pick up the bodies; perhaps they could be used as rescue services. There were no Muslims present. But that was OK because as the subject of the plot, it was better they were kept in the dark.

"Let's be a little bit clever." (Oh Ahmed, always so clever; how could you have been so stupid?) Serrated shadows of vine leaves fell across his face. The big Alawite pushed his chair back from the table. Ahmed spread his hands impresario wide. "The first thing is to identify your true goal."

"Peace in the Middle East!" I called out. This had been our old joke toast. What shall we drink to? Ah yes, Peace in the Middle East!

"Yes!" said Ahmed, surprisingly. "And what is the greatest obstacle to peace in the Middle East?"

"Israel!" "Amrika!" "Iran!" cried out different voices. (Oh Ahmed, you were a compelling motherfucker. But what whopping lies you told! Can it be that you had even convinced yourself?)

"The biggest problem," said Ahmed, slowly, drawing out his reveal, "is Saudi Arabia. The kingdom of oil that is the origin of this cancer of Wahhabism that is destabilizing everything." Everyone nodded; this was a simplistic but universally accepted truth. "And by some happy irony, the very jihad that their Wahhabism has spawned hates the Saudis too. It should not be very difficult, *non*,"— he nodded towards Alexandre, who he regarded as a great pragmatist—"to persuade jihadis, a group of them, some commander-imam with a band of Kalashnikov idiots, to turn their attention away from killing Shia and Westerners and focus their attention on the venal and sclerotic Saudi regime. This was, of course, Osama's original target, before he got distracted. And how easy to entice them and say, If you want to establish a caliphate the best and most obvious place for its capital must be—"

"Mecca!" The Alawite clapped his hands together delightedly.

"Voilà!" said Ahmed, making a small bow. "Turn the terrorism towards the Saudi royal family. Attack, suicide bombs, assassinations.

There are plenty of uncles and nephews and lesser brothers and minor ministers to pick off. Think about it. It has the same evil genius logic of the Iran-Iraq War. You take the two most dangerous and unpleasant players in the region and encourage them to fight each other in a sand pit. You can even make money selling both sides weapons. The war will go on for a long time and no one will win and no one will care."

"What you are suggesting is what the Americans tried in Afghanistan, funding jihadis against the Soviet Union," said Jean. "Congratulations, you just created the Taliban. Beware the law of unintended consequences."

"One consequence of smashing up Saudi Arabia," said Ahmed, not the least deterred by this precedent, "would be to wean the world off Saudi oil. No oil, no money, no exported Wahhabism. And the rest of the world will have to find green alternatives and so the unintended consequence of this plan is to solve global warming."

"Ha!" Alexandre clapped his palm against his knee.

"What is this pipe-dream crap," I said, "the audacity of hope? Hollow campaign promises." Ahmed ignored me.

"The corrupt Saudi royal family, an apostate Erdogan, ancestral Yemeni lands, Libyan oil fields—it doesn't really matter what you distract them with, but instead of trying to defeat them with Western ideology, which only reinforces their opposition to it, or with bombs that only enrage the hornets—you simply redirect it."

"It's a solution worthy of the Iranians," said Alexandre. I am not sure if he meant this as a compliment or a criticism. But Ahmed's gaze remained focused on the Alawite. The Alawite nodded gently as if confirming something to himself.

"Is that what you were doing in Hama," the Alawite asked, slowly, deliberately. Ahmed took a step back. He had not realized that he was the mouse and not the cat.

"As a representative of the U.N. High Comissioner—" he began in defensive remonstration.

"Talking to the Muslim Brotherhood?" The Alawite put his trump card on the table. Ahmed sat down.

"The U.N. is neutral," Ahmed replied evenly. "I talked to several groups about their participation in a conflict resolution conference to be jointly sponsored by the quadrilateral powers under the leadership of France."

"Ah yes, France—" The Alawite now turned to Alexandre, Ahmed's "friend."

"France has only the desire to facilitate and encourage whatever peaceful resolution is possible."

"Yes, we remember."

Alexandre did not take the bait. He had spent most of his career in the Middle East sidestepping the Sykes-Picot question.

"Gentlemen," said Father Angelo, attempting to defuse the conversation, "the Crusades are long over, their castles are ruins."

"They are stockpiling guns in the dungeons of Krak des Chevaliers," Brother Thomas whispered to me. "The Brotherhood in Hama will rise up, everyone knows this. We have to get rid of this Alawite—"

"Is he Mukhabarat?" I whispered back.

"No, Air Force Intelligence, I think, the scary ones, very close to the president—look at his watch." I looked. Black matte Breitling. "We have to find a way to get rid of him, otherwise he will arrest someone just to have done something." Brother Thomas got up and signaled to another monk to help him clear the plates.

The bells began to ring. Father Angelo looked confused for a moment, but Brother Thomas said quickly, "It is the hour of Compline," and then Father Angelo got it.

"Yes, yes, of course, Compline!" We all got up in a great and sudden enthusiasm to go to the chapel.

"My apologies," Father Angelo said to his guests. "You are welcome to join us in prayer."

The big Alawite drained the wine from his glass and shook his head. He stood for a moment with his hand resting on his gun and looked at Ahmed with narrowed eyes. Little Ahmed jumped up and tugged at his father's hand.

"Come and pray with us, Aba, it smells like Christmas cookies and they give you a piece of bread!" With his burnt sienna curls he looked like a Raphael cherub, imploring and irresistible. The Alawite bent down and pinched his cheek. Little Ahmed, I noticed with pride, glowered at him.

"Here's my card," said Ahmed, presenting his credentials embossed with pale blue olive branches. "Please forgive my exuberance among friends. It is only the wine talking. I am committed, as we all are at the U.N. Mission, to the stability and safety of the Syrian people." He smiled warmly and held out his hand. The Alawite hesitated for a moment. Little Ahmed pulled harder, "Come on, Aba!" The Alawite took Ahmed's hand and pressed his fingers hard.

"Another time," he said, taking the card and putting it in his pocket. "We know where to find you."

"With pleasure," said Ahmed, flashing his charming smile and turning to take refuge in the church.

We all sat close together, as if huddling from the evening chill, and listened to the voices of the Alawites growing fainter as they descended into the valley below. Brother Thomas began to recite the liturgy in the language of Jesus. Rousse held my hand and I held Little Ahmed's hand. Zorro bent his head and ran his fingers through a loop of prayer beads. I closed my eyes and prayed or tried to pray, to keep us all safe, to keep everyone safe. But I knew it was pointless and soon angry, annoyed thoughts intruded. What was Ahmed thinking, to spar with a shark? What was he doing in Hama? "Liaison" bullshit? Why was he drawn back, inexorably, inescapably, into the region's disaster, as if he could somehow solve it, as if he would remain immune? Did he think his blue U.N. passport was an invincibility shield?

Father Angelo read from 1 Peter: *Be sober, be vigilant, because your*

adversary the devil is prowling round like a roaring lion, seeking for some-
one to devour. Resist him, strong in the faith. And we nodded our assenting amens as meekly as the tortoise chewed her lettuce leaf.

Afterwards, tired and quiet, Rousse and I said our goodnights
and went up to the women's dormitory. I had found a copy of *Alice in*
Wonderland in the library and had begun reading it to Little Ahmed,
and now I took it out and opened it at random. My flashlight beam
made a feeble wobbling glow, the words seemed to lift from the page
and swim in all directions. Alice fell down the rabbit hole. Grew too
big and then too small and then nearly drowned in a pool of her own
tears. The Cheshire Cat grinned and disappeared.

"I've never seen Ahmed in full flow like that," said Rousse, splashing cold water onto her face from a zinc bowl. "It's terrifying, unstop-
pable, strangely compelling."

"I know."

"The whole evening, the dinner, had the quality of a last supper,"
she continued, considering. "Orange-blossom-scented betrayal, death
waiting in the wings, a canopy of vine leaves above, and the stars
laughing at us from far, far away."

"And the Queen of Hearts shouted, "Off with their heads!""

———

In January 2014, Father Angelo went to Raqqa to negotiate the release
of a French Syriac Catholic priest who had been kidnapped by ISIS.
He called Alexandre the day before he left from Aleppo. Ahmed and I
were having dinner at his house in Saint-Cloud at the time. I listened
as Alexandre tried to dissuade him from his self-imposed mission.

"*Ce n'est pas efficace, mon cher ami.*" It will make no difference—
another hostage, another death. "We need someone to be the hope.
Dead is only dead." I could not hear the other side of the conversation, but Alexandre must have known that his appeals would not dissuade the determined monk. Father Angelo would never count his

own soul more valuable than any other. Death *was* hope, death *could be* hope; if his effort failed, it was God's will, but without trying, there was nothing—

Anyway, there is nothing; we have not heard from Father Angelo since. Or there is hope; Alexandre says that if he had been killed we would have heard about it.

FOUR

Not long after we returned to Paris, Ahmed told me he was moving to Baghdad. He said he had been offered a promotion, and the new job would give him a roving responsibility seconded to the Iraqi Foreign Ministry to coordinate with the American Embassy. Ahmed said things were different in Baghdad now that Obama had announced the U.S. military would pull out by the end of the year. Oil prices were high, potential foreign investors had begun to sniff. There was work to be done, he said, to guide and shape Iraq's future and its place in the world.

"Business, financial infrastructure, international standards, legal codes, import-export guarantees, capacity building. It's a challenge, Kit," said Ahmed.

"You once said 'a challenge' was just an administrative euphemism for a problem."

Ahmed made a wry face.

"Back to Baghdad?" I was surprised, I was concerned.

"It's a career-defining opportunity," he said. He sounded like he was trying to convince me with bullet points from a corporate brochure.

"Are you trying to continue your father's work? Is this some kind of expiation?" Ahmed frowned. This had not occurred to him. Which didn't mean it was not a subliminal explanation, but at the same time, it was unlike Ahmed to feel guilt. I watched his face sift through several possible responses. Should he change course, sail into the wind, luff? He finally chose the one that had always been the most effective with me, faux honesty, a popcorn puff with just enough kernel of truth to be plausible.

"Paris was never my place, never my city. I know you wanted it to be. The French are so constantly, *constamment* full of disdain. I don't even think it's racist, because they have it for everyone, even for each other. There are things I miss about Iraq that I never expected to. How people talk to each other—not what they say, but the tone, as if they are making a great joke of preparing to stab you in the back—is one of them. It's my culture, after all. I am simply not in Paris enough to make it worth it to stay in the lesser job. The money will be better, I can increase my maintenance payments. I'll still be back and forth between Paris; probably you won't even notice any difference."

He gave me so many reasons that I didn't believe any of them.

"But Little Ahmed."

Ahmed only said, "We'll tell him together."

———

We took Little Ahmed to his favorite Lebanese restaurant, and over labneh and fries his father told him he was going to live in Iraq. He had thought about it, he said, and he wanted Little Ahmed to stay here with me, where he had a good school and a good life.

"*Pourquoi?*" his son asked him.

"I have business to do in Baghdad. And your grandmother Beeby is sick and I should take care of her because all her sisters are in Dubai now."

"*Quelles affaires?*"

"Important."

"*Des affaires* that are more important than me."

"It's not that."

"What is it then?"

"It's—" and then Ahmed continued to explain in Arabic.

"*Laesh?* his son asked again. It is almost impossible to outwit a nine-year-old. Little Ahmed kept asking, alternating his three languages, "*Laesh, pourquoi, WHY?*" He gripped the starched white tablecloth with two small fists and shouted at his father. His father did not answer him. To me Ahmed could dissemble as easily as he had always done. He could not bring himself to lie to his son, but neither could he tell him the truth. Cornered, he put on his pickle-jar-smashing mask and resorted to anger.

"You will sit down and behave. You will eat everything on your plate. You will make good conversation and we will have a nice time. Life is not arranged for nine-year-old children. I want the best for you, as my father wanted the best for me. You must grow up in the West."

Little Ahmed was not intimidated by this display of paternal authority.

"Why do I have to grow up in the West if you don't want to live here? Why don't we just stay together? You said we are a family. Why are you leaving me?"

Ahmed looked over the mezze at me for help. I raised my eyebrows back at him.

"All good points," I said.

"I don't have a choice," said Ahmed. He swallowed his glass of wine as if it were a lump of coal. Whatever the reason was, was his; ours not to reason why. I saw that Ahmed was genuinely torn—not conflicted, but somehow caught. I saw in the way he could not meet his son's eyes that he did not want to leave him.

I said to Little Ahmed, "It's not your father's fault," although it was. "He will come back and visit often. You can Skype together. You can get lots of presents out of him by making him feel guilty." But Little Ahmed was not the kind of child who was easily bought.

"It's not fair," he repeated, and no amount of ice cream changed his mind.

———

Before long Little Ahmed seemed to settle into a new routine. As Margot said, kids adjust to the world with which they are presented.

"Their brains are still plastic at this age," she explained to me the following summer in Brittany. Little Ahmed was learning how to surf, and Margot and I were sitting side by side on the beach, trying to see which of the seal-slick black neoprene figures poking out of the far waves was him. "They can absorb change as long as they have the constant of love and support—that's you. And Ahmed hasn't disappeared out of his life. He's not your father, you don't need to project your childhood onto his. It's not the same."

"*Ad*-just, yes," I said. "But he feels *in*-justice so keenly. He is very sensitive to inequity." I told Margot how Little Ahmed had taken our assurances of shared parenting and reasoned that he should spend half his time in Iraq with his Dad and half his time in Paris with me. When I pointed out that he had to go to school, he said, "Well, OK, I can spend six months with you and then six months with Aba and go to school in Baghdad." When I said that wouldn't work because of school attendance requirements and exams, he came up with another solution: term time in Paris, holidays in Baghdad.

"He is a stickler for fairness," I said to Margot. "If I steal six fries from his Happy Meal, I owe him six fries back—and he remembers! The next time we go to McDonald's he reclaims them from me."

"He is trying to create order in his world," laughed Margot. "He is trying to find his balance. He's at the age when he is beginning to question your rules and assert himself by making up some of his own."

"His mother's family are trying to insist that he take Koran lessons," I said. "His father is against it, but the grandmother wrote to me directly."

"I think it's a good idea," said Margot. "Don't hide his heritage from him. He shouldn't have to feel cut off from it."

"I know," I said. "But."

"I know," said Margot, simultaneously understanding and pushing my misgivings back at me, "but."

———

We surfed and swam and dug for cockles on summer weekends in Locquirec. In the winter I wrote about French political scandals, and Little Ahmed went to life drawing classes on Monday evenings and Koran school on Friday afternoons. Springtime was rain picnics, a thermos of Heinz tomato soup and a golf umbrella, homage to my mother. Rousse said the autumn was her favorite season, and she and Little Ahmed had a long-running competition for who could find the most beautiful fallen leaf.

And we still went to the Louvre every month. One Sunday, Rousse showed us one of her favorite pictures on the top floor. We had gone to look at the gallery with David's unfinished Napoleon and his portrait of Delacroix's sister, and Rousse called us to come and look at something in the corridor outside. The picture was small and people walked by without noticing it. It was framed under glass so that the natural light puddled its surface with reflections, making it almost impossible to see.

"It is *The Barricade* by Meissonier, a famous and expensive artist of his day, now forgotten," Rousse explained. Meissonier, she told us, painted in the mid nineteenth century and made most of his money selling pictures of Renaissance scenes, musicians, dice players, and other gentle pursuits, for the bourgeoisie to hang on the walls of their drawing rooms. He was most celebrated, though, for his grand battle scenes.

"Fifty years after the fact, he was painting giant historical canvases of Napoleonic victories for the flattering edification of Napoleon's nephew, the third and unlucky-in-war Bonaparte."

Little Ahmed and I looked closely at the little painting. *The Barricade* was a watercolor, brush-washed, dashed, with faint color glaze in places, sketched with bare pencil lines in the foreground.

"Meissonier was famous for his precise and figurative style," continued Rousse in her best art lecturer style. "He spent an entire year sketching a horse's fetlocks in order to realistically depict the cavalry group in his masterpiece, his painting of the Battle of Friedland. But *La Barricade* is scribbled with vigor and urgency. Look at the date."

"Eighteen forty-eight," said Little Ahmed.

"Meissonier painted it thirty years after Géricault's *Raft of the Medusa*. Géricault came from the time of the created image, Meissonier worked at the beginning of the age of photography, the reproduced image. Meissonier had been a captain in the artillery in 1848 and witnessed the massacres of the revolution firsthand. This is the evolution from Géricault, this is the next step, do you see?" I leaned close and angled my head to see behind the silvery windows of reflection. "It is reportage! Isn't it true and beautiful!" Meissonier had drawn a heap of corpses laid across the street. "Can you imagine how much better we would understand the world if we had to paint our horrors instead of taking snapshots of them. A snap takes less than a second. A reaction only, without *considération*. This barricade is so small and personal, the bodies have no glory, the violence is spent and gone and left lying there in a mess of piled-up rubble and sadness and loss. Do you know that Delacroix bought it?"

Afterwards we walked back to the *onzième*, stopping for ice cream on the way. Little Ahmed and Rousse had a long conversation about illustration and imagination, about the representation of fact and whether it was OK to make collages out of photographs and still call it reportage. What made an image true?

Indian summer sunshine. Rousse and Little Ahmed filled their pockets with yellow ginkgo leaves. What makes a family after all? Just us and a balmy afternoon.

I loved our neighborhood, on the edge of the canal, on the edge of *populaire* and immigrant, old cafés with stubbly men standing up at dented zinc bars all day buying lotto cards, the same three drunks on the corner behind the school for a decade. My mother used to call them the Marx brothers, wrapped up in sleeping bags whether rain or summer sunshine, surrounded by a little fence of empty wine bottles that acted as a tinkling alarm in case their stupor was disturbed by do-gooding authorities. There was a good *fromagerie* next to the kindergarten where we had put Little Ahmed when he was very little. The proprietor liked to terrify the kids with whiffs of Époisses. Pablo the greengrocer pretended he was Spanish, but according to Carillon gossip, he was actually part of the Moroccan fruit and vegetable mafia of the *onzième*; have you seen the price of his endive?

I didn't mind when the new bistronomies moved in and the upholsterers and the watch repairman were replaced by young designers selling thumbprint pottery and bamboo cutlery and fabric bags printed with Victorian moustaches. I liked the new Italian coffee place run by an Australian. But increasingly, when I walked down the street, I realized that I was mentally categorizing people. Before I had just thought of everyone as mixed-up locals, we of the *onzième*. Now I saw separate tribes who went to different cafés: international hipsters, bourgeois young mothers, bland professionals with blue suits and pointy shoes, older worn-down first-generation Maghrebis, hermetically un-Francophone Chinese. As the quartier had become trendy, lots of kids came day-tripping into *le vrai Paris* from the *banlieue*—skinny, chippy kids with ripped jeans and gel-spiked hair who stole glasses of beer from people's outside tables and ran off laughing. They swaggered and smoked their spliffs openly along the canal side. I warned Little Ahmed not to react if they hassled him on the way back from school. Better just to walk on the other side of the street, ignore them. He said I was being overprotective.

"They're alright," he said in a way that suggested he already knew them.

———

Ahmed would come to Paris and take his son for a few days, on the train, to Strasbourg or Dijon or Marseilles. The gaps between his visits were long. In the meantime he would call from Baghdad or Beirut or Tripoli or wherever. He sent Little Ahmed postcards of ruins. Leptis Magna, Palmyra, Baalbek, once even the Minaret of Samarra—it was some kind of a private joke between them. From time to time Little Ahmed would asked me, "Can I go and stay with my father for a while?" I was not sure if this was a rejection of me or a childish longing for something else. I did not want to ask him why he wanted to go for fear of opening up the old argument that began, "You're not my mother . . ." But eventually he stopped using this as a weapon. We had grown together, the childish recriminations were rescinded.

"I love you, Little Ahmed. Even if I'm an ogre, we have to stick together, we're the only ones each other's got in this town."

Once or twice he even conceded, "Yeah, I love you too, Kit-ma."

FIVE

When Little Ahmed turned twelve, Ahmed asked me if he could visit him in Baghdad. Since Little Ahmed was now old enough to fly as an unaccompanied minor, I agreed he could go over the Easter break. He had not seen his father in almost a year.

Rousse gave Little Ahmed a new iPhone before he left for Iraq. That winter she had a retrospective at the Jeu de Paume; her painting of an aerial photograph of the refugees packed into an open boat crossing the Mediterranean had sold to a Lebanese collector for 35,000 euros. We ate well. "Have the lobster, Kit!" She rolled her eyes at Charb and his liaisons and told me all the office gossip. Charlie was running out of money again, sales were slipping. A couple of the older well-established cartoonists put their own money in to keep it going. I don't know if Rousse did or not. But she was happy. I was happy for her.

"Take pictures of everything you see," Rousse told Little Ahmed. He beamed his special only-for-you-Rousse smile at her. "Anything you think is interesting. Even the things you think are boring. Imagine you are making a visual diary."

Little Ahmed was gone for two weeks. When he came home, he was quiet.

I asked him: "How was it, tell me about Baghdad, did Aba take you to Mutanabbi Street? What were your impressions? Did your grandmother make you her terrible doormat kibbeh?" I said, "Please tell me, because it's been years since I was there."

"It was good, Kit," he said. "I had a good time."

It was Rousse who he talked to. When she came round for Sunday brunch before we went to the Louvre, he took her into his room and showed her all his pictures. Apparently he swore her to secrecy because when I asked her about them later that afternoon, she shook her head.

"He's not ready to show them yet," she laughed. "He's still editing."

"Oh for God's sake."

I did not see the photos until some weeks later. Little Ahmed printed them into a booklet, much like the travel journals that Rousse used to make. I had expected snaps of Ahmed and his mother, I had expected to feel a pang of revisited nostalgia. But he hadn't taken pictures of people. Instead he had focused on shapes. He was interested in crescent curves that delineated one color from another. Minarets against a blue sky, the bend of a river reed, the edge of an engraved copper platter. He had found this form repeated in many different places. Palm tree sway, donkey neck, bicycle tire left as garbage, the headlight rim of an Iraqi Army Humvee, a slice of melon.

There was only one picture of another person. It was a boy about his own age, sitting in front of a dusty computer terminal in an internet café.

"Who's that?"

"Ahmed," he said, inevitably. And we both laughed because, well, it was ridiculous, this Ahmed thing. "Actually, I'm joking," Ahmed said. "His name is Thayr, he's my cousin. He was visiting from Amman and he taught me how to play *Gulf War: Operation Desert*

Hammer. It was super funny because his handle was SaddamT and he killed loads of Iraqis. I told him that he should be on the Iraqi side and not the American side, but he said there wasn't any choice, everyone had to be an American, there was no function on the game to be Iraqi. He didn't seem to mind though; he said it doesn't matter, it's only a game. He was really good at it. He had one of the highest scores in the whole café. The only one who was better than him was called SaddamA. They all called themselves Saddam. Aba let me go by myself, because it was just on the corner."

Over the following months, Little Ahmed let slip the odd comment about his time in Baghdad. When we went to the Louvre, he wanted to see all the Babylonian stuff. He asked me about Hammurabi and about Gilgamesh. He wanted to know if an Assyrian was the same as a Syrian and what was a Syrian? Weren't we all Arabs? I talked him through the patchwork polyglot of his antecedents. The land between the two rivers, Jews and Chaldean Christians, who were there long before the Arab tribes arrived. Alexander and the Mongols, the disputed origins of the Marsh Arabs, Salahuddin the Kurd. His questions came out one at a time, almost slyly, as if he were gathering the answers as individual bricks and building a wall out of them. I wasn't sure of the architecture of his thoughts. Even as I explained the cross-hatched ethnicities of his country, I knew that I was describing an Iraq that was already past. My stories seemed to have the quality of a fairy tale: *A long time ago there was a land where everyone lived in harmony* . . .

"We are Sunni," said Little Ahmed decisively one day when I was trying to tell him about the Feyli Kurds. "They are Shia." These were the poles that he had brought back from a Baghdad where you were one or the other and you better know which.

"Well—your Dad is not exactly religious."

"I know, Beeby was always telling him he should go to the mosque. She took me to the mosque, but she had to go and sit behind the partition. Have you ever been to a mosque, Kit?"

"Yes," I said, "but not to pray. I'm not religious either."

"You're a convert. I know." Something about the way he said this, emphasizing the weight of the hard consonant syllables *con vert*, a cadence of accusation, seemed to suggest the iceberg tip of a conversation between his father and his grandmother Beeby about me. I knew that Ahmed's mother wanted him to bring his son home to live in Iraq where he belonged.

"Did you pray with all the men?"

"Yes, they were nice to me. One complimented me on my prayer positions, he said I must be very pious if I was so graceful." Little Ahmed still went to Koran lessons twice a month. He loved mastering the swoops of Arabic calligraphy. "I told him I had memorized the surah of the Dawn and he said that was an easy one because it was so short."

We continued our history lessons. I tried to balance the certainty of God's revealed word with the Enlightenment, enquiry, and the Socratic method. I looked for books about the early Islamic period, but the only thing I found for boys his age were adventure stories of the Crusades. We watched *Monty Python and the Search for the Holy Grail* and then *The Name of the Rose*. He was very impressed with the burning of the witches.

"When was the last time they burnt people at the stake?"

"Not for a long time," I reassured him. "Not in Europe."

Recent Iraqi history was more of a challenge. I tried to put the British Empire into the context of the receding, sclerotic Ottoman Empire. I told him about the day his father and I had driven to Kut and walked the rows of British graves. Colonial misadventure.

"So the Turks and the British were fighting over Iraq?"

"Yes."

"Because of the oil?"

"No, the oil hadn't been discovered then."

"Why?"

I made a face. Why was the world the way it was? A twelve-year-old's consternation can tip you over the edge.

"What were the Iraqis doing?"

"There weren't any Iraqis because Iraq hadn't been invented."

"Huh?"

"The British and the French drew the lines on the map. Before, Iraq was a mix of peoples and tribes and the capital Baghdad."

"Hitler was the only Western power to offer the Arabs their independence," Ahmed replied, knitting his brow. I guessed he was repeating something he had heard from his grandmother; Ahmed's mother was old enough to have absorbed the fascist nationalism of the forties in her childhood. So through the summer, in between bicycling green country lanes and watching him ride the waves, I told him the story of the Third Reich. Hitler, the racial laws and *Lebensraum*, the invasion of France, the invasion of Russia, the Holocaust.

"Yeah, I know about the Jews," said Little Ahmed airily, "we had to learn about them in civic history."

Little Ahmed knew about the Holocaust, but not about the Fall of France or the Occupation or Vichy. The Second World War, which formed the backdrop of my own historical and cultural context, was for Little Ahmed something distant and German. Little Ahmed's generation had no such general knowledge; for them it was not a touchstone. He listened to me bang on as I went through the Pacific Theater, Hiroshima, the Eastern Front, the Siege of Leningrad, and D-Day, and he kicked at pebbles on the beach as we walked.

"So in this war," he said, grappling with the idea of horror in a continent where everyone now lived in unbordered union, "the Americans and the English were the *good* guys?"

———

When I measured him against the bathroom door that Christmas, Little Ahmed had grown taller than me. He squirmed and ducked under my hand as I marked his annual progress with a green marker pen.

"Can we stop this ritual now? We are running out of door."

He had shot up to six feet tall and his feet were growing so fast that I had to buy him new sneakers every month. He was withdrawn, he mumbled, he shut his door behind him, and stared for hours at the computer screen with his headphones on. I didn't dare check his browsing history because it was bound to be nothing but porn. I told him that porn was corrosive and corruptive, and I knew he understood this, but at the same time, Margot had warned me, the physical and the cognitive were at odds in his adolescent mind. Almost as if they were fighting against each other under his own skin. Inflamed spots burst on his forehead, and I caught him trying to shave his armpits in the shower with my razor. He was so furious at being embarrassed that he would not meet my eyes for two days.

Little Ahmed's school was a big, rambunctious, diverse place in the 19th arrondissement, next to Oscar Niemeyer's spaceship Communist Party headquarters. He was in the middle of the awkward year of the *sixième*, when the boys were twelve going on puberty, and half the class were choirboys and the other had grown into hairy rugby players. He was having a difficult time.

The school day finished at 5 p.m., but Little Ahmed often didn't get back till after seven. I could no longer meet him at the school gates because this was not done. When I would ask him why he got home late, he would reply monosyllabically and stare at the carpet. Sometimes he would say, "Walking Grégoire's dogs." Grégoire was his best friend, friendly and doe-eyed with a blinking wide stare, a shy smile, and a tendency to giggle. He was half Little Ahmed's size, still a soft-limbed boy.

Other times he said they went to the skate park. "Alright, yeah, like do you want to put a tracking device on me? Like the CIA?"

I rolled my eyes. "Don't tell me I'm some unreasonable mother. You are twelve and I am worried about you!"

"You are like the Mukhabarat, you prefer interrogation."

"Jesus, Ahmed—"

At least twice a week Grégoire would come over after school, and they would clump around the apartment interrupting my work time, eating all my good cheese out of the fridge, and playing *World of Warcraft*. Grégoire, apparently, was not allowed to play computer games at home.

Little Ahmed kept knocking things over with his elbows, which drove me crazy. "Watch where you are!" I knew this was unfair—he was still adapting to his place in the world. Grégoire and Ahmed never teased each other about their littleness and largeness. This must have required an enormous unspoken tact, and I was glad Little Ahmed had a best friend. I had a suspicion that neither of them was very popular at school. It didn't make sense to me that his peers would shun my quietly intelligent, free-thinking boy, but Little Ahmed didn't complain. Maybe these two were the brilliant outcasts who would invent wireless electricity and change the world. But this was unlikely, considering the dismal grade Little Ahmed had received on his last science report. His teacher told me he was falling asleep in class. According to his teacher, Mme Hérisson, he had an attitude "*d'indolence*." She wanted to know what time he went to bed and what my regime of discipline in the evenings was. I did not tell her that he no longer had any bedtime.

"We must make a greater effort," she told me. She wore glasses on the tip of her nose, and her hair was scraped into a bun fortified with a barricade of hair slides. I explained to Little Ahmed the word "harridan" and we laughed for about a week.

I didn't want to bug him about his "*devoirs*," which in French is the word for "homework" and "have to." And sometimes he was sunny. When he wanted twenty euros.

"What for?"

"I've got expenses." Shrug, obviously.

"What for?"

"OK, it's for this special silicon paper that is easy to make cutouts with a scalpel."

"Is this a Rousse project?"

"No, it's my own project."

———

On my birthday Little Ahmed woke me up with a pot of tea and breakfast in bed. He went out and came back in with a package under one arm.

"I made this for you."

"Really? For me? You like me, you really like me!"

"Just open it, Kit-ma."

He sat on the bed next to me as I tore the brown paper off. It was a portrait of me, made in stencil, like a Banksy graffito. The detail was as fine as a Victorian miniature silhouette and he had not used black, but Prussian blue, the color of the waves in Locquirec when the sun went behind a cloud. The image was taken from a Rousse photograph. Three-quarter profile, I was sitting at my desk, bent towards my keyboard. On the laptop screen Little Ahmed had drawn a teardrop shape of elaborately entwined Arabic calligraphy.

He translated it for me: "Sorry I ate the last chocolate digestive biscuit."

SIX

The first week of January 2015 was high cold blue skies. My morning was filled with new year errands. I had my coat on, Little Ahmed was lingering in the bathroom, and I wasn't allowed to pester him.

My phone vibrated and I ignored it. Vibrated again. It was Jean and his voice was ragged.

"Don't go out. There has been a shooting." Jean repeated, "Don't go out there has been a shooting. It's still ongoing. There are gunmen at Charlie."

I dropped my bag, took off my coat, and went back into the living room and turned on the TV news. The newsreader was talking excitedly. The breaking news banner read: SHOOTING AT CHARLIE HEBDO. 10 DEAD.

Little Ahmed came out of the bathroom, and seeing the TV was on, sat beside me on the sofa. "Kit-ma, what happened?" I hugged him close. He recoiled. He wouldn't hold my hand on the street anymore.

"Rousse?" he asked.

"I don't know." I was worried too. "Nobody knows anything."

Blue lights flashed over the ceiling, sirens screamed. Ahmed went to the window and looked out over the canal. The water was green and calm.

"I can't see anything," he said.

"Charlie is near Richard-Lenoir, the other side of République."

"Will Rousse be there?"

10 DEAD.

"I don't know." Little Ahmed sat on the sofa with his corduroy knees hugged to his chest. His eyelashes were as long as his father's, but his cheekbones were getting sharper. Soon there would be no vestige of the boy anymore, his face would grow and change and harden.

My phone buzzed. Oz was awake already in New York. There was an email: *You on this?*

I was about to call him back, but as I scrolled through recent calls on my phone, I stopped. The screen glowed with the name ROUSSE. I had called her yesterday about lunch on the weekend. I texted her. It did not go through.

For thirty minutes the TV newscaster repeated ten dead, but no other news outlet would confirm this. All we knew was: gunmen at Charlie Hebdo. Even after Charlie Hebdo was firebombed—when was that? four or five years ago?—Rousse and I had never talked about the risk except to roll our eyes at Charb's police bodyguard. I looked at my watch. It was Wednesday morning, the time of the weekly editorial meeting.

When Ahmed used to travel back to Iraq during the height of the civil war, when bodies were dumped by the side of the road with drill holes in their heads and every checkpoint was a death trap, I practiced denial as a coping mechanism. There were times when I couldn't get hold of him, and when he would finally call me back, he would always say, "Don't worry, Kitty Cat. No news is good news."

I tried to reassure myself with this mantra. It didn't work. No news was only a terrible limbo, no news was watching the news not telling me anything. The earnest young woman on the television sat behind a desk and repeated the fact of something terrible. There were camera shots of the ambulances whose sirens I could hear outside my window.

Little Ahmed was scrolling Twitter, but it was all the same there too. Gunshots heard. Police on the scene.

"Je suis Charlie," he said, looking up from his phone screen.

"What? Who is Charlie?"

"I am. I mean everyone is, suddenly. It's trending everywhere."

There was a lot of confusion. It was not clear who was killed and who was wounded and who had survived. The gunmen had shot a policeman and made a getaway, crashing into a traffic bollard and then carjacking a man, and driven out of Paris, north. The police lost them somewhere near Pantin. President Hollande went immediately to the scene of the shooting.

Little Ahmed and I stayed in front of the TV. We watched the mobile phone footage of the gunman standing over the policeman and shooting him in the head. The newsreader identified the dead policeman as Ahmed Merabet. *Another dead Ahmed.* A phrase from a different city—not here, not home, not Paris. I wondered what Rousse would have done with the image.

"He shot another Muslim just like that, for nothing," Little Ahmed said. "The *flic* was on the ground, wounded, he didn't even have a gun. *Le connard* just shot him."

"Why are you so upset about the fact he killed a Muslim when Rousse is dead for all we know?" Little Ahmed got up from the sofa and went into the kitchen to be away from me. "Don't just walk away!"

"You don't understand!"

"Understand what?"

Little Ahmed hovered in the doorway, looking back at me, a scowl masking the sadness and hurt in his face.

"For a jihadi," he said, explaining, "it should make a difference. You're not supposed to kill brother Muslims."

"So you're seeing it from the jihadi point of view—"

"No I'm not!"

"They're just killing! They don't care who they kill!"

He shut the door behind him. I heard the gas whoosh on the stove; he was making coffee, Arabic coffee, in the little brass jug he had brought back from Baghdad.

I had said the wrong thing. I was upset, he was upset, I would apologize—but then the land line rang and I answered it. It was Jean again. He said, "Rousse is gone. I'm sorry. She's gone."

There was only a hollow ringing shock. Like my ears hadn't popped yet after the plane had landed. Like the noise after the cymbals have clashed. Vacuum. Thought suspended, there was not even disbelief. Clarion clanging resounding nothing.

I said, stupidly, "Jean, what do you mean?"

"She's dead, Kitty. Dead at the scene." But I still didn't understand. The word didn't make sense, as if it was in a language I didn't know.

"Kitty, I'm sorry—" I heard a sob catch between "Kitty" and "I'm." Then I got it. Hit by a train, like in the clichés. And then the pain came.

Little Ahmed heard me shriek, and he came back into the living room, long arms hanging down, empty-handed, anger gone. He looked to me to tell him.

"That was Jean," I told him. "Rousse." I couldn't say it out loud so I just shook my head.

There was nothing to do, there was nothing that could be done. Ahmed put his arms around me and hugged close. I hadn't had such a long hug from him in a long time. I could feel his heart beating steadily against mine, out of sync, but together.

Little Ahmed brought me a ceramic cup of Arabic coffee and we sat and watched the news all afternoon. The treble urgency of the newcast bounced against our numbness. We didn't talk much, it was too awful for any words. From time to time Ahmed handed me a tissue. He put his head on my knee like a puppy and wedged his feet into the seam of the sofa like he used to do when he was small, falling asleep in front of cartoons. Tears were caught in his long eyelashes.

"How can I ever draw again?" he asked me. "I always draw for Rousse."

"You can still draw for Rousse," I told him. "You will always draw for Rousse."

I didn't write anything that day. Oz said he understood, but I could hear his irritated sigh in the email. Late that night, when I was almost asleep with three glasses of calvados numbly burning in the back of my head, as Little Ahmed slept grumpily in his blue room, humfing through his dreams, popping his cheeks . . . in . . . out . . . the familiar metronome of my nights, the phone jangled and it was Oz. If I couldn't bear to write analysis, he said, pretending to be solicitous, what about a personal essay?

I put down the phone and I tried, but my fingers cramped. I couldn't write anything at all for several days. And when I did come to write an anatomy-of piece, I had to keep Googling news reports because I couldn't remember the order in which everything had happened.

———

It was more than a week later when I forced myself to walk over to Charlie's building. I needed to make sense of the geography so that I could organize the different perspectives of the witnesses who had appeared on TV and given interviews to the newspapers. There was still police tape girdling the entrances; flowers and candles overflowed the curbs. Grim reaper of the details, still and forever mistress of the aftermath. I sat down at my laptop and, painfully, fitfully, over several long nights into the early hours, I wrote.

File: GAÎTÉ
January 15, 2015

On the morning of January 7, Saïd Kouachi woke up early in Reims, kissed his wife and baby son good morning and goodbye, packed his kit in a black hold-all, and took a shared taxi to Paris. He took the métro to his brother Chérif's apartment in Gennevilliers. There they loaded the car, a small black Citroën hatchback, with the two Kalashnikovs, a pump action shotgun, a rocket launcher, ammo. They dressed in black combat trousers and black combat webbing vests and said goodbye to Chérif's wife and son.

They drove their black car and parked it in the Allée Verte next to the building where Charlie Hebdo had its office.

The office building was a modern white rectangle that took up a block on the Rue Nicolas-Appert, a small street in a nest of small streets between the Boulevard du Temple and the Boulevard Richard-Lenoir. The building housed about twenty different businesses. There were three entrances. The Kouachi brothers approached the one at No. 10 Rue Nicolas-Appert. A sign read: FOR ENTRANCE AND ENQUIRIES, PLEASE GO TO THE GARDIEN'S OFFICE AT NO. 6. A post office woman was delivering letters. They pushed past her. They went up the wide concrete staircase to the second floor, barged into the offices of an audiovisual company, and pointed their guns at the man behind the desk.

"Where is Charlie Hebdo?" they asked, and shot a bullet through the glass door of the office for emphasis. He did not answer them.

Charlie Hebdo had their offices on the second floor in a suite at the back of the building. It had windows on only one side that overlooked a courtyard between buildings. They had no window that overlooked any of the three streets that bordered the building. It was a kind of cul-de-sac.

Charlie Hebdo held its weekly editorial meeting on Wednesday morning. It was the only time that everyone came together. Editors and cartoonists and columnists sat around the big oval table in the backroom. Charb, as editor, led the conference. All the old guard—Cabu, Wolinsky, Honoré—sat in a row on one side, the gathered sum of more than two hundred years of satire and caricature.

The editorial meeting began at 10:30. They talked, as always, of jokes and news. Charb had drawn a cartoon that morning of a jihadi with a speech bubble: "Still no attacks in France. Ah well, we have until the end of January to make our resolutions."

As usual, the conference began late. That morning they were discussing a possible cover for the first issue of the year. The writer Michel Houellebecq had just published a new novel entitled Submission that imagined a Muslim electoral victory in France. On the oval table was a cartoon of Houellebecq with lank greasy hair and ragged rabbity teeth, captioned: "New Year predictions of the Magi Houellebecq: in 2015 I will lose my teeth, in 2022 do Ramadan."

At 11:28 a.m. the Charlie Hebdo Twitter account tweeted a drawing by Honoré of Al-Baghdadi, the leader of ISIS, with the tagline, "Happy New Year: And above all to your health!"

The Kouachi brothers went back down the staircase of No. 10 Rue Nicolas-Appert, not realizing they could have simply walked along the second-floor corridor to the offices of Charlie Hebdo. They went back out into the street and tried No. 6. There they were confronted by two maintenance men at the booth by the entrance.

"Where is Charlie Hebdo?"

Chérif Kouachi then shot one of them, Frédéric Boisseau, 42, in the chest. His colleague, Jérémy Ganz, hardly had time to realize what was happening. As Boisseau collapsed, he was still conscious. Ganz pulled him back into the booth and tried to close the door. He held Boisseau in his arms, but he was bleeding heavily. The gunmen pushed past into the foyer of the building.

Inside, the Kouachi brothers found Coco, one of the Charlie Hebdo cartoonists. She had just picked up her small daughter from day care and was coming into work with her.

"Where is Charlie Hebdo?" Coco, terrified for her daughter, reluctantly took them to the second floor. She punched in the door code to the steel door with the barrel of a Kalashnikov pointing into her back.

Inside the offices of Charlie Hebdo, the Kouachi brothers pushed Coco aside and called out for the editor, Stéphane Charbonnier, Charb, by name. They turned left into a small corridor that ran past the kitchenette. At the end was the conference room. They burst in shouting "Allah O Akbar!" They kept shouting for Charb. They shot him first. Charb's bodyguard, a police officer called Franck Brinsolaro, drew his weapon and was gunned down. The brothers said, "Now you are going to pay because you have insulted the Prophet!" They recited the names of other cartoonists and shot them one by one, in turn.

A female journalist, Sigolène Vinson, tried to crawl away under a desk, and one of the brothers addressed her. "We won't kill you because we don't kill women, but you must read the Koran." Despite this pronouncement, they shot Elsa Cayat, a psychiatrist who had a column called "Charlie on the Couch," who once wrote, "I want to talk about the difficulty humans encounter in opening up to others and their differences." They shot Rousse, a painter and photographer who revolutionized the comic strip as reportage and who had recently represented France in the Venice Biennale.

They killed the grand triumvirate of French cartoonists, Cabu and Tignous and Wolinsky, artists who had woven themselves into the fabric of the French cultural tapestry. Wolinsky was eighty years old and rich and successful but came faithfully every week to Charlie Hebdo. They killed Bernard Maris, who was an economist at the Bank of France who wrote a column on finance and was known as Oncle Bernard for his sagacity. They killed Mustapha Ourrad the copy editor who had got his French citizenship just one month before. They killed Michel Renaud who was almost seventy, and just happened to be in the office that day, because he had created a festival in his hometown of Clermont-Ferrand called "Rendezvous of Travel Notebooks," and Cabu had lent him some drawings for it and he had come up to Paris to return them.

They shot Philippe Lançon in the lower jaw. Philippe was an investigative reporter. They shot Fabrice Nicolino in the leg. Riss, who would take over from Charb as editor, was wounded in the shoulder. For several days he didn't know if he was going to be able to draw again.

Luz arrived late, it was his birthday and his wife had made him breakfast in bed. The gunmen had just left the building shouting, "We have avenged the Prophet!" A neighbor in an apartment opposite filmed them on his mobile phone as they got back into their car, apparently unhurried, moving purposefully, "like trained soldiers," said another witness. The brothers spotted a policeman coming into the alley on a bicycle and they shot at him. Then they tried to drive away, but a police car was driving towards them blocking their way. One of the brothers got out and fired at the police car so that it was forced to reverse at speed. Then they drove towards the Boulevard Richard-Lenoir.

When the Kouachi brothers got to the Boulevard Richard-Lenoir, they were met by several police on bicycles. The brothers both got out of the car and started firing. They shot Ahmed Merabet, a policeman who had just received a promotion to lieutenant, in the groin.

SEVEN

We buried Rousse at Père Lachaise cemetery on Friday morning. Everyone wore red. Little Ahmed wore a red pair of jeans I had bought him the day before. I wore my secondhand red Valentino coat and red lipstick to kiss her headstone. Oscar Wilde's grave, a little further up the hill, was always covered in lipstick kisses. Rousse had taken me there one day, and we had contemplated the tender communion, lip to stone, that so many people had made.

"I love that there is still so much love," Rousse had said. "Maybe it is consolation for his alienation, his misery and fall. I think he knows that he is loved. We are lucky, those of us who can make marks on paper that people will see after we are dead. Love is everything, after all, and the only thing that endures, that can survive us."

It was cold and rainy. I gave Little Ahmed my gloves to wear because he had forgotten his. My hands were chilled, but I kept them out of my pockets, some private mark of contrition. The rain dripped down the back of my neck, but this too felt like solace. Discomfort, pain, heartbreak, seemed a pitifully small price to pay, reminding us that we were still alive and so many were not. Rousse's mother had died of cancer the year before. Her father was in a wheelchair and Jean and Zorro carried him up the steps. Little Ahmed manhandled the heavy wheelchair behind them. I tried to help the old man, but he waved me off. He wanted to make his own gesture, and I was very proud of him for it. During the eulogies he dug the sharp point of a pencil into his palm and did not cry. Afterwards everyone went up and laid red roses against the polished granite gravestone. Between their stems, Little Ahmed tucked his own offering, a plain white envelope; what was in it, he wouldn't tell me, it was just for her.

Jean had arranged for a gathering at Bar 61 afterwards. There were four TV news trucks parked outside, and the crush inside was intense. All the formalities of condolence rang hollow to me. That annoying reporter from *Le Monde* (Rousse had once had an affair with him; we nicknamed him Didier the Dickhead) engaged me in a long lecture about how he knew it was a tragic event, but what can you expect when so many French Muslims are disenfranchised and ghettoized? The Kouachi brothers were still on the run, somewhere in northern France. There was a report they had robbed food from a service station.

"They were orphans," he said, as if he expected me to be sympathetic.

Little Ahmed was agitating at my side, bored by the grown-ups. I felt angry and hot and exhausted. Dickhead's mouth opened and closed, and the words that came out of it were subsumed by the din into nonsense. I whispered to Little Ahmed, "Do you want to get out of here? Shall we go and have a McDo?"

Little Ahmed nodded and let me take his hand as we weaved our way through the crowd. We left the ritual cocktail party of mourning and went to eat quarter-pounders with cheese.

In the McDonald's on the nearby Avenue de Flandre, I gave Little Ahmed a twenty-euro bill and he went to order at the counter. I found a table in the window. Outside on the gray pavements beneath the gray sky, people were walking by, going somewhere. On the blank expanse of a dirty white wall, I spotted a silver and green mosaic space invader. Paris was dotted with these street art whimsies and Little Ahmed and I had made a game of collecting them when he was younger. Below was the stenciled gun graffito with the croissant trigger firing madeleine bullets. Take that, you soft Parisians! Let them eat cake! The sidewalks were full of Parisians in winter uniform: jeans, brown black gray jackets, drab and neutral colors that blended into a crowd. McDonald's was all red trim. I looked down at my red fingernails and had one of those strange feelings of prescience. I knew I would remember every detail of this moment, the mop leaning against the wall, the old man sitting alone with a collapsed Maghrebi face and white bristle moustache, shoveling fries into his mouth at the table opposite. Something about the way he used three fingers of his right hand made me imagine the movement as a reiteration of a childhood memory of rice pilaf heaped on a platter.

Little Ahmed came back with a tray of food and unwrapped his Cheeseburger Royale and began to take giant bites out of it. I hadn't let him watch *Pulp Fiction* yet, but we had rented *Inglourious Basterds* the week before. He had loved it. Revenge!

"Well," I'd said, watching him clap his hands delightedly at the exploding climax, "you can take the Arab out of Arabland—"

"Kit, what are you talking about? They were Jews!"

"Say *Jewish people*. In English, just *Jew* is a bit rude."

"Why?" I hadn't known what to tell him.

It began to rain again onto Paris's gray cobbles. Spiky umbrellas went up, individual shelters, shields against the sideways-sleeting world, like turtle shells.

"Why?" Little Ahmed said again, and I realized I hadn't heard him.

"Why did they kill them?" He was talking about Charlie.

"Because they were angry at the way they made fun of Mohammed."

"Is it because the Koran says you can't insult the Prophet?"

"Is that in the Koran? You would know better than me."

"The Koran has strict rules about the death penalty," said Little Ahmed.

"Yes."

"You have to have four male witnesses. And these brothers were not judges or scholars, were they?"

"No," I said. "The Kouachi brothers had not studied the Koran, they were just petty gangsters having revenge."

"Do you think they thought they were doing the right thing?" Little Ahmed chewed his hamburger and looked over to the shabby Maghrebi man who was cupping his hands around a cardboard cup of coffee. Little Ahmed had learned from his lessons at the mosque that justice was not a universal or fixed system. In the Koran and the Hadith he read that thieves should have their hands cut off, that adulterers should be stoned or lashed, that the testimony and inheritance of a woman was worth half that of a man. The imam cautioned that Mohammed preferred mercy to be shown to those who were repentant for their crimes and that he always encouraged forgiveness over vengeance. I said that these were old desert customs from more than a thousand years ago and had no place in a modern society.

For several weeks Little Ahmed pendulummed between our two authorities—probing each with the arguments of the other—before he seemed to resolve himself to the idea that bad things should be punished but that the punishment depended on whom he was talking to. Now he seemed to investigate the idea that justice could be in the eye of the beholder, that it could be weighted relative to the intention.

"It doesn't matter if they thought they were doing the right thing. It was not the right thing. It was murder."

"But who decides?"

"Well, you can," I told him. "Do you think it was the right thing?"

"But I'm not the power," he said. "I'm not the government or the police."

"Islam gives the power of punishment to the victim and the victim's family. They can decide to let the murderer go free, ask for compensation, or have him put to death. In the West we give this power to the state: to judge and jury. 'Which do you think is fairer?' "

Little Ahmed seemed to consider this and to grapple, by extension, with the awkward implications of majority and minority opinions. He wiped the ketchup from his mouth with a napkin. "The final judgment lies with Allah," he decided, finally, lapsing into Arab fatalism. Where had he got that?

"What does it matter what they *thought* they were doing? Is it alright to kill people like that?" The old man at the next table looked over at me. He made a hissing *tcht*, a clucking sound of censure. I had not realized I had raised my voice. I stopped myself—but stopped in my throat too were the old niceties and nuances of a decade of arguments and debates and conversations with bottles of beer and arak on the table and Iraqi-Syrian-Lebanese friends. The endless tug-of-war between cause and effect, provocation and reaction. What is a terrorist? One man's equivocation, another man's outrage.

I had once believed in a universal morality. Now . . .

I saw the old man looking at me with a gleam of disapproval—even, did I perceive, hostility? Should I feel reproach? Guilty that I was upset because my friend was dead? Why was I supposed to respect his sensibilities? Was he respecting mine? I felt the middle ground falling away from under my feet. No more liberal-livered justifications. They had killed people. They had killed Rousse. This was a simple and obvious fact and there was only one way to feel about it.

Ahmed was still struggling with his own logic. Thinking, he absently began to lay his fries out in a row and then put other fries across them to make boxes. After a while he snatched up a handful of fries and stuffed them in his mouth.

"They were angry about the cartoons of Mohammed," he said.

"Yes."

"But Rousse didn't draw cartoons of the Prophet."

"No," I said. "This is what terrorism is: it kills innocent people."

"Like the Americans in Iraq."

"Where did you get that?"

"The other Ahmed at school. His father is from Tunisia. He wanted to be friends with me because I was an Iraqi, but then he saw you picking me up one day and said I had a *kaffir* mother. But I told him you weren't my mother and that in any case you were a Muslim. He said that the biggest terrorists were the Americans and the second biggest terrorists were the Jews."

"The Jewish people."

"Alright, the Jewish people."

"What do you think?" I asked him. "Do you think it was right for them to go to Charlie Hebdo and kill all those people?"

"No," said Little Ahmed. "But the other Ahmed refused to be quiet when we had the minute silence in assembly. He said we didn't have a minute silence when Arab children were killed by Jews and Americans."

"Jewish—"

"I'm quoting him. *He*, the other Ahmed, said that."

"OK."

"He shouted it out in front of the whole school and Mme Tuil took him out to stand in the corridor and told him off, but some of the other kids were cheering and the headmaster was angry because the whole minute silence thing was messed up and he made us do it again."

———

When we got home, I put on the television. We had left early in the morning and I had turned off my phone all day and I hadn't seen the news. The Kouachi brothers had holed up in a printing company in a village near the airport and were surrounded by armed police. The live feed showed a helicopter overhead. At the same time, a gunman had stormed a kosher supermarket at Porte de Vincennes, just the other side of the Périphérique, and taken everyone inside hostage on the eve of Shabbat.

Ahmed and I sat on the sofa and watched TV. All over the country I imagined other families were doing the same. As it got dark, I lit a couple of candles. I poured myself some calvados. Ahmed made popcorn because it was the only thing he knew how to make and we were full of McDonald's and I didn't want to cook. Since Wednesday I hadn't even managed to buy a baguette.

"Is it hard at school?"

"You know, Kit-ma, most of the kids ignore me, unless they ask me about American TV shows or English rap lyrics. It's the other Ahmed and his fat friend Mo-mo. They are in my face the whole time: Why don't you pray, why are you eating *saucisson*, why are you eating in Ramadan? If I talk to a girl, they tell me I'm dishonoring her."

"Can you talk to Grégoire about it?"

"Yeah, Grégoire's the only one who understands. But it's like Grégoire says, you can't escape who you are, you have to be the best version of who you are, but—"

"But you have to decide who to be."

"Yeah, like if I want to be the best Muslim, then according to Ahmed and Mo-mo I am probably supposed to blow myself up and take as many infidels with me as possible and then I'll get to paradise."

It was raining outside. The branches of the big plane trees, which made such a pretty green canopy over the canal in the summer, were bare.

"You can stay home for a few days if you want," I said to Little Ahmed. "We can hang out and watch Tarantino movies and be Americanos. But we should call Mme Harridan and get Grégoire to bring you some work. I don't think it's a good idea if you fall too far behind."

"I'm OK. Jean says all the people who go on to do anything good were bad at school."

"Plenty of people who do badly at school then go on to do nothing," I said. Little Ahmed scowled. My tone of voice, I realized, had relapsed into maternal hector lecturer. "I mean," I tried to laugh, to lighten the mood, "I'm not worried. You are brilliant in a million ways. Your photographs are fantastic. You won the school portrait prize last year. You can draw like a natural. But school is not nothing. It's the preparation for university, where the rest of your life begins—and if you want to choose—well I want you to be able to choose what you want—to have lots of options, not be stuck in a second-rate place."

"Yeah, I know. But I want to go to art school."

"Art will always be there. Art is the easy thing for you. But artists—"

"I know, I know. Artists don't make any money and so I have to be a lawyer in the daytime."

"Pretty much." Ahmed made a face, but I could see he had taken on board the point. Rousse had told him last weekend—how could it only be five precious days of lifetime ago—"Of course you will be an artist, but just make sure you have a real *métier* too. A profession. Then you will be a better artist because you won't be starving."

He leaned into me on the sofa and I stroked his hair, shaved close at the back of his neck, thick and glossy as an otter's pelt. He did not mind.

We watched as the police stormed the printing house and the kosher supermarket and killed the terrorists and freed the hostages and I wondered where the hell this was going to end.

EIGHT

On the Sunday after Rousse's funeral, Jean and I took Little Ahmed to the memorial demonstration in the Place de la République. Charb's sister had said we were welcome to join the friends and family at the head of the march, but Jean had thanked her and said we didn't want to impose.

They said on the news there were four million people in the streets that day. It's notoriously difficult to accurately count crowds. This crowd was dense; it would have been frightening if everyone had not been so polite; *excusez-moi, pardon, pardon.* Polite and well heeled, cashmere scarves, stylish winter boots. We shuffled forward, en masse. The police stood to one side beside their vans, they did not interfere or try to corral or funnel people. I mentioned to Jean that this was a first for a *manif.* From time to time a wave of applause broke out, like a wind-carried ripple. People sang the *Marseillaise,* not with the vigor of triumphant nationalism, but quietly, reverently, as a hymn.

The crowd held up homemade signs and placards. *Je suis Yohan,* for the hostage at the kosher supermarket who tried to grab a gun the gunman had discarded, only to discover it was jammed, and was shot and killed. *Je suis juif*, *Je suis musulman*, *Je suis athée et tolérant*, I am an atheist and tolerant. I even saw a *Je suis Ahmed*, for the policeman they had shot in cold blood as he lay wounded in the street. I nudged Little Ahmed to point it out, "Look, everyone is Ahmed!" Ahmed made his *whatever* face. I squeezed his hand and pointed out more signs: JE SUIS FLIC, and the more polite JE SUIS POLICIER. JE SUIS FRANÇAIS.

We inched towards the monument on the Place de la République. The crowd was so crammed in, it was almost impossible to move. A group of *banlieue* kids, skinny toughs in ripped jeans, had climbed up onto Marianne's giant feet and were waving Palestinian and Egyptian and Tunisian flags among the tricolors. Jean and I were taken aback by the incongruity.

"It's a freedom-of-speech march!" I said. "What are the Middle East flags doing?"

The kids had black hair gelled into oily quiffs. One of them was trying to rally the crowd as if it were a football match. He called "Charlie!" and pointed at the crowd to respond. The crowd shuffled uneasily. "Charlie," they called back, some of them, not many, quietly, awkwardly.

I imagined Charlie, ascended, a ghost sitting upon a cloud, looking down on the massing ants holding pencils aloft in solidarity and proclaiming *Je suis Charlie!*

"But I am Charlie! Up here! I am Charlie!"

It had fallen to Luz to channel the spirit of Charlie and draw the next cover. He drew Mohammed with a big fluffy turban and tears in his eyes, holding up a sign that said ALL IS FORGIVEN.

Charlie stood on his tip toes on his cloud and shouted as loudly as he silently could.

"Forgiven? Are you fucking kidding?"

———

After the march we went to Bar 61. Jean and I drank wine; Little Ahmed had a coke. Jean had been writing commentary all week.

"I hate writing editorials," he said. "They made me write them. It's as if any journalist over sixty is pensioned off as a pundit."

"What did you say?"

"I can't remember."

"Did you write Rousse's obituary?"

"No, I couldn't face it. I wrote Charb's. I left out the good bits, the raving Marxism, the women. I was worried that without these things the readers would miss his charm, his warmth—but, you know. Respect for the dead. We are already polishing the sarcophagus."

"What's a sarcophagus?" Little Ahmed asked.

"It's a tomb," I said. "A fancy tomb."

"Like Rousse has."

"No, it's not exactly a coffin, it's made of stone and carved. Usually for kings and Pharaohs."

I told Jean that Oz wanted a long piece about the day of the attack but I hadn't been able to write anything yet.

"You just have to do it," said Little Ahmed. "Like homework."

"Not you as well," I said. "Oz is harassing me."

"Kit-ma has one set of rules for her and another for me," Little Ahmed appealed to Jean. "When she doesn't want to do her work, she allows herself to believe the excuse she makes up. But she never believes my excuses."

"Yes, the tyranny of adults against kids," said Jean, wagging his finger at him, joking, admonishing.

"You all oppress me!"

"Yeah, right," I said, and then turned to Jean. "Last night he accused me of colonizing him."

"You two need to stick together," said Jean, cuffing us both around the ears like recalcitrant children. Little Ahmed sucked all his Coke up the straw and slammed the glass down on the counter. "But she never believes me!" he said, and stomped off to a corner where there was a pile of old Tintin books to take him away from irritating adults.

"He's bound to be confused," said Jean gently. "He's suffered a great loss. He is in shock. It is a trauma."

"I know," I said. "This is what Paris was supposed to keep him safe from. Not again. Not after his mother—"

"Time heals." Jean put his hand on my arm, the father I never had. Sometimes platitudes are all there is. "Don't worry."

"I feel as if something has shifted," I said after a pause. "Little Ahmed is angry. I am too."

"The violence isn't somewhere else anymore."

"All this time I feel as if I have been earnestly trying to understand the Other, trying very hard to see the world as a universal humanity, to raise Little Ahmed to pay respect to his heritage—all that stuff that his father hates and wanted to get away from but ended up going right back to—but that all the time I was just pretending there wasn't a difference, when there is."

I recalled a conversation with Ahmed-the-Wahhabi in Beirut, after the cartoon riots. I had said, "But we are all the same, no? We are all just people trying to do the best for ourselves and our families." He looked at me very seriously, leaning forward, black-winged eyebrows coming together like ravens landing, and replied, "I can say this to you because you are also a Muslim: we do not want the same thing for our children as Americans, Europeans, the Christian people, do. We do not want them to think only of themselves and their pleasure and dishonor their religion and their family. You will know this better when you know your religion better."

Jean was tired and sad too. His eyes were hooded and the swags underneath made shadow circles. He had taught me that to be a reporter was to have no opinions, to make no judgments. Now this tenet seemed like a quaint adage from another era.

"How are we supposed to be tolerant of people who are not tolerant of us? Why *should* we tolerate them?"

"Them?"

"It's about me, you, this bottle of wine that we are sharing." I raised my chin, defiant, and cupped my hands around my breasts to make my point. *Liberty Leading the People*, her breasts bared to the world. "I want to be able to drink, to think, to be a woman, to be me, to do what I want, to say what I want, to have different opinions, to change my mind. I want to live the way I want. I don't want to be circumscribed, hobbled by political correctness. They killed Rousse and Charb. I don't want to understand their point of view anymore or how their sensibilities have been upset. This has gone too far. It is us and them now."

"Does this mean you're no longer a Muslim?" said Jean, mocking.

Just then Little Ahmed came back to the table, declaring, "Captain Haddock is a racist." The boring grown-ups were still talking. "Who's a Muslim?" he asked.

"We are," I said, grumpy, weary.

"I am, but you're not. You only said you were to marry Aba."

"So what makes you a Muslim?" I pushed back. "Maybe nobody should be allowed to be any religion until they are eighteen and old enough to decide for themselves."

"I am a Muslim because I am an Arab."

"But some Arabs are Christians."

"My father is Muslim, my mother is Muslim. So I was born Muslim." Little Ahmed would confound even a Jesuit with the logic of facts.

"Where is it written that you have to be what your parents are? Don't you want to decide for yourself?"

"Well, I am," said Little Ahmed, angrily, kicking at the leg of the bar stool with his sneakers. "Everyone says I am, so I must be. Even you say I am."

I threw my hands up in the air in exasperated surrender. "We should get home." Jean nodded, kissed me goodbye.

"This will pass, Kitty. It's natural to be angry now. We are all angry. But we have to temper it."

Now I felt like Ahmed-the-Wahhabi when he asked me how Christians could bear to turn the other cheek. "Forgive? How are we supposed to do that?"

————

Over the following weeks I found I could not engage with the debate and the handwringing, the TV panels endlessly talking about Charlie Hebdo this and Charlie Hebdo that. Charlie was now defended as a Messiah. Free speech was an article of faith, born in the satirical pamphleting tradition of the Revolution, carried through the modern iteration of France, as the essence of *liberté*. After the attacks, hundreds of Muslims were arrested and charged with "apology for terrorism" offenses. When you asked the free speech group what they thought of people being prosecuted for speaking—for example, for yelling at a policeman who was stop-searching them, "I wish they'd killed more of you!"—they only shrugged. I asked one judge about this heavy-handedness at a dinner party at Alexandre's and he was entirely unapologetic. "Well, it will discourage them from doing it again."

At the beginning of June, I had lunch with Jean at Les Editeurs. He said he was worried about the nuances of hypocrisy which crept into the debate. He was frustrated too that debate was all there was; dialogue had dropped out of the lexicon. I complained about the word Islamophobia that was being bandied about by the leftist apologists on political panel shows.

"It's a tar brush to smear anyone who raises a question about Islam or its overlap into a culture of violence. At this point it's just a form of denial. There are six million Muslims in France. A tiny few are jihadis, a bigger few—still a minority—are fundamentalists. Overlap this with the larger number that believe that drawing pictures of the Prophet is unacceptable blasphemy and should be punished, and you find you have expanded into the larger gray zone of Muslims who are sympathetic to—I mean not to violence, I get that—but if you are a proper fundamentalist Muslim you want to live under Sharia, the Caliphate is an aspiration. But the French Republic, under its banner of *laïcité*, says no, there aren't Muslims and Catholics and Calvinists, there are only Frenchmen. The French state denies the difference, and it's a difference that fundamentalist Muslims themselves can't bear to be denied. They wear different clothes, they trim their moustaches in a special way, the women curtain themselves off from the world. They want to *show* that they are different. They don't want to be us."

Jean looked up from his steak tartare.

"Have you finished, Kit?"

We ate for a few moments in silence and then he asked how Little Ahmed was coping. I heard Margot in his query. Margot and I had not spoken for several weeks. She had tried to get me to go and see someone, a psychologist friend of hers. She said Little Ahmed was worried about me and that made her worried. She and Little Ahmed had been talking behind my back. She was basically telling me I wasn't a good mother, that I was unhinged. What was I supposed to do? Carry on as normal, as if nothing had happened?

I told Jean, "He's fine." I didn't tell him that Little Ahmed had been sent home from school the week before for arguing with Mme Hérisson. When I had asked Little Ahmed about what had happened, he was entirely unrepentant.

"She's always getting at me. It's like she's the thought police for the French state." He mimicked her pinched squeaky voice. "'What are the first words of the Constitution? Monsieur Solemani?'" And just because I said, 'whose constitution?' she went into a giant tirade in front of the class about how we should all be so lucky to be educated in the French Republic of *égalité, fraternité,* blah-blah. So I said something sarcastic back and she just lost it and sent me home for the afternoon. Everyone thinks she's mean and crazy. It's no biggie."

The coffee arrived.

"I know you miss Rousse," Jean said.

He reached across the table, but he didn't take my hand in his. I looked at his outstretched fingers, black hair on his knuckles, blue veins, manicured fingernails, perfectly oval and smooth. There was a certain vanity to Jean. He was known for the creases in his chinos, even in war zones.

I did not *miss* Rousse. Missing Rousse was Rousse being away and looking forward to her return. This was only void and rage. Jean tried to convince me that her work and her talent, her pathos and wit, her sparky oddball asides, all the contradictions of depression and chutzpah, all that was *her,* spirit soul and friend, continued in us. "Love," said Jean, "is irreducible, like carbon. Many different forms, but always extant. Passed on generation to generation, love does not die. In death it continues to nourish life—" I did not find any useful solace in this—what was it? Not exactly a belief—in this *humanism.* I felt only alone and cold and furious.

"But you can't let go of what is important," Jean continued.

"What is important? Are you going to lecture me about love of my fellow man again?" There were times I knew—Ahmed (both of them) would remind me—when my voice rose to a shrill and imperious treble. I saw an expression on Jean's face I didn't recognize—disapproval, disavowal, distaste? His mouth assumed a rigidness. I had never realized he had such a thin top lip. He didn't reply. His silence made me want to retaliate.

"Do you know where my father is?" I asked, accusatory.

He signaled to the waiter to bring the check.

"You can't tell me because you don't know, or you know and you won't tell me?"

"Kit," he warned, "don't let this anger engulf you. I understand you are in pain. But being angry about it won't help. It's selfish—you let it eat you from inside and it poisons people around you. After anger comes depression. Maybe it's better, *non*, to be sad, to cry. Then you can accept. Because you must accept."

I went home and drew myself a hot bath and lay there for a long time. When the water grew cold, I turned the hot tap on my toes to replenish it. Dad was gone, Granbet was gone, Mama was gone, Ahmed had gone back to Baghdad, Rousse was gone, Zorro was away again, Alexandre was distant, Jean and Margot had condemned me. It was true, Little Ahmed probably hated me. The only warmth I could find, I would have to provide for myself.

NINE

In July, Little Ahmed went to see his father. They met in Amman and took a trip to Petra and went camping in Wadi Rum with his cousin Thayr. Left alone in Paris, I didn't want to go out and see people. Empty summer Paris suited my mood. There was still a scrim of JE SUIS CHARLIE posters pasted over the base of the monument in the Place de la République, but the candles and the flowers had been cleared away and there were no more Charlie stories in the media. Everyone had gone back to normal, as though the shock had been absorbed. Ostrich fools. I knew it was only a matter of time before it happened again.

When Little Ahmed came back, he dropped Arabic into his sentences and groaned when I couldn't understand him. We had only a week together before I left for Greece. Little Ahmed would go and stay with Jean and Margot in Brittany.

Little Ahmed shut himself in his room, hours concentrated in front of the computer. He is thirteen, I said to myself, of course he is confused and diffident. Poor kid with an absent father and an other-mother instead of a real mother. Minding the gap between worlds, from Wadi Rum to Locquirec, sand to surf.

Thirteen is the dawn of the age of discovery, of self-assertion. When I was thirteen, I read Margaret Bourke-White's *Portrait of Myself*. I found it in the bookcase in my mother's bedroom. I don't know why I was attracted to a plain volume of maroon broadcloth hardback. I read many books at that age (mostly Danielle Steele) but Bourke-White's autobiography stuck. She had been in Moscow when the Germans invaded the Soviet Union, a woman in a man's world. It tuned my ambition.

What book would Little Ahmed find? I hurried him out of his room, took him to Shakespeare and Company and pushed him through the stacks.

"Here's a novel about Tom Paine," I said. "Or what about Edward Said's memoir? Or *Homage to Catalonia*, *To Kill a Mockingbird*—" But my exemplars would not do. He did not want my heroes. What sense could I make to him when he was still struggling to make sense of himself? When his every sentence that summer week in Paris together began with a determined *I*.

"Life is like a mirror, Kitty," Granbet said long ago. "You get from a relationship what you put into it."

"Give him the tools for intellectual enquiry," Alexandre advised.

"Give him your love," Father Angelo had told me.

"It is your example," Jean warned, "that will form his worldview."

"Just keep him out of the mosque," Ahmed had once implored. "Whatever you do."

"You'll screw his head up no matter what you do," Rousse's voice came back to me. "All parents do. Don't worry about it."

As usual, he wouldn't let me see his pictures from Jordan.

"I'm editing. Rousse understood."

"Did you take pictures of shapes? How was the desert? Did you like camping?"

"It was good."

"Tell me about your cousins."

"They were OK."

"Thayr and Zaid and Leyla, isn't it?"

"Only Thayr came with Aba and me. My uncle said Zaid was too little and Leyla is older but she's a girl."

"You like Thayr?"

"He's OK. He's a year older than me, but he doesn't know anything about music, he's never even heard of Booba or Tupac or Kanye. I let him listen to some Furious and it totally blew his mind. Afterwards there was a big fuss because he downloaded some of my songs, and my uncle said it was a degenerative influence of Western drug music or something and made him wipe them all."

"Is your uncle strict?"

"Yeah. Like, not about religion so much; Thayr goes to the mosque on Friday with him, but he doesn't have to pray every day. But it's more like the classic Iraqi father, all about obedience. Aba's not like that, and it really surprised Thayr, like when he would ask us whether we thought this is a good place to camp, instead of just telling us. We talked about lots of things in the desert in the nights and Thayr said he would never talk to his father the way I talked to Aba. He got quite upset about it. And then we would argue and he didn't know how to argue because if he didn't like something we said he would just keep repeating his point over and over. He said he knew, because his father said so, that everything wrong in the Middle East was the fault of the Americans. Iraq, Syria, was all because of the Americans. And I said: How does your father know? Like give me proof of the argument, like the supporting points, and he just said, you're wrong, you're just wrong! Like just being convinced of something is enough to make it right. One time he got really upset because I said that it wasn't true that in France they didn't let Muslims pray. And then we got into the whole issue about girls wearing the veil. I said I live in France and I know, and it's only at school that girls can't wear the veil, but they can in other places. He just said it's the same thing. He was really mad about it. Afterwards, Aba said I had to apologize just to make him feel better even though there wasn't anything really to apologize for. I had just said the truth."

"Do you want peanut butter on toast? I'm making some for me."

"Haven't we got any Nutella?"

"I forgot to buy some."

"*Kus Umak*," he muttered under his breath. It was one of the few Arabic phrases I knew.

"Seriously? Ahmed, that's nasty! Don't say that to me." He managed to look a little guilty. "Is that how Thayr talks?" Ahmed nodded. "Do you know what it means?"

"Camel's woman thing." He could not bring himself to say *cunt*. Bless him. I relented, laughed, and said, "Actually it's your mother's—blank."

"Oh. Sorry."

"It's alright. For years I thought it was *sac à bordel*."

Ahmed grinned. "Instead of *sacré bordel*?"

"Yes. I mean, a bag of brothels is a better description of a fucked-up situation than sacred brothel."

"Kit, you said *fucked up*."

"Sorry."

"That means I get to say it once within the next week."

"Yes, OK." According to our swear word agreement, he was right.

"Kit?"

"Yes."

"What's a brotherly?"

"A brothel?"

"Yes. What's a *brothel*?"

"Ah. Well."

"Don't say, *When you're older* . . ."

"A brothel is where men go to have sex with prostitutes."

"Like in Pigalle."

"Yes."

We ate our tartines standing up in the kitchen. It was a hot summer day, and through the window I could see the couples picnicking along the canal. "So is it weird," I asked Little Ahmed, "to be a French boy with your cousin?"

"No, not really," he said thoughtfully, picking at a bunch of grapes on the counter.

"Don't eat those, I'm going to make grapes in cream and brown sugar brulée." Ahmed made a face.

"I'm not French when I'm with Aba, I am just an Arab like everyone else. I mean I just live in France, right, I'm not really French."

"No, I guess, really you're British, according to your passport."

"No English person would think I was English," Ahmed pointed out, bluntly practical. "Can I take my scooter to the top of Montmartre later? Can we go to Rousse's?"

———

All summer the news was the refugee exodus across the Aegean. Families crammed onto inflatable dinghies, set off at night from Turkish coves to cross the sea to a Greek shore, to Europe, to safety, to a future. Wet, salt-sprayed, mute and frightened children in their parents arms; blue sea, orange life vests littered on the beaches. Tents under pine trees, trash fires in the dark, tarpaulin flapping in the rain. Huddled masses. Hundreds, thousands, a million walked along highways, filled buses and crowded onto trains, moving north across the unbordered European Union towards Germany.

The *New York Times* sent Zorro to Greece to cover it. His pictures were more intimate than his usual wide-angled scenes. He had become famous for the grand diorama scale of his photographs, but these portraits were so close up that they were details more than faces or individuals. Strands of hair caught in the hinge of a pair of spec-

tacles, the curled eyelashes of a baby—sleeping or drowned?—razor
rash at the edge of a moustache, a howling mouth, spittle-flecked lips,
the edge of a shy smile as extraordinarily beautiful as the chipped
face of a marble goddess, a little blond girl holding out a pink sparkly
headband. Exhaustion, anguish, joy: arrival.

Zorro should have been dead. He should have died a hundred
times: Shrapnel in his head from a Baghdad car bomb, you could still
feel the nubbin just above his hairline. Smashed-up pelvis from a car
crash in the Panjshir. Recurrent malaria. He no longer had a belly
button because he had been operated on for a hernia in Tbilisi and
the surgeon had sewn him up without it. He was on and off coke and
mostly on heroin, but he had a good doctor who kept him in clean
white pills and so this was under control. Well, he was functional; he
still took brilliant pictures. That's what Jean and I said to each other
and put our worrying to one side.

We were so used to Zorro's medical emergencies—impacted
molars in Basra, an ear infection caused by a spider that crawled into
his ear canal in Erbil—that we only laughed when he'd turned yellow
after coming out of Congo. We thought it was jaundice because he
was on some strange drug for giardia, but it turned out to be hepatitis
C. The doctor said it had gone too long untreated. The doctor was
very grave; he told us, "He has six months, maybe a year. You must
understand his liver is very *fragile*." I held Zorro's hand, bruised purple from the catheter. Zorro took the doctor's words to mean he could
not tolerate wine and so he insisted on drinking nothing but vodka.
The opiate tablets, of course, continued. The doctor told him that at
this point his addiction was the least of his troubles.

When Zorro was told he would die soon, it didn't seem to trouble
him very much because he had always thought he would die soon. He
lived in war more than he lived in peace. He was more comfortable in
the shellfire chaos, where adrenaline swam with the heroin and made
him somehow happy. Home in Paris, he would sit restlessly in a café

as people walked past, people in no particular danger talking of where they were going to go skiing over the Easter break or of how annoying it was that the sofa delivery man wouldn't give an exact time. He would go to exhibition openings and trade photographers' gossip about someone getting the World Press Photo prize who shouldn't have, because everyone knew he was manipulating his shadows . . . But in this quotidian world, Zorro was bored and itchy. It was all so pointless. And then the *New York Times* would call and he would be back on a plane and up and gone to his beloved bang-bang.

Six months after he was given six months to live, a specialist prescribed a new drug regime. Unbelievably, he got better. One day the specialist told him he was virus-free, that he was cured. The new and unfamiliar idea that he was not going to die tomorrow or the next day discombobulated him. Zorro had no idea how to plan. The future is always unknown, but to Zorro it had been *unthinkable*. He had always avoided life, and now that he had been given it back, he understood that it was precious and he should not take it for granted. But what on earth to do with it?

"It's ridiculous, Kit," Zorro said down the phone from Kos. "It's refugees on the beach in the morning, beers on the beach in the afternoon. It's a good story for you."

Oz agreed but I hemmed. Since the Charlie attack I had been pulled back into political and news stories. I wanted to go back to Euroculture, visit the Venice Biennale, write about New Nordic cuisine. Oz wanted *banlieue* imams, deradicalization programs, Molenbeek, burkinis-on-the-beach, the rise of the Front National. Muslims Muslims Muslims. I was tired of listening to their indignation. I didn't note the tremor and reedy tone of their voices as I once would have done. I didn't hear their fear; my own had canceled out empathy.

I went to meet a family in Grigny for a story about immigrants in the outskirts of Paris. The husband had been run over by an ambulance the year before, and he could no longer work as a plumber. I asked if his wife went to work; he shook his head. She had tried to find a job, but around here—he waved his hand towards the small square window which looked out onto a square housing block. Gray brick blocks, gray sky. No métro, no shops. Three connecting buses took an hour and a half to get into Paris. His teenage son was on remand for a shoplifting charge in prison—in Fleury-Mérogis, a notorious jihadi breeding ground that was located only a kilometer away—and he was worried about him. "He was with the wrong people at the wrong time; he didn't steal anything, the police just arrested everyone. He's a good boy, he studies for the bac in his cell. Maybe he can still go to technical school." Dislocation, isolation, bad luck, poverty. He apologized for not having any biscuits to give me with the tea. His nine-year-old daughter came into the kitchen and sat on his lap. "Maybe we should have stayed in Mali," he told me. "But I wanted something better for her."

I left grim Grigny too late to beat the rush hour and got caught in traffic on the Périphérique. I pounded my hands on the steering wheel, stuck, irritated that I could not make a story out of this kind of mush. Maybe Zorro was right, maybe a change of scene would be good.

———

Rousse's apartment was due to be officially vacated, but neither Jean nor I had managed to find the time or heart to go and clear her things, and the supervising agent at the Bureau des Artistes had kindly said we could have until the end of September.

She'd lived on the back of the butte, in the attic space of a grand beaux arts apartment house on the Rue de Clignancourt. It was an enormous atelier with bare wood floors, and half the roof was a skylight streaked with pigeon droppings like paint drips. As an artist, she'd been entitled to this subsidized space, granted by the Mairie de Paris.

The gallery had removed her larger canvases and a few of her more polished and later notebooks. But most of her work, the backlog files and folders, giant portfolios tied up with string and piles of pasteboard that she used for her collages, were still there. Ahmed rested his scooter against the doorjamb, and I rooted around in the kitchenette for some coffee and put the *cafetière* on the stove.

"Ahmed, you should take some things of hers. The rest will just end up in storage or sold—choose things that you would like to have to remember her."

Little Ahmed hated my mother voice.

"As if I'm going to fucking forget," he said, hands clenched by his side.

He crouched down in the corner where Rousse had stacked her most recent work. She had been taking portraits of refugees and migrants making the Mediterranean crossing from Libya. She had spent a lot of time in Catania, where the boats came ashore in Sicily, setting up an outdoor studio in the camps. She asked each person to bring a possession to hold up for the camera. After a while she'd had to say "no more mobile phones," too prosaic, even though for most people it was the only possession they owned. Many of them had been rescued at sea, half naked, wet, and salt-rimmed and had nothing with them at all. But some had small fetishes, ferried and guarded all the way from grandfather to father to son, from village in South Sudan across the Sahara through camp and detention, beatings, robbings, sitting in a foot of water off the Libyan coast when the motor stalled and they had drifted for three days. A crumpled leather pouch, two swirling blue glass marbles, a carved wooden figure. One man, with a heavy brow and a blunt nose, held up a single cardinal feather.

Ahmed flicked through these, and then I heard him stop. He pulled out one of her pasteboard squares, and held it out in front of him in both hands. I walked over to see what he had found. It was a portrait of him. The picture had been taken last year, his twelve-year-old self, before his recent growth spurt and the black fur appeared on his top lip. Three-quarter-length portrait. He was bare-chested and in his hands he was holding a Kalashnikov.

PART IV

KOS

ONE

I flew to Kos the day after Little Ahmed went to Brittany. The town of Kos was pretty, blue and white and light; a ruined castle overlooked fishing boats in the harbor. In the cobblestone old town two minarets poked up over red-tiled roofs, vestiges of an Ottoman past. Zorro took me for an ouzo on the seafront the afternoon I arrived. He told me that dozens of boats were coming in every day, mostly at night. The Greeks made the refugee-migrants register at the police station before they could continue their journey to Athens.

"They all say they are from Syria," Zorro told me. "Half of them are from Pakistan. The others are Iraqis and Afghans. The Africans have the disadvantage because they can't say they are Syrian. Anyway the Greeks don't seem to care, they process them all just the same." The authorities were overwhelmed and slow; the process usually took about a week. In the meantime the wealthier ones rented hotel rooms, the poorer ones slept in abandoned houses or in tents along the seafront.

I watched the tourists walk by, French and English mainly. Vikings and Celts from the cold north with yellow hair. The women wore skimpy clothes and the soft pink rolls of their shoulders and plump bare upper arms were covered with tattoos. They strolled about with a slow aimless gait, unconcerned, dawdling, on holiday. The refugees, thin and harried, weaved among the slow-milling tourists. I wondered what it would have been like if I had brought Little Ahmed here on holiday and we were walking on the esplanade right now, among this strange mingled crowd. Would people think he was a tourist or a refugee? Which group would he identify with?

I set my alarm for midnight, but Zorro refused to wake up, so I walked down the hill to the beach by myself. The beach was a long curve of shingle. There were stars in the sky, but the moon hung too low and wan to offer any light. Below the hotel there was a line of beach recliners and I sat on one and waited.

Across the sea, the ancient Aegean, full of rotting civilizations that nourished and lapped its shores, was Turkey. It was only three or five miles away. I could see the orange necklace of lights along its coastal road. I could not see the people massing on the shoreline; I could not see the smoke from the bomb blasts or the elongated shadows of gunmen standing beside braziers or the hovels in which eight or ten people were sleeping side by side, or the hungry mother with a scrawny baby, sickly and fussing. These things I imagined, turning them over in my mind as the waves lapped over all the centuries of wars and oppressions. I laughed to myself at the banality of these thoughts and the metaphors that come along in facile trills, with nothing but the stars and the repeating rhythms of the sea to keep time and company.

I stared out to sea. Lights twinkled and blinked, elusive. I kept my eye on one, an intermittent blueish pinprick that seemed to be coming closer. Would an illegal boat have a light? I thought I could hear the faint throbbing drone of an outboard motor, but then the sound merged with the waves and was lost. It was very dark. I couldn't see anything. Further along the beach, where the line of recliners and the streetlights stopped and the shore clumped with dunes, a shore light flashed on and off. It seemed as if it would be a logical beacon to steer for.

I watched a car drive slowly along the esplanade and stop close by. A man got out and I went towards him to preempt my fear of the unknown, waving my hand in greeting. The man smiled back.

"Hello, I am a security guard, my name is Giorgios." He said he had seen two boats land earlier, both full of Pakistanis. "Sometimes you can see them when they turn on their mobile phones and the screens light up. Look there!"

A bright light was moving jerkily about, a flashlight of some kind.

"It's a boat! Get in the car!"

We drove a few hundred meters and I rushed down onto the beach, and there, caught in Giorgios's headlamps, were the outlines of figures coming up towards us. It was the very moment of landfall, of arrival. I could hear high-pitched voices, full of exclamations, urgent, triumphant, relieved.

"Hello, hello," I said, bumping among them. I reached out and found myself embracing a woman, plump and damp from sea spray. She clasped my two hands together in her two hands, a little dazed and amazed.

"Hello, my name is Kit."

"I am Mohammed!" said a young man's voice in English. "The children are all wet! And look, this woman has no shoes!"

I could see them only in glimpses between the dark and the wobbly beam of their flashlights. Perhaps a dozen people, among them two women with dyed blond hair, two or three small children, and four or five men. Their moment of joy was hustled and brief. They threw down their life preservers, took their mobile phones out of the Ziploc bags they had put them in during the crossing, gathered up the children, and began walking, at a brisk pace, towards the lights of the town. The women and the children were barefoot.

I walked with them, distributing cigarettes, which was all I had to give them. One produced a lighter and gallantly lit my cigarette for me. Mohammed was the only one who spoke English. He was young and handsome, with even white teeth and a quiff of wavy black hair that fell over one eye. "I was the driver of the boat! We were chased by the Turkish patrol. They shot at us! I swear it. They were shouting through a megaphone. Finally they said, 'OK we allow you to go!' Allow us? They could not catch us!"

"Where are you from?"

"From Syria."

"Where in Syria?"

Mohammed hesitated. I offered him a cigarette. He declined, pressing his hand against his chest in a gesture of pious refusal.

"Hama."

"Oh, I'm sorry," I said. "Things are very bad in Hama."

"Very bad."

"Is this your family?" I asked, pointing to the group trailing behind us.

"These people?" Mohammed's eyebrows drew together to make a thick black line. "These people? No. They needed a driver for the boat and so I went with them without paying. I don't like them."

"You met them in Turkey?"

"Yesterday only. The women are very rude and the men don't pray. They are bad people. They don't respect people and they don't pray. Except in the middle of the sea when the waves were coming higher and the Turkish coast guard light was shining at us and then they all started praying too much."

"How old are you?"

"I am eighteen." It could have been true, but he looked younger. Dawn lit his face soft rose; his cheeks were smooth, his eyes glittered black, his left eyebrow was striped with a scar.

"Did you bring your passport?" He made a derisory face. "Any ID at all?"

"I burnt it in Turkey," said Mohammed. "Where is the police station? Is it far?"

"No, it's not far, but it's early yet. You can begin the registration process when it opens in the morning. There will be a line. A lot of people."

"How long does it take?"

"Five days or a week." He frowned.

"They said it was better on Kos than Lesbos."

Mohammed was wearing a pair of jeans and a black polo shirt. He had no shoes. I asked him if he had any money with him. He pulled out his pockets to show me that he had nothing at all. How would Rousse have photographed him? Upturned empty palms, supplication of prayer, cupping nothing.

"There are some volunteer organizations around the port," I told him. "They can get you some clothes, some shoes, perhaps a tent."

As we came into the main town of Kos, the sun was coming up. We walked along the sea front where the Afghan refugee migrants had pitched their tents. A few women were up early and washing clothes in the sea. Mohammed took in the sight of the makeshift camp strung out along the road. A tangled family was sleeping on a foraged mattress under a canopy of bougainvillea; a row of men lay like a row of sardines on flattened cardboard boxes under a pillared portico. He looked out over the harbor where a giant white ferry was moored, as large and rectangular as an apartment building. He didn't say anything.

"Can I buy you a coffee?" I asked. He nodded. We left the others in the small plaza next to the white-washed police station and went to find a café on the harbor front that was open early.

I was thinking: scene, describe, early-morning boat landing, horizon, details, reportage, Hama, Syria . . . I was thinking about the beginnings of a story and the questions I needed to ask Mohammed.

I never liked refugee stories. They are all very sad and desperate, but they are always the same. War, home destroyed, flee . . . Report, write, repeat. The relationship between journalist and refugee is awkward, transactional, collusive. The journalist must tell the great suffering; the refugees must present themselves as greatly suffering; they are reduced to selling their package of abject despair, advertising it with tears and torn clothing and desperate quotes. "Our house was bombed!"—"They killed my husband-father-mother-sister-son!"—"We don't even have milk for the babies!"—"Look! The children are wet and this woman has no shoes!"

We found a place and sat down at a table and I asked for a cappuccino. Mohammed wanted tea. He did not put any sugar in it, which was abstemious for a Syrian. I took out my notebook.

"Would you mind?"

He did not answer, but he did not say no. He asked: "Can I please to borrow your phone? I want to call my family to tell them I crossed the sea safely."

"OK." I gave him my phone. He got up from the table and walked a short distance to the esplanade to be private.

I sat back with my coffee and took in the postcard view of the Mediterranean: sky blue sky, navy blue sea, sunshine sparkling on the waves.

I watched Mohammed walking in small circles beside a fishing skiff advertising boat tours of the island. He was smiling and nodding—affirmation, survival, good news. He finished his call and came and sat down, handing me the phone. As I took it, I looked down at the screen and saw not just a number but a name in white letters on the shiny black. It was a long-lost name recalled from another life and another place; undeleted, the number must have been transferred through my contacts list through several phone upgrades over an intervening decade: Ahmed-the-Wahhabi.

Sitting in my living room in Beirut bent over a mobile phone texting his wife to say he was OK. Laughing with Ahmed over lunch in Tripoli, throwing his little boy in the air and calling him his bear cub. I recalled his kindly face, his courteous and patient manner, as he had tried to explain to me, very gently and sincerely, his concern for my spiritual well-being. I looked over at Mohammed; I began to ask, "How?—" I saw that he was sitting back in his chair pressing his fingers together to make a steeple. It was the gesture of a vicar or a headmaster, a particular gesture, and I remembered more clearly now, Ahmed-the-Wahhabi, with his big black beard and his incongruous elegant fingertips and I felt a queasy sense of déjà vu, of time overlapping.

"Mohammed?" I asked, tentatively amazed.

Mohammed looked at me with narrowed eyes, suspicious. I was staring at him, grinning. "Mohammed, are you the son of Ahmed. From Tripoli?"

"No, I'm not," he said, reflexively defensive.

Of course he wasn't. That would be a ridiculous coincidence. "I'm sorry," I said, "but I think I know the man you called. It came up on my phone. Look." I showed him the name, Ahmed-the-Wahhabi.

"It's a nickname. I mean, a kind of joke—"

Mohammed was wary. Perhaps he was confused because I seemed to be accusing him of being Lebanese when he had told me he was Syrian.

"My father is Syrian," he said, with a certain stubbornness.

"Yes. From Hama!" I clapped my hands.

"Yes, from Hama," he repeated slowly.

"And he moved to Tripoli and married Fatima. He has a mobile phone shop."

"What are you saying?" he asked me sharply.

I told Mohammed how I had met his father (omitting the bathtub scene). I showed him the story that I had written about him on my laptop. I explained I was a journalist, that I had been living in Lebanon, that Ahmed, his father, and I had become friends.

"Your father! The same Ahmed—it must be," I said. "You just called him!" He still looked unconvinced, so I added that his father had helped me to understanding my religion better because I had just married my husband and was a recent convert to Islam. "My husband and I went to lunch at your home in Tripoli. We met! You were arguing with your sister. I think you must have been six or seven."

He nodded then, acknowledging, but still not smiling, "Yes, my father was always very hospitable with foreigners."

"How are your parents? Are they well?"

"Alhamdulillah."

"Your father taught me a lot," I said, hoping to break through his reticence. "I am very grateful to him. Let me repay his kindness. You need some clothes, I can see, and somewhere to stay."

He looked beyond me for a moment, towards the milling crowd around the harbor, as if he was looking for someone he couldn't find. Then he looked back at me, having considered his situation, and seemed to relent.

"You're not a spy?"

"No, I'm not a spy."

"And you knew my father in Lebanon?"

"I know. It's crazy, isn't it?

——

We walked to a beach shop to buy him new clothes and on the way we bought a couple of croissants. "Really, you came to my home?" he said, and shook his head. He said he could not remember the lunch in Tripoli at all.

"Your mother kept you in the bedroom with Disney cartoons the whole time," I reminded him. He frowned, but I was not sure if it was because he was trying to remember the scene or because he disapproved of Disney cartoons. I held up a T-shirt with a picture of a cartoon shark swallowing a swimmer under a sun-rayed KOS. Mohammed frowned. Frowning was his default expression. In repose his face had a drawn-down look; maybe it was just his thick black censor- bar eyebrows.

"Are there sharks?" he asked.

"Sorry, not funny," I said. I picked up a pair of shorts. Mohammed shook his head and reached for a pair of khaki trousers. He tried them on in the cubicle and turned the hems up an inch or two above his ankles so that he was satisfied. We also bought a plain hooded sweatshirt, a packet of athletic socks, a pair of blue Adidas sneakers and, the most important part of the refugee kit, a nylon backpack.

At the back of my mind was the idea that this was a really good story. The problem with refugee stories was that they were always impossible to check. The backstory was left behind in the rubble and all the compromising interesting details buried with it. Here I already had a beginning and an end. Now I just had to fill in ten years in between.

"We can get more tomorrow," I said. I carried one bag, Mohammed carried the other. He had worn the sneakers out of the shop. Less flat-footed now, a little bouncier. "Now let's get you a room in the hotel, and then go and get you registered at the police station, and then you can sleep." At this possibility, at last, Mohammed allowed a smile.

TWO

Zorro always knew the best place in town. In Kos he had made his regular spot a taverna behind the seafront called "Costas" after its owner, and we stopped in for coffee. Costas pulled up a chair, cuffed Zorro's unshaven cheek, and said, "You just woke up." Zorro did not deny it. His rhythms were anticircadian. Golden hours, dawn and dusk; the black and bright in between was no light and the worst light, so he was accustomed to sleeping through the middle of the night and the middle of the day. It was five in the afternoon. The terrace was empty. Zorro introduced me, and Costas clicked at someone to bring three glasses of coffee. Costas was big-bellied, friendly, and heavy-handed with the ouzo. His terrace was less than half full—his season had suffered with the influx of refugees—but his hospitality was undiminished. He had asked his Egyptian dishwasher to translate the menu into Arabic—and with lower prices.

"Not Turkish coffee, Greek coffee!" He winked at me, then looked at Zorro. Old jokes already between summer friends.

"In Armenia they call it Armenian coffee," I said.

"And it comes from Colombia!" Costas chimed.

"All good things come from Colombia," said Zorro.

"No, no!" Costas wagged his finger. He had a walrus moustache and this wagged too. Zorro smiled his wide, chipped-tooth smile. Easygoing, take life as it is, turn it into a joke if you can. I resented his laid-back serenity; I was jealous of it. We had shared our marmite in war-zone hovels, we had our gray London childhoods in common and our escape. We had met again in the Panjshir Valley when the Northern Alliance were pushing into Kabul. He was the very model of the dashing war photographer. A brilliant diamond shining in his own black drama, laughing till we had drunk all the vodka I had brought from Moscow. "It's easy for you," I complained. "You get to look at the world and take a picture instead of trying to make sense of it in sentences. You can live in moments, in images. *Click snap send.* Front-page splash." He told me that wasn't true. "You can't imagine what I see," he said. "What I have to look at, *how* I look." Later I came to understand the price he paid for not looking away. And then I envied him, because I had always recused myself.

We left Costas, and I followed Zorro as he looped around the police station and shot pictures of the kids playing on the seafront. Knots of migrant refugees clustered around volunteers distributing food and clothing and bottles of water. Women searched through a plastic bag of scarves. A pair of Danish sisters with thick flaxen braids and tight red T-shirts with a discreet logo were besieged by young men begging for shoes: have you size 42, size 40? They held up the rubber soles to measure against their feet.

The police station faced the harbor beneath the walls of the old fortress. In front of it was a small plaza bordered by a broken wall on one side, a police cordon on another, a line of four portacabins, and the sea. Gutter filth; garbage mulch tramped into the cracks.

The late-afternoon air was trapped by the pine trees, and the atmosphere was thick with the stench of urine, rotting figs, and the sweetish undertone of excrement. The refugee migrants milled about while the Greek police stood guard in their black Kevlar leg armor and surgical face masks.

A line of men sat on a low stone wall, eating their donated supper out of foil takeout containers. They passed the time and snippets of information: a room to sleep, the price of a tent, bus timetables, the name of a driver that would put their family in the back of a truck and take them from Belgrade to Salzburg, a photograph of a Macedonian policeman beating back migrant refugees at a train station, news from the Hungarian border. "They are putting up a razor wire fence, did you hear? At midnight anyone illegally crossing it will be put in jail for three years." "My cousin was detained in Denmark." "You can still go to Sweden, but how can you go to Sweden without going through Denmark?" "Can you buy a train ticket to Austria in Budapest now?" "I have relatives in the Netherlands, they told me—" "No, that's not true anymore. Did you hear? The Germans blocked the border!"

I sat down on the edge of the group and began a conversation with a Syrian Kurd who told me he was an English teacher. His teeth were covered in gray patches where the enamel had worn off. He told me he was traveling alone and hoped to get to a European country and then apply for his family to join him. "Ah, Paris. I dreamed to go Paris and see the Eiffel Tower." He had never seen the sea before, he admitted, "I was too frightened of it so I paid three thousand euros to go across the sea in a good boat."

"Three thousand euros!" I said. "Usually people pay twelve hundred."

"I know," said the English teacher, a little abashed, and now almost entirely out of money. "It was a yacht."

"You had the VIP voyage," I teased him.

"Yes, a Very Important Person." He managed a half smile and

then he asked politely, "I have a question, if you don't mind?" I nodded. "Is it permissible, I mean, for example, in Europe, if there is a girl, a daughter, is it possible that when she is eighteen she can go out of her family's house?"

"Yes," I told him. "At the age of eighteen, a girl or a boy is legally an adult and can leave home or do what they want."

"And if she has a boyfriend? How can I put this"—the man paused—"if she is not a virgin?"

"This is her decision," I told him. "Nobody can make choices for her, not her father or brother or even a husband."

"Do girls in Europe have more than one boyfriend?" he asked hestitantly.

I was not sure if he meant more than one boyfriend at the same time, or sequentially, so I answered, "Yes, sometimes."

"And then if there is a boy who wants to marry her? Will he still want to marry her?"

"Yes, it is quite normal for a girl to have boyfriends and then get married."

He thought about this for a moment. His mouth pursed in distaste. "We have the matter of honor," he said.

"I know," I said, raising an eyebrow in rebuke. "But in Europe, we do not have the concept of honor, we have the concept of individual rights."

I knew Oz would want a perfect, nicely desperate middle-class Syrian family with a disabled child and a mother who did not wear the headscarf who had fled ISIS. There were a few families in the tents around the park at the base of the old fortress who might fit these criteria. I copied their details into my notebook and sat in a nearby café writing paragraphs in my laptop, to be topped and tailed later on.

File: FRANKLIN D. ROOSEVELT
August 10, 2015

I met several Syrians from Hasakah who were living in the tents around the corner, by the ramparts of the Castle. When I asked them about the situation in Hasakah, they shook their heads. The government was holding the provincial capital, but they said that Daesh, the name most Syrians use for the forces of the Islamic State, had captured many of the villages. When I asked them about life under the Islamic State, they shook their heads. When I asked them about the government of Bashar al-Assad, they also shook their heads, pointed at the sky and made helicopters with their arms and mimed houses falling down. "Barrel bombs," they said. One young man told me he had left because he didn't want to be called into Assad's army. Another pointed to shrapnel scars on his legs. His friends hoisted him up like a trophy to tell his story. "He was buried, dead. He was dead and now alive!" They said it had been a miracle and they proudly showed me photographs on a phone: a rectangle of gray ash rubble and in one corner, a shape of a comma, the curve of his neck and a shoulder, barely visible in the blasted scrim. The miracle was embarrassed, but his friends made him pull up his T-shirt to show me a long surgical scar on his narrow torso.

I met an older man, also from Hasakah, who was limping. "Daesh is in my town," he told me. "I cannot go back. They will kill me for leaving. They took over my house, my car, everything they take for themselves when someone leaves. Very difficult here"—he swept his hand over the camp to take in the washing draped over the bougain- villea bushes, a man filling a water bottle from a hose connected to a main water pipe, and a woman sitting against a palm tree slumped over her sleeping baby. "I have three children. I cannot stand for a long time—my legs," and I looked down and saw that his trouser legs flapped at awkward angles. "I had polio when I was a boy, they didn't have vaccines then."

I stopped typing. Too flowery, too much first person. Oz had warned me on the phone the night before I left, "Don't let your fiction ambitions color your reporting, Kit." I had rebutted, "There's a difference between fact and truth, you know," and he had sighed his writers-are-so-troublesome sigh.

I sat for a while, nursing a melting glass of gin and tonic, watching Zorro photograph boys playing in the surf. My eyes lit on a man leaning on a rail, staring out to sea, to Turkey, back beyond. He had broad shoulders and a scar on the edge of his cheek where it glowed against the setting sun. What resolve was set in his jaw?

I had the idea that I should write a short story about an Arab who would defy the sentimental image of the poor, desperate, homeless, war-torn refugee that the happy-clappy nice and liberal Europeans were so gratified to rescue. A man who made his own luck. I imagined him as a chameleon charmer—a version of the Ahmed I had been seduced by. An antihero who would subvert the mass media narrative of victim. Not dependent, not suppliant; savvy, resourceful. Good with his fists if he needed to be, computer-clever, able to hack into banks. Carrying a secret, sent on a mission, searching for something or someone, he would have many adventures along the way . . . An Odysseus. If Odysseus had been a Trojan.

Zorro clunked his camera down on the table and fished into his pocket for his silver pill box.

"Refugees, refugees," he said happily. He chewed a little white tablet and washed it down with a sip from my drink. "It's a story that will never stop giving."

———

Mohammed had spent the afternoon sleeping, and when I knocked on his door a little after eight in the evening, he opened it only a crack. I could see that he had showered and dressed in his new trousers with the hems neatly rolled up.

"Excuse me," he said, not quite frowning, but serious. "I will come later. I must pray now."

"Oh. OK. We'll wait for you in the lobby."

"Who are you with?"

"With a photographer friend of mine."

"I don't want my photograph taken." Mohammed shut the door. I stood for a moment facing the bare wood and then walked down the stairs slowly. I had thought that we could call his father together and surprise him with our reunion. But suddenly I didn't want to share it with Mohammed. I reached the lobby and found a sofa in the corner and tapped Ahmed-the-Wahhabi's name onto my phone.

He answered warmly, expecting to hear his son's voice, calling back. When he heard instead a foreign woman, he said, brusquely, "Wrong number" and I had to talk fast to stop him from hanging up. "Ahmed? Fatima Mohammed Ahmed. Um Ahmed." I repeated all the names I could think of and then mine.

"Kitt-e-redge?" he said at last, in the three syllable, spelling-out way I remembered. I told him about meeting Mohammed on the beach. "It has been a very long time."

"Can you believe it?"

"It is unbelievable." A sigh, or was it the phone line? His voice was familiar, but there was an echo of reserve—time, distance, reticence— I couldn't tell through the static.

"So now I have rescued the father and the son," I said. I was excited by the luck of the cosmos colliding for my benefit. Ahmed-the-Wahhabi did not say anything. I repeated my little joke.

"I am glad he is safe," he said.

"I know. I couldn't believe it! It is him. He's so big now, he's seventeen? He told me he was eighteen."

"His mother was happy to hear from him. It has been such a long time—"

"Fatima! How is Fatima? Please send her my warmest regards. Mohammed doesn't have any papers, but don't worry, the Greeks are letting everyone through."

"Kitt-e-redge."

"Isn't it funny?"

"Funny?"

"I mean strange."

"Strange? Yes, very strange."

"I mean peculiar."

"Kitt-e-redge, I am sorry."

I took this to mean thank you. I kept talking. I asked, "So when did he leave Lebanon?"

"Lebanon? A long time."

"Yes. I mean I know he is Syrian, through you, but really he is Lebanese—"

"No, Syria."

"Yes, I mean it's better if he's Syrian."

"He was in Syria—"

"Syria?"

"Kitt-e-redge. A lot of things have changed and happened. What did he tell you?"

"He said he was from Hama."

"Hama, no. Impossible."

"But you are from Hama, aren't you? Originally."

"Hama is in the government's hands."

"I'm sorry."

"Didn't Ahmed tell you?" he asked.

"Ahmed?"

"Your husband."

"Oh. Yes. But we are divorced now."

"I am sorry. He didn't tell me that."

The line cut. I called back and he picked up after a single ring, but the connection was crackly and it was hard to hear him.

"Who didn't—wait, are you in touch with Ahmed?" I asked.

"Yes, we will be in touch."

"I mean have you been talking to Ahmed?"

"When he comes to Lebanon. Through Syria."

"Through Syria?" I was confused. "Ahmed or Mohammed?"

"His mother is very upset. She is very happy to hear his voice safe." Some other words followed, but I couldn't make them out.

"Hello? Hello?"

"I don't know how to say—but Kitt-e-redge, please don't tell Ahmed that you saw Mohammed."

"Why?"

"It is not safe for him."

"For Ahmed?"

"Kitt-e-redge, it's not how you think."

"Not what? What do I think?"

I saw Mohammed coming across the lobby towards me, and I felt as if I had been caught doing something I shouldn't. Zorro was right behind him. A wasp landed on my finger and I twirled the phone around trying to shake it off. Flustered, I said, "I'll call back. Bye!" and hung up.

Zorro greeted Mohammed—"Welcome, how was your journey?"—as if he had come down for the weekend by train. Mohammed shook Zorro's hand gravely. For a moment Zorro's silver skulls interlaced with Mohammed's carnelian set in a silver band.

"Shall we go and eat?" I was annoyed at Mohammed. He had none of the warmth or twinkle of his father. Why hadn't he told me he hadn't seen his parents for a long time? And apparently Ahmed had kept in touch with Ahmed-the-Wahhabi through all these years. This was odd too.

We went back to Costas for dinner. I assured Mohammed we would not order any pork. We ordered lamb souvlaki and rice and a Greek salad. He prodded it with his fork and said, "It is Lebanese food." Costas, leaning over the table, hands clasped, waiting for a compliment, made a wry face.

"Ottoman, Levant," I said. "It is all the same food empire." Mohammed looked blank.

"But Syrian food is the best," I said, fishing carefully. "I remember the cherry kebab. *Kibbeh* with quince, walnut baklava . . ." Mohammed did not respond. He remained taciturn. He resisted even Zorro's easygoing friendliness. He knit his forehead when he saw four plump sunburnt women come in wearing spaghetti-strap sundresses, laughing, orange cleavages amply on display. Mohammed looked uncomfortably marooned. I recounted the story of our meeting on the dark beach to Zorro in an effort to draw him into the conversation. Zorro asked him about the Turkish side, about the smugglers, police, the price of boats.

"They are all bad people," was all Mohammed would say.

He answered us in monosyllables. He said he had not seen his parents for a while.

"More than a year?" Mohammed nodded vaguely.

"Have you been studying?"

"Yes, studying."

"In Lebanon?"

"No, not in Lebanon."

"Your father said you had been away."

"You talked to my father?"

"I called him just before dinner. Were you in Syria?" I looked down at his hands to look for fighting scars. I noticed for the first time that he was missing the tip of the little finger on his right hand. "Were you in Hama? Your uncle was an imam there, I remember."

"What do you know about my uncle?" Mohammed's tone flashed close to menacing. Zorro intervened with a compliment.

"Your English is very good."

"My parents teached—taught—me."

"You want to go to Germany?"

"Maybe Germany. Germany first."

"Sweden is also taking refugees," said Zorro helpfully.

"Not Sweden."

"What do you want to do?"

"I don't know."

"Study?"

"Yes, study."

A large family of Iraqis arrived and sat at the adjacent table. Two brothers, their wives in flowing black robes and headscarves, and several children, two little girls in matching pink dresses with pink sparkly shoes. The men ordered beers and kebabs, and big plates of fries for the kids. They tossed a pack of cigarettes between them on the table. Three boys ran around until they were admonished by their mothers, hauled back up onto their chairs, and told to sit still and be quiet.

"Children are a blessing," Zorro said to them amicably, in Arabic (one of his friendly phrases that he had collected in several languages). The women smiled, the men offered him a cigarette. "*Shaku Maku?*" They were from Basra, they were going to Germany where they had relatives. No, they were fine, thank you, they were staying in a hotel. Their papers had been registered and they were going to Athens on the ferry tomorrow.

"Why did you leave Basra?" I asked.

One of the brothers pointed to his bottle of beer. "If you drink in Basra, they will kill you." He drew his finger across his throat and laughed heartily. "And I like beer." His brother pulled his chair over to our table and scrolled though pictures of his family on his mobile phone. Two sons and a daughter, sitting in a row on a new sofa still covered with the manufacturer's protective clear plastic. *Swipe*. A family picture, twenty-five people crammed into the frame. *Swipe*. He pointed proudly to the screen. "Me and my brother." They were standing arm in arm wearing camouflage military fatigues and carrying American M16 machine guns. "Soldiers!"

I became aware of Mohammed standing beside my shoulder. He said something in Arabic in low composed tones to the Iraqi brothers from Basra. One of them looked at me, unsure. The other stood up, as if to reply.

Mohammed nodded curtly to me and said, "I am tired. I will go now," and left before I could remonstrate.

"He is your friend?" asked one of the brothers from Basra, irritated, defensive.

"He is the son of a friend," I clarified.

The brothers from Basra sat down again, but the moment of friendliness was broken.

Zorro asked Costas to bring us the bottle of ouzo that we had been refusing out of deference to Mohammed.

"I hate prickly Muslims," I said.

Zorro laughed.

"You are a self-hating prickly Muslim."

"I know. It's an advantage. I can say it without being Islamophobic. I am fed up." I continued. "I want to sit and have a nice meal and a conversation and drink a beer. For God's sake. I don't know what he said to the family from Basra."

"The Shia militia brothers," Zorro commented. "Fleeing the pro-
hibitions of their own ayatollah."

"You see, I am not the only Muslim fed up with Islam. Calumny
heaped upon irony."

"What? You are making even less sense than usual, Kit."

The mayor arrived. Apparently the mayor ate at Costas most
nights. He was tubby and care-worn. He had an upside-down smile;
Costas' was the right way up. The mayor and Zorro had struck up
an unlikely friendship. All of Zorro's friends were unlikely. One of
his closest friends was footballer Thierry Henry. The greatest thing
about Zorro, I once realized, was that he was entirely indiscriminate
in his friendship—to all it was given equally. He could joke with a
president and talk politics with a beggar. Once—long ago, before all
the relapses; before answers got twisted around by questions—I had
a theory about Zorro. I thought that his madnesses, his addictions,
his heights and depths, were the consequence of an oversensitive
soul. Like some people have more taste buds than other people,
Zorro had more feelings. He could not watch movies because he
could not understand how it was possible to watch suffering, violence, betrayal, and war—essentially any human drama, because
drama is someone else's pain—as entertainment. He was a dande-
lion; a puff of wind could blow his halo of seed into a sunlit grove
or a mass grave. Maybe he was just more honest than most people.
Maybe he saw the world for what it was and himself for what he
was, a photographer, nothing more, nothing that could make any
difference. Maybe this is what gave him such agony.

"How is it going on Ellis Island?" Zorro asked the mayor. The
mayor reached for the ouzo by way of answer. The numbers of
migrants had been rising all summer and the number of tourists was
falling. Every day was a new problem. Tomorrow, Athens was sending
him a new police chief.

"We need more Indians," he said, "not more chiefs."

"Haven't you got plenty of Indians?"

The mayor made a not-funny face. "Plenty of Pakistanis; not so many Indians, in fact."

"How come the authorities are not making any distinction between refugees and migrants?" I asked. "What happened to the idea of processing people for asylum? Whether they have passports or no documents at all, they give their names—whatever names they want to give—they have their photographs taken, and they all get the same stamped document, take the ferry to Athens and onwards." The mayor looked up at me blearily.

"Can we be off the record, please," he said, getting up and going to the bathroom to wash his hands. "I'm off duty now. I'm not the mayor for the next ten minutes."

"They can't," said Zorro. "They are overwhelmed. Greece is in the middle of an economic crisis, the mayor hasn't been paid since April. He can't even take his own money out of his own bank account. And there are too many people coming. Last week there were more than a hundred boats."

The mayor returned.

"I'm sorry," I said to him. "It's all Merkel's fault!" The mayor allowed a wan smile. I continued, "Merkel throws her arms open and says *come!* All those pictures of people welcoming them just encourages others to take the risk. Now more people will come. Did Cameron say 'swarming'? The Hungarians know what's coming, they were always the frontier land against the Ottomans. They are putting up the fences."

The mayor said, sadly, "We are the frontline now."

Costas sat down. "My grandmother was from Smyrna," he said quietly.

"Yes," I said, "and so you know what happens when history tips over, when populations shift."

Zorro moved his chair back; it made an awful scraping noise against the terra-cotta. "What do you want to do, Kit? Let them drown? Send them back?"

"I don't know. All I'm saying is that nobody dares mention the fact that Muslims who were born and grew up in Europe are now violently rejecting its values, while at the same time their fellow Muslims are appealing to those values to let them in." I threw up my hands. Was I a politician? Did I have to come up with the answers? Wasn't it my job just to ask the questions?

Zorro tried to ignore my shrill Cassandra. He lifted up his glass of milky ouzo and said, "I raise a glass. What if there were no borders at all? Imagine if everyone could go anywhere they wanted at any time. Come and work, come and rest, come and look around. Stay if you like, move on, go home. Nation-states are a nineteenth-century invention. Burn all their flags! Tear down the fences! Shoot all the border guards!"

The mayor made a laugh-grunt. "And who pays?"

"Pie in the sky," I said.

"A man can dream."

"Or hallucinate."

"Stop being nasty, Kit." I felt the queasiness of humiliation. But I did not admit this. Instead I mustered affront.

"I'm not nasty. I am being realistic. Pretend that we are all one happy family of humanity if you like. But you'll see, they are different and they want to live differently and it won't be an easy integration. It won't be integration at all. It will be us and them."

Zorro turned on his singsong voice and recited:

"*Oh come on, Brian, or they'll have stoned him before we get there . . . Would you like to buy a packet of gravel, madam?*" And I laughed, like I always did. Zorro was the original Monty Python fan, he knew all the words. He fell back into his normal voice. "But seriously. But

not seriously. What if we refused to be their enemy? What if we for-
gave them for hating us and said that we did not hate them and we
were not afraid of them either? I've got a cunning plan:"

"Let's hear this plan of yours," said Costas.

"You let Turkey into the EU," said Zorro with a touch of both the
triumphal and the absurd in his voice. "If Turkey joins the EU, you take
away the whole argument of we-are-we and you-are-you. Take away the
border between Europe and Asia, East and West, Christian and Islam.
Erase it. Heal it. Anyone can go where they want, under the umbrella
of Brussels and Strasbourg and human rights courts and anticorruption
conferences and subsidies for minorities. International. Community."

"Don't talk to the Greeks about the community of the European
Union," said the mayor bitterly. "It used to be called Community.
Now it's just a German *Zollverein*."

"No, listen to the crazy man," said Costas, whose grandparents
had been forced to flee Smyrna when the Turks burnt the Christian
quarters of the city. "If Turkey is in the EU, they will have to allow us
to go back there! Freedom of movement!"

"You see!" Zorro poured more ouzo all around. If Zorro ruled the
world, it would be the best party ever. "Turkey wants to be part of
Europe. Give them this and they become us and stop being them.
Think further: Turkey's natural sphere of influence is Syria. Turkey installs a client in Syria to oversee reconstruction. Then after a
generation Syria becomes part of the EU—which is then given a different name—"

"Rome," I suggested.

"Mediterraneo! Who next? You might as well let the Lebanese in,
and they will be only too happy to remember they are really Phoeni-
cians and trade with everyone. And then what happens? Now who
wants to be in the club?"

"Israel!" Costas clapped his hands.

"*Voilà!*" concluded Zorro with a big grin. "And you have solved Israel-Palestine too." He sat down with a flourish.

The mayor laughed heartily. Costas clicked his fingers for another bottle of ouzo.

"Give him another bottle and he will tell us how to persuade the lion not to hunt the gazelle."

For a few moments we basked in the reflected silly brilliance of Zorro's fantasy. But the sun had set and the zephyr breeze began to gust colder and I had drunk ouzo, which made my brain clear and my mouth warm.

"Just one tiny detail," I said. "The Roman Empire needed Roman legions to enforce it. Only a monopoly of violence can ensure peace. Alexandre always says this. You need a European Army. Otherwise everything is civil war."

"All wars are civil wars," said Zorro. "And all wars are uncivil."

"And we are in the process of importing one. How are you going to enforce the peace in Zorroland? All these people desperately clamoring to come and live in our nice functional societies. Aren't they the same people who fucked up their own?"

"The people who are risking their lives to come here, they are the victims—" said Costas. "These people are fleeing! They are the ones who are trying to get away from—"

"Don't be naïve," I said. Insulted, Costas got up and went to check on something in the kitchen.

Zorro said, "Kit—" but I kept talking.

"They are coming and there are millions of them and many of them are nice and friendly and desperate and many of them are suspicious opportunists and some of them want to kill us and some of them will kill us."

Zorro shook his head. The mayor made his excuses and said good-night. Costas did not come back and sit down with us. We paid the bill and walked home past the slumbering tents and pitiful trash fires surrounded by glowing faces.

"Fucking hell, Kittredge," Zorro said.

THREE

The next morning I woke up early, first light at six. I made a cup of tea with the minikettle and the Lipton yellow tea bags in my room. I sat at the narrow table by the window and began to write my short story about Ahmed the atypical Arab.

I could not decide whether to make my fictional Ahmed into a spy or a con man. Agent, double agent, terrorist, bigamist, entrepreneur, fixer, fraudster, thief. Which of these was the real Ahmed? Which of these was my original Ahmed? What was he doing going in and out of Lebanon? From Syria?

File: LES GOBELINS

Ahmed was handsome and he was cleverer than everyone else and these two things were going to be his passport because he didn't have one . . .

I wrote for two hours before I ran out of track. My fictional Ahmed began his odyssey in Baghdad and hopscotched on fraudulent papers to Beirut, to Istanbul, to Athens, to Paris. He had many escapades along the way. He had several identities and encountered many different characters—a priest, a prostitute, a plumber, and a politician. He stole and was robbed. He deceived and was lied to. When he earned money, he spent it. His journey took him up mountain paths and lapsed in squats.

What would this Ahmed do when he got to Paris? Would he wind up sleeping on a grating outside the Gare du Nord or in a suite at the Bristol? Would he find friends and business partners or disillusionment or religion or get thrown into prison and be radicalized by a cellblock sheikh? Was he a hero or a villain? He could get a lowly job as a stockroom boy in a kosher supermarket and then save people during a terrorist attack by hiding them in the walk-in freezer. Or would he be the terrorist? Would he have a happy ending or blow himself up? (Maybe that would be a happy ending as far as he was concerned.) Was this kind of plotting corny or melodramatic, even if these things actually really happened? What if I made his story ironic so that he returned to Iraq? What would make a fictional Ahmed go back? What had made my real Ahmed go back . . .

. . . And in and out of Lebanon. *Through Syria.* The thoughts dropped like drips from the shower. The shower dripped on my forehead. What lines of usefulness might connect Ahmed and Ahmed-the-Wahhabi? What did Ahmed do for the U.N. anyway? Protocol officer special assistant to the envoy of the undersecretary . . . traveling all the time, so many SIM cards that the numbers were all crossed out and cross-hatched in my diary. I thought back to the postcards of ruins he sent Little Ahmed. Leptis Magna in Libya—when was he in Libya? What for? The ziggurat minaret in Samarra. But Samarra had been under ISIS control for more than a year. The citadel in Aleppo—a city besieged, bombed, and divided. Which side would he have—?

Cold, naked, wet, fumbling for a towel and thinking too much, I dressed and went downstairs to the lobby for coffee, stretching imagination, fictionalizing my life, replaying it with a melancholy cello score. Stories to steal. Little Ahmed had said it was not a real Kalashnikov, only a replica.

———

I knocked on Mohammed's door. I had a hundred questions. There was no answer. At reception they told me he had checked out.

A thousand refugee migrants were packed into the plaza next to the police station. Some had formed a queue of sorts, and had sat down to wait their turn in the meager shade offered by squares of tarpaulin strung up from the pine trees. A pack of men pushed against the line of Greek policemen, shouting at them to let them through. The police banged their batons against the riot shields to warn them to move back. The banging made a drumbeat and the crowd began to chant at them: "*Oh Greece, we sacrifice our blood and souls to you!*" It was a chant Iraqis used to sing for Saddam. They were mocking the police. The press of people pushed me up a side alley. Faces crowded into mine. Someone trod on my foot and I howled and elbowed my way through the crush.

Behind the police station there was a grove of pine trees in the lee of the wall that enclosed a field of Roman ruins. Pakistanis had set up little camps under the trees, sleeping on blankets spread on the soft pine-needle ground. I found Mohammed squatting on his heels, leaning against an ancient lintel. He was tapping the screen of a mobile phone and did not notice me until I was standing over him. He saw my shadow, looked up, and frowned.

"You left," I said, and frowned back at him.

He stood up and put the phone in his pocket. He avoided looking at me—whether out of piety or obfuscation, it was hard to tell.

"Are you OK?"

"Fine," he said. He made a sideways move to get past me. I blocked him.

"Look, it's obvious you were in Syria." He did not answer. I knew he was trying to escape. I tried a last-ditch tabloid scam. "I can help— my newspaper can help, with asylum, with getting you to Germany. I could come along and report the story." He stopped for a moment. Tall and glowering, he did not look like a refugee today. Perhaps the meekness of yesterday was only an act when he thought he needed me for something. Where had he got the phone?

"What story?"

"Your story."

"I don't have any story," he said.

"No, I mean your life, Syria, war, fleeing, refugee." A string of headline clichés came out of my mouth.

"I don't want to talk about it."

"You can tell me what the Americans need to understand." Usually this worked—provide an outlet for Arabs to vent their outrage at Western hypocrisy and indifference. Mohammed narrowed his eyes at me.

"The Americans are not stupid," he said unexpectedly. "The Americans understand very well." He put his hand on his heart, a formal gesture, enough, goodbye.

"But—"

"Ask your husband about Syria," he said, irritated. "Your husband is the Iraqi-American, isn't he? My father told me." He shook the phone to show he had talked to his parents.

"Just Iraqi, not American—"

"My father told you not to tell him that you saw me. But you will tell him."

"Why shouldn't I tell him?"

He didn't answer. I took my business card out of my wallet and gave it to him. "If you need anything, get in touch."

"I go."

I did not put out my hand to shake his. I knew he would not

touch it. Mohammed walked away and I was left standing there feeling wrong-footed. I had done something wrong but didn't know what.

———

Oz said, "It sounds interesting, Kit. I like the backstory. Can you follow him on the road to Germany?"

"No," I said. "He's disappeared on me."

"What about the parents in Lebanon. What do they say?"

"His father is Syrian," I said, trying to tune the story to his fork. "His uncle an imam in Hama."

"And Hama is—remind me."

"In the middle of Syria."

"But under who? Under ISIS?" Oz's tone was hopeful.

"No, under government control."

"Can we get to the uncle somehow?"

———

I rang Ahmed-the-Wahhabi in Lebanon. I told him that Mohammed had checked out of the hotel and I didn't understand why.

"My son follows his own path." Was there sadness in his voice? "We pray for him."

"Where was he in Syria?"

I heard a muffled voice in the background, admonishing tones.

"We don't know anything about his life now." There was a woman's voice in the background, high-pitched and talking rapidly.

"Is that Fatima?"

"Yes, she is here."

"Please give her my love."

"She is very worried."

"He made it across the sea, that is the most dangerous part."

"We have not heard from him in long months and now he is in

Greece—" Perhaps Ahmed-the-Wahhabi was trying to make sense of it all too.

I asked about his brother the imam in Hama, but he said he did not know anything about him. He said it in such a way that I did not quite believe him. He did not seem to want to say much. Then he asked, "Your husband is in Damascus now?"

"I don't know. I haven't spoken to him in a couple of weeks. He lives in Baghdad."

"In Baghdad? . . . *wallah Baghda . . .*" I heard Ahmed-the-Wahhabi repeat what I had said to Fatima in the background. The line faltered as I walked back to the hotel. I couldn't hear what he said next.

"He was just in Amman with his son," I added.

"Amman? . . . *wallah Amman.*" This news seemed to cause some consternation in the apartment in Tripoli. There was a pause while Ahmed-the-Wahhabi remonstrated with Fatima. Then his voice returned with a finality in the tone. "Kitt-e-redge. We will pray for you. And for the son of Ahmed."

"Pray for all of us," I said.

"*Inshallah,*" he said. And hung up.

I did not find Mohammed again. I looked for him in the plaza next to the police station, in the pine grove, among the tents pitched along the seafront. There were many young men who looked like him— amber-skinned, a sharp edge between cheek and eye socket, oil pool eyes—but they were not him.

————

I called Ahmed-the-Wahhabi in Lebanon two or three times over the next couple of days, but the phone just rang. I called my Ahmed on his Baghdad cell number, but it went straight to voicemail. I emailed *Urgent! need to talk—where are you?* A day and a half later I got a single line back: *Internet terrible here. Will be in touch when I get back to civilization.* Lines stretched and doubled back, grew slack, entangled, frayed.

The refugee migrants waiting at the police station sat on the dirty cobbles under umbrellas against the sun. They queued to board the ferry, white paper documents flapping in the harbor breeze. The line formed again in Athens and moved towards the Macedonian border in buses, in trains, in Albanian taxis. It snaked along railway tracks through Serbia. It pooled against the shiny new razor wire along the Hungarian border, tautened, and turned left towards Croatia. Thousands of people moving en masse through summer fields, tramping along motorways. Mohammed was somewhere among them.

I stayed a few more days on Kos. I went to the beach again and watched the boats come in at dawn, but the people were wary. They put their hands in front of their faces to stop Zorro taking their picture. They did not want to talk and said (in English) that they did not speak English. Zorro was withdrawn, opiated, mad at me or just tired. Like the time he came back from the front at Tora Bora and collapsed into the camp bed in the corner of the refugee tent and slept for twenty-two hours straight.

I ended up writing a story for Oz about the Danish volunteer sisters who distributed donated clothing to the refugees. Freya and Sophie were very nice and earnest and deluded. They reminded me of Soviet peasant girls on revolution posters.

File: OLYMPIADES
August 22, 2015

Father and son, Ahmed and Mohammed, set off from Aleppo at the end of June, walking to the Turkish border. They spent three nights sleeping rough to avoid ISIS checkpoints. In Turkey they took a bus to Bodrum and paid smugglers there $1,200 each for a place on a boat. They were crammed with 40 other Syrian refugees in a small inflatable dinghy. At some point during the night the engine stopped. After drifting for several hours they were picked up by the Greek coast guard. Now they are stuck on the island of Kos, waiting for a registration document that will allow them to continue their journey to Athens and then, they hope, to Düsseldorf, where they already have relatives.

They know that it is a long walk ahead. Ahmed is 65 years old, hale, and confident, but he has diabetes and suffers drowsy low-sugar episodes. His son Mohammed worries about him. Mohammed has only a pair of flip-flops on his feet. Every evening they come to the seafront in the town of Kos where different charity organizations congregate with donations of clothes and supplies and medical help. The two Danish sisters, Sophie and Freya, promised to bring Mohammed a pair of sneakers sized 45 if they could. Bigger sizes were always in demand. Their mother was bringing in another container of donations in a couple of days. Mohammed held up a plastic shopping bag containing his few possessions and asked if they had any backpacks. Freya shook her head regretfully.

"They are fleeing war," she told me, "we have an obligation as fellow human beings to help them."

I did not write about the scrum that surrounded the two blond sisters whenever they appeared. I did not write that the sisters were careful to limit their presence to half an hour. Freya had admitted to me that a couple of times they had stayed too long after dark and the crowd had become threatening. Men pushed aggressively, grabbing at them and at the bags. One had squeezed her breast so hard that she had a three-finger pinch bruise for a week. Another time a band of irate Greeks, bristly locals, probably drunk, had confronted them with sticks and told them they should stop encouraging people to come and ruin their island and their businesses. After a couple of beers and a shared cigarette, Freya, wheaten hair falling over her tanned shoulders, admitted that she was scared to be alone with the refugees. She remained determined, but she had developed the jaded ambivalence

I recognized from do-gooders in Iraq. Freya's full quote was: "They are fleeing war. I know we have an obligation as fellow human beings to help them, but sometimes it's frightening and I don't want to."

————

I left Kos dispirited. I had to change planes in Athens. I had an hour transit time, but there was a huge queue at security. Eight cordoned lanes snaked back and forth. Hundreds of people, babes in arms, patient pensioners, a headphoned Zen guy. We shuffled along, waited, shuffled along. The security officer manning one of the X-ray machines had a beard and a trimmed moustache. He barked at me in Greek. He barked again in English. "Put your bag here, no there, computer out! What is in your pockets?" I struggled to heft my bag onto the belt. Worried about missing the connection, I looked at my watch.

"Take your watch off!"

"My watch is plastic."

"Take your watch off."

"Why?"

"Security. Security," he repeated. *Security.* Meaningless. The X-ray idiots stared at green and orange jumbled outline of shapes all day long and saw nothing. The body scanner operators laughed at our bodies, just as I had once laughed at an Iraqi woman in a village who swore to me that the American soldiers had special binoculars that could see through women's clothes.

The security idiot said "security" again.

"Security is an abstract noun," I retorted. "If you are looking for a bomb, say you are looking for a bomb. Do I look like I have a bomb?" By now I was shouting. The word "bomb" detonated among the tourists. Everyone went quiet. "Why are you strip-searching all of us and letting in hundreds and thousands of God know who—anybody—and not stopping anyone. Not stopping them, rescuing them!"

I hurled my coat onto the conveyor belt and tried to march through the metal detector, but the beard blocked my way. He pointed to a sign that said aggression against security staff will not be tolerated and will be dealt with by all legal means necessary. "Am I being aggressive? Am I attacking anyone?" I swept my hands over the vast mass behind me, "Are we all terrorists? We are forced through airports like cattle! This is not security, it is fascism!"

As if on cue, two policemen appeared. They were wearing black Gore Tex uniforms and carrying submachine guns. One of them took a step towards me. I thought I was about to be arrested. I shut up. I put my hands in the air as if in surrender.

"OK, OK, OK," I said, and kept walking. (Jean's checkpoint policy: raise your hands in the air, flash a big smile, walk slowly, pretend you don't understand the instructions to stop and, most important of all, *keep walking*.) I walked through the metal detector and mercifully it did not beep. I collected my bags from the other side of the X-ray machine without looking up. Encumbered, I stuck the boarding pass in my teeth. *Keep walking.* I didn't look back. Departure flight screens, gate numbers, long strides down the corridors. My Air France flight was already boarding. I was so angry, I sat in the narrow rigid metal chair all the way back to Paris and fumed. *No, I don't want coffee, I don't want tea, I don't want your plastic wrapped slimy sandwich.* When the man in front of me leaned his chair back, I kicked it sharply.

PART V

PARIS

ONE

I heard the shots underwater in the bath. The enamel made a faint percussive ting against my inner ear, a drumbeat. When I raised my head to hear better, I heard another sharp crack, felt the weight of it, a solid sound, and then another. Ripples echoed on the surface of the water.

I leapt out of the bath and dressed fast. Checked my bag for pencil, notebook, phone, keys, passport. I put on sneakers in case I needed to run, tied the laces tight. It was Friday night, I was alone, Little Ahmed was staying with Grégoire for a sleepover. I put on my anorak and went down to the street with my hair still wet. It was early November, not cold, not winter yet. The streets were slick because it had rained earlier and the leaves were piled up in damp drifts.

Along the canal it looked as if nothing had happened: pools of yellow streetlamp light, couples sitting on the low concrete wall with a bottle of wine between them. A jaunty young man with slicked-back hair and a ready-for-it grin walked past, bouncing on the balls of his feet. The shots had stopped and I stopped for a moment to think, to reorient myself. Which direction had they come from? Across the slice of dark water, I saw the young crowd outside Le Verre Volé hurriedly scattering. One man ran and his girlfriend called after him, urgent and frightened, "Wait!" He ran past me, slammed against my shoulder, and kept going.

People were running or walking quickly in the opposite direction. A man in skinny jeans bent like a pipe cleaner over his phone, a girl raggedly pulled along by a large man. "*Yallah!*" he shouted to her in Arabic. A motorcycle roared past. A taxi crawled behind, looking for someone to pick up.

Metal shutters rattled and a face popped out beneath one and cried out to me, "Come in! Come inside!" Pale oval face, arched eyebrows, rose pink lips. I was not afraid. I kept walking. Not fast, not slow, looking all around me, behind me, up too—people had come to their windows and were leaning out to try and see what was going on.

"What's happening?" someone called down.

I turned left, away from the canal, down the Rue Albert. A man limped past me, dragging one foot. He had no jacket and there was blood on his T-shirt. He looked at me and I looked at him. I did not say anything and neither did he.

I looked at my feet and saw my navy blue sneakers against the dark tarmac street glistening with mica stars. I saw a blue pebble of shattered windscreen glass. This was all very familiar. It was inevitable. It was almost—how to explain this strange feeling of disassociation. Journalism? It was almost a relief. I had the clear sense that I was exactly where I should be.

The blue circular chips of scattered glass glittered like diamonds. How oddly beautiful! I was at the crossroads by Le Carillon. Café tables and chairs were overturned, and among them bodies had fallen in dark triangular shapes. Nobody tells you about the awkwardness of limbs when they are violently dead, bent wrong, jutting unnatural angles. Not even Géricault could render this. The worst thing of all was that some of these terrible shapes were still moving. The blood on the streets was black at night, not red as I was used to in Baghdad, but black and shiny, like oil.

A siren wailed a single note and fell silent. An ambulance crew went to work between the shadows of the flashing blue light, between awful illumination and dark matter. I stood there and watched. *I am a camera.* I did not take any pictures.

The medics knelt at each body and felt for a pulse at the neck. They waved for stretchers. One sat a woman up and bent her arm close to her chest to staunch the bleeding. Another moved among the bodies, laying tablecloths over the dead as shrouds. Slowly the scene became animated and filled up the silence with sounds. Short gasping utterances, here, here, *ici*. The police appeared and pushed back those few, like me, who had been drawn to the scene.

There was a young man next to me with a big hipster beard who was texting with great concentration. He looked up for a moment and said, "They are saying there has been a bomb explosion at the Stade de France, and at the Louvre."

"Go home!" a policeman shouted at us, agitated. "Everyone go home, get inside!" He wore black leather gloves, a riot helmet with a black protective flange that covered the back of his neck, and heavy plastic shin guards. He looked like an armored beetle.

I thought: I can walk to the Louvre from here—it's far, but not so far. I tried to call Little Ahmed, but the circuits were jammed. Call failed. I texted: *Stay inside, don't go out.* I kept walking, long strides, down the canal, towards Bastille, in the direction of the Louvre. Police cars flashed past. There were still a few people on the street; hurried exchanges—*They're shooting at bars! Where? Where?* I walked past a homeless man bundled inside a green sleeping bag and lying against a ventilation grille.

I thought: Everything is gathered here tonight on the point of a spear. I felt a crystalized determination, a confidence. Was it vindication? I reached the point where the Canal Saint-Martin is paved over with a stripe of park and it flows underground to meet the Seine. Gunfire, close and loud.

I crouched down next to a rose bush. A streetlight shone above me, like an orange sodium moon. I moved into the shadow; the rose pricked my cheek and snagged in my wet hair. There was an azalea bush nearby and I crawled underneath its branches. The glossy evergreen leaves made an umbrella. I was hidden. The gunfire continued. A lot of it, *bang! bang! bang!* Single shots, aim and squeeze. Then bursts, *ratta-tatta-tatta*, a cracked staccato rhythm I knew well. The single shots were more terrible. *Crack!* Very precise, very clear, very definite, each sound a death.

I crawled through the flower bed, twigs and cigarette butts and soft mud clots between my fingers. I was hidden, no one could see me. I pressed my tummy into the soil, and it was an enormous comfort to know that half of me was protected by the permanent, solid earth beneath. I turned my phone off; I did not dare risk it ringing or the screen lighting up to give me away.

I put my arms over my head and shuggled deeper to minimize my exposure. I conceived the idea that as long as no sliver of my white face was showing, I was invisible. I kissed the earth, felt my mouth against the clean alkaline tang of the earth. I wriggled myself into a little hollow. *Bang!* A metallic noise chipped like a pickaxe. Would it be better if they used swords, the technology available to the original armies of Mohammed? "Would you prefer to die by blade or bullet, Kitty Cat?" A typically Faustian question of Ahmed's. I didn't know. I only knew that I hated the sound, the insistent *bang-bang-bang-bang*, and I began to pray that it would stop.

It did not stop.

I felt the fear tingle in my fingertips the way it used to in Baghdad. I was not prone to panic or stasis. I was lucky. Jean said, "You get this from your father." (Certainly, I did not get my nerves from my mother.) I felt fear as a fizzing in my fingertip nerves, not as a heart-clanging clamor. *Hold me, hold me tight!* I felt my thoughts bounce through slideshow memory scenes . . . *Cut! Make it stop!* I held my breath.

It did not stop.

I began to count the shots. Fifty, sixty-two, seventy, eighty-nine . . . *bang-bang* . . . a hundred. I stopped counting. I realized I felt cold. My left leg ached. I flexed the muscle in situ. I inched to one side to stop a stone digging into my kneecap. There was a smooth pebble next to my ear and I thought perhaps I could listen to its whisperings as the water talked to me. (It said nothing.) My wet hair made a cold hat on my head. I didn't know if time had sped up or slowed down. Had I been lying there ten minutes or an hour?

The shots stopped.

I exhaled. I had not realized I had stopped breathing. Then the shots began again, a hundred and thirty, two hundred and thirty, three, four, five, six . . . Then another pause.

I inched forward on my elbows. I was cold, but there was no use in thinking about being cold because there was nothing I could do about it. It was not cold enough to freeze or to get hypothermia. Granbet appeared in my head and told me, in her practical and reassuring way, "There are three things in your favor, listen and pay attention: Little Ahmed is with Grégoire; they are safe, so do not worry in this direction. You are hiding in a bush and no one can see you. And this will end and you will be home again soon, you will come in from the cold and be warm. Nothing lasts forever."

"Except death, Granbet."

I wriggled forward, deeper into the azalea bush, which entangled itself with a thicket of incongruous bamboo. I raised my head so that I could see the street on the other side of the canal park, tiger stripes of orange light through the stalks of bamboo. I could see that I was opposite the façade of the Bataclan theater. There were groups of people in a side alley, crouching, hiding, hunched together, clinging in twos and threes.

The façade of the building was decorated as an ornate theatrical curtain, looped with swag and announcing in big billboard lettering THE EAGLES OF DEATH METAL. But there were no eagles, only pigeons cooing. A pigeon hopped along a railing on pink deformed legs, bright- eyed, head cocked to one side. Then he flew off and I followed his flapping wings up along the Quai Voltaire. He landed on a striped awning above a shuttered café. On the sidewalk there was a body lying in a pool of light, one long arm outstretched, waving slowly goodbye. The groups of people escaping down the alley began to break cover between the starburst fusillades, running away.

A big red fire engine arrived in a blaze of sirens and blue light. Two policemen appeared from behind it and advanced towards the front door with their handguns drawn. I thought to call out a warning to them, but there was no time before a volley came from an entrance and they went backwards, firing, then forward firing, *en garde*, fencing with the gunfire.

The gunman who had been firing from the entrance retreated inside and barred the door. The street filled with police vans, ambulances, and hundreds of uniforms, helmets, and automatic weapons. The police led away survivors who had been sheltering in the surrounding streets. A young man with a stripe of blue hair, shivering in a T-shirt, bent over his girlfriend. She had blood running down the side of her face. He held her so tenderly. The police were rougher, grabbing to rescue her. She stumbled barefoot. She looked up from the ground to try and make sense of where she was and she seemed to look straight at me, but her gaze was unfocused and indistinct. She was not dead, but it was as if she hadn't yet realized that she was alive.

I saw a policeman with an officer's hat stride forward and point at everyone in a muscular way to move back. But when he got back into his car, no one did anything he said. The gunshots all but ceased from the interior of the Bataclan and a strange atmosphere descended on the scene. The wounded were taken away, the police vans arranged themselves as an articulated metal vehicle screen. Police tape was stretched across the intersections. I spotted Zorro coming up the road from the direction of Bastille with his camera waving like a surrender flag. "Let me through!" A policeman in a motorcycle helmet pushed him back brusquely. I thought of texting him, but I did not dare risk the ping of a reply.

I lay there, listening to people die. After fear, anger; after anger, fear again. In this new incarnation it did not tingle with excited shock but felt as heavy as a frozen blanket, leaching cold into my hunched shoulders, cold to the bone, to the marrow of me. I could no longer see the façade of the Bataclan because there were so many police vans parked in front of it. My toes were cold. My hair had dried into stiff strands. I turned my head to one side and nestled it in the crook of my arm and let my thoughts wander where they would—as random as a pigeon. Where was my pigeon who had gone to roost above the dying man? Flown away.

I could see a small group of people, Zorro among them, a hundred meters away across the road. One man was sitting on a doorstep cradling his phone in his lap, another stood leaning against a wall with his hands in his pockets just watching the scene, like me. He had a knit cap pulled down over his forehead and wore orange sneakers. I watched him for a while watching. Did he have a friend inside? Someone he loved? I couldn't see his face well. He talked into a phone. He looked behind him down the alley. He scratched his temple. He shifted his weight from one leg to another and held his hand over his face for a few moments, in a gesture of tension or absolution. I wished him well, I hoped it would be OK for him, that his friend would be alive.

I couldn't see his face well beneath the knit cap. He was busy with his phone. He looked down at the phone and then glanced sideways, squinting at the corner of the Bataclan where the police were concentrated. He raised his head and looked up and around him. I looked up with him and saw the silhouettes of police snipers moving on the rooftops. A soft wind blew the trees.

When the police began their final assault, the sound of gunfire was interminable. I covered my head with my hands, dug myself deeper into the earth. I thought it would go on forever. When I looked back at the corner again, the man with the orange sneakers had gone.

Finally, the police began to come out of the building shepherding survivors. Their faces were blank and immobile. Some stumbled barefoot. The gunfire had stopped. There was a gap in the police vehicles, and I saw a still life framed between the white metal of the police van and the horizontals made by the foreshortened perspective of the curb and sidewalk, a motorcycle boot studded with pink gemstones and an empty green beer bottle that glowed like alien blood under the flashing blue light.

———

I got up from the dirt and walked away without looking back. The noises dissipated into clangs and thuds, like distant construction. Or maybe this was just my brain muffling the impact. I walked across the narrow park to the other side of the road. Now that it was over I felt an overwhelming physical need to see Little Ahmed, to hold him safe and tight. I turned on my phone. It vibrated violently. One hundred three missed calls. Little Ahmed, Little Ahmed, Little Ahmed. I scrolled through his texts:

> **Don't go out there is shooting**
> **Again**
> **Please**
> **Kit**
> **Don't go out!**
> **Call me**

Where are you?

You're phone is off. The circuits are busy. I can't whats app.

If you get this try whats app

If you have gone to journalist Ill never speak to you again

I will speak to you

Sorry

But Ill be very angry

I mean Im not angry

Dont worry

Just call

Dont not think I dont love you

I mean I love you you know

I love you

I held this precious rectangle in my cold hands and it rang.

"Ahmed."

"Where have you been where have you been are you OK are you in hospital are you shot?"

"I'm OK," I said. "Where were you? I called and you didn't answer!"

"YOU DIDNT ANSWER, YOU WERE NOT at home! I called Clothilde next door, I made her walk across the hall and knock on our door and she said no one was there. I called the man downstairs who woke up Batshit the concierge and he came up with the key and opened the door. And YOU WERENT THERE."

"I'm OK, baby, I'm OK. I'm sorry. I'm so sorry. I had to turn my phone off. Are you at Grégoire's now?"

"No, nearby."

"Text me the address, I'm coming now."

"No, Kit—"

"Just text me the address."

42 rue Stephenson Code 23A45 2e étage a gauche

I walked to the métro at Jacques Bonsergent. The streets were quiet but not empty. People were walking, talking into their phones. I looked at my watch. It was one-fifteen in the morning—the witching hour of the métro. Luckily it was still open. A young guy ran from behind me and jumped the barrier, barging, and my fear, held at bay, nearly home nearly to Ahmed, burst into a raw flower again.

The train rattled through the tunnel, a string of yellow lit carriages. Tunnels felt safe, which was nonsensical. I sat opposite a couple who were holding each other's hands. I studied their fingers, intertwined, a complex tangle of knuckled wrinkles, creases, interloops, shades of brown and pink.

The metro jerked in the tunnel. The world shuddered. Jean had called Charlie a fulcrum moment, when history tips into a new chapter, weighed by an incident that hardly seems more incremental than the last headline, but which somehow suddenly changes everything. Like Gavrilo Princip, he said, or all those forgotten telegrams and ultimatums of the nineteenth century. Something whispered, something misunderstood, a loud bang—and then a start, the reaction.

Is this what happened to me? When something traumatic happens, you are changed by it and nothing is the same again. Violence hits you like a billiard ball hitting another billiard ball and life goes off on a completely different angle. I saw it happen so many times to other people. Did I imagine that I was immune? Yes, I think I did.

I got out at Barbès. The pirate cigarette sellers who Zorro said were all police informers were gone. The corner that was always such a Maghrebi African market bustle of rustling paper kebab wrappers and the smell of popcorn was now weirdly quiet. I looked up at the windows that should have been dark and asleep at this hour, but they were all glowing with blue television light. I walked along the boulevard, past the encampment of migrant tents underneath a section of elevated métro line.

No. 42 Rue Stephenson was a modern block that backed up against the rail cutting that led into the Gare du Nord. The windows were small and square, the façade paved with pale blue tiles like a municipal swimming pool. Satellite dishes were bolted at intervals like ear-shaped fungi. I tapped the code and the door buzzed open. The elevator needed a key so I walked up the stairs. The lights were on an automatic timer that clicked on only when I had passed, so that the light was behind me as I walked up into the dark.

I knocked on the door. Voices inside the apartment halted, a chair scraped. I heard a man say something in sharp undertones. I couldn't catch the words, but they sounded irritated and wary. The chain tinkled and scratched and the door opened a fraction. A man stood there wearing a brown dishdasha with red slippers on his feet. He was short and tubby and had a bristle moustache and a spade-shaped beard. There was a deep furrow at the bridge of his nose and a dark disc of welted prayer callus on his forehead. I told him I was Ahmed's mother, that he'd said he was with Grégoire, and I'd come to pick him up. He did not answer but looked behind him where a bulky woman wearing a long house gown was hurriedly wrapping a black scarf around her head.

"I am Um Ahmed," she said. Her voice was thickly accented and reticent.

"I am Ahmed's mother," I repeated. I thought she was confused. "I am Mrs. Solemani." I never used this name, but I wanted to explain my formal connection to Ahmed.

"Our other son is also called Ahmed," said the father, realizing the mistake.

"Grégoire's brother?" I said. "I did not know he had a brother."

I realized I did not know very much about Grégoire. When he had first come over to the apartment a year or so earlier, I asked him if he wanted to call his mother and let her know where he was. But he said no thanks, that she wasn't expecting him until later, that it was OK. I wondered if it *had* been OK. Hadn't Grégoire told them where he went when he came over those afternoons after school? His parents seemed to have no inkling of me. I could see their discomfiture. They hesitated to ask me in.

"His name is not Grégoire," said the father, "it is Ghaith—"

"Ghr?"

"Ghaith—it is Grégoire's real name. But it is difficult for the French to pronounce it. So he uses Grégoire." He sighed as he said it, as if it was the beginning of a long list of disappointments.

Behind them on the wall of the narrow hall was a calendar with a picture of the black meteorite cube Kaaba surrounded by concentric ranks of white-robed faithful.

"Where is Ahmed? My Ahmed? I came to take him home." I took a step forward.

"They are not here," said the mother.

"He told me to meet him here—I want him to come home. The attacks—"

"He is safe," said the father.

"Where are they?"

"They are at the mosque with Ghaith's brother Ahmed."

"At the mosque?" There followed a small pause, neither of them replied. What were they doing at the mosque? "Look. Can I come in and wait for him?" Neither of them moved. "He said he would meet me here." The father opened his palms, as if to say it was out of his hands.

The mother pulled on the loose fabric of her husband's dishdasha as a signal for him to relent. She took a step backwards and moved her hand to indicate that I could enter. She ushered me into the kitchen. On the right I could see the reception room through an open door, a slice of beige sofa with orange-and-gold cushions, beige carpet with a prayer mat laid on top. On the coffee table there was a half-eaten plate of food and a tulip glass of tea with an inch of sugar in the bottom. The TV was on, the news in Arabic on Al Jazeera. I realized they were Iraqis. The details of tulip glass, the wooden prayer beads wrapped around the father's wrist like a chain around a fist. I could smell lamb fat and cinnamon-cumin. I looked down at my feet. I had tracked mud all over the carpet. I reached up to touch my face and a fine sprinkle of dried soil flaked off.

The father returned to his sofa in the other room. I heard him make a call and speak in Arabic to someone. I stood in the kitchen next to a table that was covered with a plastic oil cloth printed with roses and Mickey Mouse. The mother turned towards the stove and away from me.

"Where were they tonight?" I asked. "I thought they would be here. I did not think they would be out, on the street." I was angry about this. "Were they walking Grégoire's dogs?" The mother turned back to me with a box of tissues. Tea and a box of tissues; Iraqis were almost English in their useless niceties. When I didn't take a tissue, she touched her face to indicate that I needed to wash mine. I took a tissue because I was obliged to. I crumpled it in one hand and repeated, "Where were they all night—? A night full of attacks?" She did not reply. I thought perhaps she did not speak French and had not understood me. Frustrated, I mimed, *bang-bang-bang!* with my hand as a gun and dredged up a couple of Arabic words, *"Awlad wen?"*— Where boys?

The mother pointed to the chair for me to sit down. I did not want to sit down. That's the first thing an Arab bureaucrat will tell you: *Please take a seat, just one minute.* If you sit down, you will wait all day.

"He is safe," she said finally, forcing the unfamiliar French words with an Arabic intonation. "They are with Grégoire's older brother."

"His older brother who is called Ahmed." I said, overwhelmed by Ahmeds. Where was mine?

"But what were they doing all evening? Why are they still out?"

"Ghaith does not have any dogs," said the mother, as if I had said something ridiculous. "You live in the *onzième*, yes?" I nodded. "Near the attacks." What could I say? I had thought to go home, to take Ahmed home, where it was safe, but who knew if this night was over yet? I sat down defeated. She put a glass of tea and a saucer of biscuits on the table. I dabbed at my face with the tissue. "We were also worried," she said. "*Alhamdulillah*, Ghaith is a good boy, but the police can catch anyone at a time like this, so we were very worried—"

"Very worried. The police!" echoed her husband, appearing in the doorway.

"And the telephones were not working, so this was also very worrying."

"Finally, Ghaith answered and said that they had taken shelter in the mosque because it was not good to be on the street and the mosque was closer. And it was the time of the evening prayer, so Ghaith knew his brother would be there." Grégoire's mother spoke perfectly sincerely and I wanted to strangle her. She sat down next to me and took my hands in hers. This was unbearable.

"Don't—" I said.

"He is safe, my sister, Um Ahmed," she said. She closed her eyes and added, piously,

"*Alhamdulillah*." I withdrew my hands and stood up.

"We could not find you," said Grégoire's father. "Ahmed was very worried," he added. "He was sure you would go to the scene because you are a journalist." He drew this last word out so that it sounded like an accusation. "He was worried and they were praying."

"To pray? To pray for who?" Now I was really furious. "Do you think prayers make any difference? These people are killing with God on their side! They are killing and they are the martyrs! Yes, let's pray! I am sure that will help! Allah O Akbar and blow everything up!"

"To pray for you," said Grégoire's mother softly.

I turned to leave, but suddenly there was Little Ahmed, standing in the doorway between Grégoire and Grégoire's brother Ahmed. His face was full of shock and his green eyes glowed like Kryptonite in the dim hallway.

"Kit, stop it," he said sharply; a rebuke, telling me off, like I was the child. Turning to Grégoire he added, "You see what I mean," and I felt the cold iceberg tip of a larger, submerged complaint. Grégoire gave him a sideways glance, as if to say, not now, and put his hand out to shake mine and said politely, "Hello, Madame Solemani, I am sorry we were late."

Grégoire's brother Ahmed was tall and thin and sallow-skinned. He wore a dishdasha with a leather jacket over it and a white knit prayer cap on his head. His face was smooth but for an incipient straggly beard. He was very calm. He put his hand on my Ahmed's shoulder, as if he had authority over him.

"You see, I was right," he said to Little Ahmed. "You mother is safe, just as I said. *Alhamdulillah*." He added a phrase in Arabic in the cadence of Koranic recitation. I could not stand this. I could not stand his certitude and sanctimony.

"Did your prayers help?" I asked him. "Did God save anyone tonight or did he kill them?" The pious Ahmed blinked and swallowed. Very carefully, with infinite patience, as if explaining clear evidence to a child, he replied, "Everything is written according to God's will."

"Which is the same thing you say when you shoot people. Allah O Akbar!"

"Kit—" my Ahmed stepped forward to intervene. "You're crazy. You're embarrassing me."

"It's alright," said Ahmed the preacher, maintaining his rectitude and composure. "She does not know the right way to believe. It is not her fault."

"I can't listen to this *merde*," I said. "Come on, Ahmed, we should leave."

I moved forward to push through to the door and tried to grab Little Ahmed's hand, but he shook himself free. Grégoire's brother Ahmed put his body in front of the door to stop me.

"Madame Solemani," he said. "We have been in the mosque, place of sanctuary, to pray for you because Ahmed was worried that you would rush to the Bataclan because you are a journalist. For three hours he tried to call you and your phone was off." He spoke with eminent reasonableness, but he was not reasonable at all. "Do you think it is a good idea to take him home now to this area where there was shooting? Please consider the safety of the child." He did not say "your child" I noticed. He had already claimed Little Ahmed for himself, apart from me; I was not a real Muslim. I spat his disdain back at him.

"Do not claim to me that a mosque is a safe place," I said to him, squarely, caustic. "It is a room full of narrow-minded people who will tell you there is no other way to be in the world but their way. You are so convinced of your own divine rectitude that anything you disagree with is denigrated. Your religion forces obedience and submission as if God was a dictator. I don't want you ever to take my son to such a place again."

"It is the duty of all Muslims—" the brother began, taking a breath to absorb my outburst. I cut him off.

"I am sorry." (Why did I apologize? Some latent British gene probably.) "No more. Do you know what your religion is doing? It is killing people!"

"I do not agree with the attacks," said the brother.

"Yeah yeah. But will you condemn them?"

Little Ahmed stood without speaking. His eyes flashed from me to this other arguing Ahmed to Grégoire's mother, who held her hands to her mouth, appalled, to Grégoire's father, who shuffled forward in his slippers and tried to remonstrate by raising his hands up and down like bellows. I saw him mouth *"désolé"* to Grégoire.

"Should I ask you to condemn what Christians do?" The pious brother countered. An old liberal equivalency argument.

"What Christian suicide bombers?"

"Israeli bombs that kill Palestinian children. American drones that kill brides on their wedding days. Is this not terrorism?"

"Aha!" I had him now. "So because other people are doing it, it is OK for you to do it."

"But I am not doing it!"

"No, you are going to pray in a mosque for the enlightenment of all unbelievers and the day when the Caliphate will return to rule the world. Because of course all good Muslims should want to live under Sharia law. What's the difference between you and the terrorists? A degree of violence is the only difference; the aim is the same. In fact you are a hypocrite because you let others fight for what you believe in."

"You have insulted me and insulted my religion," the brother said starkly, as if this was the most unforgivable thing in the world.

"I can say what I like," I said. "I don't have to respect your beliefs."

"You are not a Muslim." This was, I guessed, the worst thing he thought he could say to me, the greatest insult he knew. I shrugged.

"Alhamdulillah and fuck you."

I barged through the narrow hallway and took Little Ahmed's hand and pulled him hard. He snatched it away. Still, he came with me.

We did not talk on the way home. I felt Little Ahmed's fury as he walked long strides beside me. When we got home, he went into his room and shut the door. I sat down on the sofa and poured myself a glass of calvados and shook. Oz was in my inbox. He wanted me to write something. I wrote *something something something something something* across a whole page for half an hour and sent it to him as an attachment.

——

In the morning I woke up so late that Little Ahmed had already gone to school. My anger had not subsided. The apartment closed in and I went outside. The world was lighter by daylight, but still gray. Gray cobblestones, black tarmac, motorcycles and strollers cramming narrow sidewalks. I barked at a woman in front of me, walking so slowly that I could not get past. The tall elegant windows and curlicue wrought-iron balconies were impassive observers. Baguettes in the bakeries, métro grates rumbling, dog shit and bollards. A vitrine of chocolate bonbons tied with ribbons. This is what it looked like when France fell in 1940, I thought. The day after, but just the same.

I walked up the steps of Montmartre and found myself standing in front of Rousse's apartment block. I knew the codes by heart and I took the old metal cage lift up and let myself in with my key. I sat cross-legged on the wooden floorboards amid the stacked canvases, still wearing my coat because the heating had been turned off. I flipped through the most recent pile of pasteboards again. I found the picture of Little Ahmed with the gun. Little Ahmed had said, "It was nothing really. It was just an idea she had. It wasn't a real Kalashnikov! Seriously, Kit, come on. It was a replica."

"So where is this replica now?" Little Ahmed had shrugged when I'd asked.

"Dunno."

In Rousse's portrait, Little Ahmed was still a child, with a narrow bare torso, delicate ribcage, the long slender bones of his arms were thinner than the rifle stock. He was looking back at me with an expression which I had thought was defiance or anger, but as I looked at it more closely now, staring hard enough to blur the image with my tears, I noticed a hint of amusement at the corners of his mouth. Had Rousse made him laugh just before she took the picture?

I sat there for a while, raging. At Little Ahmed and Grégoire's complicity. At Grégoire's pious, righteous brother. The anger dug deeper with every thought.

I got up from the floor and walked over to the kitchenette to make a cup of tea. A cup of tea. A nice cup of tea. My mad English mother who did nothing but drink cups of tea and watch *EastEnders* and *Crimewatch* and smoke and spout stupid platitudes when I was upset. But when she was upset, which was always, because she was depressed and neurotic and either going on or coming off lithium, she would rant and rave to her heart's content. Nevermind, have a cup of tea. I picked up the teacup and hurled it against the wall. It smashed.

I bent down to pick up the shards of china and noticed a plastic bag against the wall. Inside were three or four spray-paint cans and a stencil of a Kalashnikov with a croissant trigger and another with flying madeleines as bullets.

TWO

For the next three days, Little Ahmed endured me in silence. He went to school, he came home again and went into his room and closed the door against me.

Oz sent harrying emails. I would not be allowed to recuse myself this time. Professionalism, or something. "Your contract is coming up—" I did not tell him that I had hidden in a flower bed outside the Bataclan the whole night. I did not tell anyone. It seemed so surreal that I did not trust my memory of it.

There was some distraction in working, in running around to trace the route of the attack sites. Le Carillon was boarded up. Someone had stuck a rose through the jagged bullet hole in the window, and people politely took turns taking a picture of it. The Bataclan was cordoned off for several blocks. The strip of park where I had hidden was behind police tape. TV vans were parked up at the crossroads and stand-ups jabbered in the spotlights. I went into nearby cafés to talk to people for reaction quotes. One of them was the immigrant from Mali who had been working in the kosher supermarket during the Charlie attacks in January and saved people by hiding them in the basement cold room. It turned out he lived two blocks away from the Bataclan and had gone out that night when he heard the first gunshots and got stuck between police cordons, unable to go home.

"It's like having to go through it all over again," he said.

I wrote a story about a bartender opposite Le Carillon who had spent the night in lockdown, desperately trying to text his friends in the neighborhood to make sure they were OK. I wrote about the doctors in the emergency room at the Saint-Louis hospital who worked all night as the casualties came in. Oz pressed me to find witnesses, people who had been inside the Bataclan when the terrorists had burst in and opened fire. I pushed contacts for contacts, I cold-called. *I'm sorry my sister cannot talk. We are only existing between the telephone and the hospital room. We don't have anything else to say. I have not slept for three nights.* I did not have the heart to convince them to talk. Too raw, too soon; I knew how it was when you can't trust yourself to make sense, not to scream and cry and rail.

I went to the supermarket. Another brightly lit banality. Red plastic basket, Nutella, lardons, orange juice, speculoos biscuits, Weetabix, more calvados.

On the way home I saw three men standing next to a garage. Jeans, hoodies, puffer jackets, dark beards. One of them had a submachine gun hanging around his neck.

"Are you police?" I asked. They had no identification.

"Yes, we are police."

"But how can I tell?

———

My hands hovered over the keyboard, fingers cramped like claws. Sentences blurred before my eyes and swam together. The red numerals on the digital clock blinked 23:24. It was too late for Little Ahmed to still be out, but I didn't want to call him and face another argument. Presently, I heard his footsteps in the corridor. Crumpfing heavy Timberlands on tiptoes; he was trying to be quiet. I heard the clunky double click of the door latch unlocking and then closing. I should have called out to him, Hi, Heya—something, but I didn't trust the tone of my voice. He went into his room and shut the door. I stared at the screen, but I couldn't see the words through my tears. Tomorrow, I thought, tomorrow, I'll take him to McDonald's and I'll say I'm sorry.

I kept working for another couple of hours and fell into bed exhausted. It was still dark when Zorro woke me up to tell me that the police had surrounded the suspected terrorists in a house in Saint-Denis.

———

Drumbeats, but the rhythm was discordant. Gunshots, heartbeats, footsteps. The métro roared through the tunnels on my way home. The crowd and the sirens of the police raid receded, but left, in their wake, white noise screaming in my head.

I dressed for lunch with Alexandre and Jean at Le Grand Véfour in my severe black Dior funeral suit and wore red-for-Rousse sneakers in case I needed to run. I was nervous and scratchy. Little Ahmed had probably called Margot and told her I was going mad. I braced myself for an intervention.

I arrived a little early. I came in from the battleship gray streets, from the cold, into the surreality of warmth and light, twinkling chandeliers and shimmering mirrors.

"Madame," said the maître d', showing me to a red velvet banquette. "L'Ambassadeur Monsieur Delacroix always likes to reserve the emperor's table."

I sank into the soft cushion and looked about me. Cherubs smiled from the gilded plasterwork and peeped out from beneath the imperial swags and acanthus of Napoleon's First Empire. Roman goddesses and nymphs held platters of pomegranates above their heads; the ceiling was painted with wreaths of roses and borders of laurel leaves. The light sparkled in rubies and diamonds on the edges of silverware and the rims of wineglasses and gleamed in the antique mirrors that bloomed with silver-speckled galaxies. I saw myself reflected, refracted into three aspects; one pinkish under an incandescent sconce, one a hard-edged profile, and the last a view of myself I had never seen. A congruence of looking-glass angles had caught me almost from behind, a jowl of mottled cheek cut with a garish stripe of lipstick which some further optical trick of light and shadow had turned black.

I was a clown monster. I hated myself, but I could not help it. Drop an unseen tear, watch it spread a circle stain on the white tablecloth. When I looked up, my eyes were underwater.

Sitting alone at Balzac's corner table, almost hiding behind an urn filled with white lilies, was a strange little man wearing John Lennon glasses with yellow lenses and a rumpled corduroy jacket. *It's Charlie!* I whispered to myself. He looked sad. He picked up a red china pencil and began sketching on the snowy damask tablecloth. He drew a man with long floppy arms tipping a glass of champagne down his throat and the champagne pouring out of all the holes in his body where he had been shot through like a colander.

Alexandre and Jean arrived together. There was always a certain superciliousness to Alexandre. When he arrived, I saw that in retirement, this tendency had been indulged. He divested himself of his periwinkle cashmere coat. His face looked taut, as if he had his eyes done. He kissed me *bonjour* on each cheek and ordered a bottle of champagne and a glass of crème de menthe.

"Margot sends her love," Jean said. "She says, please call her." Rapprochement or committal?

A highball of crème de menthe appeared. The waiter poured my champagne; it hissed delicately.

"How are you doing, Kit? Did you manage to sleep a bit?" Jean asked. Kind, always so kind. "It's a horrible week, it's a horrible week for everyone."

"I'm fine."

"And Little Ahmed?"

"Ahmed is fine," I said. One corner of Jean's thin lips contracted.

"Kittredge," Alexandre tried now, as delicately solicitous as if he were treading on the toes of an ayatollah. "I know it has brought it all back. Rousse . . ." he trailed off diplomatically.

"It just reopens old wounds," said Jean.

"For all of us," said Alexandre.

"I am not wounded," I said. "I am angry."

"It's not good to be angry," Jean said quietly. "Anger is the same as shooting."

"No it's not." I had not shot anyone.

"I mean that the way we *are* in the world affects the world," said Jean.

"Yeah, yeah, and other platitudes and Margot psychological tidbits. It's not *my* fault they are killing people," I said. I swallowed another mouthful of champagne, honeycomb dissolving into a viscous, medicinal syrup in my mouth. "Before I was in the middle, trying to communicate one to the other, going back and forth from Paris to the Middle East all these years—reporting, listening, writing. But after Charlie, no. They made me choose a side. And now again—"

The waiter hovered deferentially. Alexandre ordered the duck liver ravioli. Jean, snails with chestnut purée and caviar. I was not hungry, but I asked for the sweetbreads.

"You are so like your father," said Jean. "Collecting the anguish of everyone's outrage, absorbing all the pain in the world, trying so hard to make it better and then punishing yourself for failing."

"That is what destroyed my father," I said. "He should have stayed at home."

"He couldn't stay at home," said Jean. "He was drafted."

"I didn't know that."

"It was the early seventies. It was the time of the dreaded birthday lottery. Calling people up to fight in Vietnam. He did not want to fight in that war."

"But he went to war all the same."

"Yes," sighed Alexandre. "He went to war all the same—"

"We all did," said Jean, the former second lieutenant.

"It doesn't make any difference," I said. "War comes anyway, whether we choose it or not."

"We can choose how to fight it," said Jean.

"Are you going to tell me the pen is mightier than the sword, or some such rubbish?" I glanced at my imaginary friend in the corner. *Ask Charlie if he thinks cartoons are any defense against Kalashnikovs. Writing, debating—that's the very thing they wanted to destroy!*

"This anger," said Jean, wearily, "will destroy us all." He looked at me, but he was talking more broadly. "Our response has to be different. We can't repeat Algeria. We need a new kind of humanism, a new enlightenment. It's not enough just to reiterate our old values."

"But it *is* about our values!" I said. "After Charlie, after the Bataclan. Shooting people having a drink on the terrace, in bars, at a football match, at a concert. It's exactly an attack on our values!"

"We are all swept with raw emotions," said Jean. "It's been a difficult few days. Everything will be a bit calmer in a week or so."

"No," I said. "You said the same last time and it will happen again."

The food arrived with funereal pomp. We ate in silence. I cut into my thymus and it bled a trickle of pink jus into the gutter of the plate. Our knives and forks made a hollow percussive conversation, metal scraped against china.

"This is not why we asked you to lunch," said Alexandre when they had cleared the plates away.

"You mean you don't want to lecture me about Little Ahmed and what this is doing to him, what *I* am doing to him, and what a bad mother I am."

"No." Jean looked at me, his face was slack, his mouth had lost the straight line of articulation. He looked at me almost tenderly.

"Just because we don't agree with you," said Jean, "doesn't mean . . . Kit, we gave John our word that we would watch over you. So that's what we try to do."

"I know," I said. "I know I should talk to Little Ahmed, but he doesn't want to talk to me. It feels as if I am constantly having to censor myself, as if everyone is against me, and all I'm trying to do is see through the layers of bullshit—which I am supposed to do. That's my job, isn't it? I am supposed to question and judge and figure out. But there's just so much noise. It's like we can't hear the alarm that's ringing louder and louder and louder—"

"Kit—" Alexandre interrupted with a calm insistence. I looked up from the desert of white damask. He looked straight at me, swallowed a gulp of air, and said, "Your father died six days ago in Bhutan."

I was wrong-footed by the non sequitur. How odd, I thought, how incongruous. For a moment I lost my bearings, the mirrors reflected in each other a floating world. I felt my fingertips rub against the red velvet of the banquette; corporeal, reality.

"My father is dead?"

"Yes, Kitty—I'm so sorry—" Alexandre's eyes were blue and wet against his softly powdered face.

"Yes. He died last week. In the monastery where he had been living, apparently."

"We didn't know where he was," said Jean. "I always thought he was in Burma somewhere, lost in the jungle or the mountains—and that's why we never heard from him. I think he *was* in Burma for a while, but anyway, he died in Bhutan. The lawyer in Massachusetts called us both on Friday—we should have told you straightaway—but then everything blew up. The lawyer called us because he named Alexandre and me as his executors."

He bowed his head. I did not say anything. I felt curiously light. After all this time, there was an answer.

"The house in Good Harbor Bay," said Alexandre.

"Granbet's house?"

"Yes. Yours now."

"Wasn't it sold when she died? My mother said it was sold."

"No, rented. That's what he lived on all these years. The rent from his mother's house and opium."

"My mother always said he had gone away from us because he loved opium more."

"He loved you too."

"You cannot love someone and leave them."

"You can," said Jean. "But it destroys a piece of yourself."

"I could never leave Little Ahmed."

"No," said Jean, "you haven't got your father's fatal flaw. He was the kindest man you ever knew. He hurt the people he loved more than he could bear."

I barely heard what Jean was saying. I was thinking of the only clear memory I had of my father. He was holding me up to the sea wind, roses in my cheeks, hot and cold at the same time, and I was laughing and laughing because I was five years old and I felt only pure and unbridled happiness. My sneakers were wet from racing the incoming surf, but my father did not notice. (Granbet would have noticed immediately: "Toes are very important, let's get you inside right away!") Dad said, "Ice cream!" The most beautiful words in the world. I felt his voice burring against my neck. Ice cream! He took my hand and we walked over to the diner on the other side of the dune fence, where Granbet never went because of a long-running feud with That Mister Wade who ran it. We sat at the counter on the red vinyl stools and I was allowed to order whatever flavor I wanted. I asked for chocolate.

"Good choice," said That Mister Wade. I thanked him because even if he was a mean ole custard, you had to be polite—please, Louise, and thank you, Hank.

"Chocolate is my favorite," said my father.

"Didn't expect you'd be able to come back down around here," said That Mister Wade.

"Granbet doesn't know I came," I replied, and then added, carefully, slyly protective—of my Daddy, of me—"Don't tell."

"Well, you didn't see me," said my father.

And I remember asking, "Are you invisible, Daddy?"

I hailed the waiter and asked for chocolate ice cream. It was cold on my tongue and melted into velvet pools of Madagascar mud at the back of my throat. Alexandre handed me a linen handkerchief.

"It's OK, Kitty, don't worry. We're here."

———

I walked home carrying the solace of solution in my heart. I had the idea that the mystery had been resolved and now everything would right itself. It was raining softly, but I was dry under the colonnade of the Palais Royal. Rose bushes drooped heavy rose hips, fountains sprayed water arches. I felt free to be an orphan. I felt a stirring of new resolve. The house in Good Harbor Bay—

I texted Little Ahmed to meet me at the Café Contra after school.

Little Ahmed was surly at the summons. Six feet tall, thirteen years old, everything was awkward. He sat down lumpily with a crash of heavy textbooks.

"Take the earphones out." He made his I-hate-you face and complied.

"What's going on, Kit?" he asked. He sounded grown-up, my equal.

"Something needs to change. We can't continue to live in Paris as if nothing has changed. As if our lives are not threatened, as if our way of life is not threatened."

Two pots of tea arrived, two different colored tea-bag tags hung out of the lids, green mint for Ahmed, gray Earl Gray for me. Ahmed looked at me straight on. He regarded me coolly, like an inmate under duress, but he was getting older, he would be free soon.

"They are trying to kill us." I continued. In my head my thoughts were clear, but Little Ahmed was looking at me as if I was raving nonsense. "I mean, they are trying to stop us living. Stop us going to see a movie, walking down the street and having a beer afterwards."

Little Ahmed shook his head. "Kit, what are you talking about?"

How could I explain better? "You'll understand when—"

"Don't tell me I'll understand when I'm older."

"You will. You're the child now and I'm the adult and I'm telling you—"

"Telling me? That's a joke, telling me! You're always telling me, telling me. Not *listening* to me."

"Is that Margot talking?"

"Don't try and blame her."

"Is that why you were always going to see Rousse all by yourself. Is that what you were doing with her, playing with a Kalashnikov? Do you think that's funny? Do you think that's clever? Subvert the stereotype of an Arab boy with a gun by making an image of the stereotype."

"You're the stereotype, Kit," said my son, simply. "You're the ranting right-wing nutcase." Then he said something really mean. "You sound just like Aba: Islam is stupid and ridiculous! Turn it against itself. Eradicate it!"

What had I meant to do? Extract the Arab gene, inoculate him against it? Take him away and live in a place where there was only *us*. An hour before, it had seemed obvious, simple. The house in Good Harbor Bay, mine now! Cleansing cold blue ocean, wholesome American summertime, lobster rolls and clam bakes and homey folksy can-do. My green-eyed boy with dark hair, handsome square-cut photo in his high school yearbook.

If only I could get us to some other place where we didn't have to be in the middle anymore—if only he could understand that I was just trying to protect him, take him away from—

He stood up and delivered the ringing blow. Oh, but he was magnificent.

"You are upset about Rousse and so you take all this upset and label it *Muslims*. But it's not Muslims' fault. It's not *my fault*. Blame an entire religion and everyone who believes in it. *Even me*. Blame and blame. That's your solution?"

"We need to get away—we need to go—"

"*Where?*"

"Home," I said very quietly. He did not understand me. I had not told him that my father was dead. I had never talked to him, really, about Granbet and Good Harbor Bay. My America was something abstract for him.

"There's nowhere to go, Kit. Because I will have to go with you and you'll just have to look at me: a Muslim. Every day."

"It's not you."

"Yes it is. You keep saying it's a war, it's war and *they* and *them* and we have to be on a side. But what does this mean? I mean what are you going to do about this Muslim disease? Isolate it? Put us in a ghetto. Disinfect with bleach—what do they call it, *deradicaliza-tion*—it's bullshit anyway. Expel us? Kill us? What do you want to do to solve this problem. Do you want to *kill me*?"

"Ahmed—"

"You think you know you're right. But you're really just saying that I should change and not be a Muslim. If you want me to be someone else, then you are not my mother."

He stormed out of the café. The cold air came in when he banged the door, and it bounced in its bracket and hung open.

"Teenagers," said the café man, *sympa*. I could not bring myself to smile at this. I put the coins on the counter and left.

He hated me. He was on their side. Everyone was sleepwalking into a nightmare and everything was fragile. Didn't they know how easily concrete turns into rubble?

———

Little Ahmed did not come home until after midnight. I knew he had been with Grégoire. I heard him brush his teeth and go into his room and close the door. For several minutes I tried to ignore the presence of him. I continued to transcribe notes into files named for Republican heroes whose deeds were forgotten. Who was JAURES? Or CARDINAL LEMOINE? or PHILLIPE AUGUSTE? But I couldn't concentrate.

I knocked on Ahmed's door, carefully, conciliatory, waited for a response.

"Yeah." He was arranging pictures on the desktop of his computer screen. I stood behind him; a pool of yellow lamplight made soft shadows.

"My father is dead," I told him.

"My mother is dead," he said.

"Mine too."

"And Rousse. And all of these people. Look at my pictures. Me and Grégoire went out to see all the shrines all around the cafés and the Bataclan," he said. "People have left messages, hundreds of them. Handwritten notes. It rained and splotched the ink."

"Show me," I said, and he clicked through his slideshow.

He had taken close-up pictures of the notes that people had left. Blue biro on yellow legal pad, greetings cards, block-lettered on Xerox paper, ink-blotched with tears and rain.

THREE

Banging woke me up, but before I knew what it was, there were three men wearing balaclavas in my bedroom pointing guns and shouting at me. I got out of bed very fast and pulled on a pair of jeans.

"Quick, quick," barked a man who pointed at a police badge on his chest.

"Where is my son?"

An official pushed through the police. He was wearing a dark suit, dark tie, his face that of an ordinary accountant. He held a piece of printed paper and read from it:

"Pursuant to the Counter Terrorism Act of 2014, Section 3—"

"Where is my son Ahmed?"

"We are placing you under *garde-à-vue*, pursuant to our inquiries according to the Counterterrorism Act of 2014." I did not know if this was arrest. *Garde-à-vue* is detention, but I was not sure if it was arrest. France's judicial system is different from the Anglo-Saxon versions I knew from TV detective dramas. It depends on the investigating magistrate. There's no jury trial. Just the investigating magistrate.

"I want a lawyer."

"It's not *Law & Order*, Madame L'Américaine," said one of the policemen. I asked him to turn around so that I could put on my bra. He refused. "It's *Engrenages*, it's a spiral." He twirled his finger round and round, "Heh-heh-heh."

I shouted for Ahmed, and he shouted back, "The police are taking me."

"It will be OK!" I called to him.

"Stop talking!" said the policeman roughly.

"He's thirteen-years-old," I told him, "you can't arrest him."

"You think thirteen-year-olds can't commit crimes?"

The official in the suit said, "He is being escorted by an appropriate adult."

"Who?"

"An appropriate adult."

I saw Little Ahmed pushed out of the apartment. He had obviously pulled on his clothes in a hurry, because he was wearing his least favorite green Nike sweatshirt. His face was ashen and knotted and defiant. This cut into me. I felt helpless, awful. One of the female policemen told me to stand up straight with my arms out. She searched me carefully, around my waistband, running her hands around my bra strap, and the underwires. I stared at the ceiling, seething, powerless, violated. She did not look at me.

The man in the suit asked me for my passport, my residency papers, my marriage certificate, and Little Ahmed's birth certificate. I kept these documents in a drawer in my desk at the end of the living room but the policemen barred my way.

"Tell me where they are and I will get them."

He took my laptop and Little Ahmed's laptop. I said I was a journalist. This was not relevant. He asked me how many mobile phones

I had. I said, "One." It was plugged in to charge on the desk. He took it. One of the policemen found a bag of old electronic stuff in the hall cupboard and held up two old mobile phones as refutation. I explained they were old phones I did not use any more. They put each one in a separate plastic bag. They found my box of sim cards and these were put in another plastic bag.

"Where is the boy's mobile phone?" I said I did not know.

They searched the drawer in the desk but could not find Little Ahmed's birth certificate, only the certificate of adoption. I said if it wasn't there, I didn't know where it was.

"Where are you taking Ahmed? What is going on? I need a lawyer." My questions were met only with more demands. I gave up trying to be helpful.

"Where is your French Press card?"

"I don't know. I never use it."

"We need the access code to your laptop and to your son's laptop."

"No."

The man in the suit shrugged, as if noncompliance was to be expected. He told me to put my hands behind my back to be handcuffed. Again I said "no." A policeman behind me pulled my arms behind and pinched my wrists together. He ratcheted the cold metal bracelets closed tight so that they rubbed against my wrist bones. My nose began to itch. This was the worst moment, when I could not touch my own face, when my own body was separated from itself.

They made me stand there like that for an hour while they searched the apartment. They pulled all the drawers out and dumped papers on the table and sifted through them, they pushed books off the shelves to see if there was something hidden behind them.

Eventually they put me in the back of a van. I was not allowed to take my wallet or a coat or any book or notebook with me. The van had no windows.

I was thirsty, my eyes were dry, eyelashes still stuck with sleepy dust, my hair hung straight down my cheeks because I could not brush it off my face, my shoulders hurt from the wrench, and my wrists hurt like sharp bruises where the handcuffs bit into them. My nerves cross-wired all their electrical signals in screeching rills of itchiness and aching.

I didn't see the façade of the police station because one of the policeman pushed my head down to face the pavement when we arrived. Scuffed parquet, lintel trip, tiled corridor. White tiles like a bathroom, fluorescent lighting bouncing green shadows.

The same policewoman who had searched me in my bedroom led me to a cubicle to search me again. She took off my handcuffs and told me to take off my clothes. I complied. She took each article of clothing as I took it off and turned it over in her hands, examining every seam. She put her hands into each pocket of my jeans and brought out a wad of dryer fluff, three copper coins and a lighter. She tested the lighter and it made a tall yellow flame. My socks, my shoes were examined in the same way. She took my watch.

I was chilled; gooseflesh stood up on my arms. The curtain did not pull all the way across the cubicle's entrance. The walls, once white, were dirty and starkly grim under the glare of a fluorescent bulb. My bare feet were cold on the tiled floor.

I was down to my underpants and bra. She pointed at me. "Yes, everything." I took off my underpants and my bra and stood naked because I was told to do so. I did not speak or reply. My only defense was a silent humiliated rage which was of no interest to her. She went away and I was alone.

There was no chair or bench. I examined the walls. I thought of all my kidnapped friends. I thought of all the times I had imagined my father kidnapped. I had read the memoirs of his Beirut colleagues who had spent eight years as hostages. In Baghdad I had interviewed people who had been locked up in Saddam's prisons. I had often thought about being kidnapped myself. For a while whenever I went to the toilet I would lock the door and imagine the door being locked from the outside and consider the stall space I must inhabit now—could I lie down? Was there a window, a sink with running water?

Someone had squashed a piece of chewing gun into a corner of the cubicle, a hardened knob of flesh-colored putty. I made an impression of a smiley face with my fingernail. It's important to keep your mind to yourself because it's the only thing they cannot take from you. Thinking makes us so. I looked at my companion smiley face and smiled back. I was cold and naked and frightened. They had taken my son from me. I thought: This is very interesting. This is what fascism is.

At some length the policewoman gave me my clothes back. But not my watch. She took me down the corridor into another room, where I was told to stand inside a full-body scanner. Then I was taken up one floor to an interrogation room and told to sit on a chair on the other side of the table. The room was as bland as the cubicle. There was no window. I sat there for a long time, but I didn't know how long because they had not given me my watch back.

———

"I am Frédéric Durand, your lawyer. I have been appointed by the Republic." He looked as ordinary as the official in the suit in my apartment. But it was not the same man. This one did not look at me. "I should inform you that you are not required to talk to the police but that you are advised to do so. Sign this."

"No."

"It is in your interest," he replied evenly, still not looking at me, but rifling through several pages to find the form for me to sign.

"Why?"

He spoke a paragraph of rapid boilerplate legalese. I said I did not understand.

He shrugged and collected his dossiers and left the room.

Presently another man came in with the same sallow impassive face, brown hair, and long Gallic nose. His only distinguishing feature was a mole in the middle of his cheek.

"My name is François Paltoquet. I am the *juge d'instruction* for this case." He put out his hand for me to shake it. I shook it. Firm and dry. "You have refused a lawyer."

"I did not understand him."

"You have been detained under the Anti-Terrorist Legislation Act of 2014. We can hold you for ninety-six hours without applying to a judge for an extension. I cannot predict how long it will take to find an English-speaking lawyer. If you wish, we can begin your questioning without the formal consultation of lawyer. In any case you will not have a lawyer present during questioning." He took my silence for acquiescence and continued. "You are Catherine Madison Kittredge, born July 2, 1977, Boston General Hospital, USA. Father John Adams Kittredge, American, Mother Christine Dorothea Hardwick, British citizen, died resident of France in February 2003."

"Yes."

"Please verify these details." He handed me a form in which my address, email addresses, and mobile phone numbers were written down.

"You are employed by an American newspaper, as a correspondent. Since 2003."

"Yes."

"Married Ahmed Ahmed Solemani, citizen of Iraq, in Beirut, 2005. Divorced, finalized France, April 2010."

"Yes."

"Adopted Ahmed Ahmed Solemani, son of this man, registered, France, July 2008."

"Yes."

"You are aware that Ahmed Solemani was never legally divorced from his first wife. And that you were married before her death in"— he checked the date against his typed sheet—"February 2006."

"He told me that he divorced her through an imam in Baghdad."

"The divorce was not legally registered."

"It may have been around the time of the American invasion," I said. "There may have been no formal authority with whom to register the divorce. Iraq did not regain it's sovereignty—"

Paltoquet cut me off; he was not interested in explanations. He had a fact printed in black and white on a piece of paper and this was all the truth he was interested in.

"Pursuant to this fraud, your marriage in Beirut in"—his eyes returned to the résumé of my life printed on one sheet of paper—"February 2005, is not valid. The petition for your adoption of his son, however, was uncontested by his father."

"Correct."

He paused. He put away the typed form in a leatherette folder secured with a piece of elastic and leaned his elbows on the desk.

"Did you convert to Islam at the time of your wedding to Ahmed Solemani?"

"Yes."

"Ah. Good. Yes." This seemed to confirm something for him. He left the room.

After another long while, which could have been ten minutes or fifty, the policewoman returned and brought me downstairs again to the white-tiled corridor which led into a white-tiled abattoir hallway lined on one side with cells. The cells were not solid door bang-ups like in British TV police dramas, but built with walls of metal-framed windowpanes so that the guards could see the prisoners at all times.

My cell had a cement floor, a cement sleeping ledge, and a foul *pissoir* hole in the corner. The hole did not flush and there was no running water.

"I am thirsty."

The door shut and I was alone, but not alone. There was no privacy behind the glass wall.

"Achacha!" shouted the man in the next-door cell. No one answered him either. I lay down with my hands behind my head as a pillow and examined the infinite ceiling of my inside sky. It cracked into continents; rivers ran to water-stain seas.

———

I was not in Syria. There was no torture to be frightened of. But there were other things to be frightened of. Rat scratching, trapped in its own brain. Is prison only an echo chamber for the human condition? I tried to think what the hell had happened. I rewound the last few months, half answers, defensive mumblings, slammed doors. Mounting anger. Mine or his? What had I missed, misunderstood; teenage disaffection, my fault, or something larger, worse—Little Ahmed, *habibe*, what have you done? What has Grégoire-Ghaith's brother encouraged you to do? What lies did he fill your impressionable, inquisitive thirteen-year-old head with, what false trails of God-Allah and logic and identity has he mapped in your unfolding folds of cerebral coruscations? What were you really doing all those afternoons after school?

A month earlier Little Ahmed had come back late, past eight o'clock dinner time, congealed carbonara on the stove. I had been the very model of a nagging mother.

"Didn't you think I would be worried?"

He said his phone had, uh, run out of battery. "I am only like, late, like an hour. It's not some crime!" He had an orange plastic bag with him and I asked him what was in it and he wouldn't tell me. "Stuff a friend gave me." What friend? What stuff?

What have you done, Little Ahmed? My precious Medio. (Rousse would have trusted you; but look what happened to Rousse. From a prison cell even trust can be cause for suspicion.) Where is the gun? What did you do? *Courrier*, carrier pigeon, WhatsApp intermediary, hashtag jihadi, skyping Syria . . . Did you link your uncle in Amman to a recruiter who lives on rue Stephenson? My eye caught on a tangle of dust strings high up in the corner of the cell, and I recalled the curly hairs dangling from the smooth insouciant chin of Grégoire's brother. A violent surge of impotent rage swept through me.

After an hour or two, the policewoman came and escorted me back to the interrogation room.

Paltoquet gave me a can of Coke. I pulled the ring pull with a sparking fizz. Drank. It was cold. It was bliss. Spangling bubbles over my shag pile tongue, caramel up my nose, sugar rushed into my veins. Yes, I am American, I confess, I admit everything. I want a large Coke and a quarter-pounder with cheese, please. I want to go back to the diner in Good Harbor Bay with the red vinyl stool and eat three scoops of chocolate ice cream.

Paltoquet watched me empty the can of Coke in continual gulps. A second man, young, junior, whippet thin, came in and put a thick pile of sheets of paper on the table.

"This is a list of web pages accessed by your IP address over the past year," stated Paltoquet. "Please look through these and tick,"— he handed me a pencil—"those pages which you remember visiting. If you are not sure, please make a question mark next to it. If you are very sure you have not visited this page, please draw a cross."

Paltoquet left the room. His whippet boy remained. This list was more than fifty pages long. I bent to my task.

After two hours I was taken back to my cell. I hoped for rest. In *Darkness at Noon*, Rubashov had waited up so many nights expecting the NKVD to arrest him that when they did, he curled up in his prison cot and fell, finally, sound asleep. But there was no mattress for me to lie down on and no blanket. The concrete floor and glass wall exaggerated the chill.

After an hour I was taken back to the interrogation room.

"Thank you," said Paltoquet. He scanned the list of web pages. "Now your travel."

I was asked to list every place I had visited in the previous decade, stating whether Little Ahmed had been with me or not. Separately, I was to write down a list of all the places Little Ahmed had visited, and whether he had traveled with his father or independently of me. I said such a list would be incomplete, that I could not remember every weekend in Brittany, side trips to London, which week I was in New York that autumn.

I made my concern sound earnest. I kept my fear in check. I decided to tell him as much as possible, to give him all the information that I could, to show that I had nothing to hide, which, I reminded myself, clear-headed and business-like under those flickery fluorescent lights, I didn't. (I didn't, but what about Little Ahmed? He was undoubtedly being questioned in tandem. What might he have to hide that was hidden from me? What might I say that would prove or disprove his version or another version . . . ?)

"I understand," said Paltoquet. He gave the impression of running through these details as if they were merely a formality. He had the mien of a reception manager at the Four Seasons in Damascus: obsequious, anodyne, corporate, Mukhabarat. He affected a certain apology without offering any explanation. This was nothing personal; this was simply what procedure required. His manner—cordial, aloof, officious—was expressly designed to encourage my compliance. Even though I knew this, I complied. Oh Stanley Milgram! You are right. Authority is irresistible. Paltoquet had given me a test and I wanted to do well on it. Even though I hated him, I wanted his approval.

I began to write down my travel. I had to list every town I had been to in Lebanon and Iraq. Where had I visited in Syria outside of Damascus? How had I traveled, on what dates, to what towns? Deir Mar Mikhael. "Yes. When was the last time you talked to Father Angelo?" When was the last time you went to Damascus? Why did you go? Why did you take your son with you? Did your husband ask you to bring him? How far in advance was the trip planned? How did you obtain your visa? Did your husband arrange it for you? Did your son travel on his British or his Iraqi passport?

————

I answered as best I could. My recollections sounded like an inaccurate retracing, lines that I could not bring into complete circles, things I had forgotten, chronologies got tangled, snagged. Why had I taken Little Ahmed to Syria that spring? Was it my idea or his father's?

Late—it was dark outside, I think, it was hard to tell through the drawn blinds along the corridors as I was taken back to my cell. A meal was brought. A heap of rice, desiccated chicken, two slices of bread, a pot of pink yogurt, a cup of tea. I ate it all. *With relish.* Like Solzhenitsyn's starving gulag *zeks* who found a prehistoric salamander frozen in a timeless Siberian lens of ice and ripped it out and ate it all up, *with relish.*

The Russians are very good at writing about prisons. I recalled all the Ivan Denisovich Siberias I had ever read. Exile, boredom, malcontent, cold feet, griminess, fatigue. I envied them their camaraderie, their bunk beds and their wood stoves. Alone in my cell, my brain raced, what had Little Ahmed done wittingly, unwittingly, accomplice, patsy . . . who was Grégoire's brother? What were they doing when they were walking Grégoire's imaginary dogs? What had happened last summer with his cousins in Amman?

FOUR

"**A**mman," announced Paltoquet, back in the interrogation room, a new topic for questioning.

"I told you. Ahmed went to Amman to see his father. Because it was safer than Baghdad and he has cousins there. ISIS had just captured Mosul. They went on a camping trip in Wadi Rum and to see Petra."

"And the names of these cousins."

"Thayr," I said. "I don't know the name of his uncle."

Paltoquet raised an eyebrow and looked over a sheet of paper at me. "You do not know the family name of your son's mother?"

"My husband never told me. He did not like to talk about his first wife in front of me."

"What is your ex-husband's job and who is his employer?"

"He is a protocol officer for the United Nations." Paltoquet nodded. "What is the name of his immediate superior."

"I don't know. We communicate almost exclusively about our son."

"When he was resident in France, he undertook several trips to Syria."

"In the spring of 2011 he was in Damascus a lot. Maybe that's partly why I went and took Little Ahmed. I honestly don't remember who initiated the idea. Ahmed was there because there was still a window for political negotiation. He went to Hama, I think, I remember he was talking to opposition groups about a conference—" Paltoquet cut me off.

"This was, according to his passport records, not his only trip to Syria that year."

"He moved back to Baghdad at the end of that summer. After that I don't have much idea where he went."

"He has visited France regularly since 2011."

"To see his son."

"Please write down on this piece of paper, who he sees, that you are aware of, when he comes to France. Please include professional acquaintances as well as social friends."

"What has Ahmed got to do with this?" I asked. "Why are you asking me questions about him?"

I wrote down half a dozen names. When I was finished, Paltoquet pushed a buzzer under the table that signaled a guard to take me back to my cell.

———

Aching, interminable, alone. I had no book to read or write in. I thought of the warden of the Peter and Paul Fortress in Tolstoy's *Resurrection*. What was his name? He allowed the prisoners a slate and a piece of chalk in order to write, as a pastime. This detail of obtuse cruelty was the only thing I could remember from the whole novel. What would I write if I only had a slate and a chalk? Would I write the same thing over and over to inscribe it to memory? Could I bear to wipe away every morning what I had written the day before? What was writing except remembering?

Time fractured into segments of cell and interrogation. Facts fractured between memory, imagination, and wondering. Ahmed, Little

Ahmed, all the other Ahmeds. Loops of film on a cutting room floor, jump-cut scenes, jumbled up in my head. I was not frightened for myself; I hung onto the logic of my innocence. But for Little Ahmed I felt a vertiginous terror; precipice, abyss. In my dreams his face kaleidoscoped, smiling at me, laughing at me, mocking me. When I woke, I did not know where I was, and then it came back, hard as concrete, and the fear flushed icily through me again: Where was he? Was he OK?

There was no yogurt for dessert, only a tiny box of raisins. They tasted of sweet cardboard and made me think of a mulberry tree in Aleppo and how the fruit had fallen onto the concrete paving stones and made purple juice stains like a massacre. My concrete cell floor was scuffed in places, but otherwise as dun as the desert outside of Ramadi. But there, lo! An ant!

———

I was shunted from cell back to interrogation. I tried to collect myself, to recollect, to think. Paltoquet resumed his questioning about Ahmed. What was the nature of his work for the United Nations? Why did he have an Iraqi diplomatic passport? What was the last time that Ahmed had been in Syria?

"Are you aware that he has traveled to Damascus four times in the last year." I said I was not.

He put before me a list of four names: Mahmoud, Mohammed; Masoud, Ahmed; Abdul, Hamid; Hamoud, Mohammed.

"Do you recognize any of these?"

"They are common names. They could be anyone."

He took out several photographs from a file. Faces blown up from low-resolution stills, blurry. One was in profile, another had deep shadows that blacked out his eyes. I looked closely. They seemed to be surveillance shots, one was so indistinct and striated it must have come from a CCTV camera.

"I don't know," I said.

"Look again."

"It's hard to tell. People look different in real life."

"What about this one?" He pointed to a picture taken in the dark. Black wool ski hat, pulled down like a burglar. "It's Abdelhamid Abaaoud," said Paltoquet, looking at me carefully. I opened my palms in a gesture of nothing. "This picture was taken by Zorro Thorpe, outside the Bataclan theater on the night of November 9."

"So?"

"Your cellphone was located at the same location at the same time."

"I turned it off."

Paltoquet made a small shrug, "Yes, we know that. What is your relationship to Zorro Thorpe?"

"Friend. Colleague."

"You did not make contact with him outside the Bataclan that night?"

"I was hiding in a bush in the park. He was too far away. I didn't want to cry out. There was a lot of shooting. There were police everywhere."

"You did not make contact with the police."

"No."

"We have asked for witnesses to come forward."

"I didn't see anything specific. I didn't—"

"Why didn't you tell your friend and colleague Zorro Thorpe that you had seen him?"

"I did—I didn't *not* tell him. It didn't come up."

"He was surprised to discover that you were at the same place at the same time that night. At first he denied to us that you were there. He said you could not have been there because he would have seen you or you would have told him. But you *were* there. And so was this man—"

He pointed again to the dark wooly-hatted face of Abdelha-mid Abaaoud.

"Orange sneakers," I said. I understood now, two pieces fitted together. "He was the one standing there wearing orange sneakers. Yes, I saw him. He was talking into his mobile phone. He was worried but also calm, he kept looking down the alley. I thought he must have known someone inside the Bataclan, I thought he was trying to find one of his friends."

"You did not approach him or talk to him?"

"I was on the other side of the police cordon, there were police everywhere, there was constant shooting. I couldn't have crossed the street to where Zorro and he were—"

"How long did you hide in the park?"

"I don't know," I said. "A long time."

"You were in the vicinity of the Bataclan theater for three hours and seventeen minutes," replied Paltoquet, reading from a sheet of paper in front of him. "And all that time you were hiding under a bush?"

"Yes."

"You did not make contact with anyone?"

"Make contact?"

"Talk to someone."

"No."

"Why not? You are a journalist. Didn't you need to report, find quotes?"

"I don't know." Why hadn't I?

"You have not written about that night. You are a journalist who doesn't write a report as an eyewitness to a major terrorist attack—"

"I did not see anything!"

"—who knew very well that she had seen the main perpetrator of the attack." He took a stapled sheaf of my articles out of his file and pointed at my story from Saint-Denis about Abdelhamid Abaaoud.

"I had forgotten about the orange sneakers."

"You had forgotten."

"Yes."

"What else have you forgotten?"

———

Back in the cell, the ant wandered aimlessly. The bread was soft and sliced and I rolled it into dough pellets between my fingertips. The toilet hole was calcified with solid yellow piss, but I imagined it as a tunnel to freedom like in *The Shawshank Redemption*. It is true you get used to anything. The ammonia cesspit smell had receded to a familiar fug, so that the clean air outside in the corridors smelled aseptic, razored, and unfriendly.

———

In the next session Paltoquet had a new yellow file beside his elbow. Whippet sipped a can of Red Bull. Normal service resumed. More pictures of men with black beards. Ahmeds in a haystack.

"This man," Paltoquet pointed. Charcoal-shadowed eye sockets. I shook my head.

"This one." Low V hairline.

"No."

Baby face, smirk smile, razor stripe across one eyebrow.

"No."

"Look again." I looked again. "He would have been thinner when you met him."

"Give me a clue."

"Mohammed Ahmed Khalil."

"Mohammed—"

"Yes. Several phone calls were made from your cellphone to his father's cellphone in Lebanon."

"From Kos."

"Between August fifteenth and twenty-third."

"Is that what this is about? I met Mohammed by chance."

"By chance?"

"On Kos on the beach. It was a coincidence. It turned out I knew his father in Lebanon. I called his father. That's what the calls were. His father said he had been in Syria—his father said—" But what had his father said?

"Please repeat the details of your conversation with his father."

"I can't remember. The line was bad. He was vague. Mohammed vanished on me. He disappeared."

"And you claim you have had no subsequent contact with him."

"No."

"You do not recall the surname this Mohammed used to register with the Greek authorities or the name of his uncle in Hama."

"I never met the uncle in Hama. I only heard about him."

"And your husband did not mention him to you."

"He's not my husband."

"Even in 2011 when you were in Syria together. We believe this is the first time your husband met him in Hama—"

"Is this about Ahmed?"

"Just answer the questions. You received a call from a German cellphone number at eight twenty-five in the morning of October thirty-first."

"What has Ahmed done?"

"The phone call on October thirty-first."

"I don't know anyone in Germany," I said. "I didn't receive a call from Germany."

"It is a matter of record."

"I do not remember any phone call from Germany." Did I? Had I forgotten that too?

"The call lasted forty-two seconds. The mobile phone was located in the main refugee processing center in Düsseldorf."

"I don't remember."

"You don't remember." He drew out his syllables. I could see he did not believe me."Your inability to recollect certain details creates certain discrepancies," he said.

"Why am I detained? What is really going on here? If I understood the reasons for our arrests, perhaps I could explain myself better. What is it? Is it something my son has done? Is it a connection with my ex-husband? Is it a megadata mistake because there are Daesh websites logged against my IP address? Has some algorithm connected things that are not connected?"

"Madame," replied Paltoquet firmly, as if my outburst was distasteful, emotionally inappropriate to his diligent professionalism. "I will ask the questions and you will answer them."

"Where is Ahmed?" I began to rebel.

"You told us he was in Baghdad."

"My son Ahmed."

"He is being taken care of."

"Who is taking care of him?"

"You are tired," Paltoquet looked at his watch. "I am going to send you back to the cell to sleep."

"What time is it?"

"Four."

"Afternoon or morning?"

He did not answer.

FIVE

The glass wall of my cell gave a view onto a white-tiled wall. My thoughts bounced against it, like boomerang daggers. I was caged in a see-through box. My imagination turned my ant into an antelope, a patronus, who could leap through walls. The mind is shut in a head, inescapably (on pain of death) attached to a body, now locked up in a cell—but still it can go wherever it likes. Isn't that amazing?

I lay on my tummy and considered the links in the chain that Paltoquet was forging. Think, Kitts, think hard! It's the only thing you can do. I scratched at a ragged cuticle.

Sleep deprivation is the oldest trick in the book. Rubashov himself had employed it when he was interrogating prisoners. An easily arranged torment. Perhaps I could hide behind a false wall—a mental construct. Close your eyes and build the wall brick by imaginary sheep-counting brick. The windowpane door in the glass wall clanged and a heavy bundle of keys jangled like an alarm clock. I was about to dive off the cliff to escape from Devil's Island and swim to the island of Monte Cristo. Of course Paltoquet was the devil. The mole on his cheek marked him out, like a small gobbet of shit.

I considered a hunger strike, I considered passive resistance, I considered violence. The efficacy of these options seemed doubtful. Rubashov had been a torturer himself; he understood that resignation was the only sensible course of action.

Round and round everything blurred, dizzy. Like twirling on a dance floor and trying to find a mark to keep your focus, but the scenes just shuffled glimpses. Where was Ahmed now? Baghdad, Damascus, Hama? A trail of postcards, but the postmarks never matched the picture. Phone calls that went straight to voicemail. Bleeps and clicks on the line. What was he doing all these years, to and fro, go-between, but between who and where? Parties, interests, shadows. Cross-hatching the enemy of my enemy and crossing lines. Ahmed had always been a liar.

"All Iraqis are liars." Who had said that?

———

"An Iraqi military doctor called Muntazzer—" began Paltoquet. His face was the color of uncooked pastry, doughy pouches under his eyes. His sidekick whippet's face was the same plain buff as the paper on which he took notes. There was no window in the interrogation room. The fluorescent light gave off a sickly glow. My eyes ached. My back ached. Everything hurt. Was this the second day or the third?

Paltoquet had a sheaf of paper in front of him that I could see contained my recent email correspondence. "When was the last time you saw Muntazzer."

"More than ten years ago."

"Where?"

"In Baghdad. I didn't see him after we left Baghdad."

"According to your information, your husband visited Marseilles in October 2010."

"Did he? We were divorced by then."

"Muntazzer al Samarrai was still living in Marseilles. Did you know that?"

"No."

"And your husband never mentioned meeting him there?"

"No."

"You met Muntazzer's son, Oberon, in Iraq in 2004."

"Yes."

"How many times?"

"Twice." "You were aware that he was leading a group fighting against the Americans."

"Yes."

"You are an American. And yet you did not inform the American authorities in Baghdad."

"I was a journalist. Neutral. I wrote about him. It's called protecting your sources."

"You were against the American occupation. You had sympathies with the insurgents. Perhaps this contributed to your conversion to Islam."

"You are making inferences that are not true. I became a Muslim to get married. It was entirely expedient. It was a piece of paper, it meant nothing to me."

"You did not meet Muntazzer's other sons?"

"No."

"You are aware they were also fighters."

"I guessed."

"Did you introduce your husband Ahmed to Oberon?"

"No, he did not meet Oberon with me." But he knew him—knew him from childhood—

"But your husband is also from Samarra."

"No, his father was from there. He never lived there." But he *had* visited Samarra: the cousin with the knife-sharp nose who held his wrist that day under the colonnade of the Shia shrine . . . he knew the restaurant on the riverbank with the best kebabs in Iraq . . . Oberon's childhood anecdote, cheating him out of his Lego blocks. What games was Ahmed playing now?

"Are you sure?" Paltoquet probed. "May I suggest that there are things about your husband you do not know. What do you know about your husband's work?" He sat back, studying my reaction.

"I know—" I began and then I realized I did not know, not really. "He works as a protocol officer for the U.N. Different envoys. Various missions. Sometimes short contracts; he complains about that. His expenses are always getting shuffled to different desks and then the reimbursement gets delayed. I know that, because then I don't get the maintenance checks on time and he blames the U.N. bureaucracy. Once, he said he was like a troubleshooter. People who don't want to meet for political reasons, he meets them separately, back channels."

"Are you aware that he is paid by the U.S. Defense Department?"

"No. I didn't know that."

"Are you surprised?"

"Yes. No. Maybe. In a certain way it makes sense."

"In what way?"

"He was always a great admirer of the Americans," I said. "He was—" He had been. But now?

"What are his political beliefs?"

"His political beliefs?"

"Yes, his orientation. His views on the situation in his country, for example."

"He does not like the Shia government, their corruption, their ties to Iran—"

"Go on, please." Paltoquet leaned forward, and I had the sense of having been drawn into a more liquid conversation.

I swam back a year, to summer 2014.

———

Ahmed was in Paris just for one night; he had a flight to New York in the morning. He took Little Ahmed and me out for supper. We went to Le Petit Cambodge around the corner because he said he missed Asian spice and soy sauce. He had brought Little Ahmed a present of a wooden box with the minaret of Samarra inlaid in mother-of-pearl. Little Ahmed was not very impressed: it looked like a girl's jewelry box to him, but we explained and he traced the lines of ascending spiral and nodded his approval.

"I should have taken you there," his father told him, "when I realized you were photographing nothing but curves. Samarra is where your grandfather is from. The banks of the Tigris—ah, the most beautiful place in the world—and the best kebabs in all the land! Now it's impossible."

ISIS had just taken Mosul. Tikrit had fallen, Samara was occupied. The North of Iraq was now under their control. In the west they controlled the Anbar badlands of Ramadi and Fallujah. The Hiluxes fluttering black flags were gunning towards Baghdad. I asked Ahmed what the situation was like in the capital.

"The Shia in the government are freaked out," he said almost gleefully. "The Americans are scrambling to explain why no one saw it coming. All their money into the Iraqi army and it just ran away. I've been telling them for months, but—"

"But what?"

"They stopped paying the Sunni tribes, they disengaged. It's shortsighted of course, as usual. The Americans just want to be out of it these days—that's the official White House line. But now they'll have to get involved again." It was a reasonable paragraph of analysis, but there was a purr in his tone, a certain satisfaction. Well, Ahmed had always hated the Shia parties. The oxymorons, he called them: severe and corrupt, incompetent and yet stuck-fast, in charge.

"But isn't everyone in Baghdad terrified?"

"Is Beeby OK? What about Thayr?" asked Little Ahmed.

"Thayr and his family have gone to Amman. Like lots of people, running away. Another phase of exodus. But they'll come back."

"But you're not scared, Aba!"

"No, I'm not. ISIS will stop now—there are old hands at the helm, they know the limits. They've got the Kirkuk oil fields and oil to sell. They'll make a deal with the Kurds."

"The same people making the same accommodations," I said. "Like in Saddam's time."

"It's always about the money," Ahmed said, repeating his war-as-economics mantra.

"What are you doing in New York?" I asked.

"U.N. response to ISIS summit. Watch the moon rise."

"What moon rise? An eclipse?" Little Ahmed wanted to see an eclipse because Rousse had told him that the moon was the only perfect circle in the world. Out of this world. Ahmed tousled his son's hair.

"No, Ban Ki-moon."

"Banksy Moon? Like a street artist?"

"No, like the secretary-general of the United Nations, kiddo," I said.

"He's Korean," added Ahmed. "He'll have to engage with Assad now. I've got to talk to the new special envoy. And then get him in the room with the right Americans."

"Who are the right Americans?"

"The Defense Department—they still have some operational funds at their discretion, they love to play the margins, ignore State, tell the Senate committee after the fact. They'll listen."

"Listen to what?"

"Aha!" Bowls of steaming pho arrived. Ahmed rubbed his hands together in exaggerated anticipation. "Pork belly! Oh, I have been dreaming of it."

"Listen to what?" I said again.

"My ingenious plan," Ahmed winked at his son. "I've got it all

figured out. One domino, two dominos, third domino falls and—
just remember, Ahmed-son-of-Ahmed-son-of-Ahmed of the shining
city of Samarra—I promise I will take you there one day, to the land
between two rivers, the Euphrates and the Tigris, the mighty Tigris
that flows through Samarra, the land of the original civilization and
the origin of the creation. Remember Gilgamesh! Nothing in that
Louvre of yours would exist without the first mark of man that your
ancestors made, the first writing, the first laws—"

"The cradle of civilization, blah-blah," said Little Ahmed.

"And then the Arabs conquered Mesopotamia." Ahmed had put
on a boomy fake prophet voice and turned himself into a doomsday
soothsayer of yore. I thought he was telling an elaborate joke. "The
Arabs came and there was a battle. Karbala! Idiot Shia! Making a cult
out of a defeat!" But he seemed to be serious. "A Caliphate was just
good politics. Better the Umayyeds than those fanatics."

"But we're Sunni, aren't we, Aba?"

"Yes we are. Because we are political realists. And no we're not,
because if you mix politics with religion, you get the same idiocy.
The trick," said Ahmed with a sharky grin, "is to get rid of religion.
Shia, Sunni. Everyone's natural enemy is their brother. Set them
against each other. Let them bleed each other dry and their martyr
blood will sink into the sand of the desert and be spent. Leave us
people of the river to quench our dry and shriven lands with modern irrigation, and damn the Turks if they dam our water!" Ahmed
was giddy, stirring hot sauce into the boiling currents of his broth,
hauling up tangled strands of noodles, slurping, talking at the same
time, eyes shining, chili oil drops glistened on the surface of the
soup, fine beads of sweat shone, trapped in the crease along his
forehead.

"What are you talking about?"

"Think big! Think outside the box. Blue sky!" Now he sounded
like a management consultant.

"There's no blue sky in Iraq," I reminded him. "It's white when it's hot and yellow at night."

"Or red in a sandstorm," added Little Ahmed.

"Was there a sandstorm when you were there? You didn't tell me—"

"It was amazing! It was like rust and it was so thick that when I took a picture you couldn't see anything. It looked like I took a picture of the inside of my eyelid!"

I looked over at Ahmed. "The Good Iraqi," I said sarcastically. "Are you going to arm the Sunni tribes again?"

"It worked last time," he said simply. "Trust me, Kit. What's the best way to defeat an ideology?"

"I don't know, Ahmed, tell me, since you're so clever and have the answer to all that ails us in these troubled times, what's the best way to defeat an ideology?"

"Give it enough rope to hang itself!"

———

Paltoquet was looking at me, waiting.

"What does Ahmed believe in? Whose side is he on?" he prompted. It occurred to me, fleetingly, for a moment, to recount this conversation. I did not know what Ahmed had been doing, but I had begun to connect a trail of breadcrumbs, coincidences, comments, asides. I could make my own guess—but did I want to tell Paltoquet? Screw him. Let him make his own inference. Why should I betray Ahmed to this dossier-apparatchik who was just another agent with an agenda?

"What does Ahmed believe in? Himself," I said, and then pushed back: "Why ask me about Ahmed? What has he got mixed up in?"

"As you said, he makes connections. But my question to you, as someone who knows him well, is, to what end, for what purpose?"

"He has notions," I said haltingly, as if I was carefully considering his question, trying to answer it honestly. "He has ideas. But they change. He sometimes leaps on a theory and then shakes it for a while to see what use it can be." This was true, but also vague, of little use.

"Is he an observant Muslim?"

"No, the opposite. He always says he is an atheist." Paltoquet frowned at this.

"He could have changed. Have you noticed any signs of radicalization?" Impatience had crept into his even-keel voice. "Has your son mentioned anything? In Baghdad or Jordan, did your husband take him to a mosque? Did he ever mention meeting an imam? Someone called Abu Mohammed—"

"Abu Mohammed? Seriously? That's half the male population of the Middle East."

"An imam, a sheikh, a commander. Someone he met perhaps with his father?"

"A commander?"

"Do you think that it's a coincidence that your husband and your son were in Amman at the same time as Mohammed's uncle, the imam from Hama?" I rolled my eyes to pantomime dramatic irritation. Paltoquet was asking too many questions, everything mixed up, his composure was fraying. "Also known as Abu Mohammed." I stuck my tongue out at him, exasperated. "This man!" Paltoquet jabbed his forefinger into the forehead of one of the headshot pictures. The one with a white knit prayer cap and a middle-aged indistinct face. "Abu Mohammed," he repeated, "a known Jubat Al-Nusra commander. Picked up by the Jordanians in Amman in August. Detained. Released. Turns up here, in Europe." Paltoquet was angry now, urgent. Shaking his forefinger at me. "Think, Catherine. Think. This is important."

"Where was this picture taken?"

"Brussels. Four days ago."

"Shit," I said.

"Twenty-three phone calls have been logged between a cellphone number that was in the same café where this surveillance camera caught him, and the cellphone of your friend with the orange sneakers." Paltoquet collapsed his distance. His candor seemed genuine, but maybe it was only a ploy. I was unsure how to talk him out of his narrative. He was plotting coordinates that were accidental, that were— "Can you explain these coincidences? Because I have to ask myself, are you involved? Is your ex-husband involved—well, we know he's involved, but how? Who is he really working for? And who took the phone call from the German detention center on October thirty-first? Because if the caller was this man's nephew, as we suspect, this younger nephew Mohammed who you met—*by chance*—in Kos." Paltoquet was shouting now. "If you know his whereabouts and you are not telling us, for some reason, this is obstruction, this is an offense of accessory, this is a crime that we will not hesitate to prosecute you for!" He banged his fists on the table.

The noise shattered the armor of my innocence. It didn't matter what I told them or how earnestly I tried to explain. It didn't matter that I had done nothing, that I was only me, a collection of imperfect sentences and unkind thoughts. They would make of this mess what they wanted to. He would make the facts fit their theory. People, places, dates, data, extrapolate, interpolate, random bits and bytes of information. They would arrange them into a picture and ignore the missing pixels. Because isn't this what we all do? Make up our own versions of the world to suit ourselves.

Paltoquet stared at me. The silence fell like a guillotine. What was the point in trying to convince him. I put my hands over my face and found my cheeks were wet with tears.

"I don't know," I said, mumbling a sniveling show of defeat. Let him think what he wants. Something wretched retched in me. Paltoquet handed me a tissue. For a moment the white flag hovered over the Formica surface of the table between us.

"You husband, Catherine," he said more softly now. "No inkling?

No prayer beads in a suitcase, whispers, someone who saw him at a mosque. Has he given his son any totem, anything religious, a Koran perhaps?"

I wiped my nose and shook my head. What was in a wooden box with the minaret of Samarra inlaid in mother-of-pearl, anyway? It was easy to pretend to be pathetic when I felt pathetic.

"I've never even seen him pray," I said, keeping to my own script. "He drinks in Ramadan, he eats bacon."

"You are aware of the concept of *taqiya*?"

"Yes, lying to deceive the enemy, religious dissembling. But religion, no, that's not like Ahmed."

"Are you sure? Wouldn't he conceal it from you as he has concealed so many things?"

Where better for a jihadi to hide than behind the mask of a debonair self-hating Arab? Ahmed, so urbane and international and plausible, the perfect foil.

Splinter niggled under my fingernail. I knew there were as many things that I didn't know as Paltoquet didn't know. Had I been stupid and naïve? Don't they always say you can't see what's under your own nose. How many times had I learned this lesson, seeing something and not really looking hard enough to understand.

I thought of Little Ahmed's reticence when he had come back from trips with his father—what was he hiding, protecting, not saying, not telling? Why did Ahmed go back to Baghdad? What was he doing there? Did he think he could save his country? What was all that talk of two rivers and throwing out the Arabs and making the desert bloom green again? What deals had he made with the bad guys? Would he have pulled his son in with him? Would he have risked Little Ahmed too?

I wiped my eyes and drew myself up. I thought that it was curious how comfortable plastic chairs can be after concrete, how malleable.

"Do you know how long you have been here?" Paltoquet asked. I couldn't tell what sentences were my thoughts and what I had spoken out loud.

"I have been scratching each day on the cell wall." Paltoquet did not smile at this.

"Three days," he told me. "Most people cry within the first twenty-four hours." Was this a compliment? "You are becoming confused, we will stop for some time while I verify what you have told me." He went out, and the whippet clicked the recorder off and sat looking at me and not saying anything. The female guard came to take me back to the cell. She put her hand under my arm pit to guide me, her fingers dug into me in the same place where the insurgent had gripped me when he pushed me into a room in Samarra years ago.

SIX

I sat on the floor of my cell in the corner and talked to myself in Q and A. My interrogations were stuck in this format and now my cell musings copied it too. I knew I was not quite mad; because it would not be madness to know that you had gone a little mad. Who wouldn't? Three days in jail, dragged up a spiral staircase to be questioned over and over again. At the same time, I confessed to myself (not to Paltoquet! I would never give him any satisfaction of confession!) that I reveled a little in the madness. Now I appreciated Zorro's addiction: the escape, the half delirium, the crazy thoughts that come in riffs of clouds and draw back a sucking blur as waves on a shore—there is a delicious liberty in madness, of impotence. For the moment I did not have to answer my interrogator-oppressor's questions.

But just to think.

The lights were kept on at all times. I closed my eyes and stared at the interior angry red of my eyelids. When I blinked them open, the world turned blue again, bright and inconsolable. I thought: This is what is to be a Palestinian at a checkpoint, an Iraqi in an immigration booth, a Syrian crossing a border, a son of an Algerian immigrant frisked at a French train station, an asylum seeker stopped and searched in a London high street. This is a prison cell. I am subject to the state. Unfair, indignity, wrong. Every innocent's nightmare. Walk in another man's shoes. (I have no shoes; they had been taken away three days ago and replaced with a pair of plastic flip-flops.) It is very unhappy to be unfree.

I would not let go of my self. I would not concede defeat. I hugged my knees to my chest. The state was only interested in the facts it could type on a sheet of paper and file in a dossier, but these facts don't tell you the truth. They are not the important things—they say nothing about the elements of soul or feeling. I will not concede (not to Oz, not to the insipid inspector either) that truth is in any way connected to facts.

I was comforted by this epiphany. After all, it is a prisoner's prerogative to pretend that the imaginary realm of self can triumph over the corporeal; the only thing you can claim as your own is your belief in your superiority to your captor.

I held fast to my innocence. I had not hurt anyone. I knew that Little Ahmed had not either. This I knew for certain; a mother's instinct, although Margot would have said it was only wish fulfillment masquerading as intuition. Of his father's innocence, I was less sure. I would not believe, I could not, that he had turned into some kind of terrorist mastermind jihadi. This was ridiculous. But Paltoquet had asked questions to which I did not have answers.

I ate a plastic bowl of claggy rice with three fingers of my right hand, pressing the rice together carefully, not to lose a single grain, as Ahmed's mother had once taught me.

There is another part to the privacy of one's thoughts. After the loud protestations of innocence, there is a reckoning. *What have I done? What have I not done?*

There was no chicken on the plastic food tray and I was hungry; each mouthful of rice represented a significant treasure of consideration. Ant came to say hello and navigated the rust stream from the *pissoir* hole followed by a friend. I placed a grain of rice in their path and felt myself as munificent and wise as Zeus.

Follow the trail of thought, each footfall as delicately tensile as the thin black line of an ant leg. *What if I am not right? What if I am wrong?*

I rewound the argument with Grégoire's prayer-cap brother, and analyzed my antipathy to him and his parents. I felt guilty, but why? Hadn't I only been frightened for my son? I righted my righteousness and smiled. It kept me company in that lone cell. Yes, Grégoire's family had been unfriendly. Why keep me out in the hall, why were they so hostile? And the arrogance of the brother, his smugness, his assumption of his own superiority, this was simple provocation. All reasonable justifications—

—Or only mitigations. Some other voice inside me, the interior self-god-conscience that used to answer me when I was a little girl, growing colder in my bath, whispered, "But who was unfriendly first, Kitty?" They had opened their door to a wild thing with mud on her shoes and twigs in her hair; I was dirty, my French was foreign, they did not know me. I had said rude things.

Yes, I thought, this is all true. There were two sides to this contretemps. I should at least acknowledge the existence of the other one. Perhaps this acknowledgment was enough to exonerate me. I considered this, but my guilt still niggled. Would remorse do? No, not really.

Ant and his friend were trying to carry the big lump of rice back to their home. The problem with generosity is that it is difficult for the recipient to carry. Should I have cut the rice in half? Is the God of magically appearing rice grains expected to do everything for her subjects? Isn't it enough that I am not crushing them with my thumb out of sheer boredom. I thought about doing this, but I did not because I didn't want to feel bad about it. I clung to my mercifulness as evidence of my goodness.

So you are superior because this time you decided, in your great magnamity, not to kill the ant? said the voice. I said. To me. Inside a thought, a perception of my own devising. I lay down on the concrete bench, cold balm against the lump of regret lodged in my intestine. I had insulted the prayer-cap brother. There was no denying this. I despised him and I told him so. But he had insulted me first . . . hadn't he? I was not sure . . . On closer examination, perhaps his rudeness had been unintentional, perhaps it was only my interpretation. I had retaliated. What use was my compounding insult? Shouldn't I apply the same argument of moral equivalency—condemn American killing but not jihadi killing—that I had thrown back at him, to myself? Do unto others—

The cold leached into my bones. It felt cleansing in some way, a penitence. I let go of my insult and fury; I think I was too exhausted to hang on to it. Still, I resisted resolution. Self-pity moved into the space left by anger. Poor me. I was alone in the world, without parents. This was sad, I was sad, I had the responsibility of Little Ahmed and no one to help me. How many times had I gone to sleep, to not sleep, fretting that I should not go on a reporting trip, that he needed to learn piano or how to ski or ride and that his father had not sent money for two months. The voice interrupted, "And Little Ahmed? What about his fear and worries and you shouting, crying, drinking, railing, stuck in your own hermetic ranting grief, your stupid, blinded *"It's a war; us and them."* Then I remembered Little Ahmed's face that night at Grégoire's apartment, his mouth an open O: shock, humiliation, disgust. A wave of shame crashed through me as a sudden heaving nausea. I buckled over the yellow hole in the floor and tried not to drown the ant in vomit.

"Poor me!" the voice mocked, merciless and sarcastic. And what about Ahmed? Motherless son with only-me-for-an-unmother, a terrible mother, selfish, stupid, hurtful—

Wracked; spasms shook me until I was emptied.

And becalmed. Poor Little Ahmed. For that matter, poor Ahmed in Baghdad with a killed father, a querulous aging mother, a country ripped apart and his son so far away, left behind for his own good. I had not thought of Ahmed leaving Little Ahmed in terms of sacrifice before; I had only thought about it as an abandonment. As I had been. I had so long blamed my father for leaving me, waited for him to come back and ask my forgiveness, that I had never wondered what shame and damage might keep an intelligent man from the daughter that he loved.

I felt sorry then, for myself first, for my misunderstanding, and then for Dad, because it takes two to make a misunderstanding. And then for Ahmed who was only trying to give his son what his father had tried to give him. My thoughts unwound, untangled. As I was falling asleep, a sort of peacefulness entered my heart, something unknotted. It was not a debated sequence of thoughts, there was no remonstration, but a feeling, an emotional wash, hot water warming up a tepid bath. I thought about Grégoire's brother Ahmed too, who was probably just trying to live a good life like the rest of us, and a deranged woman had come and yelled at him because she was angry with a bunch of killers who had nothing to do with him. Poor all the Ahmeds. Because we are all Ahmeds really.

———

I slept the whole night, dead and dreamless. When I was taken upstairs in the morning, Paltoquet smiled and indicated the chair opposite him, suddenly solicitous as if I was joining him at a table in a café.

"Would you like a coffee?"

"Yeah."

He handed me a Starbucks cappuccino. Some kind of civilization had returned.

"I can tell you now"—he seemed to suggest that it was with

relief—"that Ahmed, your son, was questioned for two hours and then released into the custody of Alexandre Delacroix. He has been there for the past three days. Delacroix instructed a lawyer on your behalf, but unfortunately you refused legal representation on the first day and therefore he had no authority to visit you."

"You could have told me earlier. I did not refuse legal representation. I did not understand what the man was saying."

"In any case, you will be released shortly. Your period of *garde-à-vue* has expired and there is no evidence with which to detain you further."

"What was the charge?"

"There is no charge."

"I mean what did you hope to charge me with?"

"I did not hope to charge you. My job is simply to investigate."

"Yes, but to investigate what?"

He did not answer. I noticed that Paltoquet was alone. No whippet. He sat back in his chair, as a gesture of informality.

"Tell me, Catherine. What do you believe in?" His voice changed tone, the sounds were longer and more gentle.

"I am not a real Muslim," I said. "I told you this."

"You are a Christian."

"No."

"You have no religious affiliation."

"No, that's not true. I have Christian affiliation. I am culturally Christian. But don't ask me to believe in Christianity. Virgin births and resurrection and the mysterious Holy Spirit. It's spooky and weird, this stuff. It's absurd to believe in the supernatural."

"But of them all, Christianity is the one you prefer."

"Not really, it is only the one I grew up with, so—"

"So?"

"If you are really asking me, I have no preference. All of them have their holy fools and their murderers."

"When you arrived, you said that you were not like them. When I asked about your belief and your belief in Islam, you said: *I am not like them.* Your *them* was Muslims."

"My son is Muslim, I cannot disassociate myself from the son that I love. He is not *them*."

"So who is your *us*?"

"It's all of us," I said.

"All of us, in the context of *laïcité*?"

"No, just us, just people. Who want to live the way we want to live without hurting anyone."

"Perhaps you believe in the rule of law? Something more secular?" Paltoquet suggested. This conversation was off the books. He had no dossiers in front of him.

"Not laws," I said. "The Americans make a cult of lawyers and argue every constitutional point with the same hermetic intensity as Islamic scholars debate the Koran. Every comma has its own interpretation. The British love their law and order, but for them it is a policeman with a truncheon. The policeman is the establishment, the establishment is the complicity of the majority. Step out of line and they won't kill you but they will give you a bloody nose. This they believe is reasonable and decent, what they call "cricket." But if you want to actually change something in Britain, you will find yourself an infidel apostate. In Britain you are allowed to be—and this is more insidious—an eccentric. If you think differently you are allowed to exist but you will never be taken seriously."

"So you are a revolutionary?"

"No. Revolutions require ideology and I don't like ideologies. All theories are bunk. Plus revolutions require violence and I don't like violence, because I think it only breeds more violence."

"A kind of karma," said Paltoquet.

"I don't know anything about Eastern spirituality."

"You would be a reformer."

"I would, if I could be bothered," I said. "But I am too lazy to be an activist."

"You believe in everyone equal," he said, more hopefully.

"No, this would reduce everyone to the lowest common denominator. This is communism. People are different, not equal."

"You believe perhaps, that everyone should have the same opportunity—I am thinking of your son Ahmed now—who you decided to raise in France. That the state should provide the system, the umbrella for everyone to be *treated* as equal."

"I hate umbrellas, they poke people's eyes out with their spokes."

"It's a metaphor, Catherine. That everyone should be regarded as equal."

"Utopian idiocy."

"So you believe in nothing?"

I did not reply. Did I see the edge of a smile on his pallid plain face interrupted with a brown spot? For a full minute Paltoquet looked at me closely and I looked back at him. He had a few white hairs at his temples I had not noticed before. He wore a wedding band on his left hand. The river delta of blue veins were visible on the inside of his wrist. He was nobody, a common type; almost anonymous. A cog in a machine. But a state is not a machine, it is a system, a polity, a community. And the mechanism is not operated by metal-toothed components but individuals, people. Bigger or smaller, powerful or not powerful, each of us is only ourself.

SEVEN

I was released from *garde-à-vue* after ninety-four hours in detention. My bag and our two computers and my telephones were returned to me, and I took a taxi home. The door was closed with a plastic cord taped over a legal notice. I turned my key in the lock and broke the cord and ripped off the official form. Inside was a mess of overturned boxes, papers dumped everywhere, and books toppled out of the bookcases onto the floor. The fridge door had been left open and was beeping. I closed it and plugged in my phone.

I sat in the middle of my wrecked living room and thought, What now? I sat very still for a while waiting for an answer. None came. I got bored of waiting and so I stood up and began to tidy. Books in piles, reshelved, papers reordered, furniture righted. Put it back, make it home again.

Alexandre brought Little Ahmed over that evening. I was nervous. I heard the clang of the antiquated lift stop at our floor. I wanted to fling open the door and rush out in a great excitement of homecoming reunion, but I wasn't sure how Little Ahmed would react. I didn't want to impose, to crowd him. So I waited until I heard him knock before I opened the door. Little Ahmed stood on the threshold, smiling at me despite himself.

"So they finally let you out of prison, jailbird mother—" His voice was punchy, wisecracking. He was trying to be grown-up and cool. "They arrested me too, you know. At school, I swear, I have so much street cred now it's ridiculous."

"Are you OK, my Medio?" I reached out tentatively to touch his hair. Yes, he was here, he was really here.

"Hey." He hugged me. He smelled like teenage unwashed sweatshirt left out in the rain, sweetly sour, so very much of him. "So I'm really glad you're out and everything, but it doesn't mean I'm not still mad at you."

"I'm pretty mad at me too."

———

Margot suggested we stay with her in Brittany for a few weeks. Oz gave me time off. "We'll call it book leave." I was grateful not to have to organize my thoughts into sentences and paragraphs.

It was hard to talk: I had used so many wrong words that now I mistrusted them. My moods were brittle and unsure of themselves. Little Ahmed was wary of me, as I was wary of him. I was frightened to say sorry out loud in case he did not forgive me. "Time, a little time," repeated Margot soothingly. "It will come when you're both ready." She tended us carefully. She took Little Ahmed for coffee every morning, listened, let him talk. I was jealous, but she said that it was natural for him to want to talk to someone who was not me and that it was natural for me to resent this. I submitted myself to her explanations. I did not know better.

Blue sea, blue sky. Little Ahmed went out in the waves every day with his surfboard with the other winter seals in wetsuits. I walked the beach and dug cockles at low tide, heavy wet sand under my fingernails, scraping down to find a solid walnut lump, a fleeting nugget of joy. Time passed according to the rhythms of the tides, the swell of the surf, wind, rain, sun. I swam through the days—eventually giving in to Little Ahmed's admonition and buying my own wetsuit—vanquishing the cold, embracing it, stretching broad strokes across the bay and floating back with the incoming tide, letting the sea wash me out and a hot shower warm me up again.

"I'll come swimming with you, Kit-ma," Little Ahmed said one lulled afternoon. "The waves are too small to surf." I looked at Margot and she smiled encouragingly.

"Are you sure?" I said. "I'd love to have company."

I followed him down the sandy path between the dunes. Long lean man-cub, his hair had grown longer, more surf dude. I wanted to tell him that I liked it. I wanted to tell him a million things. He was striding ahead and I called out, "Ahmed!" but the wind blew the words away. I couldn't bear the thought of going into the water with an ocean unsaid, so I ran up and caught his hand.

"What?"

"Everything!"

"What do you mean?"

But I couldn't explain. "Thank you for coming swimming with me."

"It's OK."

I bit my lip.

"I don't actually hate you, you know," he said.

"Oh thank god."

"You're my mother after all," he made a mock smile. "I have to love you."

———

Margot was right. Over the seaside weeks the space between us lessened. We began to talk to each other. At first, about waves and barnacles and what fish to buy for supper; then watching old episodes of of *Law & Order*, about lawyers and law, about prison and questioning and questions, about answers too. I said "I'm sorry" a hundred times, and every time—in one way or another, an eye roll, a kiss on my cheek, a hug, sometimes even in clear direct words, Ahmed said, it's OK, I get it, I understand.

At Christmas everyone gathered in Locquirec. Alexandre brought smoked salmon and caviar. Zorro flew in from Kinshasa with a tan. He took pictures of us, mother and son, standing apart, sitting next to each other on a big flat beach rock, coming out of the sea and struggling to peel off our wetsuits. In one, my favorite picture, I am staring off at some distant storm cloud and Little Ahmed is grinning behind my back, about to put a crab down my neck. On Christmas Eve, Margot cooked a whole turbot for dinner and we all sat around and ate it with our fingers the way Iraqis eat mazgouf.

"I don't want the New Year to come," I admitted to Margot, washing up in the kitchen afterwards. "I don't want to go home, it feels like going back is going backwards."

"I understand, these weeks here by the sea are like a holiday from your life. But it's inevitable, you have to face it again. Work and school, all the usual pressures. You and Little Ahmed will be alone together and you are finding a new language, a different way of communicating. Both of you, I can see it happening already. I know it's not easy, but don't worry too much. Of course you will argue, there will be misunderstandings, there will be slammed doors; it doesn't matter. It matters what you do afterwards, how you handle these moments. Little Ahmed looks up to you."

"Little Ahmed despises me," I said. Margot passed me a tea towel to dry the wineglasses. "Careful," she cautioned, "they were Jean's mother's."

I gently rubbed the thin tulip bowl of one of the glasses. The linen damply absorbed the water drops, the linen would dry, and the water would evaporate and fall again as rain, or tears. "I feel like the more I apologize, the more he just says "Yeah, it's OK," as if its rote and he feels like he has to say that, but he doesn't really forgive me."

"That's just his grumpy thirteen-year-old defenses, the prickly pear exterior. See how he brings you his drawings to look at. He's looking for your approval."

"But he always asks, 'What do you think Rousse would say?'"

"But he wants you to tell him. To be his bridge to her. He wants your opinion too."

"I don't know," I said. "Maybe we shouldn't stay in Paris. But then where should we go? Could we move to Good Harbor Bay? To London? Should I try and find someplace where he can see his father more often—even though, God, right now I don't want to see Ahmed ever again."

"Home is not a place," said Margot. "It's not a location. It's a feeling you carry inside, in your heart, in your imagination. You take it with you."

———

We lit the fire in the library and banked the logs. Zorro taught Little Ahmed how to blow the bellows and make the orange flame dance. Circle of radiant heat. Jean poured an old jigsaw puzzle of a nighttime seascape out onto the coffee table.

"Fifty shades of blue," complained Little Ahmed.

"I'm sure there are pieces missing," said Margot. "I think I remember from the last time we tried to do it."

"We've never completed it," admitted Jean. "I think we just said there were pieces missing as an excuse."

We found the corners first, the easy bits. Little Ahmed had answered my phone on October 31 and forgot to tell me. Fitted together the edges, made a frame. When he was arrested, Little Ahmed had put up his hands straightaway and admitted that he had been stenciling the Kalashnikov firing madeleines all over the city. A charge of *dégradation d'espace publique* was pending, but since Little Ahmed was a minor, Jean was sure the lawyer could get the matter dropped. Zorro told him he should be proud. Especially as he had maintained that he had acted alone and kept Grégoire's name out of it.

The moon shone on the patches of sea and made a white path that we managed to put together. Little Ahmed said there were no secret meetings in Amman, no imams or commanders or passed notes, no code in the postcards. Aba was ever Aba, always his father, anyway.

"Where are the dolphin tails?" said Little Ahmed. "They're gray, we should be able to see them."

Ahmed had been in Washington while I was in prison. I hadn't spoken to him—I didn't want to speak with him yet. But it was all a complicated misunderstanding, he had assured us remotely. A Defense Department official called an opposite number in the DGSE, France's external intelligence agency, an understanding was understood. Ahmed was privately told not to travel to France for the foreseeable future. He told Little Ahmed he would be moving to Istanbul soon and they could meet there. Little Ahmed was not sure he wanted to go by himself. "Yes, Aba, OK. No, she's gone out," he covered for me, "she can't talk now."

Alexandre and Jean swapped theories. Margot said they should let it go, the truth will out in its own time, but the coruscations of plot were too beguiling. Ahmed was arming Syrian jihadis for the Americans, he was coopting lesser ISIS affiliates, he was playing a long game, helping the Sunni against the Shia. "That would have the effect of dovetailing with American and Saudi strategic interests," Alexandre dissected, "and preventing a Shia landmass bloc from forming between Tehran and Hezbollah . . ."

"But at what cost?" Jean was always suspicious of theoretical diplomatics. He thought governments tended to react, like people, emotionally, knee jerk, revenge, swipe, slight, and pride. "Long-term strategic interests—I think these are the dreams of retired ambassadors."

"Maybe." Alexandre conceded. "At least for democracies. Elections make all planning subject to short-term expediency."

"But to arm the jihadis?" said Jean.

"He was already talking about it in 2011," Alexandre said. "At the monastery in Syria. He wanted to know how far in France would go, how far in I thought the British would go. If Russia was bluster or not. The point for Ahmed, I think, was always to oppose Iran. He inherited a very Baathie hatred of Iran."

"All Arabs distrust Persians," said Jean.

"But still," mused Alexandre, "to arm jihadists, to deal with ISIS . . ."

"Think about it," said Jean, "to him ISIS were not so scary. He probably knew those guys, they were Iraqis, a lot of them, from Samarra, Tikrit, they were old Saddam era officers, leftover Awakening commanders . . . Muntazzer's sons . . . they were his childhood friends."

I kept working on the foreground, putting puzzle pieces together, fitting black tab into black socket.

"He thought the Shia had to be defeated, pushed back, contained, yes," I said. Alexandre and Jean turned towards me. "But he thought that the answer to the violence, the jihad, the endless cycle of the tortured turning into torturer, was to discredit the ideology. What did he say? 'Give it enough rope to hang itself.' By inoculation. Let them have their caliphate and then everyone can see what a brutal absurdity Sharia is."

"It doesn't matter," said Little Ahmed. "Look! I found a piece of the dolphin tail!" He held up a puzzle shape triumphantly. "It doesn't matter what my father thought he was doing or what he did. I don't really care. It's the same as my grandfather. Is he the perpetrator because he was in the Baath Party, or is he the victim because Saddam killed him? He's still my grandfather. I wish I had known him. I wish I could go to see the banks of the Tigris with my father and my grandfather and eat the famous kebabs. Maybe one day I will go with my dad. Maybe one day he will be able to come here and we can walk on the beach together. Or we can meet in America, in my other grand-parent place in Good Harbor Bay. I don't care where we meet. I only wish that my mother wasn't dead and that Rousse wasn't dead, that lots of people who were killed didn't die. It would be better for every-one. The rest of us left over just have to get on with it. It doesn't make any difference what the reasons are or whose fault it all is. That's all I'm saying. Look, it goes there. The dolphin tail is making a splash—where's the white droplet piece, I saw it here a moment ago . . ."

———

On Christmas morning we walked along the beach, and Little Ahmed and Zorro drew holly leaves in the wet sand with sticks. Curves, con-cave and convex, met in a sharp point. I pondered the uselessness of metaphors and added fat round berries to their leaves.

Back at the house, Alexandre popped the champagne and we opened our presents. Books and socks and scarves piled up amid drifts of wrapping paper.

"The best gifts," said Jean, "keep us warm and feed our minds."

He gave Little Ahmed a catalogue of an Ellsworth Kelly show, because he knew Little Ahmed loved the bright colors and the abstrac-tion. Alexandre gave him a special membership card to the Louvre. Margot gave him a lithograph by a local artist of a whale with a Jonah figure crouching, gestate, inside its belly. Zorro had brought him a Congolese mask made of teak and carved with concentric grooves rubbed with red earth. The face was half monkey, half man, and had an expression of curiosity and mischief. "Somehow it reminded me of you," he told Little Ahmed, and Little Ahmed grinned and held it up to his face and we all said, *Absolutely! The spitting image!*

I gave Little Ahmed a large leather portfolio case filled with dif-ferent kinds of paper, pressed linen, cotton rag, hemp, parchment, papyrus, watercolor card, and every weight of cartridge I could find. "Blank canvases," I said as Little Ahmed ran his fingers over their planes with a quiet reverence. "Each a new beginning, each a different medium—"

"It's like I have to figure out what the paper wants," said Little Ahmed. "Water or oil or charcoal or pencil or pastel." He felt the sharp edges of the acid-free cartridge paper and the soft frayed hem of a hand-rolled Indian silk-slub cotton mix. "And to figure out what to draw too—because some are rough and some are really slippery, supersmooth. Some say jagged, because you can't draw a clean arc, it would snag on the texture. Some are so shiny it's like they are just telling me: try to draw a perfect oval egg." He came over and hugged me and kissed my forehead. Benediction. "Cool, Kit-ma, thanks." Maybe it would be alright wherever we were, two mongrel outcasts brought together by fate, by love, by absent Ahmeds.

Then Little Ahmed opened the brown paper parcel his father had sent him. Inside was a lump of bubble wrap. He gently unrolled it to reveal a small cylinder of green agate. It was an ancient cuneiform seal. Little Ahmed held it up to the fairy lights on the Christmas tree and examined the carving.

"It's a lion!"

Alexandre peered over his demilune tortoiseshell glasses. "In fact it's a winged lion. An Assyrian winged lion. It must be three thousand years old. Extraordinary."

I held the seal in my palm, felt its delicate heft, and saw how the light shone against it and through it, luminous and opaque. I was amazed at this tiny thing that had survived civilization and its ruin, the fall of empires, invasion and conquest and bandits, buried, lost, found, probably looted, to be safely delivered to a son of the land between the two great rivers.

WITHDRAWN